She grabbed the stack of mail and started to flip through it on the way to the laundry hamper in the master bedroom. A Reader's Digest. The electric bill. Some pieces that were obviously junk…

And a plain white envelope, with the name "Mary Hollister Beamer" written on it with her address.

Mary was puzzled. She examined the envelope, dropping the rest of the mail on the floral comforter that covered her bed.

The postmark was Atlanta, Georgia. Mary shivered. She couldn't ever think of Atlanta without remembering the worst summer of her life. She wondered who was writing her from there. Celia?

She opened the envelope and pulled out the single sheet of paper. When she read the two sentences written on it she stumbled against the bed, sitting down hard because her legs would no longer support her.

I KNOW WHAT YOU TRIED TO DO.

YOUR SON IS ALIVE.

OTHER BOOKS BY LAURA WARE

Dead Hypocrites
The Silent Witness

REDEMPTION

LAURA WARE

REDEMPTION

JJ Press
www.jjpressflorida.com

To Tina, my own BFF.

For being willing to drop everything and see me through my own valleys.

I love you.

ACKNOWLEDGEMENTS

REDEMPTION was born as a proposal I came up with during the 2008 Masters Class, a 2 week writing boot camp held in Lincoln City, Oregon. My thanks to the instructors and my fellow students for all the learning and encouragement provided, not only during the class, but since.

The 2010 Novel Workshop in Lincoln City gave me a lot of good input on the book. Thanks to Dean Wesley Smith and my fellow authors for your help.

Again, Tina Seward stepped up to the plate and copyedited the book. She was also helpful in assisting me with different locations mentioned. Any remaining mistakes, as always, are mine.

My husband Don probably deserves a medal for his constant support of my writing career. I am deeply indebted to him for his understanding and encouragement. And for supporting my coffee and chocolate habits.

And thanks to my readers who have been asking me when my next book is coming out. I hope it was worth the wait.

REDEMPTION

- ONE -

Martha Thompson was pleased that, on the day she'd chosen to be the last of her life, the weather had turned pleasant.

A cold front swept the state of Georgia, blowing away the sweltering heat that had baked it for weeks. Now, a fresh breeze cooled her face as she raised it to the sun, her eyes closed in pleasure.

She sighed. Pleasures were few and far between of late, thus the decision she was going to implement today. She returned to the task at hand, clipping some of her most fragrant pink roses.

The bush was old, planted in the front yard here twenty years ago when she and Peter first built the house. It lasted through storms, children, drought, and hungry deer. It outlasted Peter. It would outlast her.

Martha straightened up, wincing at the pain in the small of her back. She looked over at the forest green mailbox at the end of the driveway. The red flag was still up. She would have to wait to finish things. That was all right. She could wait a little longer.

She carried her bouquet of roses into the house. Every window in the three-bedroom, two-bath home was open, letting fresh air in. The dark blue curtains in the great room swayed gently.

Martha's sneakers squeaked on the white tile floor. Yesterday she'd swept and mopped all the floors in the house. She'd shaken out the rugs. The scent of lemon polish was a testimony to the work she'd done on the furniture the day before.

She went into the kitchen and divided her roses into the two crystal vases she'd prepared earlier. Normally Martha would cut the rose stems again under water, to help the blooms last longer. But she didn't need them to last longer than a few hours.

She carried the vases to her bedroom. One vase on each nightstand. The bed was made, decorator pillows piled on the headboard. A glass of wine rested on the stand to the left.

Martha stripped off her workgloves and dropped them on top of the laundry hamper. She went to her dressing table and picked up the picture of Peter that sat there – an old picture of him in his Marine uniform.

She brushed her fingers across the pictured lips. She missed Peter with a passion. He had been stricken with prostrate cancer, and left her two years ago. It had been painful to watch this strong man grow frail, wracked with pain at the end, a shell of who she'd married.

She wondered then if God was punishing her with Peter's death. When her doctor diagnosed her with breast cancer two months ago, she was convinced that He was determined to make her suffer.

Of course, she'd let her son and daughter know of the diagnosis. They were sympathetic, but the distance that had marked their relationship for so long was not bridged even with a serious illness.

She didn't blame her children. Truth to tell, she was the one who'd caused the distance. Her job, the job she'd held for 15 years, that had raised the barrier.

Martha shook her head. She'd told herself all those years that she was helping to provide a service for women. A legal, needed service. She even accepted the secret operation Dr. Grayson conducted, seeing it as a way for some unwanted children to find a home instead of death.

When had she begun to question? That was easy. Ten years ago, when a teenage girl was brought into the clinic, seven and a half months pregnant and in premature labor. She was brought in by her friend and the friend's mother, who explained to Dr. Grayson that discretion was needed. The doctor was all too glad to accommodate them.

Martha remembered when the girl awoke from anesthesia. She would never forget the look of horror on the teenager's face when the doctor told her the child had died. When the girl asked where she was and discovered it was the Peachtree Road Women's Clinic, she became hysterical. "I didn't want an abortion!" she cried.

Martha held the girl, weeping with her. But she couldn't tell her the truth. At the time, she thought it was better that the girl remained ignorant. Soon the girl's companions picked her up and Martha never saw her again.

But the teenager haunted her. Martha stayed at the clinic for nine years, continuing to do her job. She was efficient, compassionate. Dr. Grayson often complimented her on her work.

He didn't know that she sometimes went back to the files, and pulled the one that belonged to the teenage girl. She reread it often, to the point that parts of it were burned into her memory.

Then that reporter started nosing around. Dr. Grayson made it clear that no one was to talk to that annoying man. He tried to charm the nurses, offered to talk to them "off the record." No one gave in.

Well, Martha had. Almost. She'd agreed to meet him for coffee. But at the last minute she canceled. It was too scary. What would happen to her? Would she go to jail? Would she have to testify against friends and colleagues? She couldn't do it.

Two nights later, the Peachtree Road Women's Clinic burned to the ground. Martha could still smell the stink of burned plastic and other things as she stood in front of the wreck that had been her place of employment for 15 years. The rumors were that a pro-life crazy had torched the place.

But Martha suspected...no, she *knew*. The reporter had gotten too close. The clinic's destruction was an effort to stop any investigation.

Dr. Grayson moved out of Georgia. Martha decided it was time to leave nursing. She kept in touch with a couple of co-workers but found herself drawing away from them as time went on.

And then the diagnosis of cancer. That had tipped her over the edge.

Martha went to the front door and looked out. The blue and white US Mail truck was parked by her mailbox. The mailperson, a young woman with curly blond hair, smiled and waved at Martha. Martha returned the greeting, watching as the girl took the one plain envelope she'd left for her to take.

She hadn't seen the teenage girl's file in over a year, but she had remembered certain things. Her name. Her birthdate. Her home address. From these Martha was able to find out she had married, and where she now lived.

It was perhaps a cruel thing, the letter. But Martha felt the girl needed to know. It was all the nurse could do to repair the damage done. It was, perhaps, a way of making amends.

Martha shut the door of her house for the last time. She went back to her bedroom. The sleeping pills she'd gotten the doctor to prescribe sat next to the glass of wine. She gulped them by handfuls, washing them down with the sweet red wine.

When the bottle and glass were empty, she lay among her embroidered pillows and waited for oblivion.

- TWO -

MARY BEAMER PAUSED BY HER bedroom door to ensure that her husband Roger was up. The sound of the shower confirmed he hadn't buried himself back under the covers. Mary smiled to herself and went on to her daughter's room.

Kelly's room was painted a robin's egg blue, with rainbow decals scattered all over the walls. Mary leaned against the doorway, remembering how she and Roger had worked on that room together, with him insisting she not overwork herself. "This is our first baby," he said, "I don't want anything to go wrong."

Her smile faltered. He didn't know, of course, that Kelly wasn't her first baby. Almost no one did. Mary felt a stab of guilt as she wondered where that poor child had been buried, wondered if he or she would ever forgive her for what happened. If God would ever forgive her.

Her eyes fell to the golden head just above the Garfield comforter. God had been good to Mary, far better than she could ever think she deserved. That sleeping little girl was proof of it.

Mary stepped to the bed and bent down. "Good morning, Sunshine," she whispered.

Kelly stirred. Her light blue eyes opened and met Mary's. The little girl smiled. "g'morning, Mommy."

Mary cupped her daughter's cheek. "Who's my favorite five-year old?" she chanted. It was part of their morning ritual.

"I'm your favorite five-year old," Kelly answered. She giggled and rubbed noses with Mary. "Who's my favorite mommy?"

"I'm your favorite mommy," Mary said, kissing her daughter's warm cheek. "Time to get up, sweetie."

Kelly yawned and wiggled out from under the comforter. "School day, right?"

"Right," Mary said. Kelly had started kindergarten this year, and they were both getting used to the new schedule.

Ten minutes later Mary and Kelly were in the kitchen. Roger was already there, pouring himself a cup of coffee. "Morning, ladies."

"Morning, Daddy," Kelly said, climbing into her chair. "Today is a school day."

"Gotcha," Roger said, dropping a kiss on his daughter's head. "Today's a work day too." He went to Mary and kissed her cheek. "What's Mommy got planned today?"

"Mommy is volunteering at the clothing room at church and then doing laundry," Mary answered. She poured three glasses of orange juice and fixed instant apples and cinnamon oatmeal for Kelly. Roger was popping an English muffin into the toaster.

Breakfast went quickly, as it always did. Mary basked in the normalcy of it. Loving husband, darling daughter…she was truly blessed.

Too bad I don't deserve any of it. Mary was all too aware of her sins. Including the worst one…the one she didn't know she could ever be forgiven for. The one she could never confess, lest she lose everything important to her.

"Hon?"

Mary looked up. Roger was staring at her, concern evident in his gray eyes. "You all right?"

She swallowed, and made herself smile. "Of course I am. Just thinking, I guess."

Roger nodded as he took off his glasses and cleaned them with a napkin. "You sure?"

"Yes, of course," Mary said. She got up and began to take dirty dishes to the sink. She knew Roger wasn't buying her explanation. She also knew he wouldn't push. That was the pattern that was established in their six years of marriage.

"Well," Roger said. "I'd better get going. I have some work to catch up on at the bank." He got up and came up behind Mary, kissing her cheek. "I do love you, you know," he said in a low voice.

She blinked back sudden tears. Oh, she didn't deserve him. She turned so that she could kiss Roger on the lips. "I love you too. You're one of the best things that's ever happened to me."

The tender moment was interrupted by Kelly. "Kiss me, Daddy, kiss me!"

Roger chuckled. "I'm just so popular," he said, brushing Mary's cheek with his fingers. He then went and scooped Kelly up from her seat, kissing her soundly on her cheek and accepting an orange juice flavored kiss in return.

Mary took a deep breath. The past was the past. This was her reality. She needed to quit dwelling on what she couldn't change.

She just wished she knew how to stop.

- THREE -

MARY PULLED UP TO THE small block building that housed the Mandarin Community Church's clothing room. "Clothing room" was an oversimplification: not only did the place house donated clothes, but small appliances, furniture, and a food pantry.

The church kept the place open three days a week, from 9:00 AM to 11:00 AM. It was totally run by volunteers from the congregation and was well-known in the Jacksonville area as a place to go if you had a need.

It was ten minutes before nine and already there was a small knot of people waiting at the front door. Mary parked in the rear of the building and let herself in the back door.

The scent of hazelnut coffee told her someone was already in the building. Mary skirted the many racks of clothes that took up most of the available floor space and went into the sorting/break room. Joanne Carson, a thin energetic redhead, was already rooting through a box of clothing. "Morning, Mary!"

"Morning, Joanne," Mary answered, helping herself to a cup of coffee. "Anyone else here yet?"

"Tom will be here soon. He got a call this morning from someone who wanted to donate a loveseat," Joanne said as she held up a bright red t-shirt. She frowned. "I don't know why people donate stuff like this – we can't exactly give it out."

Mary looked over and saw the t-shirt was advertising some heavy metal rock band. Skulls were part of the logo. "They mean well," she said.

"I know," Joanne sighed. "But stuff like this just sends the wrong message."

As she scanned the volunteer list to see who else they could expect that day, Mary shrugged. "We can always rip it up for rags. The youth group wants to have another car wash – I'm sure they could use cleaning stuff."

Joanne nodded and tossed the shirt onto the off-white carpet. As she continued to sort through the box of clothes she asked Mary, "How is Kelly doing with kindergarten?"

"She loves it," Mary admitted. She grabbed a blue smock off a rack across from the brown leather couch and put it on.

With a small smile, Joanne asked, "And how's *Mom* doing with kindergarten?"

Mary laughed. "I admit, it's different not having her with me all the time. At least I can help here more."

Joanne grinned. "Yeah, I remember when James started kindergarten. One day he wound himself around my leg and would *not* let go. By the time the teacher got him away, we were both crying."

Mary felt her smile slip. "Well, it hasn't gotten quite that bad yet."

"Hey," Joanne said. "I didn't mean to depress you. I just know you're pretty close to Kelly, and this whole school thing is an adjustment for you."

Mary shrugged. She glanced at the round clock high up on the wall. "Five minutes. You want to work the front or do you want me to?"

"Since I'm already into this box, why don't you start off in front?" Joanne said. "We can switch after an hour."

Mary nodded. "That sounds fine." She headed out to the main room and sat behind the large desk Joanne's husband had put together for the clothing room.

While the old computer they used booted up, Mary pulled out the sign-in notebook and a few welcome packets. To the left of the desk was a large box filled with plastic bags. To the right was an empty box for hangers.

Mary flipped through the notebook until she came to the first empty page. She wrote the date on top of it, and put it and a pen where people coming in could sign in. As part of their efforts to make sure people coming in were truly seeking help and not stuff to unload at their garage sales, the clothing room tried to keep track of who came in and how often.

At 9:00 AM Mary unlocked the door and welcomed the people waiting outside. The first person to come in was a young Hispanic woman, who looked to be six or seven months pregnant and holding the hand of an adorable three year old boy.

Mary didn't remember seeing the woman before. *"Habla Ingles?"* she asked, hoping the answer would be yes.

The woman nodded. "*Si*. I speak some English." She shifted from foot to foot, her cheeks red. "A friend of mine told me…I could find help here. I have no one, and my *hijo*…my son…he needs clothes."

"We'll be glad to help," Mary said. "Could you sign in for me here please?"

As the woman bent over the book, her black hair falling over her face, Mary swallowed the lump in her throat. *I could have been her. Alone, with no one to help me.* Maybe that's why she was so eager to help out in the clothing room. It was a way for her to atone for a sin committed 10 years ago, a sin she'd never forgiven herself for.

A sin she'd take to her grave, and beyond. The only question she had was would she end it go to Heaven – or Hell?

- FOUR -

MARY CHECKED HER WATCH as she turned her blue Toyota Camry onto her home street. After her stint in the clothing room she'd run to the grocery store to pick up a few things they were running low on. It had taken longer than she'd hoped – it felt like everyone in Jacksonville had descended on that particular grocery store the minute she put her hand on a shopping cart.

She pulled to the end of the driveway and flipped open the white mailbox. There was a respectable pile of mail waiting for her and she eased it carefully into the car, trying not to let any spill onto the ground.

Kelly needed to be picked up in about an hour. That gave Mary just enough time to put away her groceries and get a start on that load of laundry she'd meant to run. She quickly got the groceries into the kitchen after dropping the stack of mail on the round oak table that sat in the nook.

While loading milk, shredded cheddar cheese and seedless red grapes into the refrigerator Mary looked over to where the answering machine sat on the kitchen counter. A red **2** flashed on the display.

She hit the play button and slid a loaf of bread into the breadbox she'd found at a garage sale and painted a warm yellow.

"Mary? Betty Parsons from church. Do you think you could teach Ladie's Class tomorrow morning? Evelyn called, she's caught that stomach bug that's going around. Call me and let me know, please."

Ick. Kelly had come down with the latest sickness that was making the rounds of the congregation and it had been an unpleasant 48 hours. Evelyn

- 13 -

was an older woman, her kids grown and gone. Mary hoped Arthur would be able to take care of his wife without catching the bug himself.

Mary's mind was on the Ladie's Class and whether she could put a lesson together in time when the second message clicked on. "Yeah…This is Bob Thompson? Um, I don't think you know me, but my mom…my mom Martha Thompson had your name and information, and I need to know if she talked to you. I – I don't really want to explain on your answering machine. Please call me at the following number…"

She frowned and replayed the second message, running the name through her mind. *Thompson, Thompson*…she didn't know who this could be. The call was disturbing. Why was this man calling her?

She grabbed the stack of mail and started to flip through it on the way to the laundry hamper in the master bedroom. A Reader's Digest. The electric bill. Some pieces that were obviously junk…

And a plain white envelope, with the name "Mary Hollister Beamer" written on it with her address.

Mary was puzzled. She examined the envelope, dropping the rest of the mail on the floral comforter that covered her bed.

The postmark was Atlanta, Georgia. Mary shivered. She couldn't ever think of Atlanta without remembering the worst summer of her life. She wondered who was writing her from there. Celia?

She opened the envelope and pulled out the single sheet of paper. When she read the two sentences written on it she stumbled against the bed, sitting down hard because her legs would no longer support her.

I KNOW WHAT YOU TRIED TO DO.

YOUR SON IS ALIVE.

- FIVE -

MARY WONDERED WHY her face was tingling. Why the room was getting darker. She realized she wasn't breathing.

"Okay," she muttered to herself. "Don't do this…breathe. In. Out. Get it together, Mary."

She couldn't take her eyes off the paper. The two sentences had almost stopped her heart. I KNOW WHAT YOU TRIED TO DO. YOUR SON IS ALIVE.

She shook her head. Who sent this? Why? It was ten years ago. The only people who knew about what happened that terrible summer were Celia and her mother. Mary had managed to hide it from her parents even. And of course Roger didn't have any idea.

Roger...

At the thought of her husband, Mary found herself beginning to panic again. What if he found out? After all this time? Would he understand? Would he want to stay with her?

If he didn't want to stay, would he take Kelly with him? Would she be ostracized from the church? Humiliated in front of everyone?

Mary stopped and forced herself to breathe again. She lay back on the bed, letting tears slide into her hair while she tried to gain a measure of self-control.

The phone on Roger's nightstand began to ring. Mary threw an arm over her eyes. She couldn't talk to anyone. Not now. Not until she woke up from this…this *nightmare*.

It stopped and she knew the answering machine would be picking up the call. She hoped it wasn't the school or anyone like that.

Mary looked over at the clock by the phone. She had about a half hour to get herself together. Then she'd go to the school, pick up Kelly, act as if nothing had happened to yank her feet out from under her...

She couldn't do that.

Mary sat up and rubbed her stinging eyes with her hands. She looked at the letter again, resisting the temptation to shred it and bury it in the wet garbage. With a sigh, she leaned down and picked the envelope up off the floor.

No return address. Nothing to indicate where the incriminating sentences had come from except for the postmark. Mary shook her head. *Why?*

She walked into the small third bedroom that served as a guestroom/office for the house. Roger's heavy walnut desk took up a good portion of one wall. The closet was filled with four filing cabinets and boxes of Christmas decorations, sewing projects, and boxes of papers and memorabilia.

Mary went to a stack of cardboard boxes and shifted them around until she could get to a battered one near the bottom. Scrawled in black Magic Marker were the words, "Mary – High School."

She opened it, inhaling the musty scent of old paper. There was a faint floral scent as well – it smelled like one of the sachets she put in her underwear drawer when she was a teenager. She hadn't smelled it in years.

Swallowing, trying to think past the memories, she began to search through the box. Her eyes fell on a picture of a young man and herself, grinning like fools with their arms around each other. She touched the picture, feeling tears sting her eyes again. "Harold..."

Under that was what she was looking for. A green dog-eared book with the word "Addresses" in faded golden script on the cover.

Mary flipped through the book back to the "W's". Celia's mother's address and phone number were there. Celia had gone to live with her mother that summer, and Mary went with her for a girlfriend bonding time. That's what Celia's mom told Mary's parents, anyway.

Mary found her hands shaking as she punched in the number. The phone rang a few times, and to her relief she recognized Mrs. Winters' voice.

"This is Mary Beamer. I – I was Mary Hollister?"

"Mary!" Mrs. Winters voice was warm. "It's been quite a while. Celia hasn't mentioned you for ages, dear. How are you doing?"

"I – I'm fine," Mary said. "I'm afraid Celia and I lost touch after a while."

"That's too bad. You both were such good friends."

REDEMPTION

"Yes," Mary said. She felt the hand holding the phone start to sweat. "Mrs. Winters, I got a very unusual letter today from Atlanta. I wondered if you or Celia might know something about it."

"Well I certainly don't. And if it came from Atlanta I'm almost certain Celia doesn't. She moved to Houston four years ago, didn't you know?"

"No," Mary said, her shoulders sagging. "I didn't."

"What did this mysterious letter say?" Mrs. Winters asked.

Mary swallowed. She considered just hanging up the phone. But maybe, maybe, Mrs. Winters knew something. Something that would help her.

"It said that my son was alive," she whispered.

There was a silence on the line. Mary waited, straining to hear anything. Finally, she had to break the silence. "Mrs. Winters?"

"Do you have a son?" Celia's mother asked in an abrupt tone.

That startled Mary. "No. At least . . . I don't think so."

"Then you don't," Mrs. Winters said quickly. "Dear, I understand what happened was a terrible thing for you to suffer, but it's over and in the past. It's best left there."

"But why would someone send me this?" Mary burst out. "Is it possible —"

"Mary, hush!" Mrs. Winters said, her voice suddenly harsh. "What's done is done. Don't look back. There's nothing there for you!"

Mary wanted to plead. Mrs. Winters knew something, she knew something . . .

The sound of a dial tone filled Mary's ears.

- SIX -

FRANCINE WINTERS' HAND SHOOK as she hung up the phone. *Ten years.* She'd thought that summer was gone and buried. Especially last year, when the clinic went up in flames.

She went to the kitchen and poured herself a glass of wine. She gulped half of it down, leaning against the black marble counter while she fought to calm herself.

You did the right thing, she told herself. *That girl had no business having a baby.*

She remembered the night Celia came into her room, face tear-streaked. Her best friend Mary was in trouble. Was there anything they could do to help? Her parents were straight-laced Christians, they wouldn't be any help . . .

Francine snorted. Yes, she knew the type. Her own parents had been like that, with all their rules and harping about the way she dressed, how much makeup she wore. She knew that Celia's poor friend would get no proper support from those people.

She was moving on, anyway. Her marriage to Danny, Celia's father, was at an end. He was a nice guy, but not someone to set her on fire. Francine was thirty-seven. She was too young to settle for boring.

So Francine sweet-talked the parents into letting Mary spend the summer with her and Celia. It had taken some doing – Francine *knew* that Mrs. Hollister looked down on her. After all, Francine was divorcing her husband – something that was certain to make her a woman in red to a Christian lady.

But the parents allowed it. And Francine took the two teenage girls to Atlanta, glad for the company, feeling she was doing a good deed.

Mary was a quiet thing, grateful for Celia's friendship and Francine's support. The only friction that came about was when they discussed what she should do about her pregnancy.

"Sweetie, abortion isn't really a big deal," Francine told her.

Mary's eyes filled with tears. "I can't kill my baby!"

Francine tried to hide it, but the girl's attitude bothered her. She had a problem, and an abortion would solve it. She could go back to living her life, no one the wiser, no loose ends. And then the kid has the nerve to act like it was murder!

Celia worried about her friend, which was why Francine put up with her. Celia was the one thing she didn't regret from her time with Danny, and she'd do just about anything for her daughter. So when Celia begged her mom to find a way to help Mary out of the situation, Francine felt compelled to do just that.

And she had. She knew Dr. Grayson – they'd gone out for drinks and stuff after meeting at an art gallery. Francine mentioned one time about Mary and her problem and Grayson had presented her with the ideal solution. Even offered her something for her referral.

She didn't tell Celia about that part. Figured she didn't need to know it all, she might let it slip to her friend. It was for the best, really.

So when it was all said and done, Mary got a clean slate. A way to go on with her life with no unwanted baby hanging around her neck. And Francine...well, Celia adored her for doing so much for her friend. And the money she got didn't hurt either.

With a frown, Francine refilled her glass. She didn't know who was trying to dig up the past, but they weren't doing *her* any favors. Or Mary. She hoped the girl would just forget about it and move on.

That's what Francine would do.

- SEVEN -

IT WAS ON DAYS LIKE THIS that Jack Foster was reminded of a comment an ex-girlfriend made when she walked out of his life.

"You might be a great reporter, Jack," she said as she slammed her suitcase shut, "but there are times you're just slime."

As he walked up to the front door of Martha Thompson's house, Jack guessed that visiting the home of a suicide victim hoping to get some information for an ongoing investigation fell into the "Slimy" category.

He'd noticed the dark blue rental car in the driveway so he figured someone was there. Family of some kind, he reckoned. Maybe they'd be willing to talk.

The man who opened the door wore the tired, slightly stunned expression that Jack associated with the newly bereaved. His reporter's eye clicked off the guy's appearance: probably around five foot ten, sandy brown hair, watery blue eyes.

"Yes? Can I help you?" the man asked.

"Yes, my name is Jack Foster. I was an acquaintance of Martha Thompson," Jack said, sticking his hand out. "I wanted to tell you how sorry I was to hear of her passing."

"Bob Thompson," the man took Jack's hand and gave him a cursory handshake. "I'm sorry, but this isn't a good time right now."

"I understand completely," Jack said, letting his eyes flick behind Thompson. Nothing obvious. Jack arranged his face into an expression of sympathy. "Are you her son?"

"Yeah," Thompson said, running a hand over his short hair. "Look, Mister…"

"Foster," Jack supplied. He didn't mind that the guy couldn't remember his name. Hopefully that meant his mom had never mentioned their almost meeting.

"Foster," Thompson repeated. "I'm really busy now, trying to sort out her stuff, and make funeral arrangements. I don't wanna be rude, but I'm not in a mood to be sociable."

"Is there any way I can help?" Foster asked.

Thompson's eyes narrowed. He appeared to be turning something over in his mind. "Look, just how did you know my mom?"

Foster weighed his answer and decided on a half-truth. "I met your mom around the time the clinic she worked at burned up. I know there was something about that really upset her."

The man stiffened at the mention of the clinic. "That place burning up was the best thing for her. You know what they did, right?"

I'd like to, Foster thought. Out loud, he said, "You didn't approve of Martha's working there?"

Thompson's mouth twisted. "It…it wasn't good. Not for her. Not for anyone. But she didn't want to hear it. After a while, we quit talking." His eyes filled and he dropped his head.

Foster nodded. "I'm sure your mother knew you loved her."

"I hope so," Thompson sighed. "I just wish I knew what drove her to this. I hope it didn't have anything to do what that awful place."

"Is that possible?" Jack asked.

"I wish I knew," Thompson said. "She was apparently looking for someone before she died – she had all this stuff from the Internet on her."

"Really? That sounds interesting," Jack said. "Perhaps it's a mutual acquaintance? If you give me the name, I might be able to help you out."

When Thompson frowned, Jack realized he might have overplayed his hand a bit. "Look, you seem awfully eager for information. What did you say your name was? And just how did you know my mother?"

Jack put a smile on his face. "Like I said, I knew your mom. Sorry about bothering you at this time."

Thompson studied him, and Jack was uneasy. He'd been stupid giving the guy his real name. If he figured it out…

"Yeah," Thompson said, rubbing his face. "Well, thanks for coming by."

"No problem. Again, my sympathies." Jack shook Thompson's hand and quickly made his way to his battered third-hand Ford Explorer.

As he drove towards his office, Jack reviewed what he'd learned. Apparently Martha Thompson was looking up someone before she died. He wondered who it might be. And why? He was willing to bet it had something to do with the clinic. She'd sounded very disturbed about it when she'd offered to meet that one time.

He'd have to watch for Martha's obituary and consider if there was a way to attend the funeral. He wanted to find out who Martha was looking for.

Maybe *she* had some answers for him about the clinic. And he'd finally write that award winning article he'd been researching all these months.

That was worth acting a little slimy for.

- EIGHT -

"Mommy? Mommy? Look at my picture!"

Kelly was quivering with energy as she waved the large piece of butcher paper in front of her.

Mary glanced at her daughter in the rear-view mirror. "In a few minutes, sweetie. Mommy needs to get us home first."

"But Mommy, I want you to look at it now!" Kelly whined.

"I said, we need to get home first!" Mary snapped.

She slumped as she pulled up to a red light. She turned and looked at her daughter, whose blue eyes sparkled with tears.

Oh, real good. Take your guilt out on your daughter. God, what kind of mother am I?

"Baby, I'm sorry," Mary said, reaching in back to rub her daughter's blue jean clad leg. "Mommy's feeling a little cranky today."

Kelly sniffled. "Do you gots a headache? Is that why you yelled at me?"

Mary nodded. "Yes, I guess I do." It wasn't a lie – she could feel the ache in back of her head near her neck – a tension headache for sure.

"I'll rub your head when we get home, then you won't have a headache and you won't be cranky. 'Kay, Mommy?" Kelly said. as she wiped the tears off her face.

"That sounds like a great idea," Mary said, trying to smile. A horn's honk made her twist to the front and realize the light was green. She drove forward, her hands tight on the steering wheel.

She needed to settle down. Kelly could be fooled, but Mary wasn't certain she could deceive Roger. And he wouldn't be satisfied with "I'm just cranky" as an explanation.

Once they were home Mary got Kelly in and settled with some frozen grapes and a glass of milk. While her daughter sat in the den checking out a VeggieTales video with her snack, Mary checked the answering machine, remembering that she'd missed a phone call earlier.

She realized she hadn't erased the old messages. When she heard the one from Bob Thompson for the second time, she felt herself tense. She didn't know a Martha Thompson, why would she have Mary's name and "information?" And why did her son sound so upset?

Mary quickly hit replay on the machine and grabbed a pen from its magnetic holder on the refrigerator. She scrawled the phone number on the pad that hung next to it and ripped the page off.

A glance in the den showed Kelly was totally engrossed in her video. "Sweetie, Mommy's going to make a phone call in Daddy's office. Just sit and watch your show, all right?"

Kelly nodded without taking her eyes off the screen while she sucked on a grape. Mary stopped in the bedroom where she'd left the mail. She scooped it up and brought it to the office.

She dropped most of the letters and advertisements into an untidy pile next to Roger's keyboard. She stuffed the condemning note back into its envelope and studied the room. She didn't want Roger to see it.

Finally she tucked it into the front pocket of her Bible cover. She felt a pang of guilt as she did so, as if hiding it near God's word was a kind of dirty act.

Mary took a deep breath. "Please God," she prayed, "I know I shouldn't even ask this given what I've done, but please help me figure this out."

Then she picked up the phone.

- NINE -

"THANK YOU FOR CALLING ME. I hope my message didn't alarm you."

"No, it didn't," Mary lied. She found herself twisting a blue paper clip she'd taken out of the jar on Roger's desk. "I have to admit it confused me, though. Why do you think I know your mother?"

"Well…" Thompson's voice was unsteady, which made Mary uneasy. She wondered why he was calling a stranger about his mother. Was she ill? Had she been in an accident?

"You see, Ms. Beamer…my mom…well, she wasn't well lately." There was a noisy sound of a breath on the line. "It's really hard for me to say this, but…she committed suicide."

Mary gasped. "Oh! Mr. Thompson, I'm so sorry!" She felt her stomach roil. As Thompson's words sank in, Mary remembered a night, less than ten years ago, when she sat in the bathroom she shared with her kid sister, the door locked. She sat on the cold pink tile floor, her back resting against the bathtub, one of her mother's good knives in her hand as she lightly pressed it against her wrist and thought about paying the ultimate price for her sins.

In the end, the fear of Hell kept her from it. She'd gotten the knife back into the kitchen without anyone knowing how close she'd come to bleeding out on the floor.

She came back to the present realizing that the choking sounds she heard on the phone were Thompson's sobs. Swallowing to get some moisture back in a throat that had suddenly gone dry, Mary said, "Mr. Thompson, I'm so sorry for your pain. But I don't know how I can help you."

"Please," he gulped. "She apparently searched for you on the Internet. Paid to get your information. It looks like she may have known you before you got married?"

Mary shook her head, then realized he couldn't see her doing that. "Did she ever live in Florida?"

"No," Thompson said. "No, she's lived here in Atlanta for years. Never in Florida."

Mary felt as if she'd suddenly slammed into a wall. "Atlanta?" she whispered. In her mind's eye, she saw the letter, the two sentences. Postmarked from Atlanta.

"Yes," Thompson said. "Have you ever been here? Maybe you met someplace here?"

She closed her eyes. "I was there once. Ten years ago."

"Where did you go here? Maybe you met her and didn't realize it?"

She didn't want to ask. Didn't want to know. But she had to. Mary pushed the words past the lump in her throat. "Did your mother have anything to do with the Peachtree Road Women's Clinic?"

The silence at the other end of the line was so complete Mary wondered if Thompson had hung up on her.

"What does that have to do with anything?" Thompson asked, his voice suddenly harsh. "Were you a – a *client?*"

"I –"Mary forced herself to take a breath, "It's a long story. Not what you think."

"Oh really?" Thompson's voice was tinged with anger. "You didn't ask that butcher Dr. Grayson to kill your baby for you?"

"No!" Mary cried, getting angry herself. "I didn't want to go there! I didn't *ask* to go there! You don't know me!"

Tears were sliding down her face. The door to the office opened, and Kelly peeked in, her blue eyes wide with worry.

"Mommy, who you yelling at? Why you crying?"

"I'm –" Mary wiped her face, tried to stop her voice from shaking. "Mommy's all right, sweetheart, I'll be out in a minute, okay?"

Kelly frowned. She didn't look convinced. "Can I help?"

"In a little bit, sweetie. I need to finish this phone call, then I'll let you help me." Mary tried to smile at her daughter. Kelly looked unconvinced but slipped out of the office, shutting the door again.

She wiped her eyes and fought to control herself. "Mr. Thompson, I think your mother sent me a letter before she died."

"Yeah?" he asked. There was still anger there, but her obvious distress seemed to dampen his own reaction a bit. "What did it say?"

Mary clutched the bent paper clip in a fist, feeling the ends of it dig into her palm. "It said, 'I know what you tried to do. Your son is alive.'"

There was a sharp intake of breath on the other end of the phone. "What did she mean by that?"

"I don't know," Mary whispered. "I hoped you did."

"How do I know my mother even sent it?"

"Again, I don't know," Mary said. "But you said she was searching for me. I don't know why anyone else would send me something like this. Almost no one knew about…about what happened."

She felt her heart slowing down. *Breathe*, she thought. *You can get through this. You can.*

"Can you come up to Atlanta?" Thompson asked finally. "I'd really like to see this letter."

"I'm sorry," Mary said. "I have a five-year-old daughter. And my husband . . . he doesn't know about any of this."

"I see," Thompson said. "Well, I suppose I could come down and see you after I clear up things here. But could you fax me a copy of the note? I'd like to see if it's her handwriting. It would tell me something."

"I – I suppose I could do that," Mary said. "Where do you want it sent?"

"I'll call you and let you know," Thompson said. "Ma'am…I don't know your story, but that clinic was nothing but trouble and evil for my mom. If you were part of what hurt her, I can't say I like you very much."

Mary closed her eyes. "I understand," she said, her voice sad. "To be honest, I'm not sure I like myself very much right now."

- TEN -

MARY HEARD THE FRONT DOOR OPEN as she pulled the cheesy chicken casserole out of the oven. Kelly, who was carefully decorating a tossed salad with cherry tomatoes, scrambled out of her chair. "Daddy! Daddy!" she squealed.

"Hey, how's my big girl?" Roger said. Mary put a smile on her face as she heard her husband heading for the kitchen. She put the hot dish on the stove top and stripped off her oven mitts as Roger entered, their daughter perched happily on his right hip.

"And how's my bigger girl?" Roger smiled as he gave Mary a kiss.

"Fine. How was work?" Mary asked as Roger put Kelly down. The little girl headed back to the kitchen table to resume adding tomatoes to the salad.

"Nothing really new. Just business." He frowned a minute. "You all right? You look a little pale."

Mary turned to pull a serving spoon out of a drawer. "Yes, I'm fine. Maybe just a little tired."

"Mommy was cranky today!" Kelly reported. "She had a headache and I was s'posed to rub her head and I forgot."

"That's all right sweetie, Mommy's headache went away," Mary said. *Everything's normal. Believe it and you'll look like it.* "Dinner's about ready, hon. Do you want iced tea?"

"Iced tea sounds good," Roger said, going to the kitchen table. "I'll put my stuff up and wash my hands." He plucked a cherry tomato out of the salad and popped it into his mouth.

Kelly giggled. "Daddy, you're not supposed to that!"

He grinned. "Oh yeah? Are you the Tomato Police? Are you gonna catch me?" he grabbed another tomato and trotted out of the kitchen, his laughing daughter chasing after him.

Mary leaned against the small island countertop that stood in the center of her kitchen and fought the sting of tears. Ten years ago, after Harold and the horrible summer, she thought she'd never be able to have a husband and family. She just wasn't good enough.

Look at her now. Mary wiped her eyes with the back of her hand as she poured iced tea for her and Roger and milk for Kelly. She had a life many people she knew envied. And they didn't realize it was built on shaky ground, ground that even now threatened to collapse under her.

The phone rang. Mary picked up. "Hello?"

She heard Roger's voice echo her greeting on another phone in the house (probably the bedroom phone). The caller appeared hesitant. "Ms. Beamer? This is Bob Thompson? I have —"

"Just a minute please," Mary broke in. "Roger, this is for me. I have it."

"Okay," Roger said. There was a click and Mary heaved a sigh of relief.

"Ms. Beamer?" Thompson sounded a little annoyed.

"Yes, I'm sorry," Mary stammered. "I…I just want to keep this between us for the moment, if you don't mind."

"Fine," Thompson said after a short silence. "Anyway, I have the number of a place here you can fax that letter to. Sooner the better."

Mary wrote down the number. "I'll get it and the envelope sent to you tomorrow, Mr. Thompson."

"All right," he said. "I guess I'll let you know when I've looked at it."

"That would be fine," Mary said. Out of the corner of her eye she saw Roger and Kelly coming back into the kitchen. "I have to go. Thank you for calling." She hung up the phone without waiting for Thompson to respond.

She wiped her hands on her jeans and turned around. Roger was frowning. "Hey, what was that about? You look upset."

Mary's thoughts raced. "It was one of Celia's friends," she said. "He's trying to track her down and wondered if I'd heard from her."

She cringed inside at the lie, but couldn't bring herself to tell the truth. Taking a deep breath she continued. "I still have Celia's mom's number – I talked with her earlier today. She confirmed Celia knew this guy and gave me some information to give him."

Roger nodded, though he still looked concerned. "Talking about Celia bothers you? You guys haven't been in contact for years."

Mary dropped her eyes to her hands as she twisted her wedding band. "Well, I keep thinking I wasn't a very good friend to her, was I? I never could persuade her to consider Christianity."

"Not your fault," Roger said, putting his hands on her shoulders. "You can only give the message. You can't make her listen."

Mary nodded. Kelly looked from one parent to another, frowning. "I'm hungry," she announced.

"Well then, I guess we should eat," Roger said. "What do you say, Mommy?"

Mary put the smile back on her face. "I think that's a great idea," she said. "Let's go ahead and get going."

Kelly ran to her chair at the table. Mary picked up one of the iced tea glasses and Kelly's milk. Roger reached from behind her and picked up the other glass of tea. "You are a fantastic lady and I love you," he murmured into her ear.

Mary swallowed, wishing she could believe him. Wondering if he'd still think that if he knew all she'd done.

- ELEVEN -

JACK FOSTER SIPPED HIS LUKEWARM Starbucks coffee while he waited in his Explorer outside the Thompson home.

He shifted around, trying to find a comfortable position. He'd been waiting there with the windows down for ventilation for a couple of hours, figuring the guy had to leave the house sometime. Maybe to get groceries, or make funeral plans. Or even to get out of a house that had to be getting depressing by now – Foster couldn't imagine being in a dead person's house as a cheery experience.

His cell phone rang. Foster glanced at the Caller ID: *Wheeler.* He chewed his lip as he considered answering it. With a shake of his head, he tossed the phone to the passenger seat. He really didn't want to talk to his boss at the moment. He'd want to know where Foster was and what he was doing, things that the reporter simply wasn't ready to share yet.

Finally, Foster's patience was rewarded. Thompson came out the front door and climbed into the white car in the driveway that screamed "rental." The man drove off without a glance at Foster's car.

Once Thompson was out of sight, Foster slipped out, his hands jammed into his windbreaker's pockets. He strolled down the sidewalk, noticing that no one was outside. It was a school day, so no kids played in the yards. Here and there a television program could be heard from an open window.

Foster strode up the walk to the Thompson's front door as if he belonged there. He caught the scent of roses as he took a deep steadying breath. It wasn't the first time he'd done something like this, but that didn't make him any less nervous.

He tried the knob. Locked. Not a surprise. But it had to be only the bottom lock. Thompson would've needed a key to lock the deadbolt and he hadn't done so. Foster had watched to make sure.

Using an old credit card, Foster jimmied the lock. His eyes darted to the left and the right. Nobody around to see. He slipped inside, shutting the door behind him.

The only light came from the weak sunlight coming in through the window in the front room. There was a small stack of newspapers next to the plump embroidered sofa under the window. A coffee cup sat on a doily coaster on a low oak coffee table along with a plate with a crust of toast.

Jack glanced in the room but didn't see anything particularly helpful to him. He didn't know how much time he had and so he would have to prioritize. Not that he knew exactly what he was looking for – he only knew he'd recognize it when he saw it.

The reporter went around the corner, taking in the small kitchen that had dishes stacked next to the sink and a couple of Chinese take-out cartons on the counter. A small, neat bathroom.

He hit paydirt in the second bedroom he peeked into. This room had a twin bed with a dark green floral duvet spread on it and enough decorator pillows to bury a small child. A computer sat on a small rosewood writing desk, with a printer on a gray filing cabinet.

What got Foster's attention were the papers laid out on the bed. He scanned the piles. Skipping over things that were obviously personal, such as Martha Thompson's bank statements, he came to a paper that was from an information website he'd used himself from time to time.

Quickly flipping through the pile, Foster saw that Martha Thompson had been looking for information on a woman named Mary Hollister. The older woman had managed to track her quarry to an up-to-date address and new name – Beamer. Looked like the gal had gotten married or something.

Using his cell phone, Foster quickly took pictures of all the papers in the pile. He was going to check more of the piles but he glanced at his watch first. He'd been in the house about five minutes – that was probably as long as he could risk. After he made sure the stack of papers he'd taken pictures of looked pretty much the same as it had when he first found it, he quickly got out of the house.

Just as he stepped off the walkway, he saw the white rental car turn the corner. He swore. Dropping his head, he kept up a steady pace, walking right past his car, trying to convey the impression of a man lost in thought, not a man running from the scene of a crime.

He kept walking even after he heard the slam of a car door. Turning left at the corner, he continued walking, risking a quick glance down towards the Thompson house. Everything looked peaceful.

Foster made a circuit, turning left at each corner until he was once again at his Explorer. The Thompson house looked pretty much like it had when he'd driven over to the neighborhood over two hours ago.

Once he slid into the driver's seat and started the engine, he felt the shaking begin. Foster let it happen, knowing he was reacting to the stress of what he'd just done. He was okay with that.

He headed to the office, feeling pretty happy with what he'd accomplished. That feeling went away when he remembered he probably had an angry editor waiting for him at his destination.

- TWELVE -

F OSTER!"

Jack groaned and cursed his bad luck. He'd gotten in and out of a person's house without getting caught but Marvin Wheeler, Editor-in-Chief of the *Atlanta Times* and the master of Foster's paycheck managed to nail him before he could get to his desk.

Marvin Wheeler was standing in the doorway of his office, sweat glistening on his bald head. He used a pen in his hand to point at Foster like a gun. "My office. Right now!"

Foster felt some sympathetic and not-so-sympathetic looks aimed his way as he obediently headed for his bosses' cluttered office. Wheeler waited until it was clear Foster wasn't planning a detour at the last minute and then moved back far enough to allow the younger man to enter.

Foster picked his way around the piles of paper that were scattered over the floor and settled into a chair in front of Wheeler's desk, setting his worn black laptop case at his feet. The editor-in-chief lowered his bulk into his much better chair, which groaned in protest.

With a scowl, Wheeler tossed his pen onto his desk and grabbed a pack of nicotine gum instead. "Whose stupid idea was it to say you can't smoke in the newsroom?" he muttered as he stuffed two pieces of gum into his mouth.

Foster shrugged. He knew better than to answer that one. Wheeler was always trying to quit smoking. One of the ongoing betting pools in the newsroom was how long the boss would stay on the wagon. So far this time it had been two weeks – the record was six.

Jack concentrated on studying his folded hands on his lap. He also knew better than to ask why Wheeler wanted to see him. When the large man hauled an errant reporter into his office, those who wanted to get out of there still employed kept their mouths shut unless they were spoken to.

"Foster, did you or did you not attend the Fulton County Commission special meeting last night?" Wheeler asked in a voice that an unsuspecting person might call soft.

"Of course I did, Mr. Wheeler," Jack said into his lap.

"You did?" Wheeler's voice asked. "Then why isn't there an article detailing the verbal sparring that supposedly took place on my desk at the moment ready to be put on page one!"

Jack groaned to himself. Yeah, he knew he should've had the article in by now. He'd gotten back from that rather entertaining meeting with his notes all ready to type up but he'd gotten to thinking about Martha Thompson again and the now defunct Peachtree Road Women's Clinic. There was a major story there – he knew it. And there would be something in that house to help him find it if he only could get in there…

And so the article he was supposed to write had flown completely from his mind. Until now, with Wheeler glaring at him from across his messy desk, his jaw working on two sticks of nicotine gum.

"I'm sorry, sir," Jack said, putting as much sincerity as he could into the words. "I'll have it for you in about twenty minutes." He started to stand. "In fact, I'll get right on it –"

"Sit down," Wheeler growled. "I'm not done with you."

Foster plopped back into his chair. He had a bad feeling about this.

Wheeler's small black eyes studied Foster from under white bushy eyebrows. "Were you aware that Martha Thompson, a former employee at the Peachtree Road Women's Clinic, recently passed away?"

"I believe I read that somewhere, yes sir," Foster said. There was no point in denying it, though he wondered why Wheeler had noticed.

The editor didn't leave him in the dark for long. "Wasn't she going to be your star informant on the alleged evil goings-on in that clinic?"

"Well, that didn't pan out, Mr. Wheeler, so I guess the answer is moot," Foster shrugged.

"Don't play with me!" Wheeler slammed his hand down on his desk, causing a cup full of pens to jiggle. "Are you still trying to revive that story? After I made it clear to you it's a dead one?"

"What makes you think I'd do something like that?" Foster asked, trying to keep his temper.

"Maybe because I know you, Jack," Wheeler said, leaning forward and waving a finger at the younger man. "You're good at getting out the dirt – one of the reasons I haven't thrown your rear end out the door by now. And once you have a story, you're like a dog with a bone. But this story's going nowhere. You had your shot – you missed. Let go of it."

"What if I've found some new information?" Foster asked. It was a risky question, but Wheeler was right about one thing – Jack didn't want to let go of this story.

Wheeler groaned and sat back. "You don't listen, do you? I just told you it's a dead story and you're saying you got new info. What are you doing getting info on a dead story?"

"Mr. Wheeler, with all due respect, this story doesn't have to be dead," Jack said, leaning forward himself. "Yeah, I've hit some roadblocks. But it's a big story. Major. We break it, we're talking Pulitzer."

"It's dead! All I've seen you do in this story is chase your tail." Wheeler shook his head. "And don't tell me that your obsession with this so-called story isn't the reason I'm missing an *assigned* story from you."

Obsession? Jack thought. *Is that what this is?*

But pursuing the answer to that question went places in Jack's mind he flinched from. Things he kept to himself. If Wheeler knew about some of those places…especially one…well, it was better if he didn't.

"Look, I admit I messed up on the county commission story," Jack finally said. "But like I said, I'll have it on your desk in twenty minutes, easy. Just give me a little more rope on this other thing. I'm close. I know I am."

Wheeler stared at Jack, his jaw still working on the gum, his arms folded across his chest. Jack said nothing. He just hoped he'd made a good case for himself.

"A little rope," Wheeler agreed with a frown. "But *only* a little. Consider this a called-in favor. And understand there's not a lot of those left for you."

"I understand," Jack said, relief flooding over him. He started to rise, his eyes on his boss. "So, maybe I should get started on that article…"

Wheeler nodded. "Yeah, get outta my sight before I remember I can fire you."

Jack wasted no time, grabbing his laptop case and all but running out the door. He made a beeline for his desk, finally sinking into his chair with a sigh.

Of course, no matter what Wheeler had said, Jack wouldn't have given up on the story. But having a green light – okay, a yellow one, maybe – was better.

Jack dug his notepad out of his case while contemplating checking out how old the coffee was in the break room. He would get this assignment finished, see what else he needed to do, and then look at the pictures he'd snapped. With any luck they would be a lead to the goings on at the Peachtree Road Women's Clinic.

And along with a great award winning story Jack might also get the ability to put a personal demon to rest.

- THIRTEEN -

MARY HEARD JOANNE CARSON finish up her prayer with a feeling of relief. Normally, ladies Bible class was a fun and instructional time. It was a chance to chance to spend time with like-minded women, most of whom were older than Mary – only a handful of those attending had school-age children.

Today hadn't gone very well. Mary had completely forgotten about the church secretary's call on Monday until after dinner. When she called Betty at home, the older woman said that when Mary hadn't called back she'd gotten hold of Joanne and the preacher's wife was happy to take the class.

Feeling guilty, Mary had dragged herself to class. On the way, she'd stopped at an office supply store and faxed Bob Thompson a copy of the letter and envelope she'd gotten. It was still in the pocket of her embroidered Bible cover, along with the book the class was studying. Having the two things next to each other was unsettling.

She'd gone through class in a kind of fog. There'd been the usual time for prayer requests, and Mary had barely paid attention to the names listed. She was asked to open the class with prayer, and she'd stood in the large room that was used for classes and meals, long tables going across the width of the room and folding chairs lined up behind them, and stumbled through a prayer, barely aware of what she was saying.

As she sat back down, Mary was aware of several concerned looks in her direction. She'd said nothing, her eyes focused on the book in front of her.

The class discussion flowed around her and Mary sat there, staring at a page in her book, not really comprehending the words, silent. Why had she bothered coming? Her mind wasn't there.

"Who's going to lunch?" asked Amy Martin, an older woman who had been with the congregation longer than almost anyone else in the room.

A number of women raised their hands. Mary didn't. She usually went to lunch with the women – it was a weekly treat for her. But she'd pushed her luck even being here. What made her think it was a good idea?

As she stood, she heard various restaurant names being suggested by women around her. As she tightened her grip on her Bible and purse, she realized how apart she felt from the other women today. Not a usual feeling – the women in this room had become a family of sorts. The running joke of the congregation was that if you wanted to know who was sick or who needed a visit that you just asked a member of the Ladies Bible Class.

Was Mary sick? Did she need a visit? She'd shared many things with the women around her – times of concern, times of illness, times of personal struggle. But never her biggest fear. Her biggest failing. Her biggest burden.

With a sigh Mary started to the door. A hand on her arm stopped her. "Mary?"

Joanne Carson stood next to her, green eyes filled with concern. "Is everything all right?"

Mary tried to smile. "I guess I'm just tired."

Her friend shook her head slowly. "I think it's something else. Do you have a minute?"

"I don't know, Joanne," Mary said, shifting her Bible from arm to arm. She wished her friend would take a hint and leave her alone.

"You're not going to lunch. You usually do," Joanne said.

"Come on, Joanne, it's not like it's a sin to skip lunch with the ladies," Mary said, her voice coming out a little harsher than she meant it to.

"It's not," Joanne said, taking a step back. "But it just seemed that something was on your mind. More than just being tired. I wondered if you needed to talk."

"I…I can't," Mary said. "It's fine. I'm taking care of things just fine."

Joanne cocked her head. "What is it? You look really upset."

Mary shook her head. "Nothing, Joanne." She regretted that she'd hurt her friend's feelings, but she couldn't – she *couldn't* tell her the truth. No one could know. Not even her best friend.

She felt her cheeks grow hot while Joanne stared at her a moment longer. "All right," Joanne said, brushing her red hair back from her face. "I'll let you go. You know you can call me if you need to chat, right?"

Mary nodded. "Of course," she said. "Look, I need to get home. Thanks for taking the class."

"No problem," Joanne said, giving her friend's arm a pat. "I'll see you tomorrow night, right?"

"Right," Mary said. "See you then."

Mary walked quickly to her car. Some women called farewells to her; Mary's responses were automatic, her mind reeling. Once in the safety of her Camry, Mary closed her eyes, letting her thoughts go back to the letter in her Bible.

For the most part she was successful in burying the horrid summer in Atlanta. She wanted to leave it in the past, bury it, burn it, anything to keep it from touching her again.

But somehow it was back in her life. It was teasing her, already reaching fingers into her current life, the life she'd built brick by cautious brick, threatening to demolish it.

She couldn't let that happen. She knew she didn't deserve her blessings, but she didn't want to lose them, either.

Swallowing the bile in her throat, she started her car. "Please God," she whispered, "don't take my life away from me. Even if I deserve to lose it, please, please don't take it."

- FOURTEEN -

FRANCINE PAID ATTENTION to her GPS navigator as she entered the outskirts of Montgomery, Alabama. She'd never been to this new clinic of Thomas'. She hadn't even spoken with Green since the Atlanta place had burned down, though they'd swapped Christmas cards over the years.

She pondered this trip. She hadn't been able to get Mary Hollister (*Beamer, her name is Beamer now*) out of her mind. That unwanted phone call brought up some concerns for Francine. Concerns for herself.

After the nice bonus she'd gotten from bringing Mary to Thomas, Francine had kept a sharp eye out for other girls in similar situations. She worked at an upscale clothing store and it was a place where she got to know the younger set.

Poor things . . . some of them worked so hard to conceal their pregnancies, dressing in horrible shapeless sweatshirts and baggy pants. Francine got to where she could spot them – the sad desperation in their eyes, the longing looks they gave pretty clothes they couldn't wear at the moment.

Francine befriended them, bought them sodas, listened to their tales of woe. She then offered them a way out. She knew a doctor who could help make it all away, and they could even arrange payment plans with him.

When Francine brought him a *particular* client – one whose pregnancy was seven months or later – there was always a nice little financial bonus for her. She never spoke to him about what happened following those procedures. After all, Francine was an expert at looking out for Francine. In this case, ignorance was bliss.

She pulled into the parking lot of a nice looking white building with a sign out front that had "Commerce Ave. Women's Clinic" in gold letters on a brown background.

Francine frowned at the sight of a few people standing on the sidewalk in front of the building. One man held up a sign "Abortion stops a beating heart." Two women were on their knees on the sidewalk, their heads bowed over their folded hands. Two or three others stood watching her as she parked her red BMW.

Stupid people. Didn't they have better things to do than harass women exercising their rights over their bodies? Francine shot the group a scornful look as she got out of her car. She strode into the clinic, ignoring the voices behind her. Idiots.

Inside the walls of the waiting room were painted a soothing peach. Classical music was piped in. A couple of women sat in the comfortable looking white chairs leafing through magazines.

A young blond woman looked up from the reception desk. "Hello. May I help you?"

Francine smiled. "My name is Francine Winters. I told Dr. Green I would be visiting today?"

The woman pulled a sticky note off her computer monitor. "Yes, he mentioned it. Please follow me?"

Francine was led to the back of the clinic and seated in a large office. She declined an offer of coffee and settled back in the black leather chair, looking over the office.

Thomas' office looked similar to the one he'd had in Georgia. It was a little nicer than that one, but the doctor's tastes in decoration hadn't changed in the year that had passed. He had an Ansel Adams print on the wall over his large mahogany desk. A colorful Oriental rug lay over the industrial carpet.

Francine remembered the Adams print. She wondered how it had survived the fire last year.

The door behind her opened. "Francine! What a nice surprise!"

She turned, smiling. "Thomas! It's been too long," she said, offering her cheek for a kiss.

Green was in his early fifties. His black hair showed a little more gray at the temples than last year, but he still appeared to be in shape from what she could see. He wore a white lab coat over a pair of black trousers and a blue dress shirt with a black tie.

"Please, have a seat," Green said, waving her to a black leather sofa and sitting at one end. "I'm glad to see you again. How're things back in Atlanta?"

"Nothing new," Francine said as she sat, smoothing the skirt of her print dress over her knees. "How are things doing here? I'm glad you appear to be back on your feet after that terrible fire last year."

Green nodded, running a hand through his hair. "Business is good, in spite of religious fanatics trying to shut people like me down."

Francine nodded. She chewed her lip, suddenly nervous. "Thomas, I hate to bring up unpleasant matters, but I received an odd phone call yesterday I think you should know about."

The doctor frowned. "Phone call?"

"Yes," Francine nodded. "Do you remember the first young girl I brought to your clinic? Mary Hollister?"

"Hollister, Hollister..." Green's eyes narrowed. "Maybe, Francine, but it was a long time ago. What's this about?"

"She told me she got a note from someone in Atlanta," Francine said.

Green shrugged. "A note? What did it say?"

"It said her son was alive."

The doctor frowned, his eyes suddenly hard. "Did she say who it was from?"

"She thought Celia or I had sent it," Francine said. She found Green's reaction to this news very interesting. "Do you have any ideas?"

Green's gaze turned inward. It was almost as if he hadn't heard her question. Puzzled, Francine put a hand on his leg. "Thomas?"

"Hm?" He looked at her, and smiled. "Sorry, Francine, woolgathering. I'm afraid I don't have any idea about this alleged note. Do you think this girl was making it up?"

"I don't know why she would," Francine said.

"It could be some delayed guilt," Green said. "Sometimes women experience some residual guilt following the termination of a pregnancy. Especially if some religious person's gotten to them."

"She didn't have an abortion," Francine said. "Remember?"

"Oh. Her," Green said. "Even so, all the more reason she might feel guilt. She was quite upset after losing her baby."

"I don't know, Thomas..."

"Look, I appreciate you alerting me to this," Green said with a smile. "But I wouldn't worry about it." He stood. "When do you have to head back? Can I persuade you to have dinner with me?"

Francine smiled. It had been a while, but she enjoyed the man's company. "I can stay overnight. I'd love to have dinner with you again."

"Wonderful!" Green said. "Ask my receptionist to recommend a good hotel for you – unless you've already made arrangements?"

"I wasn't sure you'd have time for me," Francine said, winking at him.

"I can always make time for a beautiful woman like you," Thomas said with a bow. "Leave a number I can reach you at and I'll let you know when I'll pick you up."

"Sounds wonderful," Francine said. "I look forward to it."

As she walked out of Green's office, she felt a warm feeling suffuse her body. The trip hadn't been a waste of time after all.

- FIFTEEN -

DOCTOR THOMAS GREEN SAT in his leather office chair and considered what Francine Winters had said. The more he thought about it, the angrier he got.

There was a leak. After all these months!

One of his nurses opened the door and stuck her head in. "Dr. Green? Ms. Masters is waiting in Exam Room 2…"

"Why didn't you knock?" he snapped.

The nurse, a young blonde thing, stiffened. She was one of his newer employees. He'd been forced to replace some people after the move from Georgia, and this woman at least didn't seem to understand simple protocol. "I'm sorry, Doctor, I saw your visitor had left and I assumed…"

"Well, don't!" he said. "Now, please, I need a few minutes … no, wait a moment. Ask Sharon to step in here for a minute."

A few minutes later there was a light tap on the door, and Green's office manager, Sharon Abrams walked in. She was a handsome woman in her mid-forties, and one of Green's oldest and most trusted employees.

She wore a smart red suit with a white ruffled blouse. She sat down and crossed long legs. "You wanted to see me, Thomas?"

Green had spent the time he waited for her thinking about how to approach the problem. "Sharon, do you ever hear from the help that stayed behind in Atlanta?"

She tilted her head. "Not really. Birthday and holiday cards. Why?"

"You know Francine Winters was here just now." It wasn't a question. There was little that went on in the clinic that Sharon didn't know about.

Sharon nodded. "Yes. I wondered about that." She smiled as she twisted a strand of brown hair. "Is she making another play for you?"

Green smiled and shrugged. "Not sure. But that shouldn't concern you, should it?"

"Only as it relates to the business," Sharon said. "You and I had our fun, but…"

"That's not why I wanted to talk to you," he said, leaning forward, his hands resting on the large desk calendar that sat there. "She brought me some news that concerns me. And it concerns Atlanta."

Sharon straightened up, all playfulness gone. "There's no sign they're reopening the arson investigation, is there?"

"No! At least, I don't think so," Green said. "But it could be something worse."

"Worse?" Sharon's eyes narrowed. "You think someone's talking?"

Inwardly, Green admitted how lucky he was to have someone like Sharon on his team. She was smart, and could be counted on in a crisis. Out loud, he said, "Let me tell you what Francine told me."

He relayed the conversation. As he did, Sharon pulled out her iPhone and began taking notes. When he was done, she took a moment to read them, her lips pursed.

She sighed. "Martha Thompson."

He blinked. "Excuse me?"

Sharon lowered the phone and frowned. "If the girl in question is the one I'm thinking of, it sounds as if Martha might be the one to have sent the note. She took that particular case rather hard."

Green shook his head. "She never said anything. She was one of our best nurses. I was sorry she didn't relocate with us."

"She did her job, but I'm telling you that case bothered her," Sharon insisted. "I even caught her looking at the file one time. She said she was checking something, but there was no reason for her to be in that chart."

"You never said anything to me," Green said, his eyes narrowing.

Sharon spread her hands. "As you said, she was one of our best nurses. I figured she worked through it to some extent. If the worst thing she did was look at an old file, we had no problems. Though why you even keep the stupid files…"

"I have my reasons," Green said. "Besides, as far as anyone knows now, the files are ashes."

Sharon steepled her fingers, tapping them against her red lips. "Do you want me to check this out?"

"Do you mind?" Green said. "Just call Martha, see how she's doing? Maybe encourage her to remember whose side she's on?"

"Not a problem," Sharon said, standing up. "I'll get right on it."

Green felt as if a weight had been removed from his shoulders. "Thanks, Sharon. I knew I could count on you." He stood. "I'm going to get back to seeing patients. Let me know what you find, all right?"

- SIXTEEN -

As SHARON ABRAMS STRODE towards her office, she paused to smile and say a word or two to patients or staff she passed. *Iron hand in glove of velvet* was her motto for dealing with the people here. Those who crossed her learned very quickly why it was dangerous to do so.

Sharon stepped into her tastefully decorated office and shut the door behind her. Dear Thomas. He rewarded those who helped him, and she'd been his right-hand gal all these years. He had been generous, that was for sure.

Her office was the largest one in the clinic - next to his, of course. She had a lovely mahogany desk, a top of the line computer system and some pretty watercolors she'd seen and asked for. A scent of lavender came from a lit candle on top of one of her cherry bookshelves.

She didn't feel a bit guilty for the perks – she knew good and well she earned each and every one of them.

Now she went to her electronic database and looked up Martha Thompson's contact information. Sharon had liked the older woman well enough, even though she thought the nurse had let her emotions run away with her when it came to what they did at the clinic. Not a good thing.

Sharon herself knew that to survive in this business you had to keep an emotional distance. See the women as clients, the fetuses as tissue, and the babies – well, that was harder, she admitted to herself. But they weren't _her_ kids, and they did serve a purpose.

Sharon took a moment to plan how she would conduct the phone call she needed to make. Once she'd run a suitable script in her mind, she picked up the receiver and dialed.

After three rings the phone was picked up. "Hello?" a man's voice said.

Sharon frowned. She knew that Martha's husband was dead. Had she started seeing someone? "Excuse me, is this Martha Thompson's residence?"

A noisy sigh came over the phone line. "Who is this, please?"

Sharon thought fast. She settled on a partial truth. "This is Sharon Abrams. I represent Ms. Thompson's former employer and was calling to inquire about –"

"Stop!" the voice said, rising in anger. "Don't you people think you've done enough damage? I couldn't stand that my mom worked at that horrible place! It's probably one of the reasons she –"the voice choked off.

Sharon was immediately on alert. This was Martha's son. She racked her brain and remembered Martha mentioning that her working at the clinic had caused some tension between her and her children. "Mr. Thompson, I'm sorry your mother's employment with us caused you some difficulties. But I do have a matter regarding some back pay we might owe her and I really do need to discuss it with her."

"Well you can't! Because she's dead! Dead like the babies your doctor kills!" Thompson shouted. "Don't ever call here again!" There was a click as the call was disconnected, though Sharon was sure he'd slammed the phone down.

Lost in thought, she replaced the receiver. Sharon opened a new document on her computer and typed up the essence of the phone call while it was fresh in her mind.

After she did that, she sat back in her chair and looked it over, grabbing her cup of mint tea from its warming pad. She read over the words again, replaying the call in her mind.

Martha Thompson was dead. How? It sounded like the son blamed the clinic for it. Why would he do that?

Suicide?

"Possible," Sharon murmured to herself. It was a guess at best, but she was good at guessing. It fit with the son's anger, his presence at the home.

Sharon thought about how she might confirm her hypothesis. A call to the police? They used to have contacts in the department while the clinic operated there – having good relationships with a few policemen went a long way in their business.

Yes, Sharon would have to make that phone call. She made a note on the document she'd started. She then saved the document with a password that only she knew. No one else was supposed to use this computer but she knew that you could never be too cautious.

Martha's death, while regrettable on some personal level – Sharon truly didn't bear the woman any ill will – was satisfactory if she was the one to send the note to the patient. It meant that particular leak was plugged.

As for the patient herself…Sharon made a note on her iPhone to ask Thomas about the woman. The note had obviously upset her, and the clinic might have to take steps to ensure that the former patient didn't raise any fuss. But Sharon would need more information before she could decide on a course of action.

"Ms. Abrams? Mr. Strickland on line two," said one of the receptionists.

"Thank you," Sharon replied and picked up the phone. Carson Strickland was the lawyer who worked with the clinic. He not only handled all their normal legal issues, but was instrumental in the *other* side of the business – the side known to only a few in the clinic.

Sharon felt very positive after hanging up from Strickland ten minutes later. She decided to check on the product, make sure there would be no problems with it. After a final sip of tea she strode out of her office.

Sharon stepped into a hallway near Dr. Green's office. There was a door here with a numeric keypad. A handful of help, all of them who'd been with Green since Georgia, had access to this area. Sharon was naturally one of them.

She keyed in her personal code and gained entry into the softly lit room.

The walls were painted a soothing blue here. Two wooden rocking chairs sat in the middle of the room. There were eight incubators, two on each wall. Equipment used for the care of newbies and preemies filled the remaining empty spaces. A humming sound from the machines filled the space.

One nurse was gently rocking a baby bundled in a yellow blanket. She looked up as Sharon came in. "Afternoon, Ms. Abrams. Everything all right?"

"Everything's fine, Nadine," Sharon said with a smile. She noted two of the incubators had children resting in them. "What do you have there?"

"This is Jane Doe 32," Nadine said, moving a fold of the blanket so Sharon could get a better look at the child's face. "She was terminated two days ago – was thirty weeks at the time."

"Gotta be grateful for those women who wait til the last minute to decide on an abortion," Sharon said softly. The child appeared well-formed and normal, albeit a bit on the small side. Her hair was dark, her complexion had an olive cast to it. "What was her Apgar score?"

"It was an eight. Not bad, all things considered," Nadine said, allowing the sleepy child to grip her index finger. "You have someone for her?"

"Possibly," Sharon said, her eyes going back to the two occupied incubators. "Is she our only female at the moment?"

"Afraid so," Nadine said. "We'll have to wait and see what comes up later, but right now, this is what we have."

Sharon nodded. "Well, I think she'll suit the client. And I'll see what we can get for the two boys."

Nadine stroked the child's soft cheek. "You hear that, little girl? You're gonna have a family after all."

Sharon left while Nadine continued to coo at the baby. It bothered her, sometimes, to watch the nurses cuddle and jabber at the infants. It wasn't professional. She didn't know how the nurses could stay detached when they did that.

She was different. She didn't let those little ones enter her heart. They were something to offer to others for the right price. That was it. That was all they could ever be to Sharon.

Otherwise, she'd never sleep at night.

- SEVENTEEN -

MARY LEANED AGAINST THE DOORWAY to Kelly's room, listening as Roger read the little girl a bedtime story. It had a large number of characters, and their daughter was shaking with giggles as Roger employed a variety of voices.

Normally this sight gave Mary peace; it served as a reassurance that God had not chosen to punish her for the rest of her life for her sins. He'd given her a husband and a child. Surely these were blessings?

But tonight the thought of another child invaded her thoughts. A boy, ten years old – five years older than Kelly.

What did he look like? Did he have Harold's chocolate brown eyes, or her own dark blue ones? Did his hair have a wave to it like hers did?

Was he at this moment in a warm bed, listening to someone tell him a bedtime story? Was he loved? Was he safe? Did he know about her?

She blinked back tears. Why had they told her he was dead? Or was the note just a huge lie, something that Martha Thompson sent to torture her with for whatever reason?

Thompson had called back just as Mary was walking out the door to pick up Kelly from school. He'd confirmed that the handwriting on the note was his mother's. "I'll let you know when I can come down," he said. "I hope you can help me clear this up."

Mary almost told him not to come. She was frightened. As she looked into Kelly's room, the blue walls with the rainbows, the oak dresser that had been Mary's when she was a child, she feared she was going to lose all she held dear because of this. And she didn't want to.

She realized that Roger had finished the story and was tucking Kelly in, kissing her good night. Mary took a deep breath and put a smile on her face. She leaned over and kissed Kelly's soft cheek. "Good night, sweetheart."

"G'night, Mommy," Kelly said, eyes already closed. Mary rested a hand on the golden head a moment before following Roger out of the bedroom.

She went to the kitchen to finish loading the dishwasher. As she began to stack plates, she felt her husband's hands on her shoulders, kneading them. "Hon, you seem awfully tense. Everything all right?"

Mary swallowed, her eyes on the plates smeared with spaghetti sauce. "I guess . . . I have a lot on my mind."

"Come here." Roger turned her around to face him, his forehead wrinkled. It was an expression Mary was familiar with. She saw it when he tried to balance the checkbook, or put together a toy. He was trying to figure something out.

"You've been really moody tonight. What's going on? Have I done something?"

She shook her head. "No – of course not. It has nothing to do with you."

"What does it have to do with?" Roger asked. "I can't put my finger on it, but something's really eating at you."

Mary swallowed, fighting back tears. She knew she should tell Roger, that she should have told him before they got married.

But she was afraid. Would he still want her if he knew? Could he forgive her? Would he understand? Roger was Mary's anchor. If she lost him, she didn't think she could survive.

"I – I can't talk about it, Roger." She placed her hands on his chest, feeling his heart beat beneath her fingers. "Please, don't push this. I'll be all right."

He pulled her to him, his arms around her. Mary rested her head against him, her arms wrapping around his waist. She felt peace and safety, as she always did in his arms. He rested his cheek on her head, and she let herself sink into his warmth.

"Can I pray for you?" he asked softly. "God knows what you're going through. I wish you'd tell me, but are you telling Him?"

She swallowed. "He does know. And yes, please pray for me, Roger. And forgive me."

His hand stroked her hair. "Mary, why can't you tell me?"

"I just can't." The tears pressed harder. "Please, Roger, please. I can't right now."

He said nothing for a moment. Mary blinked her eyes furiously. *Don't cry, don't cry . . ._*

He pulled her back a little, his fingers under her chin so she met his eyes. He was frowning. "You know you can tell me anything."

She shook her head, stepping back, the counter pressing against her body. "Roger, I don't want to talk about this! Please!"

He sighed. "I don't understand! What's going on?"

"Nothing!" she said. "Nothing's going on, can you please just leave it alone?"

Roger's shoulders sagged. She saw the look of hurt in his eyes before he dropped his gaze to the floor. "Fine. I guess I'll go into the office and look over the mail."

Mary nodded. "All right. Want some coffee?"

"No thanks." Roger headed out of the kitchen, but paused in the doorway. "I do love you, you know."

"I know. And I love you too," Mary said, trying to smile.

He nodded, then left. Mary breathed a huge sigh, feeling her arms start to tremble. It took several minutes for her to calm herself before she went back to cleaning up the kitchen.

- EIGHTEEN -

GREEN SAMPLED THE WINE the waiter brought to the table and nodded his approval. He smiled at Francine as it was poured. "I hope this place is all right."

She was wearing a red dress with a halter top that showed a lot of skin. Lucky for him, the skin looked good. Francine always knew how to present herself, he had to give her that.

"All right? This restaurant is fantastic!" she said, sipping her wine. "I would never have guessed a place like Montgomery would have something so – so cosmopolitan!"

"Yes, it doesn't seem to fit with one's view of Alabama," Green said. "But Montgomery is a big city – big for around here, anyway – and it knows to cater to a certain clientele."

They were at Le Chateau Bonne, an upscale restaurant that wasn't too far from the government district. It was decorated with dark paneled walls, fine linen on the tables, and tasteful artwork. The menu was second to none in the state. Now and then the Governor himself would dine there, along with his wife.

Green didn't come to this place that often. But he remembered that Francine's tastes ran to expensive, and wanted to please her for the moment. Especially with the news she'd brought – the more he thought about it, the more worried he got.

When the waiter set out their lobster bisque and a basket of bread, he decided to broach the subject. "I've been thinking about that young woman you mentioned – Mary, was it?"

Francine nodded as she stirred her soup. "Yes. I hope I did the right thing to talk to you about it."

"Absolutely," Green said. "Whoever sent her that note did her a terrible disservice. I'm sure it opened old wounds."

"She was pretty upset when she talked to me," Francine said. Her eyes glittered in the candlelight. "But I won't lie to you Thomas – I'm a little worried about me, too."

"Why?" Green said, trying to appear casual as he cut a slice of warm sourdough bread. "You surely have nothing to feel guilty of."

"I don't," Francine said flatly. "But someone apparently knows something. Does that mean others could too?"

He took his time, spreading butter on his bread and chewing a piece. "Others?"

She gave an impatient sound that sent the candle flames between them dancing. "Like official somebodies, Thomas. Am I in trouble?"

Green cocked his head. "Why would any of us be in trouble, Francine?"

"I don't know!" she snapped. "Look, I helped you out, right? So doesn't that mean you help me out too?"

"I believe you were paid under the table for any help you gave the clinic," Green said. He focused on not letting the spoon in his hand tremble as he ate.

The woman across from him stared at him with narrowed eyes. Then she relaxed and smiled. "Of course, Thomas, I was just being silly. Don't mind me."

"Well, I know that getting a call like that can be disconcerting." Green said, touching his cloth napkin to his lips. "Do you know if this woman confided in anyone else?"

"Mary? Tell someone else about this?" Francine shook her head. "Thomas, the girl was raised by parents who bought into the whole Bible belt way of thinking. She didn't tell them, I know that – my daughter and I had to be there for her. I doubt she's let on to anyone."

Green nodded. "Well, let's talk about something more pleasant. How long are you planning on staying here?"

Francine gave him a smile while she batted her eyes. "Well, I probably should go back to Atlanta sometime tomorrow. But if I have a good reason I could always plan a longer stay in the not-too-distant future."

"I would like that very much," Green said, raising his wine glass in a toast to her. Francine was fun in her own way, and he knew if he played his cards right he'd have an enjoyable evening with her following the meal.

As to the rest…Green was a careful man. He knew when there was trouble brewing, and he knew that this young woman who called Francine could be a potential problem. Keeping Francine close was a way to monitor that.

Green relaxed as he saw their waiter coming with their salads. *It'll be fine. I'll take care of this snag and business will go on as usual. It always does.*

- NINETEEN -

"SO, JACK!"

Foster glanced up from his computer monitor to see Tom Davidson hovering over his desk. The younger man held out one of the cups of coffee he was holding.

"Thanks," Foster said. He took a sip and grimaced. *No sugar. Figures.*

"Hey, no problem, Jack," Tom said. He took a long swallow of his own drink. "So, nice article on the Fulton County Commission meeting."

Foster mentally rolled his eyes. "Again, thanks. It wasn't that groundbreaking."

Davidson waved a hand. "Hey, we can't always write award winning, attention-grabbing, get-the-spotlight-turned-on-us stories. Some of us have to actually write *news*."

"Ha-ha, very funny, Tom," Jack snorted. "I write plenty of news stories."

"Yeah, but I know you think you're slumming – you think you're better than most of us in here."

"I *am* better than most of you in here," Jack snapped. "How long have you been in the business, Tom? How many words of yours have seen print?"

Tom shook his head. "Get off your high horse, Foster. You had your time – the rest of us will get our shots. Quit looking down your nose at us."

Foster stood, impatient. "If you want your shot, quit coming here picking fights." He held out his coffee cup. "And if you're gonna bring me coffee, at least ask how I like it!"

He suddenly realized how quiet the newsroom had gotten. With a glance around, Foster realized he and Davidson had gotten the attention of everyone except Wheeler. The only reason he didn't have Wheeler's attention was because the editor-in-chief had his office door firmly shut.

Davidson seemed to realize it at the same time. He grinned and held his cup up as a salute to the room. "Nothing to see here, people. Back to your business." He smirked at Foster. "Talk to you later, Jack." He sauntered back to his own desk.

Foster glared at the room, daring someone to say something. One by one his fellow reporters went back to their monitors. With a sigh, Foster headed to the break room and poured a generous amount of sugar in his brew.

He shouldn't have let Tom get to him like that. He knew what some of the other guys whispered about him – that he had been a great reporter in his day, but now that he didn't write the big stories anymore he was nothing more than an arrogant blowhard.

For crying out loud, I'm only thirty-five! Too young to be a has-been.

Foster had made his name with a groundbreaking story when he exposed the affair between the Atlanta chief of police and one of his officers seven years ago. Over the next four years he had written three other stories that won him a number of awards, all which were on the wall of the tiny second bedroom of his apartment he used as an office.

Then last year he hit a wall.

Foster went back to his desk, sipping the cooling coffee. If he could finish running down this story, he'd be back on top again. And that would make the idiots like Davidson shut up.

"So," he murmured as he moved his mouse, causing his screensaver of a bouncing blue ball to vanish, "let's see what we can learn about you, Ms. Mary Hollister Beamer."

He'd uploaded the pictures he'd taken of the papers he'd found at the Thompson house to his computer. Using the information he'd gotten off them, he began to put together a profile of the woman who apparently had Martha Thompson's attention before the nurse killed herself.

Mary Louise Hollister was the daughter of Benard and Donna Hollister. Her father was a research chemist for a cosmetics firm, her mother was a homemaker. There was nothing outstanding about the family that he could discover.

Mary Hollister graduated high school with honor. She played violin in the school orchestra, was secretary of the National Honor Society, and didn't appear to have any discipline issues. She attended two years at the community college. She married a Roger Beamer and a year later, their daughter Kelly was born.

Roger Beamer was an assistant manager at a local bank. Mary, like her mother, was a homemaker. According to an article in the local paper, she worked at her congregation's clothing room once a week. Foster couldn't find as much as a traffic ticket to mar the woman's record.

He looked for some kind of connection between Mary Beamer and Martha Thompson. He couldn't find one. But his instincts told him there was *something*. Not only that, he was willing to bet it had something to do with the Peachtree Road Women's Clinic.

Now all he had to do was find out what it was. And he would. That would show twits like Davidson.

- TWENTY -

S HARON ALWAYS MADE IT A POINT TO be at the clinic no later than seven-thirty in the morning. It was a good fifteen minutes before any of the day shift came in, and she preferred it that way. It was far easier to get things done when people weren't constantly interrupting her.

After checking the nursery to make sure nothing urgent had happened overnight, Sharon went into the brightly lit break room and deposited the two dozen donuts she'd picked up on the way to work. One of the nurses had started a fresh pot of coffee, and Sharon got herself a cup before going to her office.

There was a small stack of papers on her desk – things that had come up after she left yesterday that hadn't been considered important enough to call her about. She flipped through them quickly, making notes where appropriate.

There was a file stamped ARCHIVE and CONFIDENTIAL on the bottom of the pile. A sticky note was attached in front and covered in Thomas' sloppy handwriting:

"S –

Here's the info about the patient you asked about. Look over and refile under "Sensitive."

- TG

Sharon glanced at her shut door, then at the LCD clock that a drug rep had given her two months ago. The name of one of their birth control products was etched onto the clock face.

She had about five minutes before anyone else came in, perhaps ten before the intercom started crying for her attention. She turned on her computer and while it booted up she flipped open the file.

Mary Louise Hollister. Resident of Florida. Referred to the clinic by Francine Winters. Came in while undergoing premature labor at 28 weeks of gestation…*what?*

She remembered now. The girl hadn't come in for an abortion. In fact, they'd had to sedate her when she realized where she was. When she'd gone into labor, Francine Winters had taken it upon herself to bring the girl to the clinic.

Sharon tapped a bright red nail on the file. At the time, she'd been concerned that Francine had opened the clinic up to litigation or worse bringing the Hollister girl to them. But Thomas said it would be all right – they were providing emergency medical care, how could anyone be against that?

Still, Sharon had been concerned. She'd taken it upon herself to speak to Francine, impressing on the woman the need to keep the girl from doing anything that would harm the clinic. The woman assured her that Mary was so wracked with guilt she wouldn't want to do anything that would expose her being there.

The years passed and when she didn't hear anything from the girl Sharon let the incident slip from her mind. Francine had apparently been correct in her assessment. Sharon had to admit this was one of the few times she was grateful for religion, such as it was – the guilt it could make its believers feel caused them to keep secrets. And Sharon was just fine with that.

Still, she wondered if after all this time Mary was a threat to the clinic. If Martha had reopened that decade old wound, what would the woman do about it? Would she try to contact the clinic? Or – and this was what Sharon was really concerned about – would she start asking questions, even attempt to find a child that she hadn't even known existed a few days ago?

These were questions Sharon needed answers to. The sooner the better.

The intercom burst into life. One of the nurses had a question about a chart. Sharon sighed. She'd have to look over the file a bit more carefully before she decided on a course of action.

She pressed the intercom button. "I'll be there in a minute." Before leaving her office she lit a scented candle. The lavender fragrance soothed her, helped her stay calm when the day was particularly hectic – as this day threatened to be.

She took a final glance at Mary Hollister's file as she picked up her coffee cup. She'd talk to Thomas about it, but she was already forming a plan to keep the girl from being a problem.

That was something Sharon was good at – keeping problems from starting. She had no doubt that she could solve this little problem. If she tried to make trouble, Mary Hollister would not know what hit her.

- TWENTY-ONE -

MARY COULDN'T CONCENTRATE that morning.

After she'd dropped Kelly off to school, she returned home. She'd start a task – loading the dishwasher, for example – then find herself in her daughter's room straightening up her small bookcase. Then she'd leave that half-finished and sit at the kitchen table and look at the paper.

After a half hour of this, she put on a pair of sneakers, clam diggers and a Disney World t-shirt and left the house. A few minutes of stretching in her driveway and she started a brisk walk.

She was halfway down her block before the walk became a jog. She pushed herself, ignoring the pains in her shins that started despite her warming up before. She tried to empty her mind of everything except the gray asphalt beneath her sneakers and the pounding of her heart.

Don't think. Just move. Just burn yourself out.

She got to the end of the second block and turned right. An older woman stood in front of a yellow frame house, watering a flower bed. She raised a hand in greeting. Mary lifted a hand in return, then forced herself to go faster.

Two blocks…turn right…don't think…

She felt breath come in gasps. She knew she was pushing herself too hard – when had she done this last? Mary didn't exercise regularly. She thought keeping up with Kelly was all the exercise she needed.

She turned the next corner. What she saw caused her to stop dead.

A woman about her own age, her blond hair pulled in a ponytail, was coming out of a small house on the corner. She carried a small boy in her arms.

The boy was a towhead, dressed in blue overalls and a white shirt. He was babbling at the woman, placing his chubby hands on her face as he smiled. The woman smiled back and kissed his nose. The boy threw his head back and crowed his delight.

The blond woman paused at the dark blue Taurus in the driveway as she fumbled for a door handle. She looked up and appeared startled at the sight of Mary, sweaty and panting, staring at her from the end of her driveway.

"I'm sorry. Are you all right?" she asked.

Mary couldn't take her eyes off the boy. Her vision blurred as tears filled her eyes. "I – I'm fine," she choked out. "You – you have a beautiful son."

The woman kept staring at Mary, the arm around her child tightening a little. "Thank you," she said. She opened the car door with a quick yank and bent to put her child in his car seat.

The minute the woman broke eye contact Mary started running again. The tears wet her cheeks and dropped on her shirt as she hurried home.

When she stumbled into the house she went to her bathroom and looked in the mirror. The tear-streaked face she saw was older than twenty-six, the hazel eyes haunted. *I can't keep doing this.*

She stripped off her clothes and stepped into the shower. She made the water so hot it nearly scalded her, wanting to erase her anguish. She scrubbed her skin with a loofah, trying to wipe the memory of the baby boy out of her mind.

For months after she lost her baby she couldn't look at a child at the mall or the park without tears coming. She managed to hide or explain them away from her parents and friends but she always knew what caused them.

She'd mourned the loss of the life growing inside her, wondering if the child's death was God's way of punishing her for her sin. She'd dreamed of the baby she'd never seen, many times. Sometimes the child was a boy, sometimes a girl. He or she had blond or black hair (Harold's thick hair had been black), hazel eyes, and arms that sweetly hugged her. But only in her dreams.

When she got pregnant with Kelly, she'd held her breath during the nine months. After her last miscarriage she worried about the health of the new life. When she'd held Kelly in her arms for the first time, she'd wept with joy. Roger cried too, his hand cupping the blond fuzz that covered their infant daughter's head.

Now it seemed that her first child was not dead, but alive somewhere. A boy. She had a son.

Mary stepped out of the shower and dried herself off. She couldn't leave it at that. She needed answers.

It was time to ask some questions.

- TWENTY-TWO -

*W*HAT CITY?" the flat computer voice asked.

"Atlanta," Mary said, swallowing hard.

"*Thank you. What listing?*"

She closed her eyes. "Peachtree Road Women's Clinic."

"*Thank you. Just a moment.*"

Mary opened her eyes. The kitchen looked normal, except for the dishes piled up next to the sink, evidence of her failure to focus earlier. She gulped her glass of cranberry juice as she waited for the information she needed.

There were several clicks on the line, then a human male voice. "Operator. What city?"

Mary put down her glass and picked up the pen that lay beside the notepad Roger and she used for messages. "Atlanta."

"What listing?"

She shook her head. Didn't she just tell the computer this? "The Peachtree Road Women's Clinic."

"Checking...I'm sorry, ma'am, I have no listing for a Peachtree Road Women's Clinic in Atlanta."

"What?" Mary asked. This was the last thing she'd expected to hear. "But there has to be."

"I'm sorry ma'am, I show no such listing. Is there anything else I can help you with?"

"No...no, thank you," Mary said. She hung up the phone, at a loss. Had the clinic closed? Changed its name? Moved?

She chewed her lip. Picking up her glass of juice she went into the office and booted up Roger's computer.

Mary was semi-computer literate. She could handle email and a couple of sites she liked to visit that dealt with cooking or a favorite television show. But Roger was the expert. If she wanted to find out something, he could type a few keywords in and pull up pages of stuff.

But she couldn't ask Roger to look for this.

Mary opened up the web browser. There was a small box in the upper left hand corner with the word SEARCH next to it. She typed in "Peachtree Road Women's Clinic" and clicked the search button.

To her dismay, the next webpage claimed there were over 100,000 matches to her search. Mary bit her lip. How could she wade through all of them? How would she know she had the right one?

She erased what she'd typed in the search box and typed "Peachtree Road Women's Clinic Atlanta Georgia" and hit the search button again.

This time she still got a large number of matches. But the third one on the list caught her eye. It appeared to be a news headline: "Women's Clinic Burns to the Ground; Arson Suspected."

Arson?

She clicked the link. It let to the Atlanta Times website. The story, which was over a year old according to the date on the page, included a picture of the blackened shell that was once a clinic.

Stunned, Mary read the article. It mentioned that the clinic was the target of pro-life protestors who often picketed in front of the clinic. Doctor Thomas Green, the owner of the clinic, denounced what he called "the work of anti-women religious zealots" and urged an investigation.

It had burned. To the ground. That was why there was no listed phone number.

Mary shook her head in frustration. There had to be a way to find out more. *Had* to be. She couldn't give up now. Not if she really had a son out there.

Mary printed out the news story. She then did a search for "Doctor Thomas Green." She groaned as she saw that there were more hits for his name than there had been for the clinic. And for all she knew, he was no longer in Georgia.

She thought for a moment, then, gritting her teeth, typed the word "abortion" after his name.

She then began writing down any of the names that appeared likely. She knew this would take time. And she still might not find him.

But someone had told her that she had a son out there somewhere. She had to *know*.

- TWENTY-THREE -

JACK GRIMACED AS HE PULLED into the grassy parking lot of the Stewart-Wilson Funeral Home. He hated these places. On the outside they looked like they should house lawyers, not the dead and the grieving. Trying to give dignity to something as messy as death.

He took a moment to put on his tie, checking it in the rearview mirror. Ties were another abomination. Who thought it would be a great idea for a man to walk around with his neck in a noose? Maybe the same guy who came up with funeral homes.

With a sigh Jack smoothed his hair. He was out to get a story. For a story he'd do a lot. And he wasn't ready to give up on Bob Thompson. Not if he could help Jack get the dirt on Dr. Green and his burned out clinic.

He stepped through the door and felt the temperature drop along with the light. The front room was softly lit and air conditioned. Jack blinked as an elderly man in a black suit, white shirt, and black tie approached him. "Can I help you?" he asked in a soft considerate voice.

Jack swallowed back the smart-aleck answer he wanted to make. Instead, he said, "I'm here for Martha Thompson's viewing?"

The old man nodded and waved a hand to a doorway to the left. "Through there, sir."

"Thanks," Jack muttered with a nod. He paused at the small book that rested on a stand by the doorway. Not too many signatures. It didn't look like too many people were making note of Martha Thompson's passing.

Jack hesitated, then picked up the white feathered pen and signed. He hadn't disliked Martha Thompson – she'd seemed like a decent, if timid, woman. He figured she deserved at least a signature from him, however symbolic it might be . . .

He stepped into a medium sized room. A dark green couch was on one wall, flanked by two dark wooden end tables. A couple of comfortable stuffed chairs were on the other walls. There were only three or four people in the room. Bob Thompson sat on the couch, talking with a woman around Martha Thompson's age.

Jack stepped to the plain white coffin, figuring he should at least make a show of paying his respects before talking to the son. Taking a deep breath, he looked down at Marta Thompson's body.

Hers wasn't the first body he'd ever seen. Jack had attended his father's funeral several years before. Here, as then, he was struck at how artificial the body looked. Like a parody of a human being.

Even though he'd never met her in person, Jack could tell she'd aged badly. Even though whoever had made up the body (and that was one job he'd never take, thank you very much) had made an attempt to make her look good. The lines were still there, connecting her jaw and mouth. In death, she still looked like something was troubling her.

Jack sighed. He wished she'd talked to him. She came close to it, to the point of setting up a meeting with him. But she'd bailed on him. He never knew why.

Even though he wasn't a church goer, he said a silent prayer for Martha Thompson's soul. He hoped she was at peace.

He noticed a large floral arrangement on a tripod was stuck behind the coffin, blocked by other flowers. Curious, he stepped around to get as close to it as possible so he could see the card. It read, *From your friends and former colleagues. Dr. Thomas Green and Associates.*

Jack raised an eyebrow. That took some guts, to send a floral arrangement. Unless he'd misread Bob Thompson's attitude.

Speaking of whom. . . Jack turned and stepped over to Martha's son. The older woman Bob was talking to looked a little uncomfortable.

Martha's son frowned at him. "You again?" he asked, standing.

"Mr. Thompson, I want to express my sympathy to your loss. That's all." Jack stuck out a hand.

Thompson sighed. He shook Jack's hand. "Thanks, I guess. Your name again?"

"Jack Foster."

The older woman's head jerked up at the mention of his name. "You! Are you who I think you are? That reporter?"

"Reporter?" Thompson asked, looking from the woman to Jack. "Is that true?"

Jack winced. *Great*. "Yes, I am. Your mother offered to help me on a story."

"She did not!" the woman said, standing. "None of us would speak with you."

Thompson shook his head. "Okay, I don't want to talk to either of you. You paid your 'respects,' whatever you mean by that. Now just leave my family alone!"

"Of course, Mr. Thompson," the woman said. She sighed. "I was a friend of your mother's no matter what you think." She turned and left the room, her shoulders slumped.

Jack glanced at her and then jerked a nod at Thompson. "I'm sorry I've bothered you."

He walked quickly, catching up with the woman in the parking lot. "Excuse me –"

"I have nothing to say to you," the woman said, not bothering to turn around.

"I thought you said you were a friend of Martha Thompson's," Jack said.

"I was," the woman said, still walking away. "And I'm sure *you* weren't."

"She almost talked to me!" Jack yelled, still tailing the woman. "She almost did the right thing!"

That got the woman to turn around. She stopped so fast Jack nearly ran into her. Jabbing a red fingernail into his chest she spat, "The right thing was to have nothing to do with you. You tried to destroy a fine man and get us to help you! Well, it didn't work, did it?"

"A good man?" Jack scoffed. "Yeah, I guess good men kill inconvenient babies. Or maybe sell them?"

The woman's face turned almost as red as her fingernail. "Leave me alone. You hear me? You just leave me alone. I don't work there anymore, I have nothing to say to someone like you."

Jack watched as the woman stalked off to a tan Honda Acura. He sighed. That hadn't gone well at all.

Another roadblock to the story. How many did that make? A lot more than the very few productive lines of inquiry he'd managed in the last year and a half.

It was tempting to give up on it. He thought about it, especially when his efforts came to zip as they did today. Sometimes he felt as if he were the only one who even cared about what happened at that clinic.

The trouble was, he *did* care. The little he knew or suspected about what went on at that horror house disguised as a medical clinic haunted his dreams. He was going to get to the bottom of it.

And when he did, he'd write a story that would put him back on top of the heap. And the jerks like Tom Davidson would have to shut up. And maybe Jack would finally lay his ghosts to rest.

- TWENTY-FOUR -

S O THE FUNERAL WAS THIS AFTERNOON. I have a couple of things to wrap up here. I figure I can be down in Florida by Friday or Saturday."

Mary swallowed. She gripped the phone tightly as she wiped a sponge over the kitchen counter. "Mr. Thompson, I'm not sure your coming here is such a good idea. As I told you, my husband knows nothing about what happened."

"Ma'am, my mother killed herself. Before she did, she contacted you. I need to understand why," Thompson said.

"I don't know what I can tell you about that," Mary protested. "Her contacting me was unexpected."

"I still need answers." Thompson's voice sounded strained. "Look, Ms. Beamer, I don't like making threats, but if I have to, I will. I'm sure you don't want me talking to your husband."

Mary felt her mouth grow dry. "No…no, please. But that's why I don't want you to come. If my husband meets you, there will be questions raised."

"Then we'll meet somewhere away from your home," Thompson said. "But I do want to talk to you face to face. It's my mother we're talking about here."

Mary pinched the bridge of her nose, fighting the lump in her throat. "All right. But I don't even remember your mother. I don't know how much help I can be."

"You might be surprised," Thompson said. "So I'll let you know what hotel I'm staying at when I get there and we'll set up a meeting. All right?"

It wasn't. But Mary had no choice. "I guess so," she said, unable to keep the tremble out of her voice.

"I'm glad you're willing to help me out here," Thompson said. "So, I'll talk to you soon."

Mary hung up the phone. The black cordless blurred in her vision and she realized she was crying.

She leaned against the counter as she buried her hands in her face. All this time she'd worked at burying the past – and attempting to atone for her sins – and in less than a week it was all coming unraveled. And there was an excellent chance it would come out in the light, and Roger would find out she was living a lie.

What would happen? Would he leave her? The Bible said that God hated divorce. But would he want to still live with her when he knew what she'd done? And if he did, would he let her see Kelly, or take the child away with him?

And what about her oldest child, the one she hadn't known existed? Where was he? What responsibilities did she have to him?

Swallowing, Mary rubbed her eyes. She went to the sink and splashed cold water on her face. Kelly would need to be picked up in forty-five minutes. That gave her a half hour to continue with her research.

Mary went to the computer and pulled up the search page she'd started earlier. She found the last name she'd written down and began to go through the list again, noting every name that could possibly be the Doctor Thomas Green she was looking for.

Halfway down the third page on the search she came across a page titled, "Doctor Opens Up New Women's Clinic in Montgomery; Local Pro-Life Group Vows Protests."

She caught her breath. Even as she clicked the link, she suspected her search was over. Her stomach churned, and she put a hand on it to try to soothe it.

The story was more focused on the pro-life group, an organization that called itself Alabamians for Life. But Mary found what she was looking for in the third from the last paragraph in the story:

"Doctor Green is used to controversy concerning his work. He ran the Peachtree Road Women's Clinic in Atlanta, Georgia for fifteen years until arson destroyed the building. While no one was prosecuted in that fire, Green is convinced that it was the work of anti-abortionists who spent much of the time protesting in front of the clinic."

She tasted bile in the back of her throat and swallowed. She did not want to throw up. For a long moment Mary concentrated on taking deep breaths.

Mary knew she'd found the doctor who told her ten years ago her baby was dead. The doctor who'd shown her no sympathy when she protested she hadn't wanted to come to an abortion clinic.

The doctor who'd apparently lied to her.

A glance at the time at the bottom right of the computer screen told her she needed to leave if she didn't want to be late picking up Kelly. But Mary took the time to first print out the news story. She jammed it into her pocketbook as she ran out the door.

With the information from the article she should have no trouble tracking down Dr. Green's contact information.

And perhaps she would get some answers. With those, she'd be able to bury the past again – hopefully, for good.

- TWENTY-FIVE -

SHARON HUNG UP THE PHONE with a feeling of satisfaction. She dialed the extension for the nursery. When the aide in charge came on the line, she said "I need you to get Jane Doe 32 ready to travel. Mr. Strickland will be by to pick her up in half an hour."

"Yes, Ms. Abrams," the aide said. "I'm almost sorry to see her go. She's such a sweet little thing."

Sharon frowned. "She's not for us to keep. Please remember that."

The voice on the other end of the line sounded somewhat abashed. "I'm sorry, ma'am, of course."

"That's quite all right," Sharon said, softening her tone. "It's best to keep a distance with our babies. That way we concentrate on doing what's best."

"Yes Ms. Abrams," the aide said.

Sharon racked her brain and came up with a name. "Gloria? Is this your first time with the nursery?"

"Yes."

"Don't worry about it," Sharon said. "You'll learn. It takes time."

After she finished with the woman Sharon took a moment to pull up Gloria Taylor's record. The woman was a recent addition to the clinic, and her work had been satisfactory so far. She'd appeared to be trustworthy, so on Nadine's recommendation Sharon put her on nursery rotation.

Now she made a note to reexamine that decision. If the woman was going to get all sappy about the babies she could be a liability. Sharon liked to put a stop to those kinds of things before they became a problem.

Meanwhile, she had to make sure they had the appropriate paperwork ready for Jane Doe 32. And she needed to let Thomas know they had a buyer. He liked to be kept informed of those things.

She rose from her chair to get those things done when the intercom sounded. "Ms. Abrams? Call for you on line 3."

Sharon glared at the intercom but decided to take the call. Dropping back in her chair, she picked up the receiver. "This is Sharon Abrams, how may I help you?"

"Sharon? It's Darlene Grayson. I don't know if you remember me…"

"Darlene!" Sharon felt a little annoyed but hid it. "Of course I remember you. I was so sorry you couldn't join us in our move, you were a good worker."

"I know Sharon, and I'm sorry I couldn't keep working for you, but my daughter really needed me close by."

"I understand," Sharon said, wondering how to cut the call short so she could get back to work. "I'd love to chat with you, but we're very busy at the moment."

"Oh, I won't keep you. I just wanted to tell you the floral arrangement you sent for Martha was just beautiful. I thought you should know that, and I doubt her son will have the manners to tell you."

"Well, I appreciate that," Sharon said. "I'm sorry Martha's son still harbors bad feelings towards us." She hesitated, then decided to ask. "I don't mean to pry, but I heard poor Martha killed herself? I can't believe it!"

"It's true," Darlene said, sniffling. "I was shocked too, though I suspect it had to do with that awful reporter who was nosing around last year. He had the nerve to come to the viewing! Can you believe it?"

Sharon had picked up her cup of coffee and nearly dropped it at that bombshell. "He was?" she said, forcing her voice to sound mildly curious.

"Oh yes," Darlene said, outrage clear in her voice. "He had the nerve to claim he was paying his respects! Then he followed me out to the parking lot and claimed Martha almost talked to him! Can you imagine that?"

Sharon swallowed a mouthful of coffee, hoping it would warm the sudden chill that had swept over her. *Martha almost talked to Jack Foster? Was that even possible?*

Grimly putting what she knew or suspected together, Sharon decided the answer was yes. And the fact Foster had attended the viewing told her he wasn't finished with the story as they'd hoped. Another fire she had to put out…

Working to keep her voice steady, she said "Well, that is simply terrible of the man. You'd think people would be sensitive."

"I know!" Darlene agreed. "I wonder what lies he might be feeding that poor man…"

"He and Martha's son appeared to be talking?" Sharon stiffened in her chair. She didn't like the implications of that.

"Oh no, Bob seemed quite upset with him. He didn't even know Foster was a reporter until I told him." Darlene said.

"Well, I'm not surprised he'd try to deceive him," Sharon said. "Darlene, I hate to cut you off, but I have some things I need to finish up rather quickly…"

"Oh, go right ahead," Darlene said. "I understand the workload. I'll try to come by sometime and visit, would that be all right?"

"Yes, of course," Sharon said. She quickly finished the call. Once she hung up she settled back in her chair, took a deep breath of the lavender-scented air, and thought.

Jack Foster was still looking into the doings of the Peachtree Road Women's Clinic. Apparently, he wasn't letting the fact that the clinic burned to the ground get in the way of his investigation.

That was bad. She wondered what he knew. Did he have any idea that Martha Thompson had apparently contacted a former client – and not just any client, but one that could do real damage to Thomas and the clinic.

She sighed as she got up again. Sharon knew she'd have to give Thomas this news as well as the good news of selling Jane Doe 32. He'd expect her to deal with the problem, of course.

Sharon smoothed the skirt of her cranberry-colored suit. It would take some planning, but she would come up with a plan. Thomas had been good to her, and she wasn't going to let anyone destroy what they had.

Anyone. Including a meddlesome reporter and a troublesome former client.

- TWENTY-SIX -

M ARY?"

She looked up from the shirt she was putting a button on. "Something wrong?" she asked. Roger's tone sounded worried.

"That's what I want to talk about," Roger said, sitting down next to her on the couch. "Mind if I mute this?" he pointed to the television, where Bill O'Reilly was interviewing some woman about a bill concerning regulation of abortion clinics.

"Of course not," Mary said, laying the shirt she was mending on her lap. She felt a thrill of unease crawl up her back.

Roger grabbed the remote and silenced the debate going on. He held the device in his hands loosely, between his knees. She saw him bite the inside of his cheek as he appeared to debate what to say.

For once, Mary prayed that Kelly would call from her room, asking for a drink of water or a hug. She didn't want to have the conversation she knew Roger was going to start. What could she possibly say to him?

"Mare? Remember what we talked about the other night?" Roger bit his lip. "Can you tell me about it? You've seemed really depressed the last few days, and I'm trying to figure out why."

"Oh," Mary said. She tightened her fingers around the shirt on her lap. A stabbing pain in her right index finger reminded her of the needle that was still there. "Ouch!"

"Here, let me see," Roger said, reaching for her hand.

"It's all right. Just the stupid needle," Mary said, blinking back tears. Glad of the pain, as it gave her an excuse for her eyes to be wet.

Roger gently pulled her hand to him. He rubbed a thumb gently over the spot of blood on her finger. "Doesn't look bad." He lifted her hand to his lips.

She swiped at her face with her other hand. She still had no idea what to say to Roger. *Think fast, think fast . . ._*

Before she could say anything, the phone rang. She and Roger exchanged puzzled glances. It was after 9 PM; who could be calling at that hour? The only reasons she could think of a call at this hour weren't good.

Roger stood. "I'll get it. Probably some phone solicitor." He headed to the kitchen.

Mary took a deep breath, trying to get her emotions under control. What was she going to say? Maybe she could claim PMS? No, she just finished her period the week before.

"Hey Mare?" Roger walked back into the den, the black cordless in his hand. "It's a woman named Celia Morris? Says you knew her when she was Celia Winters."

"Celia?" Mary asked, surprised. "Yes, I knew her from high school. I haven't talked to her in ages."

"Here then," Roger said, handing her the phone. Mary dropped her eyes to the shirt on her lap. "Celia?"

"Well hi, stranger!" It was Celia's voice, all right: cheerful and upbeat. "How's it going? Long time no talk!"

Mary felt her cheeks grow warm. "Hi, Celia. I'm sorry I haven't tried to keep up with you…"

"Hey, no worries!" Celia said. "I haven't been the best in staying in touch, either. So how's married life treating you? I've only been at it about a year."

"M-married life is fine," Mary stammered. "I have a daughter, did you know?"

"Figures. You always were going to go the housewife/mommy route." Celia's voice held more than a hint of humor. "You did, right? I mean, let me guess: you stay at home, right?"

Mary couldn't withhold the chuckle Celia's comments brought out. Her former best friend had always been able to pull Mary out of any bad mood she was in.

Well, *almost* always.

"Yes, I'm a stay-at-home mom," Mary said. She looked up at Roger and tossed him a wink and a grin. He raised his eyebrows at her, a smile tugging at his lips.

"And Roger's a wonderful husband," she continued, her eyes still on Roger. His smile widened and he sat down next to her on the couch. "Maybe someday you guys can meet."

"Well, funny you should think that," Celia said. "See, I got your number from my mom – she said you called her earlier this week all freaked out about what happened in Atlanta a few years ago."

All the pleasant feelings Mary was feeling vanished without a trace. She was conscious of Roger sitting next to her. Fighting to keep her voice steady, she said, "Well, yes. I – there's been something bothering me."

As Roger's hand began to massage her tense shoulder, Celia said, "Well, when Mom told me that, I figured I should come and visit. You know, we can catch up on what's been going on in our lives. I can tell you all about Richard."

"Richard?" Mary said, totally lost.

"My husband!" Celia laughed. "Oh, he's a sweetheart, you'd love him. He's a big deal lawyer here in Houston, and we're pretty well off. I asked him and he's absolutely cool with me taking a flight down to Florida to see you and my dad."

"Celia, you don't have to do this," Mary said. She felt a little afraid. Why was Celia suddenly contacting her? Did her mother tell her to calm Mary down?

"Now Mary, are you saying you don't *want* to see me?" Celia's voice was teasing. "Come on, we used to be the best friends ever. I want to see you, find out how things are going."

Mary swallowed. She felt like the walls were closing in on her. "Celia, of course I'd love to see you –"

"Great! It's all settled, then," Celia said in a cheerful voice. "Give me your address and I'll use MapQuest to plot out the directions. I'll be there tomorrow afternoon, okay?"

Mary found herself giving her former best friend her address. That was the way Celia was – Harold once referred to her as "a force of nature." Once she set her mind on something, it was nearly impossible to talk her out of it.

Mary ended the phone call with Celia's happy voice ringing in her ears. She sighed and rested her forehead in her hand.

"Everything all right?"

Roger's voice jolted Mary back to the fact he was sitting right there. She took a deep breath and worked up a smile. "Oh yeah. Celia's an old friend. She decided she wants to pay me a visit and catch up on old times."

He stared at her. "That's a good thing, right?"

Mary dropped her head down, staring at her clasped hands. "It can be," she said.

He placed his fingers under her chin and brought her face up to where she had to look in his eyes. "But?"

Mary shrugged. "There's some bad memories. It's part of why we really haven't talked in so long."

Roger frowned. "Does this have anything to do with your moodiness lately?"

Mary sighed. "Honey, my 'moodiness' as you call it . . . I really don't want to talk about it right now. It has nothing to do with you or Kelly, I promise."

He cocked his head and studied her. "Mare, I'm really worried. Can't we discuss this?"

She shook her head. "Please, Roger, I asked you not to push me on this. Please."

Roger sighed. "All right, I'll drop it for now. But I'm not dropping this forever, Mare."

She swallowed. "Thanks, Roger."

He nodded and stood. "I'm gonna get ready for bed. You coming?"

"In a few minutes," Mary nodded. I just want to finish this shirt."

He leaned down to plant a swift kiss on her forehead and left the room. When he was gone, Mary sighed. She looked from the television that showed people silently mouthing words to the rumpled shirt in her lap. She found the needle in the tangle of cloth and went back to replacing the button.

If only her life were so easy to fix.

- TWENTY-SEVEN -

FRANCINE FROWNED as she looked at the balance in her checkbook. She was never good at living within her means. It took a lot of juggling of her bills to keep her head above water, along with the occasional commission she got at the dress shop. And last year, the payments she got from time to time from Thomas.

She sighed as she dropped the checkbook on the maple rolltop desk she used for bill paying. The problem was she wasn't getting as much supplemental income as she used to. The commissions were becoming harder to come by. And last week her boss had told her she just wasn't doing as good a job as she used to.

Francine scoffed. She was getting tired of that job, anyway. She'd been with this particular dress shop five years, and she was getting tired of smiling at older fat women who were trying to make themselves look glamorous. And she had to lie to them, tell them that yes, that gorgeous dress she was selling them covered up their pasty skin, the rolls around their waistline, the gray hair.

Didn't anyone take care of themselves anymore, for crying out loud? Francine worked hard to keep her body in shape, her features attractive, her hair styled and colored to make her look her best.

She knew her appearance was one of her greatest assets. When women learned she was in her mid-forties, it gave them hope they could look like her. She sold lies and dreams and didn't feel bad about it.

Francine also knew that she was tired of holding down a job, tired of having to scramble for the lifestyle she wanted. She envied her daughter –

Celia had landed a wealthy and generous lawyer. Why couldn't Francine have that kind of luck?

The conversation she'd had earlier with Celia had been a mixed affair. As wonderful a husband as Richard apparently was, he wasn't interested in supporting his mother-in-law. Celia had been apologetic and asked Francine to give her time to change his mind.

"Yeah right," Francine had said. She resented the fact that after all she'd given to raise this one daughter that the girl couldn't do this one thing for her.

She had better luck with the topic of Mary. That young woman had haunted Francine ever since her phone call. The trip to Alabama, while pleasant, had done little to ease her concerns.

So when Celia called, Francine had told her that her old friend Mary had been upset and spending too much time thinking about that traumatic summer ten years ago. Francine hinted strongly that Mary could use some cheering up from an old friend.

Celia was happy to agree to that. She talked about visiting her father as well, which Francine let pass with no comment. She barely remembered the man she'd left ten years ago and never thought of him unless Celia let a comment drop.

Francine finished the phone call still a little bit dissatisfied with the situation. That Mary could make trouble – especially if she found out what *really* happened at the clinic.

As Francine went to the kitchen to pour herself a glass of red wine, a thought occurred to her. Maybe she was looking at this the wrong way.

Perhaps instead of worrying about Mary and what she might or might not do (and Francine was of the opinion the girl was much too timid to do anything) Francine should see the situation as an opportunity.

Surely Thomas appreciated the help she'd provided him in the past. Francine smacked her lips as she sipped her wine. He seemed attracted to her… and he made good money. Perhaps she could convince him to marry her.

And if not…well, if he didn't want to do that, perhaps he'd realize her silence had value. As rich as he no doubt was, he could afford to subsidize her lifestyle, couldn't he?

Much more cheerful, Francine went back to her desk do pick which bills she'd pay this month.

- TWENTY-EIGHT -

*F*OSTER*!* Get in my office right now!"

Wheeler's voice rang throughout the busy newsroom, silencing conversations as everyone present turned and stared not at their boss, but at Jack. He tried to act as if the staring and the yelling didn't bother him, though of course it did. Jack stood and walked over to Wheeler with a casual air that wouldn't fool anyone who could hear his heart pounding.

Wheeler's face was bright red. He let Jack enter the office ahead of him before slamming the door shut. Whatever was going on, Jack suspected he was in big trouble. He waited for the editor to throw himself into his chair before sitting himself. "What can I do for you, sir?"

"Don't give me that fake politeness, Foster!" Wheeler snarled, pointing a pudgy finger at the reporter. "You're lucky I don't throw you out of here on your butt!"

"What seems to be the problem?" Jack suspected he knew what it was, but he prayed he was wrong. If Wheeler had any idea he'd broken into the Thompson house, there was a *big* problem.

The editor was breathing heavily. "Did you or did you not disrupt the viewing for Martha Thompson?"

Jack's eyebrows shot up. Okay, he could handle this one. "Not. I went to pay my respects."

"Pay your respects," Wheeler echoed sarcastically. "Right. That's why I got a call from her son complaining that you tried to question him about his mother without telling him you were a reporter!"

"I didn't question him at the viewing," Jack said. "I was polite and left when it was clear my presence wasn't welcome there."

"Then, according to *another* phone call I got, you proceeded to follow a woman and verbally abuse her!" Wheeler growled.

"Hey," Jack said, raising his hands up, "if anyone was verbally abused, it was me. I haven't done anything wrong here!" *At least, nothing I'm going to tell you about.*

Wheeler glared at Jack for a few minutes, then dropped his head into his hands. "Jack, Jack, why are you doing this to me? I need this like I need a strike."

"C'mon, Wheeler, you know how it is when you rattle the cages. People don't like it, they want you to quit."

"Give me one good reason you shouldn't quit!" Wheeler said, his voice raised. "You've been working on this story over a year, and what do you have to show for it? Bupkus!"

"I *do* have something!" Jack yelled back. He stood, running his hand through his thick sandy hair. He was furious – and not just with Wheeler. He was angry at himself, for not finding more.

Wheeler blew out an angry breath. "All right. What do you have? I need to know what you're using to justify pursuing this story if I'm gonna get any more phone calls about you. And for crying out loud, sit down before I get even madder at you."

Jack sat back down, rubbing his hands on his pants. "Okay. I discovered that Martha Thompson sent a message to someone before she died. A woman who was a patient at the clinic."

At least I think she was. But Wheeler didn't need to know that.

Wheeler frowned. "Why? What woman?"

Jack weighed how to word his answer in a way that would push Wheeler to give him the green light. "Apparently she was searching for this woman and her whereabouts. I suspect she was giving her a message in regards to the clinic. I know the son has contacted her."

Wheeler sighed, leaning back in his chair, pinching the bridge of his nose. "I'm hearing a lot of 'I suspects' and 'apparentlys' here. Anything you might know for *sure?*"

Jack sighed. "If I knew all this for sure, I still wouldn't be investigating. I'd have the story out and be waiting for my Pulitzer."

Wheeler chuckled. "Yeah, I bet you would." He grew serious. "Jack, what's going on with this? Are you treating this as a story, or is there some personal agenda here?"

"Nothing personal," Jack said, keeping his face blank. "I just think this is a great story."

Wheeler stared at him, and Jack fought to keep any emotion off his face. Finally Wheeler sighed as he pulled open a drawer, pulling out a couple of antacid tablets. "Okay, Jack, I'll give you some more rope. Keep on with this. But," Wheeler pointed a finger at Jack, "you get this paper in trouble, you push this past reasonable, and I'll use that rope to hogtie you when I throw you out a window. You got that?"

Jack nodded. "I got it, sir. Thanks."

"Yeah, yeah," Wheeler said, chewing the tablets. "Get outta here before I get over this nice attack I seem to be having."

Jack didn't hesitate to exit the office. He knew when he was being given a break, and he wasn't stupid enough to push his luck.

He felt a twinge of conscience when he remembered he hadn't been totally accurate with Wheeler. If the editor knew that, he just *might* tie Jack up and toss him out a window.

He sat at his desk and moved his computer mouse, causing the screensaver of multicolored lines to vanish. Yeah, it *was* personal. But it was also a huge story. And Jack was going to get it.

- TWENTY-NINE -

THE BLARE OF A HORN to her left alerted Mary that she was about to blow right past a stop sign. She slammed her foot on the brake, feeling her shoulder belt lock as the car quickly lost speed.

Her heard pounding, she watched as the car that had sounded the alarm took its turn at the intersection. The driver, a gray haired woman, shot Mary a dark look as she went by.

Mary's hands tightened on the wheel as she felt the blood rush to her face. She wasn't normally so distracted – she could practically drive the route from the grocery store to her home on autopilot.

But she normally didn't have a former best friend dropping by to bring unknown chaos to her life, either.

Mary forced herself to focus on the two-lane residential street as she made her way to her pale-green stucco home. The one she and Roger had bought when they found out Kelly was coming.

Owning that house, decorating it, caring for it, all once gave Mary a feeling of peace and sanctuary. Now that was gone, replaced by apprehension.

Roger's conversation with her the night before was troublesome. He wasn't going to be put off much longer. It was the second time he'd wanted to know what was going on, and the second time she'd managed to deflect him. But at some point, he'd want an explanation.

Mary wasn't sure what she could do about that.

She was pondering that when she realized she was about to drive right past her house. She hit the brakes yet again and backed up her car so she could turn into the driveway. Mary glanced at the clock on the car's console.

She'd cut it close – Celia said she'd be there at 3:00, and Mary had barely ten minutes before her friend arrived.

She quickly grabbed the four grocery bags from the front seat along with her purse and trotted to the side door. She felt the plastic handles of one of the bags begin to stretch – she prayed she could get it inside before the bag dropped.

The bag thumped down on the floor of the small laundry room. The sound told Mary that the bag had nothing breakable – probably the six-pack of soda she'd gotten. She put her other bags on the kitchen table and went back to retrieve the broken one.

She started a pot of coffee, a hazelnut flavored blend she hoped Celia would like. Mary put away the rest of the groceries except for some double chocolate chip cookies she'd seen at the bakery department. Normally, Mary liked to make her own cookies, but she'd been too busy cleaning the house top to bottom to do it, and as stressed as she was she couldn't resist the chocolate goodness those cookies promised.

There were fresh clipped roses in a small vase on the middle of the table. Mary considered moving the small blue and white metal plaque that was on a stand next to the vase. It read, "Prayer may not be allowed in school, but it is welcome at our table." Celia wasn't really that religious . . . maybe the plaque would offend her . . .

Mary shook her head, feeling a surge of anger at herself. Was she ashamed of her faith? Did she want to impress Celia more than stay true to herself?

The plaque would stay. Mary gave herself a mental shake and began to arrange the cookies on a plate. While her hands were busy she tried to pray. But she was not sure what she should pray for. Celia getting lost? Getting through the afternoon with her secret intact? Answers to the nagging questions that she had spent the week wrestling with? Her mind couldn't focus on a prayer, and she felt worse than ever.

The doorbell rang. Mary took a last look around the kitchen. Taking a deep breath, she went to the door and opened it.

Celia looked a lot like the bubbly teenager Mary had hung out with in high school. Her hair was still blond, though now with highlights that looked like they'd been done in a beauty shop. She was dressed in jeans that hugged her hips and body and a pale blue silk blouse, not unusual for her, except the clothes looked to be a little higher class.

For a moment Mary was embarrassed by her faded denim jeans and red and white patterned t-shirt. She dropped her eyes to her feet, where she saw her beat up sneakers in front of Celia's classy boots.

"Mary!" Celia screamed, throwing her arms around her friend. "Wow, you have no idea how great it is to see you!"

Mary returned her friend's hug, feeling a smile tug at her lips in spite of her inner turmoil. Once, Celia and she had been like sisters. Their growing apart wasn't only due to that horrible summer in Atlanta, but distance and different paths.

Celia pulled out of the hug, holding Mary at arm's length. "Let me look at you! Wow, you look incredible! I guess being a housewife is good for you!"

Mary grinned. "You look outstanding. But then, you always did." She waved a hand. "Come inside. We have a little bit more than a half hour before I have to go pick up Kelly."

"Kelly? Is that your kid?"

"Yes," Mary said. She led Celia to the small hallway where the bedrooms and Roger's office were, stopping by the family picture they'd had done for the church directory the year before. "This is a year old, but you can get an idea of what she looks like. And Roger, my husband."

Celia put a hand on her chin while she looked at the picture. "Hm. She's cute. I see a lot of her in you." She suddenly broke into a grin. "And Roger looks like a hot nerd. Very different from Harold."

Mary smiled even though she felt goosebumps forming on her arms. "Roger is wonderful. Are you ready for some coffee and cookies?"

"Mmm. I thought I smelled coffee. Lead on!"

Moments later they were both sitting at the kitchen table, cups of coffee in their hands and the plate of cookies between them. They talked about their lives over the past few years, filling each other in on what they'd experienced since they were apart.

Just as Mary was relaxing, Celia put her cup down and a serious expression came on her face. "Okay, enough chitchat. Why did you call my mom about that summer ten years ago?"

- THIRTY -

MARY'S GOOD FEELINGS EVAPORATED at Celia's question. She picked up a cookie from the plate and bit into it, concentrating on the rich chocolate flavor as she stalled for time. She wondered what Celia knew. Would she dismiss Mary's feelings and concerns as Mrs. Winters had?

"Hey," Celia said, reaching out to lay a bejeweled hand on Mary's. "We used to be what the kids nowadays call BFF. You could tell me anything. Right?"

"It's just..." Mary put the rest of the cookie in her mouth while she thought over what she might say. "When I called your mother, she basically told me to forget about that summer. Even though – even though I got this note..."

"What note?" Celia said with a frown.

"Your mom didn't mention the note?" Mary sighed.

"Hey, I know my mom," Celia shrugged. "She wants an easy, hassle-free life. If something comes to disturb that, her attitude is to forget about it." A look of sadness came to her face. "Believe me, I know."

Mary examined her friend's downcast face. "I thought you and your mother got along great."

"Oh, we did," Celia said. "When I was young and totally into irresponsibility especially. But then I grew up. She didn't."

"I'm sorry. I didn't know," Mary said.

"Hey, it's not your fault my mother is a totally self-centered opportunist," Celia said. "And according to my therapist, it's not my fault either, though I don't totally agree with her yet..." she paused to take a swallow of coffee. "So before you distract me up to the time you'll claim we have to go get your daughter, why not tell me what's going on?"

Mary sighed. She needed to talk to someone, and Celia seemed the best of a number of bad choices. "Let me get something to show you," she said.

Two minutes later Celia was staring opened mouthed at the note Mary had gotten less than a week ago. "Whoa. Do you have any idea who sent it?"

Mary nodded, her mouth suddenly dry., After a drink of coffee, she said, "A nurse from – that clinic."

"You're sure?" Celia asked, the shock making her voice shake.

"Yes, unfortunately," Mary said. She hesitated, then decided to tell her friend more. "The nurse's son contacted me. She killed herself after mailing me that note."

"Killed herself?" Celia asked, color draining from her face. She swore. "Oh! Sorry about that, I figure you aren't the type who likes that kind of language. You never did."

Mary waved a hand. "It's okay. I mean, I don't like it, but we have other things to worry about."

"'Your son is alive,'" Celia read from the note. "What son? They told us the baby was dead!"

"I know," Mary said, feeling an ache in her chest. "But I have to wonder Celia, why would she send that to me if it wasn't true? Talking to her son doesn't give me the impression she was a cruel woman."

"You don't know what she is," Celia argued. She tapped the note with a manicured fingernail. "Look, I know you don't like that clinic, but maybe you should call them and ask to see your records?"

"I already tried that," Mary said. "The clinic is gone. Burned down last year."

"You're kidding!" Celia said. "What happened?"

"As far as I know, they didn't figure out the cause, though Dr. Green was quick to blame pro-life groups," Mary said.

"Well, that's possible, isn't it?" Celia said. "I mean, some of those pro-life people are scary."

Mary rolled her eyes. "Celia, most pro-life people are *not* weirdoes. We just believe life begins at conception."

"Mary, that's fine for you. But I don't feel the same way. Why should I have to conform to *your* beliefs?" Celia argued.

Mary sighed and rubbed her temples. "Celia, I really don't want to argue with you about this, okay? I have enough on my mind right now."

Celia's expression immediately softened. "Oh, Mary, I'm so sorry. I guess all this must really be freaking you out."

Mary nodded, swirling her cooling coffee in its cup. She swallowed, trying to calm down.

"Hey," Celia said. "Isn't it time to pick up your kid?"

Mary looked at the LED clock on her microwave and gasped. "Oh no! We have to leave now!"

"Okay, okay," Celia said, standing and stretching. "Hey, am I welcome to dinner? I mean, are you mad at me?"

"Um," Mary said, as she fished her keys out of her purse. "Celia, Roger doesn't know anything about Harold – or the clinic. Please don't say anything about it?"

"Hey, I get it," Celia said, following Mary to the door to the garage. "My lips are sealed, girlfriend. You can count on me."

- THIRTY-ONE -

Mary passed the spinach salad she'd made along with the carafe of hot bacon dressing. "Hope everything's all right."

"All right?" Celia said, smacking her lips. "This is incredible! When did you become such a great cook? I still remember that time you broiled the cake in Home Ec."

Kelly giggled. "Mommy, why did you broil a cake?"

Roger was grinning. "Wow, Celia, I wish I'd met you sooner. You seem full of great stories about Mary."

Mary rolled her eyes. "Now I'll never live that down. Celia, as my friend, you're not supposed to reveal all my terrible secrets. I thought you knew that."

"Oh come on, that's not so terrible," Celia scoffed. "I have worse ones if you want."

Mary shot her friend an alarmed look. She had been worried that Celia would slip up somehow, in spite of Celia's assurances that she'd behave.

Celia caught her friend's look as she speared some green beans with a fork. "To be honest, compared to some stories that Mary has on me, her past misdeeds are pretty tame."

Mary stifled a sigh of relief. She sliced a part of her honey-mustard chicken breast while she racked her brain for a story to tell on her friend.

Kelly tore off a piece of her crescent roll. "Miss Celia, how long were you my mommy's friend?"

Celia smiled at the little girl. "A long time, honey. Years."

"Mommy never talks about you," Kelly said, examining a piece of roll before popping it into her mouth. "Did you stop being friends?"

Mary felt her breath stop. "Sweetie . . . "

Roger swallowed the food in his mouth. "Kel, sometimes when friends don't live near each other, they drift apart. It doesn't mean they don't care about each other, they just don't talk as often as they used to."

"Oh." Kelly poked at her green beans, looking thoughtful. "But Mommy, you and Miss Celia still like each other?"

"Yes honey," Mary said, looking at her friend across the table. She was relieved to see Celia smile and nod.

"We sure do, munchkin," Celia said, grabbing a roll from the basket in the middle. "And I promise to talk to your mom more. Okay?"

"Okay," Kelly said agreeably. "But Wendy and I will *always* be best friends. Even if she moves to *Miami!*"

"I bet you will," Celia said, wiping her mouth with a napkin. "Wow, Mary, this was all great, but I should probably go check in at my hotel. I told Dad I'd have breakfast with him tomorrow."

"Sure," Mary said, standing and gathering some of the dirty dishes. Celia took a couple of plates and carried them to the counter.

"Well, Celia," Roger said, shaking her hand, "It's nice to have met you. I hope we'll have more time to talk next time you come by."

"Thanks. I'll try not to be a stranger," Celia said with a smile. She bent down and hugged Kelly. "You're a sweet little girl. I'm glad I got to meet you."

"It's nice to meet you too," Kelly said politely. "If you want to stay here tonight, you can sleep in my room. I'll sleep on the couch."

Celia looked surprised. "Well . . . that's very sweet of you, munchkin, but I'd like to have some alone time tonight. Maybe I'll sleep over some other time."

Mary walked Celia out to her rental car. "Thanks for coming," Mary said.

"Hey, that's what friends do," Celia shrugged. She looked at Mary in the light of the lamppost that stood by the driveway. "I don't like what I'm hearing though. Something about all this with the clinic . . . it's just making my stomach hurt. You know?"

"I know," Mary said with a nod. "Part of me wants to just forget about it. But . . . if I have a son, a son I don't know about . . . "

"What if he's happy?" Celia asked, leaning against the driver's door. "Do you want to throw his life into chaos?"

"What if he isn't?" Mary countered. "What if he's being abused, or neglected, or…"

"I get it, I get it," Celia said, raising a hand to stop Mary. "Look, I'm having breakfast with Dad like I said, but I'm here 'til Sunday and I'm not holding to a rigid schedule. So if you want us to visit again, just say the word."

Mary looked down at her hands. "If you're willing . . . .there is something. This nurses' son is probably going to be in town tomorrow . . . he wants to talk to me."

"How're you going to explain that to the family?" Celia said, tilting her head towards the house.

"I haven't figured that out yet," Mary said.

"Well, if you want backup, I'd be happy to come with you to meet this guy," Celia said. "You got my cell phone number?"

Mary shook her head. Celia ducked into her car and pulled out a notepad. She scribbled the number on the top page and tore it. "Here. Call me when you know what time you guys are meeting. Tell your hubby we're spending time together. It'll be true, so it shouldn't offend your Christian conscience."

"Thanks, Celia." Feeling a surge of affection, she threw her arms around her friend. "I've missed you. You are such a great friend, and I've been so awful not staying in touch."

Celia hugged her back. "Hey, that goes both ways. We'll get through this, and be friends again. Just like your daughter and her BFF."

Mary chuckled. As she watched Celia drive away, she felt a little better about the situation. Maybe she'd be able to settle this with her old friend's help.

- THIRTY-TWO -

As HE NARROWLY MISSED REAR-ENDING yet another driver on the interstate who felt that a turn signal when changing lanes was a waste of time, Jack decided he hated Jacksonville.

It wasn't that Atlanta traffic was without its share of stupid drivers, but Jacksonville seemed to have a great deal of them. And they all seemed intent on trying to kill Jack.

He leaned on his horn, letting the driver in front of him know he was ticked off. He got a gesture back that he was well familiar with. "Yeah," he muttered. "Same to ya, pal."

Jack risked a glance at the directions he'd printed off of MapQuest. It had been easy to get to this point – finding Mary Beamer's house was going to be the real trick.

A glance up told him he was about to pass the exit the directions said he needed. With a swift glance backward, he crossed over to the appropriate lane. A blue pickup truck that had been in his blind spot blasted his horn, the accusing sound not quite muting the sound of screeching tires.

Jack felt his heart pounding from the near miss. He pulled into the first gas station on the right hand side he came to and found a place he could throw the car into park. Then he sat and rested his head on the steering wheel for a long moment, trying to settle down.

Closing his eyes was a mistake. He'd gotten up after only three hours sleep to make the six-hour drive to Jacksonville. He was planning to approach Mary Beamer and see if she would talk to him. If not, Jack thought he'd nose around, see if there was something that would give him leverage over her.

In spite of the energy drinks he'd guzzled on the drive, he was exhausted. Sleep whispered to him, tempting him to drift off, if only for a few minutes. What harm would it do?

Jack forced himself to straighten up. His back muscles protested, and his knees let him know they weren't happy with the situation either. *Oh, to be twenty again…*

Jack slowly and painfully got out of the car. He took a minute to stretch and to crack his back. The sound of joints popping was somewhat reassuring for some reason.

He leaned against his car, allowing a cool breeze to refresh him. The whispery noise of cars racing over the interstate was a soothing sound, contrasting with the ding of people pulling in to fill up their gas tanks. The smell of gasoline competed with the scent of coffee that wafted out when someone opened the door to the convenience store that ran the station.

Jack's stomach rumbled. He'd not made a lot of stops, wanting to get to Jacksonville as early as possible and make the most of his time there. Jack was pretty sure Wheeler wouldn't pay for this trip and would not be happy if Jack wasn't back at work bright and early Monday morning.

He'd at least taken the precaution of making sure his articles for the next couple of days were on Wheeler's desk before he left. It meant staying at the newspaper until late in the evening, which meant less sleep then he would have liked.

Jack rubbed his face and decided a coffee and pastry was exactly what he needed before driving the rest of the way to Ms. Beamer's house. He hoped she'd be home – he didn't want to come all this way just to find out her family was out of town on vacation.

Of course, he could've just called her up on the phone. Jack shook his head at the thought as he headed into the store. Yeah. The problem with phones was that people could hang up on you. Better to show up on their doorstep – harder for them to turn you away in person.

Assuming his hunch was correct and this Beamer gal had something to do with Dr. Green and his clinic. If not, then he'd just about killed himself for nothing. Wouldn't that be *great?*

Frowning at the thought, Jack snatched two Hostess apple pies off a shelf and poured himself a large cup of coffee. He dumped plenty of sugar into it before carrying it all to the counter, where a bored Hispanic woman rang him up without even glancing at him.

Back in his car, Jack munched on one of the pies as he reviewed the directions one more time. He got some of the coffee in him, though it burned his throat – "hot" in this case seemed to be just below the temperature of lava. But he needed the caffeine if he was going to function.

It took another half hour of driving and about three wrong turns before he found the address he was looking for. He pulled up two houses away from the pleasant almond colored one story frame house and turned off his car.

Sipping his coffee, Jack tried to get a feel for the neighborhood. Mostly one story homes, with a couple of two stories just to break up the view. Trimmed front lawns. Over there, three doors down and across the street, a tricycle sat next to a tree. A man who looked to be in his mid-sixties jogged past Jack's car, a transistor radio clipped to the waistband of his royal blue shorts.

Beaver Cleaver could live on this street, Jack thought with a shake of his head. It was the America all those family values people liked to talk about but that Jack rarely saw.

He snorted. *Family values*. If he was right about Mary Beamer, she certainly wouldn't be their poster child.

Jack drained his coffee cup. He felt a headache coming on. A glance at his watch told him it was 9:56 – probably still a little early to wake up someone on a Saturday morning.

He reclined his seat. He'd just close his eyes for a few minutes . . . recharge the old batteries . . . then he'd ring the doorbell and see what he found out. Just a few minutes . . .

It took less than five minutes for Jack to fall into a deep sleep.

- THIRTY-THREE -

MARY FOUND HERSELF TENSE THAT MORNING. Saturday was the family's day to sleep in for the most part – unless something specific was planned, she, Roger, and Kelly pretty much took it easy. Meals were informal, and the atmosphere was generally relaxed.

Except today was different. She was waiting for a phone call. Thompson hadn't called her yesterday, and she was glad of it – Martha Thompson's son and Celia's initial visit would have been a lot to handle.

Now, as she flipped pancakes and sipped a cup of hot coffee, Mary wondered when she'd get the call. And how she would keep Roger from suspecting anything. Celia's idea of a "girls day out" had merit.

"Hey," Roger said, coming up behind Mary, his lips on her neck.

She jumped slightly, and the pancake she'd been flipping slid off the spatula and landed half on the griddle, half on the stove.

"Whoa!" Roger said, stepping beside her. His hair was damp and he was dressed casually for the day in a pair of khaki shorts and a red, white, and blue t-shirt he'd gotten for donating blood. "Looks like I have quite an effect on you, Mary."

She smiled, shoving the thought of Thompson away for the moment. Scooping up the ruined pancake, she said, "I ought to make you eat this."

"Now see, this is why we should get a dog," Roger said with a grin, reaching up into a cabinet to grab three plates. "A pup would eat that mistake right up."

"Before or after he chewed up the baseboards and stained the rugs?" Mary asked lightly. The subject of a pet came up once in a while between them. Roger had been raised with dogs and really wanted them to have one. Mary, on the other hand, felt she had her hands full as it was and didn't want the added responsibility of an animal.

Roger grinned. "You know, they can be trained." He looked over the small stack of golden pancakes that already sat on a plate. "Kelly need some of these?"

"Yes." Mary waved the spatula towards the den. "At the moment, she is bonding with SpongeBob Squarepants."

Roger shook his head as he forked two pancakes onto a plate. "You know, I somehow think cartoons have lost something. Whatever happened to Bugs Bunny?"

"He's still out there somewhere," Mary smiled as she transferred the newly cooked pancakes to the plate of finished ones. She turned off the stove and wiped her hands on a paper towel. "But it's different today."

"Tell me about it," Roger said. He stepped to the doorway that led to the den. "Kelly! Got some pancakes for you here!"

The little girl wandered into the kitchen yawning, hugging a small brown bear. She was still in her pajamas. "G'morning, Daddy."

"Good morning, Princess," Roger said, putting a kiss on his daughter's head while he helped her get set up. "Would Her Majesty like milk or orange juice with her pancakes this morning?"

Kelly started to giggle. "Orange juice is fine."

Mary stood by the stove with the syrup bottle in her hand, watching the interplay between the two most important people in her life. She loved them both so much it hurt sometimes.

Watching Roger with their daughter, she wondered how he'd react to another child in their life. One he hadn't fathered.

Mary turned back to the plate of pancakes. She grabbed it and dishes for herself and Roger after fixing a smile on her face. She felt tension in her neck and shoulders and hoped Roger didn't notice it.

He took the dishes from her. "Butter?" he asked, sitting across from his daughter.

"Coming right up," she said, forcing brightness in her voice. She grabbed the margarine tub from the refrigerator and brought it with her coffee to the table.

Roger was pouring a cup for himself from the carafe on a small wooden trolley table that sat near the kitchen table. He held up the coffee pot to Mary. "Refill?"

"Thanks," she said.

The family enjoyed a few minutes of placid eating before the bombshell dropped.

Kelly licked syrup from her fork. "Mommy, Daddy, are you two married?"

Roger spat coffee back into his cup. "What?"

Mary met her husband's glance and shrugged. "We are married, sweetheart. I showed you our wedding pictures, remember?"

Coughing to clear his throat, Roger said, "Why do you ask, Kelly?"

"Well, Tommy Hughes in my class? He told me his mommy and daddy weren't married – he lives with his mommy and sees his daddy on weekends," the little girl said, oblivious to the distress her question stirred up in her parents. "His daddy's taking him to Disney World this weekend. He's gonna see Mickey Mouse and *everything*."

"Well," Mary said, trying to think of what to say. "Sometimes mommies and daddies don't get married."

"But Daddy, didn't you say that God *wants* mommies and daddies to be married?" Kelly asked, her brow furrowed.

"Yes, I did," Roger said, his voice sounding more normal. "But sometimes people don't do what God wants them to do. It makes Him very sad."

Kelly pondered this. "Does that mean Tommy's parents are bad people?"

Mary spoke quickly. "It means they're sinners, Kelly. Just like everyone. It's why Jesus came."

"Oh," Kelly said. She took a big gulp of orange juice. "Can Wendy come over and play today?"

Mary looked over at her husband. "I need to speak with your daddy about today first, and then we'll decide about Wendy coming over. Okay?"

"'Kay," Kelly said. "Can I take my orange juice in the den and watch cartoons?"

"Sure," Mary said. "Let's go wash your hands first, though, I think you got more syrup on them than in your tummy."

Kelly giggled and followed Mary to the kitchen sink. Before going to the den she gave her mother an orange juice flavored kiss. "I'm glad you and Daddy did what God wanted," she said before carrying her cup out of the kitchen.

Mary felt a twinge at her daughter's comment. A groan from Roger made her turn around.

Her husband was slumped back in his seat, a hand placed dramatically on his forehead. "Mare, if this stuff's coming up now, I'm not sure I'll survive her being a teenager!"

Mary couldn't hold back a chuckle as she came back to the table. "You're a strong man. You'll be fine."

"Uh-huh," Roger said. "You remember that song about the dad who warns his girl's date he'll be up cleaning his gun? I'm starting to think that's not a bad idea."

Mary grinned at her husband. "Now, maybe she'll be lucky enough to bring home someone like you. My dad didn't pull a gun on you that I remember."

"That's because he was a trusting soul," Roger deadpanned. "If he had known me better . . ."

"Stop," Mary said, balling up her white paper napkin and tossing it at him.

Roger caught the projectile. "Well, I'll tell you what. If our little girl is as good as her mom, then we won't have anything to worry about."

Mary felt her smile freeze on her face. "I hope she'll be better."

"That's a pretty high bar," Roger said, leaning over to giver her a swift kiss. "So, what do we need to talk about concerning today?"

Mary chose her words carefully. "Well, Celia is still in town, and I was thinking of our having a girls' day out. Would that be all right?"

Roger didn't answer right away. He drained his coffee cup and then asked, "What's up with this gal? She suddenly pops into your life after being silent for years?"

Mary took her plate to the sink and started rinsing dishes. "It happens."

"But why? And how did she know our phone number?"

"Well…" Mary decided that a little truth might keep her from telling it all. "To be honest, I contacted her mother the other day."

Roger frowned. "Her mother? How come?"

"I – I was going through some of my old high school stuff the other day," Mary said, working on keeping her voice light. "Just got a feeling of nostalgia, I guess. I came across her mother's number and decided to give her a quick call. That's all."

"You did?" Roger looked puzzled. "Why didn't you say anything about it?"

"I was afraid you'd be upset," Mary said. "It was a long-distance call, and I made it pretty much on a whim."

She could see by the confused look on her husband's face that he didn't totally buy her reason. She swallowed, wondering how she could salvage the situation.

The ringing of the phone saved her from trying. "I'll get it!" she said, grabbing a checkered hand towel and quickly drying her hands as she went to the phone. "Hello?"

"Ms. Beamer? It's Bob Thompson."

"Yes," Mary said, aware that Roger was still sitting at the table, watching her.

"I'm at the Embassy Suites Hotel off of Southside Boulevard," Thompson said. "Would it be convenient for you if we meet for brunch? Say, at 11:30?"

"That would be fine," Mary said. "I'll see you then."

"All right," Thompson said, his voice uncertain, no doubt due to her brusqueness. "I'll be wearing dark blue Dockers and a bright green polo shirt. Look for me in the lobby."

"That's fine," Mary said again. "Thank you for calling."

She hung up the phone and took a minute to compose her face. She felt Roger's hand gentle on her shoulder. "Mare? What was that about?"

"Just something about the clothing room," Mary said. She felt horrible for lying, but what else could she do at this point?

Roger stared at her and she did her best to meet his eyes. Finally, he sighed and squeezed her shoulder. "Okay. I don't understand what's going on, Mare, but I guess I'll have to trust you."

Mary swallowed. "Please, trust me Roger," she whispered. She kissed him, holding him tightly.

Roger hugged her back. "Okay. Well, go call Celia and have your girl's day out. The princess and I will hold down the fort."

Mary nodded. She hurried to get her cell phone to alert Celia that they had a meeting.

- THIRTY-FOUR -

J ACK'S HEAD JERKED UP at the sound of a car door slamming. He frowned at the sight of a fairly new-looking Acura parked in front of him. A woman was walking away from it, heading toward the Beamer home.

He gave the woman an appreciative once-over. She was young, blond, and good-looking, with legs that seemed to go forever and a confident bounce to her step.

Mary Beamer? Nah, he decided. Especially as she appeared to ring the doorbell. Jack glanced over at the car in front of him. He saw it had a Florida license plate and looked incredibly clean. A rental? He grabbed his notebook and jotted down the plate number for future reference.

Out of the corner of his eye he saw the blond woman go into the house. Jack tapped his steering wheel, thinking. Who was this new person, and what part did she play in all this?

He yawned. According to his original plan, he was going to knock on the door and confront Mary Beamer in the hopes she would give him some clue that would let him break into the story. Now he wasn't sure that was the best move.

A few minutes later, he saw the blond woman come out again, followed by a darker-haired woman who looked to be about the same age. Jack took a good look at the second woman, suspecting this was Mary Beamer.

His reporter's mind clicked off details. Dark shoulder-length hair pulled back. Jeans and a bright red buttoned blouse. Matching red flats, a black shoulder bag. Appeared a little apprehensive.

Jack watched the two women climb into the Acura. He waited 'til it turned at the pulled away and turned the corner before he started his car and followed. He caught up with it and faded back til there was about ½ block distance between the two of them.

He was playing a hunch. Jack knew that this could turn out to be a huge waste of time. But he'd gotten where he once was in the world of journalism by trusting his hunches. Given what was at stake with this story, it was madness to abandon that trust now.

He followed them onto the interstate, grimacing. Here it was harder to keep the car in sight while watching the other drivers on the road, many of whom thought turn signals while changing lanes were unnecessary. Jack cursed at his fellow drivers while working to keep the Acura in sight.

As it was, he nearly missed them exiting. Jack was in the middle lane and had to work to get over, earning himself an angry horn honk and a hand gesture. He ignored it, concentrating on swerving onto the off ramp and pulling up behind his target in the left hand turn lane.

When the light changed, he kept behind them. It was a risk, but he didn't know the area and if he lost them here Jack was fairly certain he wouldn't be able to find them again.

They pulled into the parking lot of the Embassy Suites hotel. Jack drove past them as they parked and found an empty space two lanes over. He got out of his car, wincing at the ache in his legs and back – he'd been sitting way too long.

Jack kept a distance behind the two women as they entered the lobby. He stepped inside, scanned the spacious area, and got the shock of his life.

Bob Thompson stood from a brown leather chair and extended his hand to the two women. He wasn't facing Jack, which gave the reporter enough time to duck behind a large green plant near the doors.

So, he thought, tapping his pen against his notepad. *Bob Thompson's down here meeting with Mary Beamer. The question is, why? And how do I find out about it?*

- THIRTY-FIVE -

WHEN MARY SAW THE MAN she assumed to be Bob Thompson stand up and approach her, she had to wipe off the sweat that suddenly gathered on her palms. Her heart went into full gallop mode.

Celia, on the other hand, appeared totally at ease. She reached over and took the man's hand. "You're Bob Thompson, I assume? I'm Celia Morris, pleased to meet you."

Mary took a deep breath and extended her hand next. "I'm Mary Beamer, Mr. Thompson. We spoke on the phone."

"Yes," Thompson said, shaking Mary's hand while his eyes darted from face to face. "You didn't mention you were bringing anyone, Ms. Beamer. That makes me somewhat uncomfortable."

"*You're* uncomfortable?" Celia said. "I was with Mary at the clinic that summer. And given how you pretty much blackmailed her into this meeting in the first place, I don't think you have much room to talk about discomfort here."

Thompson raised his chin. "And how do I know you aren't a lawyer? Or worse, a reporter? I've already had one of those sniffing around my mother's place, I don't need another one."

"A reporter is involved in this?" Mary felt nausea crawl up her throat. "Why? How?"

Thompson's expression softened slightly at Mary's obvious distress. "I don't know. I'm pretty sure it has something to do with that clinic. But my question stands: how do I know I can trust you?"

Celia rolled her eyes. "Look, I'm not sure we can trust *you*."

"Celia, don't," Mary said in a weak voice. She looked Thompson in the eye. "I am not trying to deceive you – as a Christian, that would be wrong of me. Celia is my friend and was at the clinic when . . . when I lost my baby. She may have seen and spoken to your mother as well."

Thompson pursed his lips as he studied the two of them. Finally he nodded. "All right. Fair enough. I guess we're just going to have to trust each other for now." He gestured towards a hallway. "The hotel here has a decent restaurant. Shall we?"

Mary and Celia followed Thompson to the hotel's restaurant. They were swiftly seated at a table with a white tablecloth and linen napkins. After they were handed menus and asked for coffee everyone concentrated on studying their choices.

The prices caught Mary by surprise. She nervously tried to remember how much cash she was carrying – she didn't want to put this meal on a credit card.

Celia leaned over. "Relax, girlfriend. Lunch is on *moi*."

Mary felt her cheeks heat up. "You don't have to . . . "

"Hey, I want to. Although," Celia said flipping a hand towards Thompson, "if he was a *real* gentleman, he'd pay for both of us."

Thompson arched an eyebrow. "And if you were real ladies, you wouldn't have been in an abortion clinic."

Mary felt as if she'd been punched in the gut. "I didn't *want* to be there!"

"I'm sure," Thompson said, his voice heavy with sarcasm. "You just couldn't raise the child or give him the life he deserved, so you killed him instead!"

Mary felt tears spill down her cheeks. "I didn't want to go there! I didn't even know it was an abortion clinic until . . . until . . . "

Celia's arms went around Mary's shaking shoulders. She glared at Thompson. "She's telling the truth. My mom took her there when Mary went into premature labor. When Mary found out where she was, she totally freaked out."

Mary noticed that people at nearby tables were glancing in their direction. Their waiter hovered a few feet away, a look on uncertainty on his freckled face. She closed her eyes, wishing she could just pass out or maybe have a heart attack.

"All right," Thompson said. Mary opened her eyes and looked at the man. He seemed to be aware of the attention they were getting because his voice was lower. "Obviously, there are issues for both of us here. Let's all calm down and listen to each other's stories. That okay with you, Ms. Morris?"

Celia was rubbing Mary's back. She still glared at Thompson but kept her voice at a normal level. "Of course. Just please follow your own advice here."

The waiter apparently felt the coast was clear and approached the table. After they placed their orders, Mary mentally scrabbled for a non-controversial topic of conversation. "Do you live in Atlanta, Mr. Thompson?"

"Boston," he answered. With that conversation focused on neutral topics such as places visited and movies seen. Mary started to feel calmer. Thompson still radiated unfriendliness but at least he wasn't attacking her.

She was grateful for Celia. Her friend managed to keep Thompson from any more snide comments and had funny stories to tell that lightened the mood at the table. Mary knew if she'd tried this alone she'd never have gotten through it.

Once they were sitting back enjoying coffees and waiting for cheesecake (Celia had insisted that Mary indulge) Thompson grew serious again. He reached down into the briefcase he'd carried in and pulled out a photograph. "This is my mother," he said, his voice soft with emotion as he slid the picture across the table.

Mary frowned as she studied the face. The woman pictured was perhaps in her 50's or 60's. Her blue eyes looked kind, but a little sad.

Mary had avoided reliving the details of that summer ten years ago as much as she could, though she couldn't prevent the occasional nightmares. Now she forced herself to go back in her mind, trying to see if this woman's face was part of that picture.

Something . . . she remembered when she'd been told her baby was born dead. When she learned that Celia's mother had taken her to an *abortion* clinic, of all places. She had wept, the full weight of her sin heavy on her.

And a nurse had been there. A nurse, who had tears streaming down her own face as she embraced Mary, weeping with her, telling her it was for the best, she must believe that . . .

Mary looked up at Thompson, feeling a weight on her heart. It was hard to go back to that day, even harder than she'd thought it would be. "Your mother . . . I think she was there when I was brought there. She held me while I cried."

Celia had leaned towards Mary to study the picture. "Yes, I think you're right. She was with you when Mom and I came to pick you up, right? She seemed awfully nice and the only one there who felt bad about it."

"She did?" Thompson said, looking surprised. "I mean, she was gung-ho about her work there. Said she was performing a 'service'." His mouth twisted on the word "service" as if it brought a sour taste.

Mary took a deep breath, trying to fight back the emotions that threatened to overwhelm her. "I take it . . . you and your mother didn't get along?"

"That's putting it nicely," Thompson said, plucking at his napkin. The waiter appeared with their desserts and the three of them fell silent while the cheesecake was served.

When the waiter left, no one moved to pick up their fork. The silence stretched for a long moment. Then Thompson cleared his throat.

"Let me tell you about my family."

- THIRTY-SIX -

"MY MOM," THOMPSON STARTED, "had been a nurse for years. When my sister and I were born, she took time off to be a stay-at-home mom." He glanced at from one woman to the other. "I guess that's not in style anymore."

"I'm a stay-at-home mom," Mary said softly. She studied the triangle of cheesecake on her plate, decorated with sliced strawberries with a chocolate drizzle over it all.

"I see," Thompson said. "What about you?" This to Celia.

The blond shrugged. "No kids yet. Don't know if I want any."

Mary's eyes slid to her friend's face. Celia's answer surprised her. "What? Celia, why not?"

Celia shook her head, her eyes not meeting Mary's. "Not now, Mary. Okay? Right now I want to know why Mr. Self-Righteous here wasn't on good terms with his mom."

Thompson stared at Celia. "You know, Ms. Morris, I don't think I like you."

"The feeling's mutual, Mr. Thompson," Celia answered coolly. "I tend to think that people who blackmail friends of mine aren't very nice."

"I need to understand!" Thompson said with an oath, slamming a fist on the table. "My mother killed herself! It seems to have been tied to that horrible clinic! And you seem to have a tie!"

"Why care now?" Celia asked, picking up her fork and plunging it into her cheesecake. "You've said you didn't get along."

Thompson glared at Celia. "Ms. Morris, have you ever lost a parent?"

"Divorce count?"

"Celia, don't," Mary said, putting a hand on her friend's arm.

"Mary, I don't think this guy deserves the nice-Christian-girl routine."

"It's the only one I know," Mary said with a sigh. She turned to Thompson, desperate to keep the man talking in the hopes he could shed some light on the note. "Please, I understand you're upset – to lose a parent must be difficult. I'm sure you loved her, even when you disapproved of her."

Thompson's eyes widened. He stared at Mary for a long moment, then his cheeks flushed. "Forgive me, Ms. Beamer. I formed an opinion of you that I see was incorrect."

It was Mary's turn to blush. She picked up her fork and drew the tines across the top of her dessert. "Please. I need to know, if you can tell me – why would your mother send me that note? Why would she say I had a son that was alive somewhere?"

"That's a good question," Thompson said, rubbing his temple. "She always defended her work at the clinic. My sister and I . . . we're not religious folk, you understand. But we never thought that abortion was right. I mean, just because the baby's little and inside his mom's no reason to kill it."

Celia shifted in her seat, and Mary put a hand on her friend's arm, hoping she wouldn't start defending abortion now when it appeared Thompson was willing to talk.

To keep Thompson talking, Mary asked, "So you all fought with her about her work?"

"Yes," Thompson nodded. "My sister and I said some terrible things, terrible. After a while we only spoke on holidays. And when my father died."

"I'm sorry," Mary said. She didn't know what else to say.

"My mother found out she had cancer two months ago. She let me and my sister know, of course. But . . . " Thompson rubbed his eyes. "I didn't come see her. I figured . . . I figured there was time, you know? But then I get a call from the police, and they told me..."

Mary took a bite of cheesecake, not because she particularly wanted it, but to give the man across from her a chance to compose himself. She wished he hadn't forced this meeting, but she couldn't help but feel sorry for him.

Celia wiped her mouth with her napkin. "I get it, Mr. Thompson. I'm not totally in love with my mom, but if something happened to her, I'd be a little freaked out too."

Thompson stood. "Will you ladies excuse me for a moment?" Without waiting for an answer, he left the table.

Celia shook her head. "What a mess this is." She nudged Mary with her shoulder. "How're you holding up, girlfriend?"

Mary sighed. "I don't know. I'm so confused, Celia." She looked at the photo of Martha Thompson that was on the table. "Why did she kill herself? Why did she send me that note? We still don't know about that!"

"Ma'am?"

Mary turned to see a middle-aged man standing by the table. His clothes were rumpled and there were dark circles under his eyes. "I'm sorry, were you speaking to me?"

"Yes." The man shot a nervous glance in the direction that Thompson had gone in. "I don't have much time, and I hope I'm not making a mistake, but I need to talk to you. I think I can answer some of your questions."

"What?" Mary was stunned.

"Hold up, hold up, who are you?" Celia asked.

"Here," the man put a smudged business card on the table. "Take this please, and call me when you're done here – my cell phone number. And don't let Thompson know I was here, please." He gave a final look around the restaurant before walking away.

Mary didn't know what to think. She looked at the card. It had a name – *Jack Foster* – and three different phone numbers. One was labeled as his cell phone number.

Celia leaned over to get a look at the card. "Well, well, well . . . this name looks familiar to me, wonder why." She used a polished nail to tap the phone numbers. "Those have an Atlanta area code."

"Are you sure?" Mary asked.

"Yeah, I have to dial it once a week for my duty call to Mom," Celia said. She pursed her lips. "Looks like Thompson's heading back. What do you want to do?"

Mary slid the card off the table and into her bag before Thompson sat down. He took a deep breath. "Well, sorry about that." He gave them both a sharp glance. "Something wrong?"

Mary swapped glances with Celia. Her friend spoke up. "Mary was just concerned about you. She knew you were upset."

Thompson nodded. "Thank you, but I'll be fine." He sipped his water. "Ms. Beamer, could you please explain to me how you came in contact with my mother?"

Mary gulped. She'd known she would have to talk about this. But she never had before. This story had remained in her heart. Now she was supposed to give voice to it to this relative stranger?

Celia placed a hand on her shoulder. "You up for this?"

Mary looked at the man across from her, looking for answers. She thought of the son she never knew she had, who might be out there.

With a deep breath, she started to talk.

- THIRTY-SEVEN -

W̶HEN I WAS SIXTEEN," Mary began, her hands around her coffee cup, "I fell in love with a boy in my high school. His name was Harold Edge."

In her mind's eye, she saw Harold's face in her mind. Black hair that flopped over his forehead into his eyes, chocolate brown eyes that melted her heart.

"We dated for a while. He...he took me to his parents' house. They weren't there. He . . . . " she felt her eyes fill. "I was raised in a Christian home, taught about being pure until marriage. But Harold...he was so *sweet*. And I was in love."

Thompson looked uncomfortable. "Are you married to him?"

Mary felt as if she'd been slapped. "No. Harold and I broke up after . . . after Atlanta." She grabbed her napkin to blot her eyes. "He went into the military . . . he died in Afghanistan."

She remembered hearing about Harold's death in the news. Roger had been surprised at her tears and she'd said that Harold was a friend from high school. It was part of the truth, at least.

Thompson signaled their waiter for a refill of their coffee. After he left, Thompson asked, "So, am I correct in assuming that this Harold got you pregnant?"

Mary shook at the question. "Yes. I didn't know it at first, but I missed my . . . my period," she blushed at mentioning that to Thompson. "Celia bought me a home pregnancy test and I took it while spending the night at her place . . . it was positive."

"So, you're a good Christian girl, sixteen and pregnant," Thompson said. "What did your parents say?"

"They didn't know," Mary said softly. "I didn't tell them. I knew . . . I knew they'd be ashamed of me. Of what I did."

"How could you hide something like that?" Thompson asked skeptically.

"Loose clothing covers a multitude of sins," Celia quipped. She tipped her head at Thompson. "Don't tell me you've been a Boy Scout."

Thompson sighed. "Fine. But she's the one who keeps mentioning she's a Christian."

"I know it was wrong," Mary said. She wanted to flee the table. This was not a conversation she'd ever wanted to have.

Celia shook her head. "Look, she made a mistake. That makes her human. Do you want to hear her story or would you rather make snippy comments?"

Thompson raised his hands in defeat. "All right. So you were living in Atlanta?"

"No," Mary said. "My family lives in this area. But Celia's mother was moving to Atlanta, and she knew what had happened . . . she talked my folks into letting me spend the summer with them."

She looked around, suddenly afraid that someone from church would be there, would somehow hear her spill her worst secret. There were plenty of diners – a few older couples, a noisy family of 4, a couple of women her age – but no one she recognized.

The strange man who'd spoken with them wasn't in sight either. Mary wondered what he wanted from her. She had a sinking feeling she wasn't through telling this story yet.

Thompson put his coffee cup down on the table, looking puzzled. "What were you going to do? I mean, as clueless as your folks apparently were they might have noticed if you came home with a baby."

Mary winced at the insult to her parents. "I didn't know. I was frightened – you have no idea how frightening it was to be pregnant and not able to tell people I trusted. Celia's mother kept urging an abortion, but I – I just couldn't. I thought that this was my fault, and an innocent baby shouldn't be punished for it."

Thompson shook his head. "So you just marked time?"

She found his constant sniping at her irritating. "Mr. Thompson, I was sixteen. Perhaps, in your eyes, I was naïve. I was trying to find a way out for me and for the baby would be the best for both of us."

"So what happened?" Thompson said. He glanced at his watch. "I still don't understand how my mother figures into this."

"I'm getting to that," Mary said. She had to gather herself for a moment. The next part of the story still visited her nightmares.

"I woke up after a nap one afternoon," she said, her voice shaking slightly. She could see and feel it as if it had happened yesterday instead of ten years ago: the wrenching, agonizing pain . . . the blood that stained Ms. Winters' blue pastel sheets . . . trying to walk, Francine on one side of her, Celia on the other, the two of them all but shoving her into the back seat of the silver Nissan Maxima...

"I started bleeding," she said, her eyes on the white tablecloth, the coffee stained spoon catching the light above, "Ms. Winters and Celia got me in the car and – and drove me to the clinic."

"Why?" Thompson asked.

"I don't know," Mary said softly.

Celia cleared her throat. "Mom said it would be the fastest way to get Mary cared for," she told Thompson. "I wasn't about to argue – Mary was whiter than this tablecloth and I was scared out of my mind."

"I don't remember much about the drive," Mary said, almost to herself. "I – the next thing I remember clearly I was in a bed, and your mother was standing next to me, adjusting an IV. I asked her what happened and she looked upset and said she'd get the doctor."

Mary felt the tears again. "She came back with Dr. Green. He was – he was very blunt. He told me the baby had been born dead and it was the best thing that could have happened to me."

Thompson's face darkened. "I'm not surprised. I've never met the man, but I never had a good impression of him."

"Your mother . . . I remember she looked shocked at what he said," Mary said, sniffling. "I was tired and confused . . . they'd knocked me out, I think."

Celia was hunched over the table, her expression grim. "Yeah, my mom and I were waiting outside. They finally let us in, and that's when I heard about the baby."

"I asked where I was," Mary said, fighting the sobs that wanted to choke her. "The doctor told me I was at . . . an – an abortion clinic. I was so upset!" She looked at Thompson, his face blurred by her tears. "I know what you think but I never would have killed my baby. Never!"

Thompson plucked at his napkin. He shook his head. "I can't believe your friend's mom carted you to an abortion clinic. Are you sure the doc just didn't kill your kid for you?"

Celia glared at him. "Look, my mom's no angel, but she'd never do that to Mary!"

"Your mom," Mary interrupted, her eyes still on Thompson. "I couldn't stop crying. I – I remember your mom, she wrapped her arms around me, she was crying right along with me. It was almost like my mom was with me. I don't remember when she left."

"You cried yourself to sleep," Celia said, sprinkling some pepper on the tablecloth and moving the grains around with a finger. "I remember. I was standing there bawling for all I was worth."

Mary put a hand on her friend's arm. "I left the clinic as soon as I was able," she told Thompson. "At the end of the summer I went back home and tried to go on with my life."

Thompson's shoulders sagged. "That's it? That's all you have for me?"

"That and the note your mother sent," Mary sighed. "I don't understand it."

"Do you?" Thompson asked Celia.

Mary's friend shrugged. "No. I have no idea what your mother meant. For Mary's sake, I wish I did."

Shaking his head, Thompson signaled for the waiter. "I don't get it. My mom . . . something about you stuck in her memory. It's like there's this big secret she had, and I don't understand what it was!"

"I don't have a lot of answers for you," Mary said sadly. "But your mother was there for me when I needed someone. I hope that helps you."

Thompson glanced at the check before pulling out his wallet. "I'm not sure it does. But so Ms. Morris has a slightly better opinion of me, I'll pay for lunch." He laid a credit card into the black folder and placed it on the table. "If you think of anything else, will you call me? I still feel as if I don't understand what drove my mother to suicide."

Mary twisted her hands together. "Of course. If you – you learn anything, anything that might explain your mother's note? I don't understand why she told me I have a son."

Thompson nodded. "Of course." He waited until the waiter returned with his credit card and signed the check. Standing, he took a deep breath and said, "Ms. Beamer, perhaps I've thought of you in a worse light than you deserve. Please forgive me. I just . . . I just hate that doctor and everything he stood for. I think he destroyed my mother."

Mary stood, feeling a surge of relief that the meal was finally over. "I understand. I hope – I hope you find some peace regarding your mother."

"Thank you," Thompson said. "I hope you find your answers as well."

I hope so too, Mary thought. But she was discouraged. She was no closer to solving this mystery than she had been before lunch.

- THIRTY-EIGHT -

So," Celia said as she started her rental car, "what's next?"

"I don't know," Mary said, resting her head back. The car smelled nice – nicer than hers, which, thanks to Kelly, often carried the aromas of chicken nuggets and French fries. "This felt like a big waste of time."

"I dunno," Celia said, her nails drumming on the steering wheel. "We got a decent meal out of it."

Mary had to chuckle at that. "Yes, I guess we did." She pulled out the business card the strange man had handed her. The numbers on the light brown rectangle seemed to mock her. "What should I do about this?"

Celia checked over her shoulder before pulling into traffic. "Depends. You want to let this drop, now that Thompson was a big zero?"

Mary considered it. Then she shook her head. "I can't, Celia. Even if I wanted to. I may have a son out there who needs me."

For a couple of minutes neither woman said anything. Then, to Mary's surprise, Celia whipped into a shopping center parking lot. The shops there were higher end – she noticed a Neiman Marcus, Nordstrom's, and Underwood Jewelers -- places that were so expensive she was afraid to even browse in them.

Celia pulled into an empty parking space but didn't turn off the engine. Puzzled, Mary asked, "You want to go shopping?"

"No," Celia said with a sigh, "I just can't have this conversation and concentrate on the road here at the same time. People still drive like maniacs here, you know that?"

Mary glanced over at the road, where cars whizzed by oblivious to her plight. "I think it's a requirement for living here – you have to be willing to ignore the rules of the road."

Celia laughed quietly, then sobered. "Would you have kept him?"

"What?"

"The baby," Celia said. "That whole summer, you never made up your mind if you were going to keep him or give him up for adoption."

Mary turned the card over in her hands. "You know what I was going through, Celia. I was frightened – I didn't know what was best."

"I know that and I'm not trying to make you feel guilty about that summer," Celia said. "But you've had 10 years to think about it now – would you have kept him? Or given him up?"

"That doesn't matter now," Mary said, shaking her head.

"Wrong. It *does* matter," Celia argued. "If you'd given him up for adoption, things would be the way they are now – he'd have a family you'd probably know nothing about. So if you were okay with that, why the urge to track him down now?"

"If he'd been adopted, the family would have been checked out," Mary said. "Who knows what that clinic did?"

Celia rested her elbow on the dashboard and propped her head in her hand. "It could still be a sick joke. You heard what Thompson said – his mom was dying. Maybe she went crazy."

"Maybe," Mary said, her tone doubtful. She bent a corner of the business card. "Celia, I have to know. I have to know if he exists, if he's all right…"

"What then?" Celia asked. "Will you tell Roger?"

Mary cringed. She'd forgotten about Roger. "I – I don't know. I don't know how he'll take it. He doesn't know about Harold."

"You realize the more you poke at this the bigger the chance Roger will find out," Celia said. "Are you sure you want that to happen? How do you think he'll take it?"

Shoulders sagging, Mary bit her lip. "I don't know. But all the more reason to contact this guy. If I don't head him off, he might try to catch me at home. And if he finds Roger first…"

"What makes you think he'd do that?" Celia asked. "You don't even know who he is."

"But he seems to know me," Mary said. She gave Celia a pleading look. "If I can get him to talk with us today, will you come with me? I know I'm asking a lot, but you're right – I don't know him, and I probably shouldn't meet him alone."

Celia tapped the steering wheel. "Well, I think it's a bad idea, but yeah, I don't want you to meet a weird guy by yourself – that's not a good idea."

"Okay," Mary said, pulling out her cell phone. She took a deep breath to calm herself, and dialed the cell phone number listed on the card.

It only rang twice before it was answered. "Foster."

"Yes," Mary said, her voice shaking despite her efforts. "This is Mary Beamer. You spoke to me earlier?"

"Yeah," the man's voice sharpened. "Yeah, Thompson's not around, is he?"

"No," Mary said, gripping the phone tightly with one hand while her other hand bent and rebent the business card. "I'm with my friend. You said you wanted to talk to me. When would be a good time?"

"Now would be great," Foster said. "Where? Your place?"

"No," she said quickly. Mary shot a look at Celia. "I'm not sure where a good place would be…"

"Ask him if he can find the Residence Inn on Baymeadows," Celia said, putting the car into Drive. "My room number's 3221."

After Foster confirmed he could find the hotel and promised to be there within an hour, Mary hung up and rested her head back on the seat. "Thanks, Celia."

"You need to check in at the home front?" Celia asked.

"Probably," Mary sighed, really not wanting to. She wasn't sure how she'd be able to talk to Roger without giving anything away.

She prayed silently for a moment, asking God to steady her nerves and her voice. Then she dialed home.

As she spoke to Roger she could hear little girls chattering in the background. He assured her that everything was fine and Kelly and Wendy were busy dressing up their dolls and planning on fixing cookies later. "You'd better pray for me," he laughed. "I'm not the baker in the family – I'm hoping I don't burn the house down!"

Mary chuckled. "You'll do fine, I'm sure." She got serious. "Are you sure you don't need me to come home?"

"It's fine," he said. "You enjoy yourself. I'm sorry if I came across unhappy with you having a day off – I know you don't get the chance to have time for yourself very often."

She swallowed. "I – I appreciate that, Roger. I don't deserve you."

"You say that now – just wait til you see the kitchen!" Roger laughed.

She laughed with him. "Well, I'll call you later. Good luck with the cookies."

"Thanks, Mare. Love you."

"Love you too," Mary said. She hung up, feeling happy and guilty at the same time.

Celia had been quiet through the phone call. She looked at Mary out of the corner of her eye. "You okay?"

"I don't deserve him," Mary said. "He's so good to me, and – and understanding."

"But he wouldn't understand Harold?"

"I don't know," Mary repeated, her eyes on her black flip phone. "Celia, have you ever had something so special you didn't want to risk losing it?"

Celia nodded. "I hear you. But Mary, remember what I said earlier. The more you dig, the bigger chance someone will get a clue. You might want to consider that as we talk to whoever this guy is."

"I know," Mary said. She looked out the car window. "I'm just hoping I can fix it before it comes to that."

Celia shook her head. "I hate to say it, but some things can't be fixed like that."

"I have to try," Mary insisted. They pulled into the Residence Inn parking lot and Mary closed her eyes for a brief prayer; *Please let me fix this and keep it a secret. Please.*

- THIRTY-NINE -

FOSTER GRUMBLED WHEN HE REALIZED he had made a wrong turn off Interstate 95 and was heading away from the Residence Inn. *This city is insane! How did anyone get anyplace around here?*

He finally got to the hotel and parked. He snorted. Nice place. Of course, not somewhere he'd be sleeping that night – right now he was hoping he could find a clean place for under $40 or he'd be bedding down in his car in a parking lot someplace.

Foster pulled out his tape recorder and notepad. After being sure his junker was locked (though it would be a favor to him if someone stole it) he went inside the hotel and headed for the elevators.

On the short ride up he considered the best way to approach this. He knew this all might shape up to be a huge waste of time – just another dead end like all the other dead ends he'd run into with this story. But his gut told him otherwise. Thompson's meeting with this woman after his mother killed herself and *that* was after Ms. Thompson was apparently trying to get in touch with Ms. Beamer…well, it was enough confirmation of his gut for him.

He got to room 3221 and knocked, straightening his shoulders and trying to look confident. He decided he'd try to imply he knew more than he did – that might get her to talk some.

The door was opened by the woman who'd been with Ms. Beamer – the well-dressed blonde. She raised a penciled eyebrow. "Mr. Foster?"

He nodded and stuck out his hand. "I'm afraid you have me at a disadvantage, ma'am."

"Celia Morris," she said, shaking his hand. "Come in."

He stepped into a two room suite that was huge. A mini-kitchen was to the left, the right had a nice looking bathroom complete with Jacuzzi. Further in the room was a glass-topped table with four iron-wrought chairs. The primary colors in the room were red and white.

Mary Beamer sat at the table. She gave him a wary look as he approached. "Ms. Beamer, a pleasure to meet you at last."

Apprehension flickered on her face. "How did you know my name?"

He shook her hand. "I found out Martha Thompson was looking for you," he said, sitting down. "So I did some homework."

"Homework?" Ms. Morris said. Foster had sat next to Ms. Beamer. The blonde woman sat on her other side and shot him a not-quite-friendly look.

Foster sighed. "Okay. Cards on the table. I'm an investigative reporter —"

He stopped talking as he saw Mary Beamer stiffen. "What?" she stammered. "What – what are you investigating?"

Ms. Morris' eyes narrowed. "Mary, let me see that business card a second."

"Here," Foster said, pulling out a card. "You can have one of your own." To Ms. Beamer he said, "I didn't mean to upset you – I've been doing an investigation of the Peachtree Road Women's Clinic in Atlanta."

He saw she was shaking. Her eyes darted around the room, and he knew if he wasn't careful she'd up and leave without giving him anything. She was pretty close to doing it just finding out this much.

"Ms. Beamer, I assure you I don't intend you any harm —'

"I don't want to talk to a reporter," she stammered. "I'm sorry, but I can't."

"Ms. Beamer," Foster said, trying to keep the desperation out of his tone, "I'm just trying to bring the bad guys to justice. I believe terrible things went on in that clinic, and Dr. Green and his people got away with it."

Ms. Morris looked up from his card. "Wait a minute. Are you the Jack Foster who found out Police Chief Richards was sleeping with one of the cops who worked under him?"

He nodded. "Yes. That was quite a while ago."

Her mouth quirked. "Yeah, but my mom couldn't stop talking about it for a while. You kept the gossip mill humming for months."

He chuckled. "I suppose that's a good thing." Sobering, he leaned forward. "That's the kind of thing I want to do with this story. Bring the wrongdoers into the spotlight. Make them pay."

Ms. Beamer looked down at her hands as they twisted with each other, leaving marks on the glass table under them. "Mr. Foster —"

"Please, call me Jack."

"Jack —" she sighed. "Please understand. Almost no one knows about my...experience with that clinic. I have personal reasons to keep it that way. That's why I can't talk to you."

Foster chewed his lip. "What if I promised to keep your name out of it?"

"You're asking me to take a huge risk," she argued. "My husband doesn't even know about what happened! I can't risk him finding out."

Foster tried to tamp down the anger that blazed in him. He was so close..."Ms. Beamer, don't you want that doctor to pay? Do you understand what he did? Not only to you, but to other women?"

She shook her head. "I – I wasn't like those other women."

"Can you at least tell me why Martha Thompson tried to contact you?" he pleaded. "She almost talked to me once, but backed out."

"So exactly why didn't you want her son to know about you?" Ms. Morris asked with a raised eyebrow. "I take it you bugged him, too?"

Foster sighed, fighting the temptation to yell at these two stubborn women. "Look, I'm an investigative reporter. People don't always want the truth found. So, yeah, I have to step on some toes. I'm not gonna apologize for it."

"I'll take that for a yes," Ms. Morris said, rolling her eyes. "Look, Mr. Foster —"

"Jack."

"Okay, I'm Celia then," she said. "I know you're a good reporter – or you were once. That doesn't give you the right to march in here and demand that Mary give up her secrecy."

"You said you'd talk to me," he reminded Ms. Beamer.

"I didn't know you were a reporter," she countered. "That . . . that changes things."

Foster ground his teeth. "Look. I've been chasing this story for over a year. Green ditched me once already – torched his own clinic to try kill the story. People think I'm crazy to keep trying. But I can't quit. I *won't*."

Mary Beamer had that deer-in-the-headlights look again. "I can't help you. Please understand that. I wish I could."

"You can!" he insisted. "Look, you're my last clue. I *know* you know something. Please, don't turn your back on me."

Celia blew out an irritated breath. "Look, she said 'no.' Don't you get that?"

His eyes narrowed. He'd hoped he wouldn't have to play this card, but he wasn't going to give up this source. "Fine. Maybe your husband will have some information." He stood up.

Mary Beamer's chair skittered back as she stood as well. "No! You can't!"

"I'm going to find out what I need one way or another," Foster said, hardening himself to the part of his brain that was calling him all sorts of names for tormenting this woman. "I'd rather you told me of your own free will, but if you won't..." he shrugged.

Celia Morris was on her feet as well. If looks could kill, he'd be ready for a morgue. "You are a vile human being! You can't really intend to –"

"Please," Mary Beamer whispered. "Please, he doesn't know anything... please don't contact him..."

Jack resisted the urge to put a comforting hand on the white-faced woman's shoulder. "I'm sorry. Give me something, and there'll be no reason for me to make the call."

"If you don't leave this instant," Celia Morris said, "I will call security. Get out!"

Foster's shoulders sagged. He'd played his last card. "If that's your decision." He was frustrated beyond belief. Her whole reaction told him he'd been right – there *was* something. Now he'd have to force the issue. He started for the door.

He was almost to the door when Ms. Beamer called out, "Wait!"

Keeping his face calm, he turned. Beamer was still pale. Shaking, she swapped a long look with Celia Morris. Then, straightening her shoulders, she looked at him with a forlorn expression.

"Please sit down," she said, her voice matching the dread he saw in her eyes. "I'll talk to you."

- FORTY -

L OVE YOUR ENEMIES.

Mary repeated the verse again and again as she talked with Foster. It was one of three things that kept her from slapping the reporter and stalking out of the room.

Celia sat on the edge of her seat while they talked. Mary could practically hear her friend's teeth grinding.

The mini tape recorder sat in the middle of the table. Mary kept glancing at it. She tried not to think of her words going on the tape. Even though Foster had said he'd keep her name out of things she had no reason to believe him.

The other reason was Roger. She imagined his discovering about Harold, the pregnancy, the clinic...she couldn't deal with that. If laying out her sins to this nasty man would stop that from happening then that's what she'd do.

Foster was also scribbling notes in a notepad. His face was screwed up in concentration as he wrote down her story. He seemed almost . . . happy. She found it disturbing.

She'd started at the beginning, telling him about Harold, the unexpected pregnancy, the trip to Atlanta. The nightmare at the clinic.

Foster shook his head. "You didn't *know* you were going to an abortion clinic? Just how naïve are you?"

Celia rolled her eyes. "What is it with you guys? Is today Have-to-Deal-With-Insensitive-Jerks day?"

Mary rubbed her eyes. She was feeling the effects of the stressful week. Foster wasn't helping matters. "Look, I was sixteen and yes, perhaps naïve. It doesn't change what happened."

Foster flipped the pages in his notepad. "So that's where you met Martha Thompson?"

"Yes," Mary blinked. "Celia, do you have any pain reliever? And maybe a soft drink?"

"Sure, hon," Celia said. She gave Foster a dirty look and didn't offer him anything to drink as she stood.

Foster gave a faint grin. "You don't like me, do you Ms. Morris?"

Celia didn't bother answering him. Mary felt a faint grin of her own cross her lips.

After Celia returned with a Diet Coke and some ibuprofen, she sat down and resumed glaring at Foster. Mary swallowed the pain reliever, washing it down with soda from the can.

"Okay," Foster said. "What I don't understand is why Ms. Thompson contacted you after 10 years. It looks like she made some effort to find you – what did she want to say to you?"

This was the third thing. She was going through with this, talking to this stranger she had no reason to trust, baring the darkest parts of her soul, because Martha Thompson had sent her a note.

"She told me . . . " Mary swallowed. This wasn't getting easier to say, no matter how many times she said it. "She sent me a note. It said my son was alive."

Foster's head jerked up. Instead of surprise, there was a fierce smile on his face.

"I *knew* it," he said. He looked like he wanted to do a victory dance. "I knew it! I knew you'd be able to help me!"

Mary was stunned. She swapped a look with Celia, who was equally puzzled.

Foster saw their expressions and chuckled. "I'm sorry, ladies, I really am. It's just that . . . I've been searching for someone like you for over a year. Someone to confirm what I suspected. Someone who could shut that so-called doctor down!"

Celia shook her head. "Look, Foster, why don't you pretend we don't have a clue what you're talking about – because we *don't* have a clue what you're talking about – and let us in on the joke?"

The reporter settled down, though he appeared unable to keep a silly grin off his face. "Again, I'm sorry. I guess that you don't understand my attachment to this story. Or what I think I know about it."

"What you *think* you know?" Celia echoed, an eyebrow rising.

The grin turned into a grimace. "Believe me, Ms. Morris, if I had all my facts I'd have blasted this all over my newspaper and covered myself in glory.

Unfortunately, I have very little verified, but a lot of ideas about what Green was up to. I just need to be able to back them up."

"What ideas?" Mary asked. "And what does any of this have to do with me?"

He smiled at her. Mary didn't like it – she felt as if he was looking at her through a gun's scope. "You get a note, saying your son is alive. Ten years ago you're told you've had a miscarriage. By the way, did they ever show you a body?"

Mary squirmed, not wanting to go back to that day. "No," she said. "I was so upset and drugged, I didn't think to ask about it. By the time it crossed my mind I was already at Celia's place."

"So the only evidence you have of you having a miscarriage is the doc's say-so, right?"

"Yes," Mary said, "but you're not answering Celia's question. What do you know? Or think you know?"

Foster rested his chin on his fists. "Okay, let me explain. Dr. Green's little clinic came to my attention about a year and a half, two years ago. I heard things . . . things that led me to believe that there was something going on under the radar there."

"What does this have to do with Mary?" Celia asked.

"Simple," Foster said, leaning forward, his eyes bright. "I think that you *did* give birth to a live baby."

"But why would he lie about that?" Mary asked. "What would he have to gain?"

"Simple," Foster said. "He got a baby. One perhaps he could sell to someone at the right price."

Mary felt her stomach drop. "S-sell?"

Foster nodded, all evidence of good cheer gone. "That's what I think. I wanted to get one of the nurses to confirm it. Ms. Thompson almost met with me, but cancelled out at the last minute."

Mary looked down at her trembling hands. Celia put an arm around her. "You – you think they sold my baby? But you don't know for sure?"

"Not yet," Foster said. "But with what you've told me, perhaps I can put together enough evidence to investigate further." He fiddled with his tape player. "I'm not gonna lie. I'll need help with this. Anything you'd be willing to offer."

"I – I don't know," Mary stammered. "I can't – I just want this over."

Foster sighed and sat back. "Look, if I'm right, you have a kid out there. Don't you have a responsibility to him?"

"Look," Celia broke in. "You've hit us with a lot of information here. I think giving her time to process is reasonable."

"Fine," Foster said, frowning. He pulled out another business card and pushed it across the table. "Look, can you give me contact information? So I can keep you posted, at least?"

Mary picked up the card, frowning. "I can't let you tell my husband anything. You can't tell him about this."

He sighed. "I give you my word as a gentleman."

Celia snorted. "As a what?"

He rolled his eyes. "I will keep your secret. But please, don't dismiss the option of helping me out. You might find it heals you as well."

Mary scribbled her home and cell phone number on the back of the card. "Just let me know what you find. If it's anything related to my son."

"Will do," Foster said, pocketing the card. "Thanks for talking to me."

Mary sat staring through the glass on the table, barely hearing him. She was aware of Celia speaking to Foster, the hotel room door opening and closing. Then the scrape of a chair as Celia sat next to her.

"You okay, girlfriend?" Celia asked softly.

"I don't know," Mary said. "This is all too much." She felt tears fill her eyes as she pressed her hands against them. "Celia, what if he's right? What if they sold my baby? What do I do?"

Celia rubbed her friend's back. "The best you can, hon. That's all anyone can ask. Even God."

Mary choked back a sob. She wasn't sure Celia was right.

- FORTY-ONE -

FRANCINE SIPPED HER GLASS OF WINE. "Thomas, this was a wonderful dinner. Thank you so much."

Green nodded, looking quite handsome in his dark suit and navy blue tie. "You are more than welcome, Francine." He sat back in his chair, his eyes gleaming in the candlelight. "I want your visits to be memorable."

She licked her lips. The restaurant was indeed fine, with its linen tablecloths, wine cellar, and five-star chef. She could get used to this. Indeed, she intended to.

"You know," she ventured, sliding her hand across the table to brush his fingers, "I don't just have to visit. I could . . . stay."

The corner of Green's mouth quirked. He pulled his hand back, picking up the small leather covered dessert menu. "Francine, I know how much you love Atlanta. I wouldn't dream of taking you away from that."

She waved a dismissive hand. "Atlanta is just a place. I'm sure I could think of a couple of reasons to relocate."

She saw he was examining her again. That was fine – she'd dressed just for that reaction. Francine was glad she'd worked to keep her body attractive – she knew that the black dress's plunging neckline set off her assets quite nicely.

"Francine," Thomas coughed. "I'm – if you're saying what I think you're saying, I am very flattered."

She smiled, leaning forward. "You are quite an attractive man, Thomas. I think I'm falling in love with you."

He flushed. "I – I – Francine, you are a lovely woman and I enjoy your visits, but –"

"Thomas," she said, caressing his name with her lips. "I hope you're willing to consider what I'm saying."

She saw his Adam's Apple bob. "Francine, I need to be honest with you. I hope I haven't said or done anything to make you think this was more serious than it is."

She kept her lips curved in a smile while she felt her temper fire up. *Oh, really. So you want the milk but don't want to pay for the cow, eh?*

"You know," she said, keeping her voice low and sweet, "I *love* being with you, Thomas. But I really need some stability in my relationships. At this point of my life, I can't be content with an occasional visit."

Thomas sighed, putting down the dessert menu and adjusting his glasses. "I suppose I can understand that. I'm sorry to hear it, but I understand." He reached across the table and laid his hand on top of hers. "So I suppose this is goodbye?"

She took a deep breath. Maybe she was pushing things, but she was tired of waiting. Thomas was her shot at the life she wanted – she wasn't going to let him get away that easily.

"Well, Thomas," she said, batting her eyes. "I suppose that if you were willing to support me, I could – could sacrifice and keep things as they are."

The doctor frowned. "Francine, I'm not sure what you're asking here. You want money?"

She stroked his hand. "Thomas, I want to be available for you, when you need...female companionship," she said, kissing her fingers and brushing his hand again. "If I didn't have to worry about making a living, I could be at your beck and call."

She saw his eyes narrow, and his lips thin. "Well, Francine, I never thought of you as someone who would settle for being a 'kept' woman."

"You just thought I was a woman you could use and drop like a used tissue?" she asked, tilting her head.

He snorted, pulling his hand back. "I *thought* you were a mature adult. It's possible I was mistaken in that assumption." Green looked around. "I'll just get our check and we can go our separate ways."

Francine felt the blood rush to her face. "Oh, Thomas," she said, dropping her voice so almost a purr. "You're not my only option, you know."

"I'm glad of it," Green said, finally catching the eye of their server. "Maybe you'll have better luck with someone else."

"You don't understand," she said. "I was referring to the media."

She heard Green's neck creak as he whipped his head around to face her. "What are you talking about?"

She smiled, feeling that she was gaining the upper hand. "Well, Thomas, I have a certain lifestyle to maintain. If you aren't willing to provide it directly, perhaps my knowledge of your...operation will grant it to me."

He shook his head as the waiter came to the table. "Have you all decided on dessert?"

Green opened and closed his mouth. Francine tossed her head, letting her hair bounce. "We just need a few more minutes, please," she said, smiling as Thomas shifted in his seat.

The waiter looked puzzled but said, "All right." and left them alone.

When it was just the two of them, Green appeared to find his voice. "You wouldn't go to the media," he hissed. "You don't dare. You've been a part of this yourself."

She waved a hand. "I'm sure that the media — and the authorities, for that matter — would see me as a small fish compared to you, Thomas." She smirked. "I could even contact Mary again and tell her what I know. Let her know that whoever sent her that note was telling her the truth."

Green shook his head. His face was quite pale, sweat beading on his forehead. "Francine, it won't work. They won't find anything. I've been careful."

"Then why are you sweating?" she said with a smile. "I've told you what I want, Thomas — I want to be supported in a comfortable lifestyle. We both know you have the money, so that's no issue. If you want me to stay out of Alabama, I'll do it. As long as I'm paid."

He wiped his face with his hand, a hand that was shaking. "I need time to consider this."

Francine snorted. "Do you take me for a fool, Thomas?"

"Please!" he begged her. "I — I have to figure out how to do the payments, so they don't raise suspicion. And yes, I'm well-to-do, but I don't have money simply lying around for me to hand over to you."

She cocked her head. "How much time?"

"At least 48 hours," he said. "This is the weekend, I might not be able to get things all good to go until Monday anyway."

Francine thought about that. Could she wait 48 hours? Was he sincere? Or just trying to stall for time while he tried to worm his way out of the situation?

"You would be my guest at the Hilton while you wait," he said. "I would be happy to arrange for a nice room for you."

Francine smiled as she picked up her wineglass and took a sip. "I'd love to, but if we aren't going to be together, I am supposed to be at work on Monday." She licked her lips as she pulled the dessert menu towards her. "If only I had a reason to stay. Now, why don't we get something sweet to counteract all the ugliness we just experienced?"

As she bent her head over the menu, she failed to witness the look of rage that twisted Green's features. When she looked up at him his face had smoothed out to a neutral expression.

"Do you have a preference?" he asked as he took the menu from her. He knew he had to play the part of calm, unworried man, at least until he could get this blackmailing witch into a hotel room.

After that he'd have to figure out what to do about the problem that was now Francine Winters.

- FORTY-TWO -

"Iɴ Jᴇsᴜs' ɴᴀᴍᴇ, ᴀᴍᴇɴ," Roger said. With the closing prayer said, the silence in the auditorium filled with the murmurs of people talking to those sitting near them, the cheerful cries of children allowed to release the energy that had built in an hour of sitting, and the rustle of Bibles and papers being gathered up as members of the congregation prepared to leave.

Kelly smiled at Celia. "Didn't my daddy do a good prayer?" she asked.

Celia nodded at the little girl. "He did, hon. One of the best I've ever heard."

Mary was glad her daughter's back was to her so she couldn't see her mother grimace. Mary had been surprised when Celia called her early this morning, asking if Mary could squeeze some together time before it was time for Celia to head for the airport.

When Mary mentioned worship services, Celia said, "Okay. Can I meet you there?"

Since Celia had never expressed interest in attending church before, Mary was somewhat surprised. Nevertheless, she gave her friend directions to the community church

Celia breezed in five minutes before service started, dressed in black slacks and an emerald green silk blouse. Kelly was happy to see her. "I'm glad you came to church, Miss Celia."

Crouching down so she was at the child's level, Celia said, "You know what, Kelly, I don't go to church very often. Do you think I can sit next to you and you could show me what to do?"

"Sure!" Kelly said, excited. Celia grinned and winked at Mary as she straightened up. Mary simply shook her head. Celia had certainly managed to charm her little girl.

Mary tried to give her attention to the service, but couldn't help watching her friend out of the corner of her eye, trying to gauge her reactions to things.

Celia followed Kelly's directions when it came to sitting, standing, and bowing her head to pray. She shared a songbook with the little girl, even though she didn't sing. During the sermon, she watched as Kelly drew in a small notebook she used during services.

Now Roger joined them where they'd been sitting, about five pews from the rear of the auditorium. "So, do you have time for some lunch, Celia?"

Celia shrugged. "I have about an hour before I need to head for the airport – I'm already checked out and everything."

"Are we going out to lunch?" Kelly asked, her eyes lighting up.

Before Mary or Roger could answer, Celia spoke up. "Actually, I was wondering if you and your dad minded if I took your mom out to lunch. I'm not sure when I'll be back, and I'd like a few more minutes to chat with her."

Kelly's face fell a little. "I *guess* that's okay," she said, a small pout forming. "But I haven't been to McDonald's in *forever.*"

"Tell you what, Princess," Roger said, reaching over to smooth his daughter's hair and narrowly missing dislodging the dark blue bow in her hair, "How about you and I go to McDonald's, and we'll let Mom and Miss Celia go someplace they want to go?"

"You don't mind?" Mary asked. She was feeling guilty about the weekend – he had taken a lot of the burden of Kelly, and they hadn't had much couple time.

"It's fine," he said. "Celia's not here every weekend."

Celia held her hand out. "Thanks, Roger. It was great meeting you – I'm glad Mary has such a great guy for a husband."

Roger shook her hand. "Nice meeting you too, Celia. I hope you have a safe trip home." He turned and kissed Mary's cheek. "I'll see you in a little bit, all right?"

Mary nodded. She picked up her Bible and the black purse she'd selected that morning. "Thank you, Roger. You've been wonderful this weekend."

He smiled. "Just remember this next Super Bowl weekend. I intend to make a party of it, especially if the Jaguars make it there."

Mary laughed. "All right, be sure to remind me."

"Yup," Roger said. He picked up Kelly's pink backpack. "Come on, Kelly, kiss your mom and let's get going."

Kelly climbed up on the green cushioned pew and wrapped her arms around Mary's neck. She kissed her mom. "Have a good lunch, Mommy. I love you."

Mary hugged the girl tightly. "I love you too, sweetheart."

Kelly turned and hugged Celia. "Thanks for coming to visit, Miss Celia. You be a good friend to my mommy, okay?"

Celia returned the hug. "I'll do my best, little one. Thanks for all your help."

Mary watched as Roger and Kelly went out to the foyer. When she turned back to Celia, she saw her friend was studying her.

"You really love those two," Celia said.

"I do," Mary said, feeling her cheeks heat up. "Did you think I didn't?"

"No," Celia said. "I'm just wondering if you realize how much you're risking with this Green guy."

Mary hugged her Bible tighter to her. "Believe me, I know," she said softly.

Before she could continue the lights in the auditorium went out. "They're getting ready to lock up," Mary said. "Did you have a particular place in mind for lunch?"

Celia pulled her black designer bag over a shoulder. "Something that we won't have to wait forever for would be nice. You know of a good quick place?"

"There's a soup and salad place not too far from here," Mary said. She and Celia started for the parking lot. "You know you didn't have to stay and have lunch with me."

Celia smiled a little. "I wanted to," she said. "I'm finding myself kind of fascinated with the life you've built here. Makes me wonder if I should listen to my biological clock and have a child of my own."

"Kelly is a gift from God," Mary admitted as the pair made their way to Celia's rental car. "You're welcome to visit anytime, Celia. You know that."

"I do," Celia said, pressing a button on the remote that unlocked the vehicle. "But I don't know when that'll happen. And I'd like to be sure before I leave this time I haven't made things worse for you."

Mary sighed as she got into the vehicle. Once Celia started the car she gave her friend directions to the restaurant. She said very little besides that, focusing on her hands in her lap.

When they pulled into the parking lot of the Souper Garden Restaurant, Celia spoke up. "You're thinking about where to go from here, aren't you?"

Mary nodded. "Any thoughts?"

Celia sighed as she got out of the car. "My knee-jerk reaction is to say let sleeping dogs lie. Just write this all off to a particularly bad dream."

Mary shook her head. "That would perhaps be the easiest thing…but I'm not sure it's the *best*."

"Somehow, I'm not surprised you think that," Celia said as they walked into the restaurant. They were soon led to a round white table near the windows and offered menus. They both quickly decided on tomato soup and Caesar salads.

Mary sipped her mint iced tea and tried to work up her courage. "Celia, I was wondering if you could do me a favor? I mean, you've done so much already, I'll understand if you say no."

Celia shook her head. "What do you want? I don't mind helping – I feel a little responsible for the whole thing anyway."

Mary took a deep breath. "Would you ask your mom about this?"

"Whoa," Celia said, sitting back in her white wicker chair. "You meant a huge favor."

"Yes," Mary nodded. "But she won't talk to me about it. Maybe she'll tell you what she won't tell me."

"Don't bet on it," Celia warned. "Mom has a way of looking after herself. If she thinks telling me isn't in her best interest, she won't."

"But maybe she knows something," Mary said. "Something that will debunk Foster's version of events. Or even –"she stopped talking as the waitress showed up with their meal.

Celia sighed. "Okay. Tell you what. I'll go ahead and talk to her. But no promises on it accomplishing much, okay?"

Mary nodded. "Thanks, Celia. You really are my BFF, you know that?"

The corner of her friend's mouth went up. "Yup, sure do." She picked up a fork. "Now how about doing your prayer thing so we can eat and I can get to the airport before my plane leaves?"

- FORTY-THREE -

T HOMAS, I THINK YOU SHOULD CALM DOWN," Sharon said. She stood and went to the small bar she kept in the corner of her living room. "Scotch?"

He stared at her. "It's not even 10 in the morning!'

"Medicinal purposes," she said with a cocked eyebrow. "You're so tense you're practically vibrating."

The doctor ran a hand through his hair. "Fine. But I think I have every reason to be alarmed, Sharon. I wouldn't be here otherwise!"

She tossed a smile over her shoulder as she poured him a Scotch. She brought it to him where he sat on one of her black leather couches.

"You know," she said, tucking one of her legs under herself as she sat next to him, "you used to have more fun reasons to come here."

He frowned before gulping down a third of his drink. "I thought you said you were okay with it being over? And I don't need you hitting on me right now."

Sharon sighed. "I'm just trying to lighten the mood, Thomas." She reached for the mug of coffee that sat on the low table in front of them. "So Francine is trying to blackmail you?"

"Well, first she tried to persuade me to let her move in," Thomas said, staring at the white terrazzo floor under his shoes. He was in a terrible mood – he'd spent most of the previous night tossing and turning. When he'd finally dragged himself out of bed, he'd thrown on some clothes and gone to his office manager's condo.

Sharon sipped her coffee. "Perhaps you should have permitted that."

Thomas rolled his eyes. "Please, Sharon. Francine is fun once in a while, but let her move in? The woman is a leech."

Sharon tapped her black mug, her eyebrows knitting. "A leech...so one payoff won't do it?"

"I doubt it," Thomas said with a shake of his head. He looked out the glass doors to the oak deck that stood over an impressive view of a park

"Then we have to take care of her," Sharon said. She stood up and walked to the glass doors and gazed outside, steam from her mug lightly fogging the glass.

The doctor straightened up, a look of alarm on his face. "What do you mean?"

She chuckled and turned around. "Thomas, Thomas, don't you trust me?"

He sighed and sat back in the couch. "I do, Sharon. But I'm concerned. We've finally built the business back to its former profit levels – I'd hate to have to start over again."

"I understand," she said. Sharon quickly walked into the small but modern kitchen and picked up a notepad that sat next to the phone. Plucking a pen out of a plastic cup, she started writing notes down as she came back into the living room. "Is she still in town?"

"Probably," Thomas said with a snort. "Checkout at the hotel I put her up in isn't until noon, and I'm sure she's going to stay as long as she can."

"Nice place?" Sharon said, a small smile on her lips.

"Hilton," Thomas answered as he drained his glass.

"All right. You need to call her right now and tell her you want her to stay for a few days while you consider her..." Sharon thought a moment and then finished with a chuckle, "...*proposal*."

"I tried that!" Thomas snapped. "She told me she had to be at work on Monday."

"So allow her to think you're changing your mind," Sharon said. "You have no problem lying to her, I'm sure."

"Of course I don't," Thomas sighed. "But why keep her here?"

"Because she's out of her element here. And it buys us time," Sharon said as she continued to make notes to herself.

"Do you have any idea how much it will cost me to keep that woman in the Hilton?" Thomas asked with a raised eyebrow.

Sharon smiled at him over her notepad. "Think of it as an investment against future losses." She tapped her pen against her mouth. "I need to know everything you know about her. More, if possible."

She noticed Thomas had not taken out his phone, and she frowned. "Thomas, I'm serious. Call her before she decides betrayal is her only option."

He grumbled but pulled his iPhone out of his pocket. Sharon drifted back to the counter that stood between the kitchen and the living room and picked up her coffee again. She studied her notes while she listened to Thomas' half of the conversation.

He hung up with a heavy sigh. "Done. She's thrilled." He stood and gave Sharon a dark look. "You realize she'll expect me to wine and dine her while she's here."

"That's not all she'll expect," Sharon said as she finished her coffee. "She's good in bed, right?"

She laughed as Thomas' cheeks got red. "Yes."

"I never took you for a prude, Thomas," she said. "Look at it this way – this won't be totally without some fun for you."

The doctor stepped up to Sharon, invading her personal space. She took two steps back, feeling the granite counter press against her back.

He grabbed her face and kissed her, hard. Sharon didn't try to fight him, just let it happen. When he finally pulled away, his eyes blazing behind his glasses, he asked, "Was that a prudish kiss, Sharon?"

She wet her lips. "Of course not," she said. He leaned towards her again but she slid past him, putting the counter between them. "Thomas, I'm not questioning your manhood. You don't have to prove anything to me in that area."

He stared at her, hands flat against the counter. "I hope not. Just as I hope you realize who is the boss here, and who is the valuable *subordinate*."

Sharon smiled at him. "I have no question about my standing here, Thomas. It's just that part of my job is protecting you so you can do *your* job to the best of your ability."

He nodded, his face clouded. "Well, I suppose I should be going – unless you'd like to join me for brunch?"

She shook her head, leading the doctor to the door. "I have things to do. Go do something relaxing. When you aren't quite so agitated write down everything you know about Francine Winters. I'd like it on my desk first thing tomorrow morning if possible."

Thomas ran a hand through his hair. "Of course." He paused to look Sharon in the eyes. "Whatever you have in mind…"

"That's not something for you to concern yourself about," she said calmly. Sharon leaned forward slightly and gave Green a chaste kiss on the cheek. "I'll talk to you tomorrow."

"Fine," Thomas said. He still looked unhappy as he headed for his black Lexus.

Sharon shut the door and leaned back against it for a moment. *Square breathing, In for the count of four...hold for the count of four...out for the count of four...hold for the count of four...*

She felt the tension she'd been hiding from Thomas ebb. After a few minutes she went back to the kitchen and poured herself another cup of coffee. She pulled a plastic container filled with a fruit salad she'd gotten from the deli on Friday and spooned some out into a cereal bowl.

I shouldn't be surprised. Sharon picked a strawberry slice from the salad and popped it into her mouth. Something like this was bound to happen – she supposed the surprise was it hadn't happened sooner.

The continual prying of the reporter over a year ago had been a problem. It had taken drastic steps to come out of that one. Burning down the clinic had ensured that most of the evidence was out of reach of the people who could damage them.

This was different. Sharon felt a twinge of annoyance as she thought of Thomas and his shortsightedness. Francine wasn't ugly. Expensive, perhaps, but he might have been able to manage her. By summarily rejecting her overtures he'd made the problem worse.

No matter. And perhaps it was better this way. Sharon would have to come up with a more permanent solution for Francine.

Could she do it? It certainly wasn't something she could trust to Thomas.

Sharon carried her fruit and coffee to her cozy office in the condo. She sat down at her top of the line computer and booted it up.

Her first stop was Google. She thought for a moment, and typed the word "poison" in the search box.

Sipping her coffee, Sharon leaned forward and began her research.

- FORTY-FOUR -

CELIA SMILED AS SHE FELT Richard kiss her. "Mmmm," she said, opening her eyes and looking at her husband's grinning face, "I thought I already showed you how much I missed you last night."

Richard chuckled. His ginger beard tickled her chin as he gave her a peck on her nose. "We didn't get much of a chance to talk last night. I thought you could fill me in on things while I got dressed for work."

Celia gave him a mock pout as she glanced at the clock on the nightstand. "5:45 AM? The birds aren't even up!"

He laughed as he straightened up, the lace from the canopy brushing his bushy hair. "Come on, Cee, I'm worth it, aren't I?"

She grinned and sat up, pushing two feather pillows on the headboard to support her back. "Absolutely. Did I thank you last night for letting me make the trip on such short notice?"

"Oh yeah," he said as he buttoned up a pale blue dress shirt. "About a hundred times. But please, don't stop."

Celia laughed. She liked watching Richard get dressed in the morning. It felt good to be back in their large master bedroom, snuggled in the comfortable king-sized bed. Yup, she liked her life.

"So," Richard said as he stepped into his walk-in closet, "how's your dad? Visit go nice?"

She nodded. "Yes, though I think I was cramping his style. He was almost relieved I was spending time with my friend – I think he's seeing someone."

"Oho," Richard said, coming out with a red silk tie in his hand. "You getting a stepmom?"

Celia's eyes widened. "Oh, please, I hope not! My own mom is enough of a chore!"

"You said it, I didn't," Richard said as he stood in front of the mirror on top of the cherry dresser and began to tie his tie. His green eyes met her blue ones in the reflection. "How about your friend? You seemed pretty worried about her when you talked about this trip."

She sighed as she weighed how much to say. Wrapping her arms around her knees she admitted, "I'm still worried about her. She went through a bad patch about 10 years ago, and it looks like it's coming back to bite her."

Richard frowned. "Legal trouble?"

Celia chewed her lip. "It's…complicated. I'm not sure how to answer that question."

Richard came and sat on the bed next to her. He studied Celia's face. "I didn't pry before, because I sensed you didn't want to say much. But you look really worried, hon. I don't like you being worried."

She rested her chin on her knees. "Richard, let me ask this. Is there a way to find out if a doctor in Georgia's been sued for malpractice?"

"Sure, there's an online database," Richard said. "I'll have Jenny email the link to you when I get into the office." He tucked a strand of hair behind Celia's ear. "Can you tell me? Or is there some BFF confidentiality clause I don't know about?"

Celia laughed. "No BFF clause, but Mary hasn't even told *her* husband about it. Not sure how she'd feel about me telling mine."

"Fair enough." Richard kissed her and gave her a quick hug. "I'm going to be in court today – hopefully I'll be home by six."

"Sounds good," Celia said as she swung her legs out of bed. "I need to see how backed up I got from taking the weekend off. Anything special you want for dinner tonight?"

"Nope, just maybe something that didn't come in a paper bag," Richard grinned.

She chuckled as her feet found her light blue slippers. "Why do you revert to law student eating habits when I'm gone?"

"Old habits die hard," he said with a smile as he slung on his jacket. "See you tonight."

Celia went into the large master bath to start her day, her lips still curved into a smile. She'd lucked out – Richard was one of the good ones, and he was all hers.

She thought Mary had also lucked out. Roger seemed like a decent guy. And Kelly was a little doll-baby. Celia and Richard hadn't talked a lot about kids, but after the past weekend she could see herself with a little one of her own…

Thinking about that reminded her that Mary had asked Celia to call her mother and interrogate her. She groaned. No way she was doing that before she had coffee and food in her system. After a hot, mind-clearing shower of course.

A half hour later, Celia was downstairs dressed in her working attire: comfortable jeans, sneakers, and soft cotton blouse.. One of the advantages of being a freelance computer programming consultant was that she could work from home more often than not which meant she could dress any way she pleased, thank you very much.

The coffeemaker had done its thing and Richard had left plenty. Celia poured herself a cup of hazelnut, taking a moment to inhale the fragrance. Sometimes just smelling the coffee started her brain going. Other times, like this morning, her mind refused to start doing its job until she got some of the caffeine into her body.

After warming up a croissant and putting it, her coffee, and some butter and jelly on a tray, Celia carried it all into the room she and Richard had set up as her home office. She saw the pile of mail on the cherry writing desk she used for correspondence and sighed. Hopefully there were some checks in that pile. It wasn't that they needed the money. But she was good at what she did and that meant she should get paid.

The fax machine had some papers piled in it and she glanced at them after setting her tray down on the writing desk. Nothing appeared urgent. When Celia had decided on her little trip she'd let a few clients know she would be out of town and might need an extra day on some orders. Since this was a rare occurrence the clients were accommodating.

Celia sat in front of her computer and booted it up. She'd seen a few emails pop up on her iPhone but had tried to stay work-free over the weekend. Especially when she'd spoken with Mary and discovered just how bad things were.

A call to her mother's home went to her answering machine. When Celia dialed her mother's cell phone it went to voice mail. As she ran a hand through her still-damp hair Celia glanced at the clock on her computer. She quickly did the math in her head and figured her mom might be at work.

She didn't know why she wasn't answering her phone, but if she wasn't at home, she had to be at work. Celia pulled up the number for the clothing shop her mom had worked at for years and punched it in.

An associate Celia didn't know answered the phone, and when she asked for her mother the woman seemed to hesitate briefly before asking Celia to hold on. After a few moments being subjected to awful elevator music Celia was relieved to hear her mother's boss on the line. "This is Rebecca Carter. Who's calling please?"

Celia frowned. When she'd first met Rebecca Carter during a week she and Richard had spent with her mother (and it had felt like two) the woman had struck her as warm. The voice on the other end of the line was anything but.

"Rebecca?" she felt herself hesitating. "I'm Francine's daughter Celia. We met a few months ago."

"I see," the voice warmed a few degrees, but wasn't that far from freezing. "Why are you calling?"

"I – I was looking for my mother," Celia stammered. "Is something wrong?"

There was a brief silence on the phone, then Celia heard Rebecca sigh. "I'm sorry, Celia, it's not your fault. Your mother called me late last night and informed me she was quitting, effective immediately."

"What? Why?"

"Celia, I really don't want to talk about it. I'd rather not say bad things about Francine to her daughter. You're looking for your mother? She's not here. Is there anything else?"

"Uh, no," Celia stammered.

"Then I need to go. Thanks to Francine, I'm shorthanded today."

Celia sat in her padded office chair staring at nothing for several minutes after Rebecca Carter hung up. *What was going on here?*

- FORTY-FIVE -

FRANCINE SIGHED IN CONTENTMENT as she wrapped herself in the thick white robe the Hilton offered their guests. Oh, yes – *this* was the life!

Thomas' phone call yesterday had been a small surprise – she really hadn't expected him to cave in so easily. She'd accepted his offer of dinner, thinking she'd have to watch and see if he was trying to play her.

During a fabulous Maine Lobster dinner, she tested the waters. "Thomas, I know I upset you last night. I hope you can see things from my perspective."

He'd sipped his wine and slid a hand across the table to caress her fingers. "I understand that you are in a difficult situation. I was...hasty in dismissing your proposition outright. I *do* enjoy your company, Francine. I could see getting used to it."

She smiled at him over the candlelit table, even as she jeered at him in her mind. *Thinking with your pants, bub. Men are so easy to manipulate.*

When she invited him up into her room, he came without hesitation. And she made sure he enjoyed himself – Francine knew that she had to assure him the deal wasn't one-way, that he'd be getting something out of it.

Thinking about the night before, Francine wet her lips. Before he left, he begged her to stay as long as she wanted, until they finalized their future "arrangements." Of course she'd agreed – Francine was no fool. The fish was hooked, and it was simply a matter of time before she reeled him in.

Though she liked to sleep in, Francine requested a wake-up call early enough so she could have the pleasure of calling her slave driver of a boss and tell her she wasn't coming in. Not today, not ever.

"Francine, you can't do this!" Rebecca said. "You know your contract requires you give me two weeks notice –"

"You know what you can do with your contract, Rebecca," she answered, a big smile on her face as she rested back on the thick pillows. "I'm not coming back, not even to pick up my check."

"That's fortunate, since I'm withholding your final paycheck," Rebecca said icily.

"Put that check with the contract, Rebecca," Francine sang before hanging up.

She smiled as she combed out her damp hair. Oh yes, that had been fun. She wouldn't miss that place. She was through being a working girl.

When Francine walked back into the bedroom, dressed in tight white pants and a hot pink silk blouse, she noticed a light flashing on her phone. Checking, she saw she'd missed a call from her daughter.

Oh yeah. Celia had said something about talking to Mary and seeing her dad that weekend. Francine tapped her phone, thinking about that. Mary. Would she be a help in this – or a problem?

She'd threatened Thomas with the girl. If that was going to carry weight, she'd have to prove she could control her. Celia could be very informative on that angle.

After ordering room service – all on Thomas' account of course – Francine called her daughter. To her surprise, Celia was upset.

"Mom, is everything all right? I've been trying to locate you! I even called the shop and they told me you quit?"

Francine rolled her eyes. When did her daughter start treating her like a child? "Sweetheart I'm perfectly fine, as you can hear. I'm out of town for a few days, on . . . personal business."

"You quit over personal business?" Celia asked.

"Well…" Francine stretched her legs out on the bed as she considered how much to tell her daughter. She decided to be careful – that son-of-law of hers might take issue with what she was doing, and she wouldn't put it past the man to cause trouble.

"I'm visiting a very close friend and he may have a better opportunity for me," Francine said. "I can't really talk about it yet, but I'll let you know how it turns out."

"Okay," Celia said, skepticism clear in her tone. "Well, do you have a minute? I'd like to talk to you about something."

"Of course," Francine said, wishing she had some coffee. Hopefully room service would hurry.

"I spoke to Mary this weekend," Celia said. Francine was grateful her daughter didn't bring up her father – the less said about *him* the better.

"I'm glad you did," Francine said. "How is she? Is she feeling better? The poor thing seemed quite upset when she called me last week."

She heard her daughter's noisy sigh. "The thing is, Mom – I'm starting to think she's got a reason to be upset. She does, doesn't she?"

Faint alarm bells were going off in the back of Francine's head. "Well, getting a strange letter from an obviously disturbed woman is certainly not something to settle you –"

"Mom, is it true?" Celia asked bluntly. "Does Mary have a son?"

"Sweetheart, I wouldn't know. Did you visit her? You probably know more about her family than I do –"

"That's not what I mean, Mom," Celia said.

Francine frowned. Surely Celia wasn't taking this seriously? She couldn't possibly know anything about what really happened. No one would have told her. Francine sure didn't.

"Mom," Celia said, her voice strained. "When we went to the clinic – did you see the body?"

"What body?": Francine asked, feeling her chest tighten.

"The body of Mary's baby."

Francine chewed her lip. A knock on the door bought her some time. "Celia, hang on just a moment, room service is here."

She dropped her phone on the bed as she went to the door. As she watched the waiter come in and set her breakfast on the table by the window, Francine forced herself to calm down. This was her daughter, for crying out loud! Surely she could handle her!

Even so, Francine's hands were trembling as she poured herself a cup of coffee. She picked up the phone and spoke as she sat down at the table. "I'm sorry, sweetheart. What did you ask?"

The tension in Celia's voice practically made Francine's phone vibrate. "I asked if you saw the body of Mary's baby."

"Oh, that's right." Francine took a moment to stab a ball of honeydew melon and eat it. "Well, that was ten years ago, honey. I really don't remember."

"You don't remember?" Celia's voice rose.

"Celia, calm down!" Francine snapped. "I certainly don't want to remember that horrible summer any more than I have to. It was a terrible thing for Mary to go through."

"I guess that's just like you, to forget something that's not about you," Celia muttered.

"Now, don't talk like that or I'll have to hang up," Francine warned. The Eggs Benedict smelled delightful and she really wanted to eat them before they got cold. "Since it's apparently so important to you, I'll give it some thought and call you back if I remember something. All right?"

"I'd appreciate it," Celia said, her voice a touch less hostile. "Mom, I think something worse than we thought happened at that clinic. I'm really getting freaked out."

"Don't worry about it," Francine said, trying to be soothing. It wouldn't help her to handle Mary if she alienated her own daughter. "You just take care of yourself. You're back home?"

The conversation ended with unimportant chatter. Francine sighed in relief and tossed her phone back on the bed. As she began to give her full attention to her breakfast she hoped that Thomas was going to sincerely take her up on her offer. She didn't look forward to having to deal with Celia and Mary if he didn't.

- FORTY-SIX -

MARY HAD TRIED HARD TO PAY ATTENTION during the ladies Bible class. It wasn't easy. Her mind kept circling the events of the past weekend, what they might mean. Especially if the truth was exposed for everyone to see. Roger. Kelly. Her fellow Christians here.

She'd hoped class would help her center herself. In the past, when Mary was troubled, the older women in this room had been there to hold her hand and help her with her burdens. When Kelly was born, they'd taken turns bringing meals for a solid week. Last year when Mary's father had suffered a stroke they'd sent cards to him and to her.

They loved her – she knew that. But she still didn't test it by sharing her biggest secret.

"Hey Mary?" Joanne rested a hip on the table Mary sat at. "You going to lunch with the gang?"

"Hm?" Mary realized that class had finished. Women were talking in small groups here and there, Bibles and purses in their arms.

"Hey!" Joanne said with a smile, waving her hand in Mary's face. "Earth to Mary, Earth to Mary, come in!"

Blushing, Mary put a grin on her face. "Sorry about that. I guess I wasn't paying all that much attention."

"I could tell," Joanne said. "You were like this last week, too. So, what are you planning on doing now?"

Mary drew on the leather cover of her Bible with a finger. "I guess go home."

"Hm," Joanne said, staring at Mary. "How about you guess you come to my place for a private lunch?"

"Oh, no, Joanne, that's okay," Mary stammered, quickly plopping the small spiral notebook she used at services and Bible classes on top of her Bible. "I don't want to put you out . . ."

"It's not," Joanne said. "I have a ton of chili from last night and if you really want to go decadent Evelyn made me her Death By Chocolate dessert for taking the class last week."

Mary felt her mouth water. Evelyn Miller's Death By Chocolate dessert, a trifle layered with crushed chocolate cookies, two different kinds of chocolate pudding, and whipped cream, was legendary among the congregation. Once, when a dessert auction was held to raise money for holiday baskets, the confection was sold at a breathtaking $75.

"I must really look pathetic if you're willing to share some of *that*," Mary told Joanne, her resistance crumbling.

"I wouldn't go quite that far," Joanne grinned. "But it's not like you're not doing me a favor – if I keep snacking on that thing I'll weigh a ton!"

Mary chuckled as she stood. "In that case, I'll be happy to help save my Christian sister from temptation."

"Thank you so very much," Joanne said with mock gravity.

Since Paul was the preacher, the Carsons lived in a house owned by the congregation that was next door. It was light green in color, with shutters and a roof that were a darker shade of green. Daffodils under the front windows waved at the two women as they headed for the door.

"Just toss your purse and Bible on the couch," Joanne said as she crossed the small living room. A green basket with folded laundry sat in front of a black leather sofa.

Mary placed her Bible and pocketbook on the opposite end of the couch and joined her friend in the small kitchen. The white refrigerator was covered with colorful drawings, several with the name "James" written in across the top. She smiled. Her fridge at home looked similar, except Kelly was the artist there.

Joanne was spooning chili into two white and blue bowls. "I'll heat these up, and I can fix some rice if you want. There's diet pop in the fridge or lemonade."

"Something cold sounds good," Mary said. It was October, but the warm weather that clung to the South persisted. It was over 80 degrees out and not even noon.

She pulled out a can of diet soda. "Do you want soda or lemonade, Joanne?"

"Lemonade would be great, thanks," Joanne answered. Mary heard beeps as her friend programmed the microwave.

She pulled out the glass pitcher of lemonade and set it on the counter. Joanne was pulling a box of instant rice from a cabinet. A box of saltines sat in front of her, and as Mary watched she pulled one out of the package and popped it into her mouth.

Joanne turned to her and Mary saw a huge smile on her friend's face. "Listen, I've got something to tell you, but I need you to keep it quiet for now."

Mary looked into Joanne's sparkling eyes and knew what she was going to say.

"You're pregnant!" Mary cried, grabbing Joanne's arms.

Her friend laughed and grabbed Mary back. "Yes! I did the home test yesterday and it was positive. I'm seeing my doctor tomorrow."

For a moment the two of them acted like teenagers, screaming and jumping up and down in the brightly lit kitchen. Paul Carson's amused voice brought them back to themselves.

"Hm, let me guess – you told Mary."

Mary blushed a little but couldn't stop smiling. Joanne giggled and went to her husband, kissing him on the cheek. "Yes, I did. She's my best friend, and she knows how to keep a secret."

Mary was glad the two of them weren't looking at her at the moment. Joanne's last comment – *she knows how to keep a secret* – reminded her of the secret she'd been keeping for ten years. A secret that might well be exposed before too long.

"Hey, Mary, you all right?" Paul asked. He was tall, with black hair and blue eyes that twinkled behind black frame eyeglasses. Those eyes were sharp, able to read people well. It made him a good preacher.

Mary forced herself to concentrate on Joanne's good news, hoping it would affect her expression. "Sure. I'm happy for you guys. Why the secrecy?"

Paul smiled as he gave Joanne a quick hug. "Just being careful. We want to make sure everything's okay. But Joanne was going to explode if she didn't tell her mom and you, so I figured letting you two in on it was better than an exploded wife."

Mary nodded in agreement, a sudden lump in her throat keeping her from speaking. The two of them looked so happy. And she was happy for them – she knew that Joanne and Paul had prayed for a second child.

But at the moment it reminded her of a child she might have out there. Not only that, her hand dropped to her own abdomen as she recalled how many times she'd hoped to be pregnant again, only to be disappointed.

When Mary had been pregnant with Kelly, she'd sworn her obstetrician to secrecy, even from Roger, concerning her previous miscarriage. He'd honored her request, something she was grateful for even as she cringed at asking someone to lie for her.

After Kelly was born the doctor assured her there was no reason she couldn't have another child. But as weeks turned into months and still no pregnancy, she wondered if this was yet another judgment from God for what she'd done. Perhaps He'd closed her womb, as He'd done with women in the past.

The microwave beeped. Mary was tempted to tell Joanne she couldn't stay for lunch after all. Before she could say anything, Paul spoke up, looking from the microwave to the women. "Ah, I didn't mean to intrude. I'll fix myself something quick and take it over to my office."

"If you two want to have lunch —" Mary started, but Joanne shook her head.

"No, I want to have lunch with *you*. I can share a meal with this guy —" she nudged Paul's arm, "- anytime. So, did you decide you wanted rice?"

"That would be fine," Mary said, feeling defeated. As much as she liked Joanne, she really didn't want to talk to her now. She knew her friend would sense that Mary was holding back tears.

Or – and Mary felt her chest tighten at the thought – what if she couldn't hold them back now?

- FORTY-SEVEN -

MARY WATCHED AS JOANNE spooned out a generous portion of Death by Chocolate, feeling relieved that so far her friend didn't appear to have a clue about the emotional storm going on inside Mary's heart.

The relief died as Joanne handed her a bowl and a spoon. "Mary, I really didn't mean to hurt your feelings."

"Huh?" Mary blinked. "What are you talking about?"

"I'm not blind, Mary," Joanne said with a sigh as she led Mary to the couch in the living room, carrying her dessert in one hand and a cup of coffee in the other. "Something's bothering you – something's been on your mind for a week now, but today . . . I upset you when I told you I was pregnant, didn't I?"

"Joanne, no!" Mary said as she sat on the smaller couch that was perpendicular to the one Joanne sat at. "I'm happy for you, I really am."

Her friend sighed. "But it brought up something sad in you. I could tell. And you've been really down all through lunch."

Mary carefully set her cup down on the floor. Stirring the chocolate trifle in her bowl, she bit her lip as she decided what to say. "Well, you know that Roger and I . . . we've been trying . . . "

Joanne looked apologetic. "Oh, I forgot! I'm so sorry, Mary. How could I be so self-centered!"

"No, don't," Mary protested. "Of course you should be happy. And what kind of friend would I be if I couldn't be happy with you?"

"Still, I should've remembered," Joanne said. Both women were quiet a moment, enjoying the chocolaty dessert. Then Joanne sighed and put her bowl in her lap. "Mary, I owe you an apology."

Mary paused while licking her spoon. "Joanne, I said it was okay."

Her friend shook her head. "Not about the pregnancy thing. About . . . " she took a deep breath. " . . . about why I invited you to lunch."

"Oh?" Mary had a sinking feeling. She should have guessed. Joanne was perceptive.

"Look, I'm not trying to pry," Joanne said, placing her dessert dish on the floor and shoving aside the laundry basket so she could sit closer to Mary. "But I can tell something's really wrong. You've looked like you're carrying the weight of the world all this time, and I'm worried."

Mary quickly spooned some trifle into her mouth, stalling for time. How could she tell Joanne the truth? Joanne, a preacher's wife, a woman who had probably been a virgin when she married her husband, who hadn't kept a dark past from everyone . . .

She opened her mouth to say something – anything – but all that came out was a sob as tears streamed down her cheeks.

Joanne was next to her in an instant, arms around Mary. "Okay, okay, go ahead and cry, it's okay."

"It isn't," Mary gulped, shaking her head. She put her bowl down on the floor and buried her face in her hands. "It'll never be okay. I . . . "

But she couldn't say it.

She felt Joanne's hand on her back, gently rubbing. "What is it? You and Roger are okay, right?"

Mary felt her chest tighten at the mention of her husband. "I don't deserve Roger."

"What do you mean?" Joanne frowned at her.

"I don't deserve him," Mary repeated. She closed her eyes, the darkness behind her lids feeling appropriate. "I don't deserve Kelly, I don't deserve you, I don't deserve another child, which is probably why God isn't letting me get pregnant . . . "

"Whoa!" Joanne interrupted. "Mary, I don't know what's going on, but you are *not* a bad person. Where is this coming from?"

Mary shook her head. She opened her eyes and focused on her hands, clasped together so tightly the diamond in her wedding set cut into her fingers. "You don't know what I did, Joanne. I'm not the person you think I am."

For a moment, there was silence. Mary felt her heart pounding. She was so discouraged. Everything was crashing down on her. God couldn't possibly love her. Not after all this. No one could love her.

"Mary?" Joanne's voice was soft. "Look at me."

She didn't want to. She just wanted to leap to her feet and run. Run and run until she dropped from exhaustion. Until she was at a place no one knew her.

Her friend's fingers grasped her chin and forced Mary's head up. Joanne's green eyes were flashing.

"I don't know what you did, and I don't care. I know who you are now. And you, Mary Beamer, are a good Christian wife, mother, and sister. If someone is telling you something different, they are lying to you."

"You don't know that," Mary protested. "If you knew what I've done, what awful things —"

"Are you saying God's grace isn't large enough to forgive anything you've done?" Joanne argued.

Mary shook her head. She didn't want to hear that God loved her and could forgive all her sins. She wanted to believe it. She really did. But . . .

Joanne sat back, resting an arm on the back of the couch. "Mary, there's something going on that you haven't told anyone about, isn't there? Not even Roger?"

Mary swallowed. She nodded, unable to look at her friend.

They sat there in silence. Mary heard her friend shift position on the couch, the leather squeaking as she adjusted her leg. Mary concentrated on breathing, on keeping the tears from falling. She was so tired of crying.

"Mary," there was a careful timbre to Joanne's voice, as if she was tasting every word before saying it, "I don't know what's going on. I'm guessing you don't want to tell me."

"I —"Mary found herself being careful with her own words, "I'm afraid to, Joanne. No one knows, I can't risk it." She bit her lip. "It – it happened a long time ago, and some people who do know about it are trying to bring it up again."

"You're afraid," Joanne repeated. "Of what?"

"That . . . " Mary blinked hard and finally looked at Joanne. The redhead's expression was unreadable. ". . . that people won't love me anymore. That I'll be alone. I'm not even sure God loves me after all this."

Joanne stared at her for a long moment. Then, with a sigh, she leaned over and put a hand over Mary's clasped ones. "I won't try to tell you God loves you – I have the feeling you won't accept it. But I *will* tell you that I don't care what you've done, I don't care if you've committed every sin possible to commit. I will never stop loving you, Mary. Never."

"But – but you don't know –"

Joanne leaned forward, her eyes unblinking as she stared into Mary's face. "I. Will. Never. Stop. Loving. You. Deal with it."

Mary stared into her friend's green eyes. Tears swam in them. And for the first time, Mary thought she might be wrong, that revealing this sin might not cause a fellow Christian to turn away from her in disgust.

"You can't tell Paul," she said, her voice coming out in a whisper. "Please, Joanne. Roger doesn't know, no one at church does. If you can't do that for me, please don't ask me to tell you. I'm begging you."

Joanne bit her lip. "I don't usually keep things from Paul, but I think he'd understand this. All I can promise is I'll do my best, Mary. Is that good enough?"

Was it good enough? Mary drew a shuddering breath. She knew Joanne meant what she said. The preacher's wife was no gossip. And she *was* her best friend. Perhaps it was time. Time to share her burden with a fellow Christian.

Mary held Joanne's hands tightly. And there, in the small living room with laundry and dessert dishes, she talked about that summer in Atlanta.

- FORTY-EIGHT -

As Sharon stepped into the parking garage of the Hilton, she felt a thrill of excitement mingling in with the fear that made her stomach gurgle. What she was about to do was risky, and for some reason she found that exhilarating.

She'd worked all Sunday to come up with a plan to deal with Francine Winters. After some exhaustive research on the Internet, Sharon had sat at her round kitchen table, covering pages of a yellow legal pad with notes. By the time she'd gone to bed at one AM, a plan had begun forming in her mind.

On Monday she'd started to get together what she needed. Her first stop, even before going to work, was to a nursery that helped with plants for the clinic.

Sharon wandered the rows of plants – purple violets, yellow sunflowers, roses of different hues and smells – telling the girl who usually helped her she wanted to look around for some ideas for her place. She stopped every now and then to bend closer to a blossom, giving the impression that she wasn't in any hurry.

As she walked around the outdoor plant area, Sharon kept her eyes open. 15 minutes went by before she found what she was looking for – a dirty white plastic jug with the words Parathion – warning: poisonous! wear gloves when handling! stamped on it in black letters sat under one of the long tables of plants.

She allowed herself to walk past it the first time. Sharon walked down two rows before pausing before a pot of bright yellow roses. When a quick glance showed her that no one was watching, she snapped a latex glove onto her right hand.

As she headed back to where she spotted the parathion, she pulled out a notepad and a pen and started to write something down. After taking one more look to see if anyone was watching, Sharon allowed the pen to slip through her fingers and land on the ground.

She made an impatient sound and bent down to retrieve the pen. It lay close to the jug of pesticide. She pulled a cloth handkerchief from her trench coat's pocket and dipped it into the jug, holding it between two fingers to make sure it was submerged.

Sharon pulled it out and wadded it up, sliding it and her gloved hand back into her pocket. She hated ruining the black Burberry coat – it was one of her favorites. But sometimes sacrifices had to be made.

She walked back towards her car, keeping her hand in her pocket. Once inside, she pulled out two plastic bags. She placed one over her left hand like a glove, and then eased her right hand, still clutching the soaked cloth, into the other.

Carefully she peeled off the latex glove, leaving it in the bag with the cloth, which she sealed. She then grasped it with her left hand and pulled the final bag over the first one. She then dropped it all into a small cooler that sat on the floor of the passenger seat.

Sharon carefully examined the skin on both hands. Once she was satisfied that none of the pesticide had touched her skin, she cleaned her hands with some waterless sanititizer.

When she got to work, she headed to Thomas' office and shut the door. The doctor gave her an annoyed look. "I have been quite busy appeasing Francine. How much longer do I have to do this? That woman will spend me into bankruptcy!"

Sharon shook her head. "Don't tell me you're not getting anything out of it."

"A prostitute would be cheaper and have fewer expectations!"

Sharon sat down in front of her boss' desk, pulling out her iPhone. "Thomas, I'm getting everything arranged. With a little help from you, Francine Winters will be a non-issue by tomorrow night."

Thomas took off his glasses and gave Sharon a wary look. "What kind of help?"

She glanced at the notes she'd transferred to her phone that morning. "I assume she's convinced that you are strongly considering honoring her request?"

"Yes," he sighed. "I've done everything I can to persuade her without actually making a commitment."

"Are you seeing her tonight?" Sharon asked.

"Of course I am,' Thomas said, shooting his office manager an angry look. "That's what this is all about, right?"

"All right," Sharon replied, ignoring Green's tone. "Tonight, tell her you really want to say yes, but you want to do some research on a place for her. Ask her to give you until tomorrow evening to finalize things."

"What?" Thomas said, standing, his face reddening. "Sharon, I do *not* want to put up with that woman!"

She arched an eyebrow at him. "Thomas, you want me to make this go away, correct? Well, it's going to take some cooperation from you. Not much, but enough."

"And just how is my giving in to her going to make this 'go away?'" Thomas asked, his arms folded across his chest.

Sharon didn't answer for a moment, digging into her messenger bag for the pages she'd printed off the Internet. She handed a couple to Thomas. "Think she'd find something like one of these condos satisfactory?"

Green looked at the printout with a grimace. "Waterfront property? Of course she would. Why these? Because they're the most expensive?"

"No," Sharon said, "because they're about 30 minutes away from her hotel and on the water."

Frowning, Green asked, "Why is that important?"

Sharon stood, smoothing wrinkles from her black dress slacks. "That's not something you need to know, Thomas. Just be ready to do what I ask tomorrow."

Now, here in the Hilton's parking garage, wearing light colored latex gloves she hoped wouldn't show up as gloves on a security tape, Sharon took a deep breath. A professional would probably not be at all nervous right now. For that matter, a professional would have found a much better way to get the job done.

But, Sharon mused as she spotted Francine's car, her plan wasn't that bad, all things considered. She glanced around and saw that the garage was pretty deserted at the moment. She pulled out her phone and called Thomas' pager, adding "911" to her cell phone number.

He called her back within five minutes. "What?"

She smiled. He was irritated as anything, but she understood. As long as he did what she instructed, that irritation would be a thing of the past very soon. "I need you to call Francine and tell her you've found a place to rent for her at that place I told you about yesterday."

"That's all?" he asked sarcastically.

"No," Sharon said, ignoring his tone. "Ask her to go ahead and drive to the address. Explain you need to finish some stuff up at the office and you'll meet her there."

"And then what? Meet her there?"

"No," Sharon said, keeping her voice calm in spite of Thomas' stress. "Call me back when you've finished with her. Then just do what you need to do at the clinic and wait for my call."

"Fine," Thomas huffed. "I hope you know what you're doing."

"Relax, "Thomas. It's almost over," Sharon said. "Now hang up and make the call."

She hung up her phone and lifted a hand to adjust the black wig she'd put on for this occasion. That and a pair of reading glasses would hopefully disguise her enough if there were questions.

Of course, if things went according to plan, there would be no questions.

She walked through the parking lot, her set of keys out. Every now and then she'd stop and turn in a slow circle, huffing and tapping a foot in feigned irritation. As Sharon neared Francine's red Grand Am, she stuck her hand in her pocket, fingers wrapping around the parathion-soaked handkerchief she'd kept in a sealed bag until she entered the parking garage.

When she was next to driver's side of the Grand Am, Sharon pretended to stumble, pulling the handkerchief out and pressing it on the handle of the door, as if steadying herself.

She shook her head and muttered under her breath, trying to look like a frustrated, klutzy patron of the hotel. She gave the door handle a good wipe with the handkerchief before slipping it back into her pocket.

Echoing footsteps were the only warning she had. Sharon walked quickly to a concrete column and slipped around it, hiding from whoever was heading in her direction.

Now she heard Francine's voice. "All right…yes, Thomas, I understand…this is so exciting!" The woman strode into view, dressed in a short leather skirt and a sea green blouse that was too tight in Sharon's opinion. Her black stiletto heels tapped quickly as the woman who had posed a threat to Sharon's boss pulled out a key fob and unlocked her car's doors.

Still talking, Francine grabbed the door handle that Sharon had wiped down only seconds before. Sharon held her breath as Francine paused, frowning as she looked down at her hand.

Thomas must have said something, because Francine shook her head slightly and said, "I'm fine. Something wet was on my car door...wonder if there was a bird or something in here."

Francine looked around, but Sharon could see all the woman had on her was a small tan purse slung over her shoulder. With a shrug, Francine grabbed the door handle again and opened the door, wiping her hand on her skirt as she slid inside.

Sharon pressed her lips together to contain the shout of victory that threatened to come out. Instead, she walked quickly outside to where she'd left her own car and got in. She tossed the reading glasses on the seat next to her and started her Lexus, pulling out and keeping a sharp eye out for the red Grand Am. She needed to see this with her own eyes.

Her phone rang as she caught sight of Francine's car. "She's on her way," Thomas said. "She said there was something wet on the door handle?"

Sharon pressed down on the accelerator, wanting to keep the red car in sight. "Don't worry about it, Thomas. Now, just sit tight. I'll call you back shortly."

She hung up her phone and dropped it next to the reading glasses as she continued to tail Francine Winters. After cruising under a yellow light so as not to lose her quarry, Sharon glanced at the digital clock on her dashboard. It hadn't been long enough yet – a relief, actually, because the last thing Sharon wanted was for Francine to succumb while there was a lot of traffic around.

After a few minutes the two women turned off onto the interstate. Sharon was glad to see that she'd picked a good time of day for this – there were some cars here and there, but nowhere near as many as there would be when rush hour rolled around.

Sharon punched the knob to her car stereo, tuning in the classical music station. Beethoven's 9th symphony was playing, and she let it sweep over her as she drove.

Five minutes later, Francine's car drifted to the breakdown lane and then jerked back to where it had been. Sharon held her breath. Only a matter of time, now...

The car drifted again, bouncing off the metal side rail that separated the interstate from a grassy slope. It sped up suddenly, narrowly missing a dark green minivan before bouncing across the median to the opposite lane of traffic.

Sharon slowed down some, wanting to keep Francine's car in sight until it was all over. *If there was a God*, she thought, *I'd ask Him to – yes!*

A semi was barreling down the left lane on the opposite side of Sharon. There was a screech of airbrakes applied too late and the stench of burning rubber as the driver of the truck tried to stop.

The left front bumper of the semi smashed into Francine's car. The vehicle rolled once, twice, three times before it settled bottom up on the median, smoke rising from the twisted metal.

Sharon sped up. She felt her palms grow damp with sweat on the wheel and had to force herself to take deep breaths. She glanced in her rearview mirror and saw the driver of the semi stumble out, his body language clearly anxious.

She let herself regret the nightmare that driver would be going through. But it looked like an accident, and no one would blame him for what happened.

Of course, Francine had been dead by the time the truck hit her. The parathion took twenty minutes to a half hour to work, but once it did, death was inevitable. The subsequent auto accident probably erased any traces of the pesticide from the car.

Problem solved.

As she got further and further from the scene, Sharon found herself calming. There was nothing to trace her to the crime, and Thomas had an alibi. She grabbed her phone and called the doctor to give him the good news.

"Just a minute," Thomas said. A few seconds of silence, then, "All right, I'm in my office."

"Francine Winters is no longer a factor," Sharon said. She took the next exit off the interstate. "You will probably be getting a call from the authorities."

"Why?" his tone was guarded.

Sharon pondered how much to say. "You know why."

She heard his sharp intake of breath. "How…what did you…"

"You don't need to know," she told him. "One thing – they'll know you talked to her recently. Your story is she told you she was looking at the condo. Act upset. You've been acting as if you have feelings for her – you have to sell it."

"Believe me, acting upset won't be difficult," Thomas told her grimly. "Are you coming in?"

"In a bit," Sharon said, spotting a Cracker Barrel. "Don't worry, Thomas. Everything's going to be fine."

She hung up as she pulled into the parking lot of the restaurant. Suddenly she was famished.

She wondered if everyone felt that way after killing someone.

- FORTY-NINE -

JACK SAT AT HIS DESK, looking over his notes from the weekend for what seemed to be the thousandth time since he got back into town. So much. Yet so little.

Mary Beamer was the first tangible piece of evidence of what he'd suspected for the past several years. Up til then he'd had rumors, anonymous tips, and the fact that the good doctor and his staff stonewalled him at every turn to go on.

"Foster!" Wheeler shouted from his office doorway.

Jack rolled his eyes. He'd managed to duck his boss for the past few days, even going as far as to catch up on some other assignments. He'd hoped that would keep him off Wheeler's radar for a while.

Apparently, it hadn't worked.

With a sigh, Jack grabbed his notebook and walked to the office. Wheeler dropped into his office chair, frowning. "Have a seat. I want to know how your little field trip went."

Jack eased himself down, trying to come up with the best spin on his information. "I spoke to Mary Beamer this weekend."

"And this is the gal your dead nurse contacted?" Wheeler took a swallow of coffee from his black mug that had "BOSS" in big white letters.

Foster went over the interview he'd had with Mary, trying to emphasize the fact that they now had corroboration that something underhanded was going on in Thomas Green's clinic. The note, her experience, all added up to something shady, in Jack's eyes. He wanted Wheeler to see it.

The editor shook his head and set his mug down on a pile of printed emails. "You're making a lot of suppositions here, Jack."

"The evidence supports them," Jack argued.

"Look, let me play devil's advocate here, okay?" Wheeler said. "For one thing, how do you know that this woman isn't stringing you along for some agenda she has?"

Foster frowned. "You didn't see her. She's very upset about this. In fact, I had to be very persuasive to get her to say anything to me."

"How persuasive?" Wheeler's eyebrows shot up. "Money?"

"No, she really isn't that kind of a person," Jack said with a shake of his head. "To be honest, she really just wants this to go away. I'm gonna have to handle her carefully if I want to use her as a source."

"Great, she's reluctant?" Wheeler threw his hands up in the air. "You realize she could spook and leave us high and dry."

"Not if she thinks a child of hers is involved," Jack said. "According to the note she received from Martha Thompson, there is."

"And have you seen this pretty important note?" Wheeler asked.

Jack sighed. "Not yet. She didn't have it with her."

"So, for all you know, there is no note."

"Give me a break!" Jack snapped. "I know that Martha Thompson contacted Mary Beamer. If not to tell her about her son, why?"

The editor rubbed his face. "Maybe she owed her money. Maybe she got religion and just wanted to tell the woman she was sorry for helping her kill her baby. Maybe the woman was crazy. The point is, you don't know!"

"I know something was going on in that clinic!" Jack shouted. "And I got so close to it they torched the place to stop me!"

Wheeler's face was bright red, and he was on his feet, a finger aimed at Foster. "Do *not* take that tone with me! I've let you run with this, given you plenty of leash. Another editor would have your butt in the street by now!"

Jack clenched his fists, glaring at the floor. He'd lost his temper, the kiss of death in the newspaper office. Silence filled the office as he tried to control his breathing, tried to calm down. Ticking off Wheeler wouldn't help him get the story.

He heard a chair creak as his boss sat back down. "Jack, I know you keep saying that this has nothing to do with Lisa —"

"Don't go there," Jack said, his eyes still focusing on the cheap commercial carpet under his feet.

"I have to," Wheeler said, in a far calmer tone than he'd been using. "If this is getting personal, I need to know."

"You keep asking me that and I keep telling you no," Jack muttered. "When will you believe me?"

"When I'm convinced. Which I'm not," Wheeler said. "And I'm still waiting for something to encourage me to let you continue this."

Jack rubbed his face, his stubble scraping his hand. "Look. Here's the thing. This woman had contact with the clinic. A reluctant contact –"

"According to her," Wheeler interrupted.

"According to her," Foster repeated with a sigh. "But a contact, nonetheless. She was told she miscarried, but never saw a body. Years later, one of the attending nurses sends her a note saying her child is alive."

"According to her," Wheeler repeated.

"What do you want from me?" Foster snapped. "I did the interview, I recorded it. Listen to it, and you'll see she seems to be the real deal."

Wheeler rubbed his temple. "Let me ask this. Green's not in our state anymore. He's in Alabama. Why should we, a Georgia paper, care now?"

"Because what he did was wrong!" Jack said, slamming a fist on his leg. "There's still fallout from it! Women who thought they got abortions have live kids out there somewhere."

"Kids they didn't want," Wheeler said. "That's why they were aborting them."

"That makes what Green did okay?" Jack said. He fought the urge to get up, scream, and throw something through the glass walls in Wheeler's office.

"What you *allege* he did," Wheeler shot back.

Foster took a deep breath. "I'm not giving up on this story."

Wheeler's eyebrows went up. "And if I tell you to drop it?"

"I won't."

The editor swore. "Are you serious? You're willing to toss your career over this?"

"What career?" Jack shrugged. "Right now I'm doing stuff any college graduate with a journalism degree can do."

"Is this what this is about? You think you're being wasted here?" Wheeler shook his head. "Jack, you're a good reporter – one of the best. You don't have to always break the big ones."

"Look," Jack said. "I know I can break this story. I know Green's dirty, and he's playing dirty. I've run into some dead ends, but the story's there. I'm not ready to quit on it. Don't make me choose between this and my job."

He kept his eyes on Wheeler, doing his best to hide the nervousness that made his heart pound. He really didn't want to lose his job – he was kind of addicted to eating – but he couldn't let go of this story. Not wouldn't; couldn't.

The editor sighed, rubbing his eyes. "Okay. I must be drunk, but I'll give you a week. One week — and you either come up with something concrete or you bury this with whatever emotional baggage is tied to it. You understand?"

"Yeah," Jack said, unable to keep the enthusiasm out of his voice. "I got it."

"And don't let me catch you being late on other assignments!" Wheeler grabbed his coffee cup and waved at his door. "Now go do something that justifies my paying you."

Jack had to force himself not to bolt out of the office. Relief and concern warred within him. Relief, because he had time to get what he needed. Concern, because he knew Wheeler meant what he said about a deadline.

Well, he'd get his story. Because it was a good story. Not because of any so-called emotional baggage. Not because of Lisa.

Not at all.

- FIFTY -

MARY SANG "RED HIGH HEELS" as she ran the vacuum around Kelly's room. She liked lively songs when she was housecleaning – it seemed to give her energy when she was doing chores.

She ran the cleaner under Kelly's bed and heard a clatter that meant she'd picked up something. With a sigh, Mary turned off the vacuum and checked under the bed, wondering what had gotten shoved under there this time.

Mary caught a glimpse of something white and reached out to grab it. A dice that was a part of one of several board games that sat on a shelf in the closet. Mary thought she knew where another one was.

She unplugged the vacuum. Before she could open it up, she caught the sound of the phone ringing. Mary stood up, taking a moment to brush the dust off her jeans and jogged over to her bedroom, grabbing the phone before it could go to the answering machine.

It was Joanne. "Just seeing how you're doing after yesterday. Are you okay?"

Mary sat down on the bed, reaching out to adjust one of the white decorator pillows that shifted. "I'm all right, I guess. Thanks for listening, and not yelling at me."

"Mary, I told you yesterday – God loves you no matter what. Yes, what you did was wrong, but you repented," Joanne said. "But you do have to stop lying about it."

"You promised you wouldn't say anything," Mary said, feeling her throat close. "Joanne, you *promised*."

"I'm not going to gossip about it or get the church office to put it in the bulletin," Joanne said. "But Mary, the lying isn't good. Especially lying to Roger."

"I don't know if he'll understand," Mary sniffled. "He thinks I was a virgin when we got married. How will he take this? He'll probably be furious."

"I won't lie to you, Mary – he's probably going to be angry at first," Joanne said, her voice gentle. "Wouldn't you be?"

Mary snatched the pillow she'd just adjusted, wrapping her arms around it. "I guess. But what if he wants to leave me?"

"Mary, he'll be angry, but I doubt he'll leave you," Joanne said. "I'm not saying this won't be a strain on your marriage, but it's the only way you can make it better. Hiding this can't possibly be good for your relationship."

"I've been hiding this for years," Mary said. "I don't know if I *can* tell him."

"Can you continue to live a lie?" Joanne asked. "You know what God says about lying."

Mary bit her lip. "I don't think God will forgive me for any of this anyway."

"How can you say that?" Joanne said. "If you really believed that you wouldn't come to church and do the things you do."

"I hope He'll forgive me," Mary said. "I've tried to make up for it – but then this I got this note and I feel as if God is punishing me for it still!"

"Perhaps this isn't a punishment," Joanne responded. "Perhaps this is a chance to make things right."

Mary shook her head. She realized she was rocking back and forth on the bed, the pillow crushed to her chest. "I don't know if I can. And then – what if it's true? How can I explain to Roger I have a son out there somewhere I knew nothing about until last week?"

"One step at a time," Joanne said. "Here's my advice: pick a day out of the next three and make an appointment with yourself to tell him on that day. If you pick Saturday, I'll see if we can take Kelly for the day – that way it'll just be the two of you."

"I feel like you're pushing me," Mary snapped.

"I *am* pushing you," Joanne agreed. "I'm trying to help you do what's right, and it seems to me you need a little pushing right now."

Mary tried to calm down. "I shouldn't have said anything to you. This is why I have to keep it quiet – people will judge me!"

She heard her friend's sigh. "I'm not trying to judge you. Mary, do you really think lying about this and hiding it is what God wants?"

"David lied," Mary said, her voice becoming defensive. "And he was a man after God's own heart."

There was a brief silence after that statement. Then Joanne spoke, her voice not quite as kind as it had been. "Mary, I don't think this conversation is going anywhere good. I'm going to go and I'll be praying for you. Please though, consider what you're saying and what you're doing."

"I will. I *have*," Mary said. "Joanne, please don't be mad at me."

"I wish I wasn't," her friend replied. "But I see a good woman doing bad things, how am I supposed to feel?"

Mary stood up, the pillow falling to the floor. "You're right. We should stop talking."

"Okay," Joanne said. "I love you, Mary. See you tonight."

Mary hung up the phone. She couldn't tell Joanne she loved her too – she was too upset. Nor could she say she'd see her at church – at that moment Mary wasn't sure she could ever set foot in a church again.

She picked up the pillow from the floor and placed it back on the bed. She couldn't help studying the soothing blue and green quilt that covered it – a gift from her mother years ago.

Mary put a hand on the cool fabric. She let herself think about the many times Roger had made love to her in this bed. What if he never wanted to touch her again? Did she deserve to be loved?

The phone rang again, interrupting her thoughts. Mary picked up the receiver. "Hello?"

At first all she could hear was sobbing. Then a voice gasped, "Mary?"

"Celia?" Fear gripped Mary and she sat down on the bed again, this time because she started shaking. "What is it? What's wrong?"

"My mom…" more sobs.

"Your mom?" Mary prayed that Celia wasn't calling for the reason she suspected, the reason that sent her heart hammering in her chest.

"She's dead, Mary," Celia cried. "The police just called. Mom died in a car crash yesterday."

- FIFTY-ONE -

THOMAS GREEN'S HAND trembled slightly as he picked up his cup of coffee. "Are you sure your victim is Francine Winters?" he asked the two men sitting in front of his desk.

Both men wore business suits. The one to his left was in charcoal gray, with a navy blue tie and a white shirt. The one on his right, who Green thought might be a little younger than his partner, wore a navy suit with a bright red tie.

They'd given him their names when they showed him their badges a few minutes ago. Detectives Underhill and Richards. The two of them had come to the clinic over an hour ago and said they would wait until he could break from patients.

When Sharon had found out they were sitting in the waiting room, she'd escorted them to the employees' breakroom/kitchen and served them coffee and some leftover cookies a drug rep had brought on Monday. When she told Green that they were waiting for him, he thought he would pass out. "Why are they here?"

"Don't worry about it," she told him. "Just remember what I told you yesterday, and it'll be fine."

Now, with police sitting in front of him with their notepads and questions Green was having trouble remembering his name, much less anything Sharon had said.

"I'm afraid there's no question," Underhill said, his blue eyes appearing to study Green. "The dental records match. I'm sorry."

"This..." Green swallowed, trying to stop his voice from shaking. "This is terrible news. Francine...she was a good friend."

"Just a friend, Doctor?" Richards said, leaning forward slightly.

"I'm – I'm not sure what you're implying, Detective," Green stammered.

The young man shrugged. "It's just that you apparently were paying Ms. Winters' tab at the Hilton. Not a small amount of money to toss around."

Green felt a blush creep up into his face. *At your age?* He asked himself. *Don't let this guy upset you!*

"If you're asking if my relationship with Francine was…romantic in nature, I would have to say it was," he answered, allowing a touch of frost to creep into his voice. He found some of his nervousness vanishing as he glared at Richards. "I cared about her very much."

"Easy, Doctor," Underhill said in a soothing voice. "We have to ask these questions."

"Why?" Green looked from one man to the other. "I thought you said it was a car accident?"

The two detectives swapped glances. "Yes, it appears that it was," Underhill said, flipping a couple of pages in his notebook. "But Ms. Winters apparently was driving erratically before the semi struck her car, and we aren't sure why at the moment."

Green frowned. "I wish I could help you on that. But I wasn't with her."

"Yet you placed a call to her cell phone about a half hour, forty-five minutes before the accident," Richards said, raising an eyebrow. "Was she upset? Did the two of you have a lovers' quarrel?"

"No, nothing like that!" Green protested. "I was asking if she'd go look at a condominium that was up for sale. Francine had expressed a desire to move here, and I was helping her find a place."

"Where was this condo?" Underhill asked.

"Here –" Green shifted some folders on his desk and pulled out the brochure that had the address he'd sent Francine to.

Underhill took it and glanced at it before handing it to Richards. "That's expensive real estate, Doctor."

Green tried to sound casual. "It was something I thought Francine would like."

Richards whistled. "Wow. I sure couldn't afford this." He looked up at Green, his black eyebrows knitting together. "Did you know Ms. Winters quit her job on Monday?"

"Yes," Green nodded. "She wanted to move here, wanted to live closer to me."

"And do you have any idea how she expected to pay for her new home?" Richards asked, holding up the brochure.

Green clenched his hands together under his desk, where the detectives couldn't see them. For a moment he wanted to curse Sharon – what had she done? Did she really expect to pull it off?

With a sigh, he pulled off his glasses and rubbed his eyes. "Gentlemen, I was planning to pay her expenses. Francine and I...we had an understanding."

Underhill tapped a pen close to his mouth. "What, exactly, was understood?"

Green played with his glasses, his eyes on the metal winking under his office lights. "You see, I was not ready for someone to live with me. I've never married, and I'm quite used to living by myself." He glanced up and saw that both men were giving him their full attention.

He ran a hand through his hair. "Francine understood that. She'd been married before – it did not end happily, I'm sorry to say. We agreed we couldn't live together, but thought perhaps she could move here and we could have a satisfying relationship."

"You mean she'd be a mistress," Richards snorted.

Green frowned at the younger man. "We were not breaking any laws, Detective. Unless you are one of those who believes sex outside of marriage to be a crime, which I most certainly do not. As I've said, I cared deeply for Francine; naturally, I wanted this move to be something she would enjoy."

Underhill scribbled something in his notebook. "So you're saying that you wanted her to move here? And you were willing to support her?"

"Yes, that's exactly what I'm saying," Green nodded.

Richards scratched his ear. "She didn't sound upset? Or sick?"

"No," Green said. "She was excited to go look at the condo." He arranged his features into a mask of sadness. "This is so tragic. Francine was so full of life."

"Just one more question, Doctor," Underhill said, straightening up in his seat. Green noticed the younger man doing the same. "Can you account for your whereabouts yesterday between – let's say nine AM and 3 PM?"

Green spread his hands. "I was here," he said. "I had a fully booked schedule."

"Didn't even go out for lunch?" Richards asked.

"No, I ate at my desk," Green said. "If you question the staff, I'm sure they'll corroborate my statement."

"We intend to question your staff," Richards said, standing up. "You mind if we set up in the break room?"

The doctor blinked. "You mean you intend to question them today? But why?"

Underhill stood, looking apologetic. "We're just concerned about the fact that Ms. Winters apparently lost control of her car before crashing. We're just trying to find out what happened to her so that her family can have some closure. I'm sure you can understand that?"

"Of course," Green said, standing himself. He was happy that he was no longer trembling. "If you'll allow me to send for my office manager, I'll have her make arrangements for you to question our staff. I only ask that you show consideration for our patients here while you do so. Many of these women are in crisis, and they don't need to feel harassed."

"Of course, not, Doctor," Underhill said with a nod. Richards merely stared at the doctor, his arms crossed in front of him.

Richards will bear watching, Green thought as he picked up his phone and dialed Sharon's extension. The sound of his office manager's voice angered him yet again. *As soon as these officers leave, we're going to have a serious discussion on exactly what she did.*

Until then, he'd play the sad lover and wait.

- FIFTY-TWO -

SHARON BREATHED A SIGH OF RELIEF as she locked the door behind one of the file clerks, a 50ish woman who hardly waited for the clinic door to shut before pulling out a cigarette and lighting it up.

The office manager took a moment to rest her head against the door. It had been a long, tense afternoon. And Thomas had dropped it into her lap to make sure the police only learned what they wanted them to.

Of course, she understood that taking care of things like this was part of her job. She ran the clinic. She kept it safe.

So why had Thomas acted as if he wanted to bite her head off all afternoon? Why had she gotten a terse email from him near the end of the day, informing her that they needed to discuss recent events?

Who did he think he was, anyway?

She straightened up, taking a moment to run her hands through her hair and smooth out her gray pencil skirt. A quick stop in her office to touch up her makeup, and she headed to Thomas' office.

His brusque "Come in!" when she rapped on the door did not bode well. Sharon allowed none of her concerns to show on her face as she entered. "Well, the last of the office crew is gone, and I've locked the front door."

"The police?" Thomas asked. He'd loosened his tie and opened the top button of his white dress shirt. The lines around his eyes seemed deeper than usual, and he tapped a pen nervously on the stack of files in front of him.

"The police left a half hour ago," Sharon said, sitting down and casually crossing her legs.

"How'd they seem?"

She affected a relaxed posture. "Well, the younger one appeared somewhat hostile – he didn't say anything overtly critical but I'd bet he's one of those religious people who see abortion as murder. I was polite and hospitable and made sure I mentioned how a woman's right to choose depended on men such as themselves who upheld the law."

Green didn't seem impressed at her political maneuvering. "And the staff?"

"Thomas, relax," she said, allowing a hint of annoyance to creep into her voice. "You and Francine Winters were powering half the gossip mill the past few days – I swear a couple of the nurses were swooning about how the good doctor was falling in love!" She rolled her eyes. "The only ones who knew Francine was a problem were you and me. And I had no problem answering the officer's questions."

Thomas shook his head. "I wish I could say the same thing."

"What possible problem could you have?" Sharon snapped. "You knew the story to give them – "

Thomas swore and slapped a hand down on the files, the noise sounding as sharp as a gunshot. "You *murdered* Francine, Sharon!"

She couldn't stop herself from flinching. "I solved a problem," she said through gritted teeth. "Don't sit there and try to pretend you didn't know what I intended to do!"

Green shot to his feet, his chair rolling back to slam into the wall. "I didn't tell you to kill her! Do you have any idea what you've caused? The police were here! If they'd found the nursery – "

"They didn't," Sharon broke in. She stayed seated, though her feet tapped in anxiety. She'd never seen Green so agitated.

"This time!" Green snapped. He began to pace. "Do you realize how risky this was?"

"Do *you* realize," Sharon said, allowing some irritation to creep into her voice, "that letting her live was at least as risky? You're the one who insisted we couldn't pay her off!"

"Don't put this on me!" Green stopped and pointed a shaking finger at her. "I had nothing to do with this!"

Sharon got to her feet. "No? Tell me, Thomas, when did you realize what was going to happen? What did you think was going to happen yesterday when I told you to call her?"

He ran a hand through his hair. "I – I don't know."

"Yes, you do," Sharon said, taking a step towards the desk. "You knew. The only reason you're upset is because the police showed up."

"You don't think that's a good reason to be upset?"

Sharon sighed. "Thomas, of *course* the police were going to visit us. You've been her sugar daddy the past few days. But they have nothing that would cause them to suspect anything other than what we've told them."

Green shook his head, but Sharon noted he'd stopped pacing. "It's dangerous." He looked past her, his eyes unfocused as he thought. "Perhaps it's time to consider relocating."

"It's not necessary," Sharon argued. "And relocating is sure to bring us under the authorities' radar. We're fine, Thomas."

He tapped his fingers on the desk. "And that girl – that Mary person – what if she causes trouble?"

"Why would she?" Sharon asked. "From what I understand, she wants to forget about what happened to her. I say we let her do so."

Green picked up a file from his desk and flipped it open. He shot Sharon a warning look. "I suppose I have no choice but to trust you in this. But you need to be careful."

"Thomas, you know my first priority is the protection of this clinic," Sharon said.

"I hope so," Green said. "I won't let my work be destroyed because you swatted a fly with a sledgehammer."

Sharon narrowed her eyes. "Don't threaten me, Thomas. You need me far more than I need you."

Green glared at her. "Are you threatening *me?*"

They swapped stares for almost a minute. Then Sharon sighed. "Thomas, it's been a difficult couple of days. In spite of that, let's remember we're both on the same side. We want the clinic to continue and prosper. The rest of it is merely a difference of opinion."

He shook his head, eyes down on the file. "The death of a woman is a difference of opinion?"

"Her death means we can continue to provide a necessary service to women," she said, smoothing her skirt. "We both know that sometimes sacrifices have to be made for the greater good."

Thomas' jaw tightened, but he didn't answer her. Sharon decided not to press the matter. "I'll be in my office if you need anything," she told him.

Once in her office, Sharon sat down and closed her eyes. Thomas' reaction to her actions had taken her by surprise. What did he think she was going to do? And was it too much to ask that he exhibit at least a small amount of gratitude for the risks she'd taken for the clinic? For *him?*

She rubbed her pounding temples. She'd get done what she needed to do here and then go out for a drink. Or maybe a couple of drinks. She certainly deserved them.

Hopefully Thomas would come to realize that she'd done him a great service. The clinic would prosper. And so would she. There wasn't a person out there that would prevent that.

If someone tried, Sharon knew she could deal with them.

After all, she'd dealt with Francine.

- FIFTY-THREE -

M ARE?"

Mary raised her head off the pillow. She saw Roger standing in the doorway, frowning. "What time is it?"

"It's ten after six." He came to the bed and sat down next to her. "I just got home from work. Where's Kelly? Why are you in bed?"

Mary groaned and rubbed her eyes. "Joanne has Kelly. I – I just needed some time."

Roger's expression made it clear he didn't understand what was going on and didn't like the fact. "Time?"

She let her head drop back to her pillow. She was so tired. It all felt like too much. The argument with Joanne, the terrible conversation she'd had with Celia, her friend choking her words out between sobs, the note . . . that awful note that started it all . . .

Mary knew she owed Roger some sort of explanation. Coming home before Bible study on a Wednesday night to find Kelly gone, her in bed, and no dinner made was out of the norm for them.

But she honestly had no idea what to tell him.

He put a gentle hand on her cheek. "You've been crying? Mary, what's going on?"

She closed her eyes. Crying reminded her of Celia's call. She heard herself speak. "Celia called. Her mom died yesterday."

"Oh, Mary, I'm sorry to hear that," he said, wrapping his arms around her and pulling her close. She felt the slight stubble on his chin brush her forehead before he tucked her face into his chest. "I take it it was unexpected?"

"It was an accident," Mary said, her voice muffled by Roger's pale green dress shirt. "According to Celia, she lost control of her car and was hit by a semi truck."

"Well, I can understand you being upset," Roger said as his hand brushed her hair. "Tell you what, why don't you and I pick up some fast food on the way to Bible study?"

Mary swallowed. While Joanne had been kind when Mary asked her to take Kelly, their earlier phone conversation hung over them. It hung like a weight on Mary's mind and heart.

"Actually . . . " she moistened her lips. "I was thinking about packing a few things and meeting Celia in Alabama."

Roger pulled her back so he could see her face. "What?"

"The body . . . " Mary took a deep breath and started again. "Celia's mom is in Alabama. She needs to go there and identify – and collect the – the body. She could use a friend."

"What about her husband?" Roger asked with a frown. "I mean, come on, Mare, you haven't spoken to her in ages. Surely she has people in her life who can be there for her."

"*I* want to be there for her," Mary said. She clenched her fists. "Celia asked me to. She'll pay for my flight and help with expenses, so it won't cost us very much at all."

"This isn't about the money," Roger said, shaking his head. "This is about us. You want to take off with almost no notice? What about Kelly?"

"Joanne can help," Mary said. "She has before."

Roger ran a hand through his hair and glanced at his watch. "Look, we're going to be late for Bible study if we don't hurry. We can talk about this later." He stood and started for the door.

Mary stayed on the bed. He got to the door before he realized she wasn't following him. He looked over his shoulder, looking at her. "Mare?"

She swallowed. "There's nothing to discuss. I'm going."

Mary watched as Roger turned to face her, his eyes wide. She cringed inside. Mary knew what the Bible said about wives submitting to their husbands. Never, in their years of marriage, had she taken such an opposing stand against Roger.

He took a step towards her. "What are you saying?"

She gripped her hands together and let her gaze drop to Roger's black shoes. "Roger, I don't want to fight about this. But I'm going. I'm sorry if you don't like it, but my mind is made up."

"And if I ask you not to?" Roger asked, the words practically vibrating with tension.

Mary forced herself to look at her husband's face. "I'll still go. I'm sorry."

"*Sorry?*" Roger repeated, his cheeks reddening. "What is going on with you, Mary? You've been acting strangely for almost two weeks now! You won't talk to me, you're upset all the time, now you want to take off whether I want you to or not?"

"I – " Mary bit her lip. Crying now wouldn't help matters. "Roger, I can't tell you. I wish I could."

He shook his head, glaring at her. "I don't believe you. I think you don't *want* to tell me. And for the life of me I can't understand why." His fists clenched, he turned to leave the room again.

Mary felt as if her life was spinning out of control. She jumped to her feet, took a couple of steps toward her husband. "Roger – it's not that I don't love you –"

"Then what is it?" Roger spun around to face her, and to her horror she saw tears in his eyes – tears! "If you love me, Mary, please tell me what's going on!"

She felt tears slipping down her face, in spite of her trying to stop them. "Roger, I – I…I'm afraid. I love you but I'm so afraid."

"Of what?" Roger asked. "Of me?" His voice broke. "Mary, are you afraid of *me?*"

She tried to come up with an honest answer. She didn't think Roger would ever lay a hand on her, but she *was* afraid of him – afraid that if he knew the truth, he'd walk away from her forever.

A choked sound distracted her from her thoughts. Roger's face was wet, his mouth twisted. "I – I see."

"No!" she took a step towards him.

To her dismay, he took a step back, a hand raised to stop her from approaching him. She froze on the spot, but couldn't stop talking. "Roger, I want to explain –"

"No," he said, shaking his head. "No, I can't – I can't talk about this now. I – I can't." He fell back a couple of steps, was in the doorway. "Mary, do what you want. Obviously, I can't stop you."

The door shut between them. Mary heard her husband's footsteps recede as he walked away. Away from her.

She buried her face in her hands. It was what she'd tried to prevent, ever since she met Roger. It's why she'd kept her secret, had done everything she could to keep it.

And he'd left anyway.

"I'm sorry, God," she whispered into her wet palms. "I'm sorry. I know I deserve this. But I wish he'd come back. Please make him come back."

She stood there, whispering the same prayer over and over again. When she looked up, she saw the room was a lot dimmer as the sun set outside.

And Roger was still gone.

Mary wiped her hands on her jeans. Crying wasn't going to change a thing. And Celia needed her.

Swallowing back a final sob, Mary went to her closet and pulled out a suitcase.

- FIFTY-FOUR -

MARY, I'VE FOUND A RED-EYE FLIGHT that'll be leaving at eleven," Celia's voice sounded somewhat choked, as if she were still crying. "Going to the airport now, you'll have to wait a long time."

"That's all right," Mary said. For once she was grateful that rush hour was running late and traffic on the interstate was so slow. It would give her time to think – and make some decisions.

Her cell phone beeped, indicating an incoming call. She saw it was Roger again, as it had been the last two times. And again she chose to ignore it.

"Mary, you're not telling me something," Celia said. "Are you sure Roger had no problem with this?"

The white Acura in front of Mary rolled forward a few feet, and she did likewise. "I told you, don't worry about it. It's fine."

"Then why do you sound as if you have a cold?" Celia asked.

Mary swallowed. She wondered what part of the body held the deep spring from which all the tears she was shedding came – she'd thought there was no more liquid inside her given how much she'd cried lately.

"That's what I thought," Celia said with a sigh. "Mary, you didn't need to get in a fight over this."

"I didn't plan to," Mary said, feeling her chest hurt at the memory of Roger's face before he left the bedroom, "but it all went out of control. I couldn't tell him, Celia. And now I don't know if he even loves me anymore."

"He loves you."

"You didn't see the look on his face," Mary said, wiping her eyes with the back of her hand. A green highway sign informed her that the airport was 15 miles away.

"Mary, come on, you guys have a good thing going," Celia said. "Maybe, later . . . maybe you *should* sit down and tell him about this."

"I tried, Celia!" Mary said. "I tried and I couldn't get the words out. I think my leaving's a good thing at the moment – it'll give us both time to – to think about things."

She heard Celia's deep sigh. "Look, I'm not going to lie – I'm glad you're gonna be with me in Alabama. Something about this feels so funny to me."

"Did she ever tell you who she was seeing in Alabama?" Mary asked.

"No," Celia said. "I hope I find out when I get there. I want to know if they said or did something to upset Mom. Maybe she'd had a fight with this dude before she started driving."

"What do the police say? Did they call you back?" Mary asked. The traffic ahead was still creeping along and she got a glimpse of flashing lights on the side of the road. There had been an accident – no wonder it was taking so long.

"Not yet," Celia said. "Listen, I need to start getting ready for my own flight. Go to the United counter, I got you a first-class ticket."

"What? Celia, you didn't have to –"

"Don't argue," Celia said. "It's the least I can do for you for dropping everything and meeting me in Alabama. It means a lot to me."

"It's okay," Mary said. "You're my friend."

A few minutes after the phone call ended traffic had moved along enough for Mary to see the accident that was slowing down traffic. A dark green Ford Windstar sat on the edge of the median, a large dent marring its sliding door. A few feet down the road, a silver Taurus pointed in the wrong direction, a headlight smashed, the hood sticking up and blocking view of the windshield. Broken glass sparkled in the glare of headlights.

Mary saw an ambulance, fire truck, and several police cars, their rotating lights giving the scene a sense of unreality. Several people stood about but only one stood out in Mary's mind; a girl, looking perhaps nine or ten, blond hair a tangle down her back, her eyes large and unblinking as she clutched a blanket to her chest and stared at the van.

I'm that little girl, Mary thought as she finally was able to speed up. I'm watching an accident and I'm too stunned to do anything about it.

She was a mile from the airport exit when her phone rang again. She saw it was Roger. Mary gripped the steering wheel as her cell rang two, three times. Then before she could think about it she grabbed the phone and hit the talk button. "Roger?"

"Mare! Where are you?"

He didn't sound angry – he sounded frantic. Guilt caused her face to flood with warmth. "I – Roger, I'm almost at the airport, Celia has a ticket waiting for me."

"You're okay though, right? You have enough cash on you?" She could tell from his voice he was pacing and an image of him rose to her mind; Roger, in shirtsleeves with the top button of his dress shirt unbuttoned, going back and forth in their bedroom while he ran a nervous hand through his hair.

"I didn't take any cash, didn't think you'd like that," she stammered. "I have about twenty-five dollars in my wallet."

"That's not enough. Find an ATM at the airport and pull $200."

She was confused. "Roger, they'll charge a fee."

"That's all right," he said. "Look, Mare…"

He fell silent. She took the exit for the airport and slowed down so she could keep an eye out for the signs that would direct her to the correct parking area and still talk on the phone. "Roger, I know you must hate me right now. I'm so sorry –"

"I don't hate you," he said. "I'm not saying I'm happy – to be honest, Mary, I'm furious. But I talked to Joanne tonight, and she told me that there's something you're scared to tell me."

Mary felt her heart start to pound. "What – what did she tell you? She promised she wouldn't say anything!"

"She didn't tell me what it was – believe me, I just about got on my knees and begged her to," Roger said, a touch of anger finally showing in his voice. "But she told me you were afraid – afraid I'd stop loving you, that I'd look down on you."

Mary bit her lip. "That's true. And I saw it tonight. I saw –"

"You saw me hit with a tremendous shock," Roger said. "Mary, how did you expect me to react? You've been acting so strangely! I even thought at one point –"

"Just a minute," Mary said. "I have to put down the phone."

She saw the parking garage coming up and she was afraid of losing the call. She also needed to take a moment. Before Roger finished that statement. She wasn't sure she wanted him to.

A few minutes later she pulled into a parking space between a Ford Tahoe and a blue four door sedan. Taking a deep breath, she picked up the phone again. "Okay, I'm parked."

"Okay," Roger said.

The silence stretched between them, becoming almost a tangible thing she could touch. "I – I probably should go check in."

"Okay," Roger said. "But I have to say something."

She closed her eyes and braced herself for the blow she was sure was coming. "Okay."

"I'm mad, Mary," he said. "I'm mad and hurt and I don't know what's going on. But I want to. I want you to come back when you can and talk to me. Because no matter how mad and hurt I am, I think I still love you. I want us to try and survive this."

The tears spilled out of her closed eyes. "I love you too," she whispered. "And I'm so sorry. You might not feel the same way when you know the truth."

"I think I'm willing to risk it," he said. "Pray about us, Mary. I'll be praying too."

"I will," she promised.

"I love you. Call me when you land, no matter what time it is."

"Love you," she whispered.

The phone dropped into her lap as she tasted her tears.

- FIFTY-FIVE -

JACK SLAMMED HIS HAND DOWN on his alarm clock and rolled out of bed with a groan. It had been a bad night, and not just because of Wheeler's deadline.

He'd dreamed about Lisa. It had started out as a replay of one of the good times — a picnic in the park, just the two of them. She'd made meatloaf sandwiches and oatmeal cookies and brought a thermos of sweet tea to drink.

They'd spread out an old tattered blanket that stayed in the trunk for times like this. They'd kicked off their shoes and taken their time eating, watching some boys toss a Frisbee around and a man and woman who looked on at their young child tottering about the grass, expressions of wonder on their face.

That was when the dream took a dark turn. Lisa had walked over to the toddler, her shoulders tense. Jack had tried to call her back to the blanket, but he couldn't get his voice above a whisper. He tried to stand, but his legs seemed heavy.

He watched as Lisa bent down to the child. The little girl looked up at Lisa, golden curls spilling down her back. The blue eyes stared unblinking at identical blue eyes.

Then Lisa fell onto the grass and the child ran away, laughter trailing behind. Her parents had vanished, along with everyone else in the park. It was just Jack and Lisa.

He suddenly could move. He ran towards her, calling her name. Dropping in his knees in the wet grass, he started to turn her over and then realized he was kneeling in blood.

Lisa rolled onto her back. He looked at her –

And that was when he woke up, screaming into the fists he tried to cram into his mouth. He'd sat there in the dark room, shaking and crying, sweat pouring off him even though the air conditioning was cranked high.

That had been four hours ago. Jack had managed to doze now and then, but for the most part he'd stared at the black ceiling above him, cursing Wheeler for bringing up Lisa. That was why he had the dream, he told himself. Because Wheeler brought up a bad memory.

Certainly not because Wheeler might be right.

Jack splashed cold water on his face. He decided he needed coffee before he took a shower. He headed to his tiny kitchen and pulled out the cheap instant he always bought. A glance in his cupboard revealed a half-filled box of Pop-tarts, which meant he could have breakfast too.

While he waited for his water to heat in the microwave he munched a strawberry-filled pastry and considered his options. He needed to nail down Mary Beamer. She gave his story the weight it needed. Without her, Wheeler would probably just toss it all out, along with Jack.

He smirked at the last piece of Pop-tart in his hand. He was very accustomed to eating; unemployment was not something he needed right now.

He looked at the microwave clock as he removed his cup of hot water. She was probably up, getting her kid ready for school. Maybe he'd give her a call, remind her that he needed her to stand up and work with him. Maybe lay on a little bit of guilt.

He sipped his coffee and grimaced. Tight budget or not, next time he went to the store he was getting some decent coffee. He went to the cluttered desk that sat in the corner of his bedroom and grabbed his cell phone. While his computer booted up, he looked up Mary's cell phone number and began dialing.

The call went straight to voicemail. Foster frowned, then dialed again. Same thing.

Maybe she was cooking or something and the phone was in another room. Maybe she was driving the kid to school and didn't want to talk to him where little ears could hear.

Or maybe she didn't want to talk to him.

Foster did a quick search on the internet and got her home number. She wouldn't be happy he was contacting her this way, but he didn't really care. He needed to get her to help him on this story, and if that meant he had to rattle her a little, so be it.

The phone rang three times and then a harried male voice answered. "Hello?"

Ah, the hubby. "May I speak to Mary Beamer?"

"She's not here."

Foster leaned back in his rickety medal folding chair and considered what he was hearing. Whoever this was talking to him, he was obviously in a bad mood. And Mary not home at this hour, when most good little housewives would be serving breakfast to their family? Something was up. Question was, was it something Jack could use?

"Do you know when she'll be home?" he asked, keeping his voice cordial.

"I'm afraid not," the man said. His voice got fainter for a moment. "Kelly, finish your cereal please." Now the voice was back to a normal level. "I'm sorry, can I take a message?"

"Is this Roger Beamer?"

A short silence. "Yes. Who is this?"

"My name is Jack Foster. I'm a newspaper reporter in Atlanta, Georgia."

A longer silence. Jack grabbed a pen off his desk and began tapping it against his leg.

"What do you want? How did you get this number? Do you know Mary?"

"We've met," Foster said. "She didn't mention it?" He knew good and well she hadn't, but wanted Roger to think he was surprised.

"Why did you meet?" Beamer's voice had an edge to it. "Are you planning to see her in Alabama?"

"Alabama? Why, no," Jack said. "We spoke this past weekend in Jacksonville. She didn't tell you?"

He could hear Beamer's harsh breathing on the phone, and felt a twinge of guilt. Whatever was going on, it was apparently wearing on this guy and here Jack was, twisting the knife.

"Why?" Beamer asked.

"Well, it's probably not something to talk about over the phone," Jack said. "And I'm sure you understand that I need to respect your wife's privacy. If she hasn't been open with you..."

He focused on the tune he was beating out on his ankle with his pen and let the silence stretch some more. What, if anything, had Mary told her husband? And how could Jack use this to his advantage?

"Something is wrong," Roger said. "You know what it is, don't you?"

"I can't tell you that," Jack said. "Sorry, wish I could."

"Can you at least tell me if she's in trouble?" A rustle, and then Beamer's voice fainter again. "Okay, sweetheart. Go wash your hands and we'll go."

"Tell you what," Jack said. "You tell me what your wife's doing in Alabama and maybe I can answer your question."

"She's meeting a friend of hers there. The friend's mom got killed in a traffic accident in Montgomery." The words spilled out in a rush, as if Mary's husband was afraid he'd change his mind. "Now tell me something!"

"All right," Jack said. "The answer to whether or not your wife's in trouble depends on you – and how much you and your God are willing to forgive. That help any?"

A pause, and then anger filled Beamer's voice. "Not much at all."

"Sorry about that," Jack said, hanging up the phone.

He tossed the pen back on his desk. Montgomery…something about that city tickled the back of his brain. Mary Beamer went there to help out a friend whose mom had died there.

It sounded awfully convenient to Jack. From what the husband said things were getting a little uncomfortable on the home front. Had she decided to run? He didn't know her well enough to guess at what she'd do.

There was, of course, one way to find out.

Jack searched online for a Montgomery newspaper. He figured he'd have to check back over a couple of days, since Beamer hadn't told him when the accident had occurred.

There were several traffic accidents reported in the Montgomery area. But Jack knew he'd found the one concerning Mary when he read "Francine Winters, from Atlanta, Georgia…"

Jack went to the bathroom to take a shower. He needed to think it all through – perhaps a drive over to Montgomery was in order. He started the shower and glanced at his reflection while he waited for the water to heat up.

The hard look on his face surprised him. While he gazed at himself he saw a flush fill his cheeks as he thought about the way he'd treated Roger Beamer, simply because Jack thought he could use him to get his story.

He shook his head and stripped, getting into the shower. He was doing his job, that was all. The fact it sometimes involved him doing and saying things he wasn't proud of was part of the price for being successful.

With an effort, he pushed his shame in the back of his mind, along with his memories of Lisa. He had a story to chase. No matter what.

- FIFTY-SIX -

Mary rubbed her eyes as she sat up in bed. There were voices outside the bedroom door. Celia was talking to someone.

Curious, Mary pulled on her blue cotton robe and peeked into the den/dining area of the two bedroom suite Celia had reserved for them. Celia, dressed in a sleeveless white blouse and a pair of lemon yellow walking shorts, was signing something while a hotel employee stood next to the glass dining room table where a light breakfast was laid out.

The room was as beautiful as Mary remembered it when she stumbled in late last night, physically and emotionally spent. The carpet was a grade or two up from the commercial stuff she saw at the motels during those rare occasions she and Roger stayed at them. A huge cherry wood cabinet hid a television to the left, and the couch across from it was blue striped and plush.

Celia turned to look at Mary as the hotel waiter left the room. "Morning, Mary."

Mary saw her friend's eyes were ringed with dark shadows and her pale unmade up face showed traces of tears. Mary hurried over and enveloped her friend in a hug. "You should have woke me up when you got in!" she protested.

"No, I've already disrupted your life," Celia said, resting her head on Mary's shoulder. "I figured you needed the rest."

Mary pulled back and gave her friend a critical look. "I'm not the only one."

Celia shrugged. "Believe me, I tried." She sighed. "I just couldn't turn off my brain."

"I understand," Mary said. "I'll do whatever you need me to do. I'm here for you."

A smile tugged at Celia's lips as she picked up a silver coffeepot. "I appreciate that. Coffee?"

"Please," Mary looked over the spread at the table. A basket of breads and pastries was flanked by two bowls of fruit salad. Various small jars held jellies and honey. Two plates were stacked next to a pair of napkins that were rolled around silverware.

Celia handed Mary a china cup filled with a heavenly smelling liquid. Mary took a deep breath, feeling brain cells perk up at the aroma. "Wow, this is how the other half lives? I've been missing out."

Celia slid into one of the chairs and reached over for a plate. "I guess that's one way to see it."

Mary felt chastened. "I'm sorry, Celia, I didn't mean to offend you."

"No, don't worry," Celia waved a hand at her friend while she considered the basket of baked goods in front of her. "I'm touchy. I know it."

Mary sat down and picked up one of the fruit bowls. Strawberries, banana chunks, and grapes lay beneath a sprinkling of cocoanut. She picked up one of the dark green napkin rolls and handed it to Celia before pulling out her own silverware.

"Do you mind…if I give thanks?" she asked Celia quietly.

Celia had plucked a banana muffin out of the basket and was slicing it open as Mary asked her question. She shrugged and tried to smile, though she couldn't hold it. "At this point, I need all the help I can get. If you think God can do something, pray away."

Mary nodded and bowed her head, trying to think of the words that would reflect what was in her heart. "God, thank you for this food and your blessings. Please help Celia during this terrible time in her life. Help me to be a good friend to her. Be with Roger and Kelly today. In Jesus' name, amen."

"Amen," Celia echoed. She spread butter on her muffin. "How long did you tell Roger you'd be here?"

"I didn't," Mary said with a sigh. She speared a plump grape with her fork. "We never got to that point."

For a few minutes both women concentrated on their coffee and food. Then Celia put down her cup and stared at Mary. "If Richard called your husband and told him I was freaking out and he was afraid if you didn't meet me in Montgomery I'd just go insane would it help?"

Mary blinked. "But that's not true."

Celia shrugged. "Roger wouldn't know that."

With a sigh, Mary refilled her coffee cup. At her friend's nod, she added some to Celia's cup as well. "I'm tempted…but I don't think it'll help. This is bigger than just my coming to Montgomery."

"Yeah," Celia said. She bowed her head for a moment. Mary heard a telltale sniffle and shifted over so she could draw the woman in a hug.

"I'm so sorry," Mary whispered. "You don't need to worry about me. Just get through this."

"I was such a terrible daughter," Celia sobbed. "I said some awful things to her the last time we talked."

"No," Mary soothed. "I know you think you were a bad daughter, but you loved your mom. I never doubted that. I'm sure she didn't doubt it either."

Celia shook her head, wiping tears on Mary's robe. "I asked her about the baby ten years ago. She said she didn't remember. And I – I told her she was self-centered." Sobbing loudly, she wailed, "If I'd known it was the last time we'd talk –"

"Shh," Mary said, rubbing Celia's back. "You couldn't know. And you can't keep blaming yourself for the past. You can't change it. Forgive yourself and move on."

Celia choked out a half-sob, half-chuckle as she lifted her head to look at her friend. "Look who's talking."

Mary felt as if she'd been punched. She heard the words she'd said echo in her mind: *You can't keep blaming yourself for the past. You can't change it. Forgive yourself and move on.*

Did she really believe that? Or was she just mouthing empty words to sooth a sad friend?

If Celia noticed that her comment had rocked Mary, she hid it. Wiping her face with her napkin, the grieving woman spoke in a voice that still trembled. "We should get ready to go. I need to i-identify the body. And pick up her things at whereever she was staying." Celia shuddered.

Mary nodded, struggling to keep her whirling thoughts from showing on her face. "Yes, that makes sense." She stood quickly. "I'm just going to take a shower, and I'll be ready to go in about 15 minutes. Okay?"

Celia nodded without looking up. "That's fine." A deep breath, and Celia looked up at Mary. "Thanks again. I'm glad I can lean on you right now."

Mary squeezed Celia's shoulder before heading to the bathroom. She came out a few minutes later, her hair wrapped in a thick white towel. Celia was no longer in the living area, and Mary suspected her friend was taking a few moments to steel herself for the difficult day ahead.

She saw her phone flashing when she came into her room. Picking it up off the nightstand, Mary saw she had a voicemail from Roger.

She hesitated before listening to it. She'd called him late last night when the plane landed in Montgomery. The call woke him up, which added to Mary's already towering sense of guilt. They'd had a brief but courteous conversation, and Roger asked her to call him when she had a clearer idea of her plans.

Mary chewed her bottom lip and then set the phone back on the nightstand. It wasn't an emergency; Roger would have tried calling several times if it was. That meant the message could wait. As she pulled out a pair of jeans and a pink t-shirt, Mary thought that was best for the moment. She needed to concentrate on Celia at the moment.

Roger – and whatever he wanted to say to her – could wait.

- FIFTY-SEVEN -

MARY SQUINTED BEHIND HER SUNGLASSES as she looked down the row of cars. "I think there's a parking spot at the end here," she told Celia.

Celia nodded without speaking. Mary glanced over at her friend and noticed that she'd already chewed the lipstick off her bottom lip. Her hands shook slightly as she turned into the space Mary had seen. After putting the car in park, Celia sat still for a moment, looking out the windshield.

Mary put a hand on her friend's arm. "What can I do to help?" she asked softly.

Celia's knuckles whitened on the steering wheel. Mary watched as her friend swallowed, but said nothing.

Not knowing what else to do to ease her friend's pain, Mary bowed her head and silently prayed. She couldn't imagine what Celia was feeling now. As awful as the past couple of weeks had been for Mary, she knew it was nothing compared to her friend's emotional turmoil.

Finally, Celia turned the car off. "I guess – I guess we'd better get this over with," she said in a choked whisper.

Mary nodded. She slid out of the car and took quick steps to walk next to her friend towards the building the operator at the Montgomery police station had directed them to. The large brick building contained the city's morgue. And the morgue . . .

Mary gulped as her stomach rocked a little at the thought of the morgue. She'd seen dead bodies at funerals but they always had an unreal quality to them. It was easy to see them as an empty shell, albeit a cleaned-up one.

She had no idea what Francine would look like.

Looking over at Celia's pale features, Mary suspected that her friend's thoughts were traveling in a similar direction. She reached over and grabbed Celia's hand, squeezing it. Celia's fingers gripped back, and together they mounted the stone steps that led into the building.

Mary and Celia produced their ID's to a uniformed officer sitting at a metal desk. After passing through a metal detector, they were met by a petite woman with thick black hair cascading down her shoulders who introduced herself as Officer Gomez.

"Please follow me," she said, her words laced with a Spanish accent. Mary felt Celia grab her hand again as they walked down a cold hallway lit with fluorescents.

They finally came to a wall with a large window that was covered in white vertical blinds. Officer Gomez paused a moment as she lifted a receiver off the wall. "Are you ready Mrs. Morris?"

Mary glanced at her friend. Celia's eyes were filled with tears, and she pulled her hand out of Mary's to grip her friend's arm, her nails biting into the flesh. "Yes," she whispered.

Gomez nodded and spoke into the phone. The blinds were pulled to the side. A young man with Asian features stood in front of a table. The body on the metal surface was covered in a white sheet.

Mary swallowed. She could feel breakfast crawling up her throat and she forced herself to breathe through her nose. Celia needed her to be strong right now.

At a nod from Officer Gomez, the young man reached over and lifted the sheet.

"God," Mary breathed. It was nothing less than a prayer. Beside her, she felt Celia start to shake.

When she saw Francine Winters in her mind, Mary always saw a woman who took pride in her appearance, her makeup done to perfection, her hair styled in a way that suited her face. Even living with her and Celia that summer Mary could not recall seeing the woman not looking beautiful.

There was nothing beautiful about what she saw now. The blond hair was matted with blood – what was left of it, anyway. The right side of Francine's face was scorched, her eye looking out from the blackened skin. The left side was nearly intact, that eye mercifully closed.

"Mrs. Morris?" Gomez was looking at Celia with some concern. Mary pulled her gaze from the body on the table to examine her friend.

Celia was as white as the blouse she wore. Her eyes appeared to fill her face, tears streaming unnoticed down her cheeks. "It – it's my m-mother . . . oh, I have to . . . I have to…"

"Bathroom that way," Gomez said, pointing to a door across the hall. Celia turned and stumbled to it, Mary on her heels.

Mary swallowed her own nausea as Celia collapsed into one of the stalls. She pulled her friend's hair off her face and breathed through her mouth as Celia retched.

Officer Gomez came in after a couple of minutes and dampened a paper towel, handing it to Mary. With a murmur of thanks Mary began to wipe Celia's damp forehead.

After a bit Celia leaned back against the side of the stall. She looked up at Mary and the officer. "That…" she gulped. "That's my mom. That's her."

Gomez crouched next to Celia. "I'm sorry for your loss, ma'am. When you feel up to it, there's some paperwork for you to fill out, and we have some of your mother's belongings."

Celia nodded. "Okay. Just . . . I need a few minutes, okay?"

"Of course," the officer said. Mary heard the woman's knees pop as she straightened up. "I'll just wait outside."

"Mary?" Celia asked as the woman walked out. "Could you please flush the toilet? I'm going to throw up again if I keep smelling that."

Mary nodded and reaching past her friend, hit the lever. "You want me to get you a soda?"

"Not yet," Celia said over the sound of flushing water. She took the paper towel from Mary and wiped her face. "I can't believe it. It doesn't seem real."

"I know," Mary said, sliding down to sit across from her friend. The space was cramped, and Mary hugged her knees to her chest. "I'm really sorry, Celia."

"Thanks," Celia said, sniffling. "I guess . . . I guess I have to decide what to do now? Like where she should be b-buried?"

Mary sighed and reached out to rub her friend's knee. "One thing at a time. Officer Gomez probably can help us with things like that."

Celia nodded. She pushed herself to her feet, walked to one of the sinks and splashed cool water on her face. "I'm glad you're here, Mary. Richard wanted to come, but . . . "

"No worries," Mary said, squeezing her friend's shoulder. "Let's get this taken care of. When can you call him?"

Celia looked at her watch. "Not for another couple of hours." She glanced at Mary. "What about Roger?"

Mary remembered the voicemail. "He tried to call earlier and left a message. I'll check it later."

As she took in her friend's pallor and swollen eyes, Mary decided she needed to take charge. "Come on. Maybe her stuff will tell us where she was staying. We can get this started."

Celia nodded and let Mary lead her out of the restroom. As they headed towards Gomez, Mary was relieved to see that the blinds were once again over the window. She prayed she would never have to look through such a window again.

- FIFTY-EIGHT -

SINCE CELIA'S NAME WAS THE ONLY ONE on the car rental agreement, Mary couldn't help out with the driving. She apologized several times on the trip from the morgue to the Hilton.

"It's not your fault!" Celia said, fatigue making her sound snappish. "Let's just get her stuff and go back to the hotel. I need some down time."

"Sure," Mary nodded. She turned to look out the window so that Celia didn't have to talk to her if she didn't want to. This was Mary's first time in Montgomery, and she was somewhat curious about the city.

They pulled up to the Hilton that was on the partially burned stationary that was in Celia's mother's purse. Something had been written on it, but it was impossible to decipher given that most of the writing had charred off.

Mary stretched as she got out of the car. It was warm, but it didn't feel as heavy here as Jacksonville did sometimes. She tilted her face to the sun, eyes closed, feeling as if she'd been awake all day and half the night instead of a few hours.

She remembered Joanne saying once that intense emotions were just as fatiguing as physical labor. At this moment, Mary believed it. A cold soda and a soft bed sounded very attractive about now.

"Hey."

Mary opened her eyes to see Celia standing in front of her, frowning. "You okay, Mary?"

Straightening up, Mary cocked an eyebrow at her friend. "Shouldn't I be asking *you* that question?"

Tears filled Celia's bloodshot eyes again. "Poor Mary. So many troubles of her own and I have to come and add to the load."

"Stop," Mary said, feeling guilty that Celia was crying about her. "You haven't done anything wrong. If anyone dragged anyone into their troubles I'm the one who pulled you into mine. I'm glad to pay back."

Celia shook her head and wiped her eyes. "You sure you don't drink? Because after this I think we could both use stiff ones. Or maybe fruity ones."

"That probably won't do either of us much good," Mary said, hoping her smile softened the words. "Let's get this done and then I think you've earned a break, okay?"

"Right," Celia said, taking a deep breath. "Okay. Let's get this over with."

Both women entered the large decorated lobby of the Hilton. Mary's eyes darted around, amazed at how upscale everything looked. "Celia, could your mom afford a place like this?"

Her friend frowned. "On her salary? No. She mentioned she was seeing someone here, maybe he was paying for it."

"She was seeing a man here?" Mary was shocked.

Celia ran a hand through her hair. "Mary, not everyone's a Bible thumper. My mom definitely wasn't." She headed towards the dark paneled registration desk without another word.

Mary shook her head, angry at herself for being surprised. Of course Francine Winters could legally do whatever she wanted in that regard, and if she didn't hold to the Biblical view of marriage and sex it would be in character for her to be here with someone.

Sometimes I'm so naïve I wonder if I should be let out of the house, Mary thought to herself with a sigh as she followed Celia to the counter.

Celia was trying to explain the situation to the clerk who was frowning and shaking her head. "Ma'am, I'm sorry, but I can't give out that information."

"But she's my mother!" Celia snapped.

"I understand that, ma'am, but without any evidence that your story is true, my hands are tied."

Before Celia could scream at the tanned woman, Mary put a hand on her friend's arm. "Call Officer Gomez with the Montgomery police department," she said. "I'm sure she'll be happy to verify our story."

The woman frowned at Mary but reached for a phone. While she made the call Mary kept an arm around her shaking friend and watched as the clerk's long red fingernail tapped the cream-colored countertop.

"Thanks, Mary," Celia whispered.

"No problem," Mary whispered back. "You want to sit down a minute?"

Celia shook her head but didn't move away from Mary's comforting arm. Finally the well-dressed woman hung up the phone. "The police have verified what you've said. If you could provide some form of identification I'll look up the information."

Celia dug out her driver's license while Mary looked around the lobby. She wasn't sure what she was looking for — did she really expect to see Francine walking in after seeing her in the morgue?

"Thank you, Mrs. Morris," the young woman said, moving to a computer keyboard.

Something about the woman's attitude irritated Mary. "Excuse me, what's your name?"

The woman frowned. "Carmen."

"Well, Carmen," Mary said, taking a deep breath. "If you talked to Officer Gomez you know my friend's mother died in a car accident. You may or may not know she just had to identify her mother's body at the morgue."

She felt Celia wince next to her. Carmen's olive completion seemed to pale a little. Mary felt a stab of satisfaction and continued.

"I understand you're doing your job. But perhaps it wouldn't be too much to ask you to show a *little* compassion to my friend here."

Now the woman's cheeks reddened. "Of course, if your mother was a guest here, we are sorry for your loss, Mrs. Morris," the woman murmured with a shade more emotion in her voice than Mary had heard previously.

"Thank you," Celia murmured. "Just, please, I need to finish this."

"Of course," Carmen typed on her keyboard some more, then nodded. "Here she is. Francine Winters, room 2205."

Celia pulled a credit card from her wallet. "Let me go ahead and take care of any outstanding charges she has on her room . . . "

The clerk shook her head. "That's not necessary, Mrs. Morris."

Mary felt a little better about the cool woman behind the counter. "That's very gracious of you."

Carmen shook her head. "It's not the hotel you should thank. Dr. Green has been covering all Ms. Winters' expenses here."

Mary felt herself freeze. *Dr. Green . . . ?* "Dr. – Dr. Thomas Green?" she stammered.

"Yes, it's all here," Carmen said. "Dr. Green made it clear that we charge anything Ms. Winters spent to his account." She pulled a drawer open and pulled out a ring that held keys and a white keycard. "I'll escort you to your mother's room, now, Mrs. Morris."

"Just a minute," Celia said. Mary felt her friend's arm go around her. "Mary? Come on, girl, breathe."

Wasn't she breathing? Mary realized from the tingling in her face that maybe she wasn't. She dragged in a breath, then another. "Celia . . . Dr. Green . . . "

"I know," Celia said. "Mary, I need you to focus. I need your help here. Please."

Mary nodded as she took another breath. "Okay, right. I'm okay."

"I know you're not," Celia said. "But please, keep it together a few more minutes."

"Right," Mary said. She shook her head to clear it and straightened up. "I'm good. Let's go."

She knew Celia was right. Mary was far from good. But she had to lay it aside for now. Celia needed her.

Later, she'd try to figure out what it all meant.

- FIFTY-NINE -

S HARON TOOK A FINAL BITE of her chicken Caesar salad as she scanned the financial reports on her desk. She smiled. Thomas would like this.

The report that a trusted accountant had put together for her covered both the cash flow of the clinic and the monies taken in from its hidden source. Together they painted a picture of positive income that was better than it even had been in Atlanta.

Sharon tapped her chin thoughtfully. Perhaps it was time again to give raises to those who'd been sticking with her and Thomas all this time. The income would cover it, certainly.

She sat back, her smile growing. Perhaps it would be a wonderful opportunity to get a raise for herself. Maybe now that things appeared to be settling down she could consider a vacation. Sharon was reading a book written by a woman who had bought a summer house in Italy; the thought of traveling through that country and enjoying wine and cheese at some small café was a pleasant one.

Her phone buzzed. She leaned forward, punching the flashing button. "Sharon Abrams."

It was Nadine, who was working the front desk today. "Ms. Abrams, I'm sorry to bother you, but I have a Celia Morris on the line. She claims to be Ms. Winters' daughter."

Sharon felt her smile slip. Wine and cheese under an Italian sun vanished from her mind at the news. "What does she want?" she asked, keeping her voice calm and professional.

"Well, she's asking to talk to Dr. Green," Nadine said. "I've explained he's busy and she could leave a message but she said she's willing to come down to the clinic and wait."

"She's here in town?" Sharon asked. A twinge of unease went through her. She folded her lips and willed it away.

"Apparently," Nadine said. "She sounds rather upset, Ms. Abrams, and…and I know Dr. Green was seeing her mother and that she –"

"You didn't mention that to the daughter, did you?" Sharon asked, her voice sharp.

"No – no, of course not! I have her on hold, I don't know what to tell her…"

Sharon took a deep breath. It was time to be calm. She could deal with this. "Tell her someone will speak to her in a moment. Then put her back on hold."

"All right," Nadine said. "She's on line three."

"Thank you," Sharon said, though the words were merely reflex. She wasn't thankful for this phone call. Not at all.

She pulled open a drawer and grabbed one of the many memo pads drug representatives left at the clinic. This particular one was white with a band of blue across the top and the name of a birth control pill. Sharon took a few minutes to scrawl some quick notes to herself. It helped her to calm down and get her thoughts in order.

After a sip of her sweet iced tea, Sharon took a final deep breath and picked up the phone, pushing the blinking button next to the number 3. "Ms. Morris? This is Sharon Abrams, how may I help you?"

There was a brief silence, then a hesitant voice. "I thought I would be speaking to Dr. Green."

"Dr. Green is with a patient at the moment," Sharon said, keeping her voice brisk and businesslike. "I'm his office manager, perhaps I could be of some assistance?"

"Well…" she heard the woman speak to someone else. A female voice answered, and Sharon strained to catch any words.

"Ms. Abrams, I have a couple of reasons to speak to Dr. Green. One is personal, and…well, a friend of mine has some questions she needs to ask him."

"Am I correct in assuming the personal reason has to do with your mother?" Francine asked. "We were saddened to hear of her accident here."

"Yes…thank you…" the woman's voice caught.

Sharon's mind was racing, trying to figure out the best way to keep this woman off balance. What did she want? Could she be pacified without seeing Thomas?

"Ms. Abrams," Ms. Morris' voice was shaking. "I'm sorry, but you can understand I'm rather upset right now…apparently Dr. Green was paying for my mother's stay here, and she'd said some things to me that made me wonder…if perhaps…"

"I understand," Sharon said. "And yes, this is a matter for Dr. Green, certainly. If you will give me a number he can reach you at, I'll be sure to have him call you back."

"My friend and I can come and wait at the clinic," Ms. Morris said. "I'd really like to speak with him today, if possible."

"Well, we're quite busy today, and I'm not sure how long you'd have to wait," Sharon said, fighting to keep her voice from sharpening. She had to find a way to put this woman off, at least until she could speak to Thomas. "You said your friend had some questions? I'd be happy to answer them right now if you like."

"Well…" Ms. Morris hesitated, and again there was a barely audible conversation. Sharon gulped down more of her tea, grimacing as she felt an ache begin at the base of her neck and wind up to the back of her head.

Then a new voice was on the phone. "Ms. Abrams?"

Sharon shook her head to clear it. "Yes. Who am I speaking with?"

"My name is Mary Hollister Beamer."

For a moment, panic set Sharon's heart pounding. *Her! What was* she *doing in Montgomery? With Francine Winters' daughter no less!*

"Hello?"

Sharon realized she'd been silently gripping the phone, looking at the black and white photo of the Montgomery skyline across the room. *Get a grip!* she told herself angrily. Another swallow of tea, and when she spoke her voice was calm.

"I'm sorry. Someone here was trying to get my attention. How might I help you, Ms. Beamer?"

"Well…"

If Celia Morris had been hesitant, Mary Beamer was more so. She sounded as if she were ready to hang up the phone and bolt – something Sharon wished she'd do.

Instead, she kept talking. "Were you with Dr. Green in Georgia ten years ago?"

Sharon bit her lip to keep the profanity she was thinking come spilling out. "Yes, I was. May I ask what this is in regards to?"

"I guess you don't remember me?"

The best defense was a good offense, Sharon decided. "I'm afraid not, my dear. Dr. Green has helped many patients over the years. I'm sure you can understand how difficult it would be to remember all of them."

"I – yes, I suppose so," Ms. Beamer said in a small voice. "You – you wouldn't have any records of that time, would you?"

Sharon began to breathe easier. Maybe, just maybe, they could get through this. "Unfortunately, we lost a number of our records in a fire a few years back. I can check, but there are no guarantees. I'm sorry."

"I see," Ms. Beamer said. "Well, my friend and I will come down. Perhaps while we're waiting for Dr. Green you could check?"

"There is no reason for the two of you to come down here," Sharon protested. "If you'd just leave me a number –"

"Thank you, but we'd really just like to get this over with," Ms. Beamer replied. "Thank you, we'll talk to you soon. Goodbye."

"Now, wait –" but the woman had hung up.

Sharon swore loudly and slammed the receiver down. She didn't want those women anywhere near the clinic! It had all the earmarks of an unacceptable risk.

Grimly, she paged Thomas. They were going to have to deal with this. Quickly.

- SIXTY -

"ARE YOU SURE ABOUT THIS, MARY?" Celia asked, leaning her head on her hand.

Mary looked up from her plate. She plucked a soft breadstick from the basket between them, breaking it in two and trailing it through the salad dressing that remained on her plate. "I don't know." She sighed. "It's not exactly a place I <u>want</u> to go, you know?"

"I get that," Celia nodded. "But something feels wrong about this. You'd think Dr. Green would *want* to talk to me if he really cared about Mom."

Mary shrugged. "I don't know what to tell you." She bit her lip and decided to ask the question running in her mind. "If I wasn't here – if this wasn't Dr. Geen and the whole thing about my past – would you push as hard?"

Celia didn't answer right away, picking up her glass of iced tea. Mary sighed and bit into her breadstick, feeling horrible. Didn't Celia have enough to worry about?

"Look, Mary," Celia leaned forward. "I'm not saying that I wouldn't handle this differently if you weren't involved. But Mom was all weird on the phone the last time I talked to her – talking about an 'opportunity' and claiming she didn't remember what happened at the clinic."

"Maybe she didn't," Mary sighed.

Celia shook her head. "I didn't get that feel from her. I think she knew something, and she was trying to keep it under wraps."

Before Mary could respond to that, her cell phone rang. A glance at the display indicated it was Roger. "Just a sec," she told Celia and answered the phone.

"Mary? I've been waiting for you to call," Roger asked, speaking faster than he normally did. "Didn't you get my message?"

She felt a wave of guilt hit her. "Oh, honey, I'm sorry. I saw it, but I haven't listened to it yet. We've been running around and taking care of things."

"Oh." The word carried a ton of hurt with it, and Mary felt sick.

"Roger, I said I was sorry. Is everything all right?" she started to feel concerned. "Is Kelly all right?"

"She's fine," Roger said. "You got a call this morning – from a reporter."

Mary closed her eyes. *Oh, no.* She wet her lips. A corner of her mind noted that Celia had straightened up across from her, staring.

Somehow she found her voice. "What did he tell you?"

"He said he was talking to you," Roger's voice grew harsh. "What are you both talking about? This – this *thing* you can't share with me?"

"Roger," she struggled to keep her voice calm. "I know this looks terrible, but I didn't go to him – he came to me. He threatened to expose me if I didn't talk to him…"

Celia's eyes widened and she shook her head at Mary, mouthing the word "no." Mary realized her poor choice of words. "Roger, I'm sorry, I…"

"Exposed?" Roger's voice was trembling. "Mary, what's going on? I feel like I don't know who you are anymore! What is this about?"

She shut her eyes, bracing her head on her hand. "Roger, I – we shouldn't do this over the phone."

"Well when will we do it, then?" Roger snapped. "Are you even coming back?"

Mary jerked up, alarmed. "Of course I am! How can you think I wouldn't?"

"I don't know what you will or won't do anymore!" Roger said. She heard him taking one deep breath, then another. "But I think doing this now is a bad idea."

"Roger," Mary said, unable to keep the tremor out of her voice, "I do love you."

"I hope so," Roger said. "I love you too, Mary…but I can't think straight about you or us right now. I'll call you back tonight."

Mary wanted to ask him not to hang up. She wanted to beg him to come to Montgomery. She wanted to flee the city and all the grief and trouble that she struggled with there and run to his arms.

Instead, she whispered, "Okay."

"I have to go," he said. "Talk to you later."

"Good," she said. "Roger – I love you!"

There was no answer and Mary pulled her phone from her ear. The call had been disconnected. Mary sighed, the effort sending a shudder through her body. "I don't know if he heard me say that."

Celia reached across the table and brushed her fingers on Mary's arm. "What happened? Are Roger and Kelly okay?"

Mary blinked and snatched her napkin from her lap to blot her eyes. "They're fine. Well, fine considering that Roger doesn't know what to think." Her hands tightened on the white piece of cloth, suddenly remembering what Roger had wanted to tell her. "Foster spoke to Roger."

Celia's eyes narrowed. "That little twit did *what?*" she hissed.

Mary's sorrow was quickly morphing into anger, Celia's outrage feeding the flame. "He called the house looking for me. He didn't tell Roger anything except that I'd spoken with him."

"He shouldn't have called the house!" Celia snapped. "He's trying to push you, Mary. What's with him?"

"I'm going to find out," Mary said. She rifled through her purse until she found the card Foster had given her. It took two tries to punch the correct number into her phone. She listened to it ring, each buzz making her anger rise.

Finally, she was treated to a brief "Foster."

"What did you think you were doing?" she burst out. Celia's eyes widened from across the table and made patting motions with her hands. Mary saw a couple of people at other tables looking her way and forced herself to lower her voice. "How *dare* you call my house!"

"Now, Mrs. Beamer, let's just take a deep breath here," Jack said.

"Don't tell me what to do! I've a good mind to never speak to you again!" Mary hissed.

"That won't help anything," Jack said. "Look, I'm sorry you're upset, but I have a deadline on this story now, so I need you to help me out."

Mary pinched her nose. "Did my husband tell you I'm helping a friend out in Montgomery at the moment?"

"Yes, he did. It's Mrs. Morris, isn't it?"

Mary gasped. Celia had been watching her closely and leaned forward. "What?"

"He knows you're here too," Mary whispered. How deeply could this man get into her life? Why wouldn't he leave them alone?

Celia's eyes narrowed. "Look, tell him you'll call him back in a few minutes."

"What? Why?" Mary was confused.

"Trust me," Celia said. She began scanning the dining area.

Mary bit her lip but decided to do what her friend suggested. "I'll have to call you back in a few minutes."

"Yeah?" Jack sounded annoyed. "You wouldn't be lying to me, would you?"

"No!" Mary said. "I *will* call you back. Just wait." She stabbed the red button on her phone, ending the call.

The waiter had responded to Celia's arm waving and was at the table, asking about dessert. "No thanks," Celia said, pulling out her credit card. "Just the check, please."

Mary waited til their server had disappeared and asked her friend, "What are you thinking?"

Celia gave her friend a half-smile. "I'm thinking that Foster is a creep, but he's a creep that can be useful. Knowledge is power, and maybe he can give us some info on Dr. Green to help us deal with him."

Mary's eyes widened. "I hadn't thought of that." She fell silent as the waiter brought the check. Once he left again, she asked, "Do you think he'll want something in return?"

"I think he'll be happy to know we're going to come face-to-face with the good doctor," Celia said, standing. "And if he wants any hope of a story, helping us will only increase the odds."

Mary nodded, but still felt some doubts as she followed Celia out of the restaurant. This was still going to lead to dealing with what happened 10 years ago. And she wasn't sure her marriage would survive it.

- SIXTY-ONE -

JACK WANTED TO PACE. But that wasn't advisable in the newsroom, where everyone would notice and make comments. He settled for letting his right knee bounce while he drummed his fingers on his desk.

Something was going on. Something that would give him the path he needed into the story and let him splash it all over the front page. He was close to nailing Dr. Green to the wall.

He glanced at his watch. Mary Beamer had said she'd call back six minutes ago. He knew there was a risk she'd blow him off. But he didn't think she would. She was all tied up in this good Christian shtick. She said she'd call back, she would.

He let his thoughts travel to Lisa. He knew it was self-indulgent. But while he had to wait, what harm was there in it? Her memory helped fuel him when he got tired or discouraged.

She wouldn't approve of my methods.

He frowned at the intruding observation. Lisa hadn't been a goody-goody, but she had possessed a high moral standard. Sometimes, when he was deep in working on a story, he'd catch her looking at him with a small frown, her eyes darker than normal, unasked questions floating in them.

But she never said anything. It was something they never discussed. He suspected she didn't approve, but didn't want it to be confirmed with words. It was a small shadow in their relationship, and neither of them was willing to risk it growing.

Jack rubbed his eyes, sorrow intruding on his memories. That was something else to thank Green for – he couldn't think of Lisa without sorrow showing up sooner or later.

His cell phone rang. He glanced at the display this time – yup, Mrs. Beamer was calling back like she said. He activated his earpiece so he'd have both hands free to type. "Hello again."

There was an echoing quality to her voice. "Mr. Foster, I have you on speakerphone so that Mrs. Morris and I can speak with you."

"That's fine," Jack said, opening a new document on his computer. "So, what are we talking about?"

"Well . . . " Ms. Beamer paused, her voice uncertain.

Jack clamped his mouth shut. He'd let the silence work for him this time.

Ms. Morris' voice cut in. Not as strong as when he last spoke to her – grief would do that. "Mr. Foster, we'd like to perhaps swap some information. You might be able to help us, and perhaps we could return the favor."

"Really?" Jack was intrigued. "What do you possibly need from me?"

"Information about the clinic," Ms. Beamer said. "About Dr. Green."

"What do you want to know?" he asked. "And more important to me, why do you want to know it?"

"Dr. Green . . ." he heard Ms. Morris swallow, her voice thick, ". . . Dr. Green apparently was seeing my mother before she died."

"He's there?" Jack grinned. "So that's where he wound up!"

"We're going to go to the clinic and see him," Ms. Morris continued. "That is, if we can get past his office manager."

Jack straightened up. "That wouldn't be Sharon Abrams, would it?"

"Yes," Ms. Beamer said. "Do you know her?"

"Unfortunately," Jack said, grimacing. "She's a tough gal. She gave me all kinds of trouble when I was trying to pursue this story here in Atlanta. She lives and breathes that clinic."

"So what do you suggest?" Ms. Morris asked. "Our plan is to camp out in their waiting room until he *has* to talk to us."

Jack sighed. He looked at his watch again. "You could do that…but they'll give you a verbal runaround. Claim they don't remember you, Ms. Beamer, and that they don't have your records. I'm sure Abrams has made sure that Geen has a good story about your mother, Ms. Morris."

"Why would he need a story?" Ms. Morris sounded upset. "What are you implying?"

"Well . . ." Jack stared at the sea of white that his notes had barely penetrated. A thought had been cooking in the back of his head, ever since he'd read the newspaper story about Francine Winters' death. "Ms. Morris, no offense, you're sure your mother was killed in a car accident?"

"What?" he heard both women sputter and wasn't sure who'd spoken first. Then Mary Beamer's voice, clearly disturbed. "Are you suggesting that . . . you can't be!"

"Look, I know it sounds farfetched . . . " Jack was interrupted by Celia Morris' outraged tone.

"It's ridiculous!" she snapped. "You're implying my mother was murdered?"

"Is there going to be an autopsy?" Jack asked.

"I . . . yes, because they want to know why she lost control of her car," Ms. Morris said, her tone still filled with anger. "But that doesn't mean someone deliberately made that happen!"

Jack chose his words carefully. They wanted information from him, he needed them to get his story. No point in giving them a reason to run. "I'm sorry, I didn't mean to upset you, Ms. Morris. Part of getting the story is asking all kinds of questions, even insensitive ones."

"That question is awful!" Mary Beamer snapped. "You really think these people are capable of murder?"

"Don't you?" Jack asked. "I mean, you think abortion's murder, right? What's the difference?"

Silence. Jack typed a few more words, waiting. He chewed his lip, wondering if he could get them to wait to go to the clinic until he could get to Montgomery. Probably not.

"All right," Ms. Beamer sounded upset, but at least she hadn't hung up. "What should we look for at the clinic?"

Good question. "Keep an eye on their body language. See if the outside of the building fits the inside. Ask for a tour."

"Ugh," he heard Ms. Beamer mutter.

"Look, you asked," Foster said. "If they give you paper records, great. They'll probably be fake, but it's something."

"Why would they keep records from ten years ago?" Ms. Morris asked. "Especially if they're incriminating?"

"They might not," Jack admitted. It was something that concerned him. If the records were truly gone . . . "But they might. If nothing else, they might have decided to hang onto records to blackmail people to keep their mouth shut."

"Blackmail," Mary Beamer echoed faintly.

"If you push them enough, maybe they'll attempt that," Jack said. "You have to be prepared for it."

"I see," she said.

Jack wondered if she did. She struck him as so naïve. Hopefully Ms. Morris would be able to rise above her grief enough to help her out. "Look, you guys be careful. Let me know how it goes."

"Don't worry about us, Mr. Foster," Celia Morris said, a chill in her voice. "If we need to talk to you again, we'll be in touch."

"And please do not call my home again!" Mary Beamer snapped. "There's no need for that."

"Gotcha," Jack said, making no promises. He was still after this story.

After he hung up, he looked online to see how long it would take to drive to Montgomery. It looked like he was going to take a trip.

- SIXTY-TWO -

SHARON HAD BEEN FORCED TO WAIT until Thomas finished with a procedure. That had not set well with her. She had an emergency, it wasn't like the patient was going anywhere!

Finally he tapped on her door, his stethoscope looped around his neck. "Sharon? You said it was urgent?"

"Yes, I did," she said, not hiding her anger. "And if you'd taken me seriously we'd have talked about this already!"

Green frowned as he shut the office door behind him. "Now there's no need for you to take that tone with me. I've given you a lot of responsibility, but I'm still the boss of this clinic!"

She stood up, fighting the urge to start shouting at him. "Thomas, please sit down. We have a situation that will have to be handled delicately."

His eyes narrowed. "What sort of 'situation?'"

She sighed and leaned against the cherry wood bookcase. A small jade green dragon stared at her from the top of the shelf. "We're about to have visitors."

Thomas reached for a chair and sat down. "The police?"

"I wish!" Sharon said, rolling her eyes. "Try Francine Winters' daughter! And Mary Hollister Beamer!"

The doctor frowned. "The girl who got the note? What is she doing here?"

Irritated, Sharon pushed off from the bookcase. "Apparently she came with Francine's daughter! Now they are both headed here, determined to talk with you. I'm sure you can guess the topics of discussion!"

He paled. A sheen of sweat glistened on his forehead. "What…I'm not sure I should speak with them." He shook his head. "Just inform the front desk to tell them I can't see them. Put them off!"

"I seriously doubt that will make them leave," Sharon said, beginning to pace. "They both implied they'd camp out in the waiting room if they had to!"

"Call the police!" he snapped. "Tell them the two women are anti-abortion agitators and that they need to be removed."

"Are you out of your mind?" Sharon said, her jaw dropping. "Do you want to give either of these women an excuse to get in front of a camera? If they start talking about what happened ten years ago, get someone to pay attention…"

"All that happened ten years ago is that I helped a sick and troubled teenager who presented with an ongoing miscarriage," Green said. "That's the only story out there!"

"And if Ms. Beamer shows that note around?" Sharon countered. When Green didn't answer, she sighed and ran her hands through her hair. "I underestimated the trouble she could cause. And If Francine Winters' daughter has any questions about her mother's death…"

"She shouldn't, should she?" Green asked. "You were careful, weren't you?"

"Do you really want details, Thomas?" she asked as she sank into a chair next to him. "I thought you didn't want to know."

"I *don't* want to know," he said, rubbing his eyes under his glasses. "But apparently I need to. What did you do, Sharon?"

She studied him. Thomas could be strong when it came to dealing with the business they were in, but problems such as the ones they were discussing – no, then he had trouble coping.

Sharon remembered when that stupid reporter was nosing around, getting closer and closer to the truth. Thomas had started losing sleep, drinking more. Sharon had to step in and come up with a solution.

She'd saved them then. It had been *her* idea to hire someone to burn the clinic to the ground and then toss blame on anti-abortion agitators. The press had been happy to eat that up. Once the memory of the clinic had faded from the Atlanta consciousness, it had been a simple matter to relocate and set up shop once again.

Thomas had been horrified at what she suggested but trusted her then. Could she trust him now?

"I poisoned her," she said with a shrug. "Smeared some pesticide stuff on her car door handle. She probably lost consciousness on the road. Never felt a thing."

Green's eyes widened. "That was – Sharon, other people could have been killed!"

"It was a risk," she shrugged. "But I kept an eye on it. If there'd been a major accident I'd have gotten police and ambulances there quickly."

He stood up, bending over her, his face reddening. "It was careless and thoughtless! And poisons can be traced!"

She leaned back in her chair (and noted in the back of her mind how hard these wooden chairs were – maybe they needed some padding?), surprised at the intensity of his voice. "Thomas, it was a small risk. And it's so obviously an accident, why would they look for poison?"

He straightened up with a snarl. "You – how could you be so stupid?! I assume she lost control of the car before the 'accident?'"

She shot to her feet, forcing him to take a couple of steps back. "Don't you *dare* call me stupid! Your little business would be over if it weren't for me! You'd be rotting in a Georgia prison!"

"So would you!" he barked. "Your hands certainly aren't clean in this!"

"Because someone has to get them dirty, and you refuse to!"

They stared at each other, chests heaving, faces red, hands clenched. Sharon felt a powerful urge to punch Thomas right in his face. How dare he belittle what she'd done for the clinic? For *him?*

He broke the stare first, sagging back against her desk, her penholder shifting as he pressed against it. "Sharon, if she was driving erratically, they'll run tests to see if she'd been drinking or doing drugs," he said, his voice much lower than it had been seconds ago. "It's standard."

She shook her head slightly, trying to bring her temper under control. Her office was far enough from the waiting room there was little chance of a patient hearing their exchange but that didn't mean the staff needed to catch wind of it. "All right, they'll do an autopsy. They won't find anything conclusive. Without any other evidence – and there *isn't* any other evidence – they won't have any reason to investigate further."

Green closed his eyes. With his head bowed, he looked like someone praying, though Sharon knew good and well that wasn't what he was doing. Still looking at the floor, he shook his head. "You took a huge gamble, Sharon. With strangers, no less. There must have been another way."

There was a knock on her office door. "Not now!" she shouted, her eyes still on Thomas.

The door opened a crack and Nadine stuck her head in. "Ms. Abrams, I thought you'd want to know –"

Sharon whirled, thankful to have a target for the anger that still bubbled. "Are you deaf? I said not now! Shut that door or I swear you'll be on the street before an hour's up!"

Nadine's eyes widened in fear. She shot a look at the doctor. When he didn't acknowledge what was going on, the nurse quickly left.

Green looked at the door, then at Sharon. "Do you think she heard anything?" he asked.

She shrugged. "Maybe. But Nadine has been trustworthy throughout the process – I doubt she'll stop being so at this point."

Thomas sighed, rubbing his temples. "This is all turning out so badly. I thought we were over threats to the clinic."

"There will always be people who want to stop our work," Sharon sighed. She went to the top right drawer in her desk and pulled out a small bottle of ibuprofen. After shaking out four of the brownish tablets, she handed two to Green. "Here. I think we both have headaches."

"I certainly do," Thomas said, grimacing has he swallowed the pills. He glanced at his watch and shook his head. "This little discussion has put me behind. We'll have to finish it after hours."

"And if Celia Morris and Mary Beamer show up?" Sharon asked.

He groaned. "Just find a way to get rid of them for now. We'll come up with a plan later. I have work to do."

Sharon watched Thomas leave, her arms crossed. She had work to do as well.

As she thought about that, she suddenly thought she knew why Nadine had come to the office. Hoping she was wrong, she paged the nurse on the intercom.

Nadine came in, her shoulders slumped, her eyes not quite meeting Sharon's. "I'm sorry about before Ms. Abrams. I just thought you –"

"It's all right," Sharon said quickly. She took in the nurse's posture and decided some velvet was in order. "I'm the one who should apologize. I was upset with Dr. Green and I took it out on you. Please forgive me?"

"Of course, ma'am," Nadine said, her head bobbing up and down.

"Now," Sharon said, coming over to put a hand on the older woman's shoulder. "What is it you needed to tell me?"

"Ms. Morris and Ms. Beamer are both in the waiting room," Nadine said, her voice a whisper. "I explained that the doctor had a full schedule, but they said they'd wait for him. I thought you'd want to know."

"You were right – I did want to know," Sharon said, forcing a smile on her face. "As long as they don't bother the other patients, let them be for now. I'll let you know what to do in a bit."

"All right," Nadine said. Sharon waited until the woman left the office before going back to sit at her desk. Pulling a notepad to her, she began to sketch out some ideas on dealing with the latest threat to the clinic.

- SIXTY-THREE -

"THANKS FOR MEETING ME FOR LUNCH, PAUL," Roger said as the two men sat in a booth at Red Lobster. A basket of Cheddar Bay biscuits sat between them. The aroma would normally make Roger's mouth water.

But normally his wife wasn't off somewhere with some deep, dark secret.

Paul grabbed one of the biscuits. "No problem, Roger. I could tell over the phone something pretty urgent is going on."

Roger sighed. "Urgent? More like catastrophic."

"Really?" Paul's eyebrows shot up. "I noticed Mary wasn't at Bible study last night. And I got the impression she and Joanne had a pretty heavy heart to heart talk the other day."

Roger rubbed his face. He'd barely slept the night before. The call from the reporter that morning hadn't helped any, either.

"Did Joanne tell you what they talked about?"

"Not specifically," Paul shook his head. "Apparently Mary asked Joanne to keep this between the two of them, so Jo wasn't big on telling me exactly what was going on."

"Well I guess she told you more than she told me," Roger sighed, leaning his head in his hand.

The blond young man who was their waiter came up to the table with their Caesar salads. When he left, Paul picked up his fork and began to mix the greens. "I don't think you'd really want Joanne just spilling everything to you."

"Don't bet on it," Roger said, stabbing a crouton.

"Look at it this way," Paul said. "What if you were having a crisis and came to me? Would you want me running to Mary and telling her everything we talked about in private?"

Roger shuddered. "All right, I see your point." He turned his glass of water round and round on the coaster, watching his fingers make clear impressions on the frosty glass. "But I don't know what's going on! And I'm afraid, Paul."

He brought the glass to his lips, drinking half the lemon-flavored water in one long swallow. "I'm asking myself – is there someone else? Are they threatening to come to me and reveal themselves?"

"Whoa there, Roger," Paul raised his hands up. "Whatever this is, I'm pretty sure it's not an affair. Do you really suspect that?"

With a sigh, Roger ran a hand through his hair. "I would never have thought Mary would do something like that – but that's what all this seems to point to!"

Paul plucked another biscuit out of the basket. "Eat. No offense, but you look like you haven't slept in a week, and I bet you skipped breakfast this morning."

With a wan smile Roger said, "I thought you were a preacher, not a psychic." He took the offered biscuit and bit into it.

The two men finished their salads and talked about their kids for a few minutes. Roger allowed Paul to back him away from the frightening thoughts he was having until their entrees were placed in front of them.

"Here's what I know," he said as he sampled his baked stuffed flounder. "One, Mary has been jumpy and upset for over a week. Two, an old high school friend appears out of the blue last weekend and they spend Saturday doing who knows what. Three, she just takes off – against my wishes! – to Montgomery to help said friend in a crisis. Four, my wife apparently can talk to Joanne but not me. And five, some guy calls the house this morning claiming to be a reporter who's been talking to Mary about a story!"

Roger took a deep breath. "Now, I don't know what it all means, but affair would fit."

"Except for the fact that we both know Mary," Paul said after a sip of water, "and that she adores you and Kelly too much to do something like that."

"I thought I knew her," Roger muttered.

His friend and preacher studied him for a long moment as Roger picked at his food. Paul wiped some Alfredo sauce off his lip and spoke gently.

"Here's what I think you need to consider. Now, understand I'm talking as a preacher who's known you and Mary a few years and observes people as part of his job, okay?"

Roger nodded, forcing himself to take a bite of potato. "All right."

Paul steepled his fingers. "Taking what Joanne's told me and what you just said, I think this has something to do with Mary's past."

"What?" Roger said. "I don't know what you mean. Mary's past – well, according to her parents and her, it was pretty normal."

"When was she baptized?"

Roger chewed thoughtfully on his flounder as he thought. "She was around 14. Her folks told me they worried about it for a bit – a lot of her friends had been baptized by then."

Paul sighed and shook his head. "They didn't pressure her, did they? I mean, she made the decision to respond to the gospel because *she* wanted to, not to please her folks?"

"Yes," Roger nodded. "Her congregation made a habit of sitting any potential convert down and having them write why they wanted to be baptized. It gave them something to reflect back on if they had questions when they were older."

"Wow, that's not a bad idea," Paul said, spearing a shrimp and winding noodles around it. "So you've seen this?"

Roger smiled faintly. "She showed it to me while we were dating. Mary wanted to make sure we wouldn't pressure any kids of ours to become Christians – that we would let them make the decision when the time was right."

Paul waved and Roger turned to see an older couple that attended their congregation being seated across the room. Roger added his wave and smile as the couple called out "Hello!" He hoped they wouldn't come to the table. He didn't want this spread.

"The reason I ask," Paul said, bringing Roger's attention back to the conversation, "is I've had the feeling that Mary isn't all that secure in her salvation."

"Why wouldn't she be?" Roger asked. "I mean, she's always been an example of a good Christian wife and mother – at least until recently."

Paul nodded. "Yes, she does a lot of good things – but when I talk to her sometimes I get the feeling she's doing what she does to make up for something. It's nothing I could put my finger on, you know? But with what Joanne and you are telling me, I wonder if I might be more right than I realized."

"You think whatever this is it's about something in her past?" Roger asked. "Why would she hide it?"

"Fear," Paul said. He paused as their waiter refilled their water and asked if they were interested in dessert. Both men declined the offer.

Roger picked up the bill the young man had left on the table. "Fear of what?"

Paul pulled out his wallet. "Fear that you won't love her anymore, for one thing."

"That's ridiculous!" Roger snapped. "Hey, put your wallet away, I'm buying."

"You sure?" Paul asked.

"That what you're saying makes no sense or that I'm paying for lunch?"

"Actually, both," Paul answered, leaning forward. "Roger, I'm not trying to jump on you, but look how you've reacted to her crisis already – anger, suspicion . . ."

"Paul, that's not fair!" Roger argued as he placed his blue debit card on top of the check. "She's been acting so strangely!"

"I'm not saying your reactions aren't normal," Paul said, replacing his wallet into his pocket. "I'm saying that they might be reinforcing her fear – that if she tells you the truth, you'll up and leave."

The waiter placed a small machine on the table and explained to Roger how to use it to pay the bill. As Roger punched numbers on the keypad, he muttered, "Okay, what do you think I should do?"

"You have any vacation time?" Paul asked.

Roger looked up, puzzled. "Yeah, some. Why?"

"Your wife is in Montgomery, struggling with something big. She needs to know you're on her team. Why not join her?"

"What?" Roger sputtered. "I can't just up and go – what about Kelly?"

"I bet Jo won't mind if Kelly stays with us for a couple of days. The kids will have a blast," Paul grinned. "Granted, sleep might become a luxury . . ."

Roger shook his head slowly. "Just go into work and tell them I'm taking off for a few days . . . I've never done something like that."

"Tell them you have a family emergency to deal with." At Roger's wide eyes, Paul shrugged. "It's not a lie, Roger. This is a family crisis if I've ever seen one. You're the head of your house – you need to take steps to deal with this."

Staring at his clasped hands, Roger thought about what his friend was telling him. Yes, this was a crisis. That was one of the reasons he'd asked to talk to Paul in the first place.

With a nod, he got up from the table, tossing his crumpled napkin on top of his plate. "Call Joanne and make sure she's okay with this. I'm going to go talk to my boss." He hesitated, then asked, "Please pray for us."

Paul put a hand on Roger's shoulder. "I already am, my friend."

- SIXTY-FOUR -

MARY HATED SITTING IN DR. GREEN'S WAITING ROOM. She stared at the latest issue of *People* magazine in her hands without really reading the words. She was unable to concentrate. But she still kept her eyes on the magazine, because looking at anything else at the moment made her feel sick.

When she and Celia walked into the clinic, they had to walk past some protesters on the sidewalk. One woman that caught her attention was wearing a black dress, her knees resting on a folded white towel on the grassy strip that ran alongside the street. Her gray head was bowed and her hands were folded in prayer.

Amid the energy and shouts of the other protesters, this nameless woman was a quiet island. Mary found her eyes drawn to the praying lady as she and Celia trudged up the walk, calls of "They're murdering babies in there!" ringing in their ears.

Mary understood how the protesters felt – she shared their views. But she cringed at the harshness these sign-waving men and women had in their voices. The lack of love troubled her. Didn't the women who came here need compassion and alternatives, not vitriol?

The waiting room in the clinic reminded Mary of a similar room at her own doctor's. The walls were painted a soothing pale green, with generic prints of flowers painted in pastel colors. A water cooler sat in a corner near the paneled check in counter, a cup dispenser hanging on the wall to its left. Chairs with blue patterned cushions and wooden armrests lined the walls. Magazines were fanned out on a long low wooden table in the center of the room.

Celia marched right up to the counter. "My name is Celia Morris. I and my friend here need to talk with Dr. Green."

The woman behind the desk nodded and pointed to a clipboard on the counter. "Please sign in and have a seat."

"You don't understand," Celia said as she shook her head. "We don't have an appointment."

The graying woman blinked. "I don't understand . . . ?"

"My mother was Francine Winters," Celia said, her eyes drilling into the nervous receptionist. "And my friend has questions about her experience with Dr. Green a few years ago."

"Oh," the woman said. "I believe we spoke on the phone, Ms. Morris. As I told you then, our schedule is quite full today. If you'd like to leave a number we can call you . . ."

"We'll wait," Celia said. She turned and led Mary to a pair of chairs at the end of the left hand row.

As Mary turned to follow her friend, she caught the troubled expression on the receptionist's face. She felt a little sorry for the woman, who looked like Mary's picture of a grandmother – gray, plump, silver bifocals. Mary could see the woman in a kitchen making snickerdoodles for a couple of bouncy toddlers, instead of working *here*.

Mary picked up a copy of *People* and sat next to Celia. She let her eyes scan the room, and felt a lump in her throat as she did.

There were about seven other women in the room. Several of the women appeared to be at the clinic by themselves, like one dark-haired woman in a cranberry business suit busily thumbing buttons on her dark red Droid phone.

The person that upset Mary the most was a girl who looked to be fourteen or fifteen, wearing a baggy t-shirt with a picture of Edward from the movie *Twilight*. She rested her head on the arm of an older woman who could have been her mother. The woman sat stiffly, her eyes glued to a paperback book, her lips in a thin line.

The girl – whose short blond hair was a frizzy cloud around her head – met Mary's eyes. The girl's blue eyes were bright with tears, shadows under them aging her beyond her years.

Mary gasped. Celia followed her friend's look, and then jabbed her elbow into Mary's side. "Don't stare!" she hissed.

Mary looked down at the magazine in her hand. She felt dirty sitting in this peaceful, pleasant waiting room, as if she was performing abortions herself. But she knew Celia was right. She couldn't look at these women and especially not at that girl. If she did, she'd throw up – or stand up and start screaming at the other women there. *Don't you know what you've doing? Is this the only solution for your life? Don't you realize there's a precious life inside, a life that has done nothing to deserve what you're doing to it?*

She didn't have the courage – or perhaps the rudeness – to challenge these women. So she flipped her magazine to a random page and stared at it, trying not to think.

The minutes passed with all the speed of thick syrup crawling across a pancake. Mary checked her watch several times, wondering why it was taking so long. Every once in a while, a white clad nurse would enter the waiting room, file in hand, and softly say a name. One of the women in the room would get up and follow the nurse through the door.

When the nurse said "Megan," the teenager with the haunting eyes stood, a little hesitant. The woman next to her snapped her book shut, stood, and placed a hand on the girl's shoulder. As Mary watched out of the corner of her eye, it seemed the hand was there not for comfort but to make sure the girl went through the door.

Bile filled her throat. Mary had to force herself to pull enough air into her lungs so that she didn't hyperventilate. She didn't know how much longer she could sit there.

When she snuck a look at Celia, she saw that her friend was apparently perfectly comfortable. She had a *Time* magazine in her lap and seemed to be actually *reading* the thing. The only thing that indicated that her friend was less than peaceful was that at times she looked up and sent a glare to the check-in counter. The gray haired woman appeared to be doing all she could not to meet Celia's flashing eyes.

Finally, the door opened again and a woman who looked to be in her early forties stepped out. She wore a gray pencil skirt and a dark red blouse. Her eyes surveyed the waiting room, which with comings and goings now held about five people, including herself and Celia. The plump gray-haired woman pointed at Mary and Celia.

The woman strode over to the friends. "Ms. Morris, Ms. Beamer, I'm Sharon Abrams, Dr. Green's office manager. Please come with me."

Mary stood up, the magazine sliding off her lap in her haste to leave the waiting room. However, Celia remained seated, crossing her arms and staring up at Ms. Abrams. "I hope you're taking us to see Dr. Green."

The office manager smiled a tight little smile. Her voice pitched low, she said, "We'll see about that. I thought we could chat first."

Celia made no effort to lower her own voice. "And I think I would like to speak the man who was apparently having an affair with my mother, who I remind you passed away while here visiting him."

Mary felt heat rush to her face as she saw the eyes of everyone in the room turn to the three women. She saw Ms. Abrams' eyes narrow as she seemed to size up Celia.

"Ms. Morris," she said, her voice still low but now with a bit of fire threading through it, "you understand that regardless of any relationship Dr. Green had with your mother, he is under no obligation to see you or your friend here."

Mary flinched when the office manager's hand flipped toward her. She felt on display in this place she didn't want to be. She reached down and snatched the magazine off the floor.

"Celia, let's just please go with her," she whispered through clenched teeth as she straightened up.

Celia gave her a startled look. "Mary, we need to make a stand if we're going to see the doctor," she said, her voice dropping for the first time since Sharon Abrams entered the room.

"Not in this room," Mary begged, swallowing back the burning in the back of her throat. "Please, Celia, I have to get out of here."

Her friend studied her for a few seconds, irritation giving way to concern. "Okay, Mary. We'll let Ms. Abrams run the show. For the moment."

"Thank you," Mary breathed.

She rethought her gratitude when she noticed a gleam of triumph in Sharon Abrams' eye before the office manager turned to lead them out of the waiting room.

As Mary left that pleasant yet horrifying waiting room, she wondered if she'd lost a battle she didn't know she was fighting.

- SIXTY-FIVE -

MARY STARED AT THE BACK OF CELIA'S HEAD, trying to focus on individual strands as they went down the hall of the clinic. She felt a stinging on her palms and realized she was digging her nails into the skin.

She did not want to look at the doors they were passing. She did not want to dwell on what might be going on in those rooms.

Even though she averted her eyes she couldn't stop up her ears. A murmured conversation from the door on the left. Two down and to the right, soft sobbing.

She smelled that sharp, antiseptic smell she associated with doctor's offices and hospitals. Mary wrapped her arms around her, gooseflesh popping up. She saw Celia rubbing her arms up ahead.

Sharon Abrams opened a door and waved them in. "Have a seat. Can I get you anything to drink?"

"No," Celia said. Mary just shook her head. She sank into one of the offered seats, trying to figure out how to regain her power of speech.

She caught a whiff of lavender and noticed a white votive candle in a glass holder on top of an expensive-looking bookcase. The room looked as if it should be the office of a successful CEO, not the office manager of a clinic.

Celia sat down, her spine ramrod straight. She placed her folded hands in her lap. "All right, Ms. Abrams, when can we speak with Dr. Green?"

The office manager settled behind her desk. "I understand you want to speak to the doctor. What I'm not clear on is what you hope to accomplish."

Celia frowned. "I want to know what was going on between him and my mother!"

Abrams smiled as she raised a penciled eyebrow. "Forgive me, Ms. Morris, but your mother was an adult, was she not?"

"What does that have to do with anything?"

"Well, while it might be disconcerting for you as her daughter to realize she might have an active sex life, is it really your business?"

Mary saw her friend go pale except for two red spots on her cheeks. She put a hand on Celia's arm while staring at Abrams. "There's no need to be crude."

"I wasn't trying to be crude, Ms. Beamer," Abrams shook her head. "Just trying to understand your purposes here. The doctor is quite busy and I won't interrupt him lightly."

She turned back to Celia. "I'm not sure what Dr. Green can tell you. And while I understand your grief at the moment, you need to realize he is also grieving."

"Is he?" Celia's voice was icy. "Funny that he's managed to keep working."

"Not everyone deals with loss in the same way," Abrams said, her chin lifting slightly. "I can tell you that when the police informed him of your mother's accident he was quite shaken."

"Did he see her yesterday?" Celia asked through gritted teeth. "Talk to her? Maybe *upset* her?"

"Ms. Morris," the office manager's voice made the temperature in the already chilly room drop several degrees, "I'm not sure what you're implying, but I will be generous and assume your grief is causing you to ignore normal manners."

"Is it really too hard to understand that Celia might want to talk to someone who was close to her mother and may have been the last person to speak with her?" Mary asked. As much as she tried to give the office manager the benefit of the doubt, Mary found the woman's lack of sympathy off-putting.

"Well, that's not what I've been hearing," Abrams said, switching her gaze over to Mary. "I'm hearing a lot of anger and desire to place blame."

The office manager held a hand up as Mary opened her mouth. "And if I recall correctly, you're also wanting to make some sort of accusations about Dr. Green over his care of you years ago? Frankly, my seeing the two of you is a courtesy – another person might have simply thrown you out."

The mention of Mary's mission to the clinic had the effect of a bucketful of cold water to the face. Mary had to remind herself to breathe and now Celia had a comforting hand on her friend's arm. "I have . . . questions," she said softly. "Some things have come to my attention . . . . and I need some answers."

"Are you saying someone from this office has been in contact with you?" Abrams asked, a skeptical frown on her face.

"She used to work in your Atlanta clinic," Mary said. "She sent me a note."

"Who is she?" Abrams asked, turning slightly to look at the flat screen monitor on her desk.

"Martha Thompson," Mary said. "But she's dead."

Abrams paused, her fingers over the keyboard. "Oh."

"Oh?" Celia echoed. "What does that mean?"

With a sigh, Abrams turned to face the women again. "Martha was a kind woman, and a good worker . . . but she apparently became mentally unstable. Her children opposed her working for Dr. Green, and I think that caused severe mental stress."

"Her son didn't mention any mental instability," Celia argued. "We talked to him – I bet you didn't."

"He didn't try to contact us," Abrams said, throwing an annoyed look in Celia's direction. "But would you say that a person who committed suicide was mentally stable?"

"Perhaps guilt was the problem," Mary said, twisting her hands in her lap, wishing she'd never come to this office and met this chilly woman. "She told me . . . well, she said . . . that . . ."

She felt Celia's hand rubbing small circles between her shoulder blades. Abrams leaned forward, hands folded on top of her very neat desk, and asked, "What did she say, Ms. Beamer?"

Mary swallowed. She'd shared this with Francine Winters, Celia, Foster, and Joanne. But speaking the words in this extravagant office was a Herculean task.

"She said she knew what I'd tried to do," she choked out, "and that my son was alive."

Abrams studied her for a moment, her expression calm. No start of surprise. No immediate denial. Just a gaze.

Finally, the office manager asked, "What do you think she meant by that?"

Mary couldn't maintain eye contact. She looked down at her hands, trying to stop them from moving. "When I was brought to your clinic ten years ago, I was in labor. Dr. Green told me my baby died, that – that I had a miscarriage."

"And you believe that he lied to you?" Abrams asked. "Dr. Green is a respected physician who provides medical care. You are taking the word of a distraught woman over his?"

"I didn't want to come to the clinic!" Mary burst out. "I wanted to have the baby! Why would Martha Thompson lie to me about this? Why would she contact me?"

She felt the tears coming again, and she to take deep breaths to force them back. She would not cry again. Not here. Not in front of this woman.

Celia's hand tightened on Mary's shoulder. Mary felt grateful for her friend's support. It helped her steady her racing heart. Looking straight into Sharon Abram's cold eyes, she said, "There's a simple way to determine the truth."

Abrams cocked her head. "Oh really? And what would you suggest we do?"

"I want to see my medical records, " Mary said.

With a sigh, Abrams shook her head. "I can't do that."

"They're her records!" Celia snapped.

"Please," Abrams held up a hand. "I realize this is quite upsetting for you, Ms. Beamer, and you'll forgive me if I haven't been as sympathetic as you think I should be."

She gestured to her computer monitor. "While we have computerized our records, I'm afraid the fire that destroyed our Atlanta clinic also destroyed some of our older records. Including those of a decade ago. I'm sorry."

Mary felt her shoulders slump. Hadn't Foster told her there would be a denial of records? She glanced over at Celia, who was frowning as she contemplated the office manager.

Abrams stood and walked around to the front of her desk. She leaned against it, looking less hostile then she had moments ago. "Unfortunately, though I'm sure neither of you intended this, your appearance and demands have . . . have raised unpleasant memories for me. Those memories have colored my responses to you."

"Do you remember me?" Mary asked in a small voice. "Were you with the clinic 10 years ago?"

Abrams shook her head. "I really don't remember you, Ms. Beamer. Or the incident you describe. If you were brought here against your will, I'm truly sorry, but it was not this clinic's doing. Who brought you here, if I may ask?"

"My mother did," Celia said, her voice strained.

"Ah, it goes back to Francine," Abrams said thoughtfully. "Strange."

For a moment none of the women spoke. Mary heard faint voices outside the office door. The lavender scent was soothing – she had bath salts that smelled the same that she'd use at night after a stressful day.

Were they at a dead end? Had Mary put her marriage at risk only to come up empty handed? Was she condemned to wonder about a 10-year-old boy who might or might not exist?

Abrams sighed. "Tell me, ladies, how long are you staying here in the Montgomery area?"

Celia raised her head. "How long do we need to stay to find our answers?"

"Look," Sharon said, her hands raised. "I think we all want to end this peacefully. I may have misjudged you both – you must admit you both were rather aggressive."

Mary winced. Celia stood up, hands on her hips. "If you think this is aggressive . . ."

Sharon rolled her eyes. "Ms. Morris, hear me out. I will speak to Dr. Green again. Perhaps I can persuade him to speak with you. And, Ms. Beamer, I will personally search through our records. Perhaps I can find something – something that will give you peace of mind?"

"When?" Mary said, standing as well.

"I will be in touch with you the very first thing tomorrow morning," Abrams said.

Celia crossed her arms. "And we should believe you because . . ."

"Ms. Morris, you could make things very uncomfortable for us," Abrams said. "I would hope you weren't that type of woman, but if you wanted to cause a scene that would embarrass us in the community we both know you could. All I'm asking for is a chance."

"Fine," Mary said quickly. "You have our phone numbers?"

"Wait a second – " Celia protested.

"Celia, let's just go!" Mary pleaded. "If she doesn't call us back we can always call –"

"All right!" Celia broke in. "Fine." She turned to Abrams. "You know how to contact us?"

The office manager looked from Mary to Celia, her mouth half open. She closed it when she saw Mary staring at her. "Let me jot them down," she said, picking up a pad from her desk.

Minutes later Mary was all but running out of the office, Celia at her heels. The waiting room was empty and she felt a surge of relief that there were no more eyes to avoid. But just as she reached the door the gray-haired nurse put a hand on her arm.

"Are you all right?" the woman asked.

Mary felt a piece of paper being pressed into her hand. She frowned at the nurse but the older woman just shook her head slightly, her eyes boring into Mary's.

"Yes," Mary stammered. "Thank you."

Celia said nothing until they got to the car (the protestors had apparently decided to go home) and were buckling seatbelts. With a sigh she asked, "What was *that* all about?"

"I had to get out of there," Mary said. She looked down at the pink wad of paper that was crushed into her palm. It blurred and she realized her tears were back.

Celia started the car. "You know we'll never get any answers now. That Abrams witch is a slick one."

Mary swallowed back a sob. "I couldn't be in there any more. It's a horrible place."

"It's just a place," Celia argued as she pulled into traffic. "You shouldn't let it get to you."

"You don't understand," Mary said as she unfolded the paper in her hand.

Celia glanced over. "What's that?"

Mary stared at the hastily scribbled note that was on a telephone message slip. "Celia, can you find a Starbucks on 15th street?"

Celia glanced at a street sign as she passed it. "I think so – I'll have to turn around." The traffic light ahead of them turned red. Celia pulled to a stop behind an old pickup truck. "What's going on?"

Mary couldn't take her eyes off the note. Another note – another nurse.

Meet me at the Starbucks' on 15th at six pm. Important!

- SIXTY-SIX -

SHARON WENT TO THE FRONT DESK OF THE CLINIC. The waiting room was empty; Nadine was tidying up the counter while she nibbled on a granola bar. "Any problems?"

The nurse shook her head. "No ma'am. I just have a couple of things to finish up."

"Fine," Sharon nodded. "I appreciate your help with the desk this week. With Claire on vacation we were a little short-handed."

"That's all right, Ms. Abrams, I was glad to do it," Nadine said. "I'll just finish up here and go home."

"That's fine," Sharon said. She studied the older woman; Nadine was keeping her eyes focused on the smooth tan countertop, her hands fluttering from the appointment book to the telephone message pad. "Are you all right? Did those women cause a problem?"

"I'm fine," Nadine said quickly, glancing up at Sharon. "And the women were fine." She sighed and dug into the black purse that was slung over her chair and pulled out a roll of mints. "I'm just ready to go home, I guess."

"Well that's fine," Sharon said, frowning. She suspected there was more to it, but couldn't quite put her finger on it. And there were other matters she needed to attend to. "Let me know if you're having any problems. You know we'll help you."

"Yes ma'am, I know," Nadine nodded. She offered the roll of mints to Sharon, who shook her head. "I'll see you tomorrow, Ms. Abrams."

"See you tomorrow," Sharon echoed. Still thoughtful, she left the front desk and headed to Thomas' office.

At his weary "Come in!" Sharon entered the doctor's very pleasant office. A pale blue silk rug lay in front of the massive library desk. A top of the line sound system played classical music softly – Sharon thought it might be Mozart.

Thomas had removed his jacket and tossed it over one of the two leather chairs that sat just behind the blue rug. He was reading a chart, a hand supporting his head. "Just a minute, Sharon. I want to finish this note."

"Of course," she said, sitting in the empty chair. She pulled out her iPhone and went over some of her messages while she waited. It had been a trying day, and she was behind on some business dealings.

Finally Thomas set down his pen and flipped the chart shut. "All right. Did you talk to Francine's daughter?"

Sharon put her phone in its holster and folded her hands on her lap. "I did. I think if we are calm and smart there will be little to no fallout from this."

"I wish I could agree with you," Thomas said with a sigh. He grabbed the dark blue cup he used in the office and took a gulp of coffee. "Both her and that other woman could make things difficult."

"Of course they *could*," Sharon agreed. "But I think they won't."

"And why is that?"

Sharon chose her words carefully. "Well, I think you should meet with Ms. Morris. Express your sympathy, give her the impression that you and her mother had fallen in love and that you share her sorrow."

Thomas swallowed. "I'm not totally comfortable with that. Playing the lover with Francine was difficult. Her daughter's already suspicious – if she sees through my act –"

"I don't think she will," Sharon said, leaning back in the chair and crossing her legs. She's upset and grieving. I think if we respond to that grief, make her believe we share it, she'll go away."

"And she won't suspect a thing," Thomas said, his voice full of doubt.

"Oh, she may suspect," Francine shrugged. "But she won't have anything to back up those feelings. If we manipulate her carefully, she'll come away from here grateful you gave her mother a few last days of happiness."

"And you think I can do that."

"Thomas, Thomas," Sharon shook her head. "You manipulate women every day when they come here for your services."

The doctor frowned at her. "I am providing a service, Sharon – you know that full well. A much needed service. And as a bonus I'm able to give families who find traditional adoption difficult a chance for a baby."

She pursed her lips, wondering how hard to push. This side of Thomas – she always thought of it as his "women's rights crusader" persona – came out at times. Sharon never could figure out if he truly believed the words he spoke or he was trying to convince himself it wasn't just a very profitable business.

"We both make a nice living off of it," she finally said aloud, just to gauge his reaction.

He flinched. "Are you complaining?"

Sharon smiled. "Not at all," she said.

She knew herself. She was no zealot, no bra-burner. Sharon had found a way to use her talents to get what she wanted. It was as simple as that. The morality of it wasn't something that bothered her all that much.

"Fine," Green sighed. "I do a song and dance for Francine's daughter. That doesn't solve the problem of her friend."

"Yes, I know," Sharon said, picking up her phone and pulling up some notes. "I think we can perhaps deal with her by applying a little subterfuge and, if necessary, blackmail."

Green began to toy with a silver pen that caught the overhead light, sending little bright winks Sharon's way. "I'm listening."

"Well, first I think we need to pull up her medical records and change them somewhat."

"Her medical records? You still have them?" Green's eyes narrowed.

Sharon blew an impatient breath out. "Yes, we had offsite backups, don't you remember?"

"I thought we destroyed them!" Green said, still glaring. "I told you to do that! And I told the state of Georgia they were gone!"

"Yes, you did," Sharon said. "But you were wrong. Those records can be useful to us. They have been, as a matter of fact. How do you think we were able to contact former patients?"

Green was breathing heavily, as if he'd just run a mile. "Those records could be toxic, Sharon. Do you have any idea what's in them?"

"Oh, Thomas, don't be an idiot!" she snapped. "Of course I do. That's why they're on my hard drive, protected. I'm the only one with access to them. No one else has any idea they still exist."

The doctor shook his head. "I want you to destroy them. Tonight, before you leave the office."

Sharon felt the blood rush to her face. She stood up and folded her arms across her chest. "No."

His eyes widened. "What?"

"I said I will not destroy the records," she repeated, forcing calm into her voice. "You do your job, Thomas – performing services for women – and I'll do mine – ensuring that our little business continues."

Green stood slowly, staring at Sharon as if she were something new and alien. "Are you forgetting who is in charge of this clinic?"

"Not at all," she answered. Sharon planted her palms down on Green's desk and leaned forward, her eyes blazing. "Are you forgetting if it weren't for me we'd have lost everything not once, but twice now? You're facing something very difficult with these two women, Thomas. You need me to fix it, and you need me to fix it the best way I know how."

"Or what?" Green scowled, but she saw a hint of fear in his eyes as he stepped back, putting his leather office chair between them. "You can't blackmail me, Sharon. I go down, so do you."

She smiled. Saying nothing at first, Sharon reached over and picked up the doctor's coffee cup. Her eyes still on his, she took a sip, grimacing slightly. "I do hate the way you take your coffee."

She watched him as he studied her, gauging her reactions. Still smiling, Sharon let her hips sway slightly as she rounded the desk to approach him. She laughed a little as he stumbled backing away from her. "What's the matter, Thomas? Are you afraid of me?"

"No," he croaked. Clearing his throat, he repeated, "No. But I'm not sure I can trust you anymore."

She shook her head and perched a hip on his desk. "You have that exactly backwards. You can trust me to do what I say I'll do – and you should be very, very afraid of me."

Sharon was amused to see Thomas' Adam's apple bob as he swallowed. She smelled the fear rolling off him, and to her surprise found it very stimulating.

"Why – why should I be afraid of you?" he stammered. "You're good at your job, Sharon, but you're my employee!"

She let a long red fingernail draw patterns on the felt of his desk blotter. "I *am* good at what I do. For example, because I do have these records, it wouldn't be difficult to alter them to prove I was coerced into helping you with some of the more…private aspects of the clinic." She cocked her head. "And I am sure I could convince the DA that you'd threatened to kill me unless I did away with Francine Winters."

He froze. Sharon said nothing, just let her words sink in. She swung one leg back and forth, frowning at the small run in her stocking that started just behind her knee. That was it for this pair.

Thomas exhaled, his shoulders sagging. "I – I don't believe you. You'd really destroy what we've worked for?"

"Only if you give me no other option," she said. "I'm no Francine Winters, empty-headed and careless. And you're no me, able to deal with a potential disaster. We stay together on this, Thomas. But you're going to have to let me solve the problems the best way I know how."

The music that had leant a soft undertone to the argument stopped as the CD ended. Again, Sharon chose silence while she gauged Green's reaction.

In truth, her going to the authorities and handing them Thomas was what she considered a doomsday scenario. While she was certain she could escape the worst of any criminal investigation, she knew that jail time would be likely. It wasn't something she looked forward to.

But she couldn't let Thomas know that. So she kept a placid expression on her face and continued to trace random patterns on the blotter while she waited.

At last Thomas spoke, his head down. "All right. This last time. But once this crisis is over we need to talk about this."

It was less than full capitulation, but Sharon knew it was the best she could manage. She nodded and stood. "That's fine."

"Fine," he muttered. "Now, if you'll excuse me, I have a few things to finish up before I leave."

"Of course," Sharon said. She turned and walked out of the office, relieved that her hands didn't start shaking until she was almost at her office.

- SIXTY-SEVEN -

JACK WENT UP TO THE COUNTER of the dingy convenience store in Auburn, Alabama carrying a large container of molten coffee. After a moment's hesitation, he grabbed two Three Musketeers' bars and added them to the drink on the stained countertop.

"That it?" the dark young man with an Arabic accent asked.

"Gas on pump four," Jack answered, pulling out some of the cash he'd withdrawn from his account a few hours earlier. He frowned – the gas had cost more than he'd expected, and he wasn't left with much after paying for everything.

He trudged back to his vehicle, listening to the swish of cars on the nearby interstate. He felt like he'd been driving forever, that perhaps he wasn't getting closer to Montgomery – maybe he was dead and in Hell the roads went forever.

You're getting old. Lisa's voice, teasing, affectionate, played in his head. *When you were younger, this was an adventure and you had no problems keeping up with it.*

Yeah, he silently told the voice. But I'm not younger and this ceased to be an adventure when I lost you.

He dropped into the driver's seat. Before going into the convenience store he'd stuffed most of the trash into a Burger King bag and placed it precariously on top of the full garbage can by the door. Now he placed his cup in the holder, sighing in relief as he removed his fingers from the hot container.

After starting up the car and watching the gas gauge's needle slowly climb to FULL he doubled checked his map and the directions he'd printed off Google. Assured he was still on track, he pulled into traffic and merged back onto the interstate.

The sun was setting and positioned perfectly to send bright beams of light into his eyes. With a snarl of impatience, Jack pulled on his sunglasses and spent of couple of minutes trying to get his visor to block out the worst of it. The blare of a car horn to his right made him abandon the attempt and concentrate on his driving.

When his cell phone rang he pulled it off his belt and checked the display: Wheeler. Jack considered letting it go to voicemail – he'd already done so twice – but figured doing it a third time might push his boss past the limit. With a sigh he flipped it open. "Hey, boss."

"Jack?" Wheeler sounded annoyed. "Where've you been? I haven't seen you around since lunch."

"Working on a story, sir," Jack answered. He braked briefly to let a hotshot in a red convertible slide in front of him. The traffic was heavy, so he had to be extra careful.

"Oh really? That's funny because I don't recall assigning you a story," Wheeler said. "In fact, I've been looking for you so I could do just that."

Jack took a deep breath, feeling his fingers tighten on the phone. "Well, I apologize, Mr. Wheeler, but I'm kind of busy right now with this particular story."

A brief silence. Jack noticed red taillights brightening in front of him and braked carefully, hoping there wasn't a huge delay coming up.

"Foster," Wheeler's voice was measured, "where are you at the moment?"

"I'm on the road," Foster answered. He came to a stop behind a dirty white pickup and took the opportunity to gulp some coffee. He bit back a yelp as the hot liquid burned his tongue.

"Where on the road, exactly?"

Foster drummed his fingers on the wheel, trying to look past the blinding sun and sea of brake lights to estimate how long he'd be held up.

"Well, I got a lead today, and time was of the essence, so I decided to make a run to the area and check it out."

He heard Wheeler sigh over the phone. "Jack, is this about Green and the abortion clinic?"

Jack watched as the truck in front of him rolled a couple of feet. "You gave me a week."

Wheeler swore. "That didn't mean I gave you permission to take off whenever you wanted! You'd better not expect the paper to pick up your travel expenses! In fact, you'd better not expect to be paid while you're AWOL, period!"

Jack grit his teeth. "Believe me, I'm assuming that I'm on my own dime on this. Not that I have many dimes left."

"Whose fault is that?" Wheeler snapped. "Not the paper's. Don't you dare try to pin your financial woes on us!"

"Not assigning blame," Jack said. He saw a hole open to the right of him – he swung his car into the faster moving lane, earning an extended blast of a horn from the car behind him. "I'm stating fact. You gave me a week – it's not like I have a lot of time for this."

"What lead are you following up?" Wheeler asked. "And why didn't you tell me about it before you left? What are you hiding, Jack?"

Don't lose your temper, Jack told himself. If he let his anger take over, Wheeler would have his job, no matter how the story turned out. He made an effort to keep his voice calm as he replied, "I found out where Green's been hiding. Apparently he's up to his old tricks in Montgomery."

"And you're going there?" Wheeler asked. "What's your plan? You do have a plan, don't you?"

"Ms. Morris and Ms. Beamer are there," Jack said. The cars in his lane moved forward for a bit, then slowed to a stop. He sighed.

"And the reason you chose to keep this to yourself?"

Jack thought about it, and decided to be honest. "I wasn't sure you'd approve the trip."

"So you decided to go anyway," Wheeler growled. "Jack, I've a good mind to fire you here and now. What makes you think you can get away with this?"

"Sir," Foster struggled to keep his temper – it was getting harder the more Wheeler ranted. "you know this could be a big story. I need you to give me this. This could be the thing that breaks it wide open. And the door may be closing – if those women spook the clinic, Green could go underground again. Then I'd never get the story."

Wheeler was silent for so long Jack checked the phone to see if they were still connected. The traffic began to pick up speed – apparently whatever had been holding things up was gone.

"All right," Wheeler said. "Answer one question. Give me an honest answer, and you've got your shot."

Jack tensed. He suspected what Wheeler would ask, and it was the one question he didn't want to answer.

"Does any of this have to do with what happened to Lisa?"

Foster closed his eyes briefly. He'd *known* that's what Wheeler would ask. He wrestled with himself, argued silently as he sped down the road. The sun ducked behind a stand of trees and he blinked the spots out of his eyes.

"Jack?"

"I don't know," Jack blurted out.

After a few seconds of heart-stopping silence, Jack heard Wheeler sigh again. "That strikes me as pretty honest. Okay, Jack. You got my belated permission for your field trip. Be careful, and good luck."

Jack stammered his thanks and gratefully ended the call. He tossed his phone on the seat beside him, and grabbed a candy bar with a shaking hand.

He had a chance to finally finish this story. He hoped it would be the only chance he needed.

- SIXTY-EIGHT -

MARY HUNG UP HER PHONE after a brief conversation with Foster. She'd let him know where they were staying and the address of the clinic but ended the call in a hurry. She glanced at her wristwatch – 6:07.

Celia sighed and stared into her chai latte as if there was an answer to her sorrow in its depths. "Maybe she was just . . . I don't know, maybe she changed her mind."

Mary leaned her head on her hand, letting the growl of the coffee shop's bean grinder run through her. There were people crowded at the counter – some glancing at a newspaper, a couple of younger people swaying to whatever music was playing in their ear buds.

The door opened again and Mary straightened up. "Celia, it's her."

The older woman looked around the shop and spotted the two of them. She appeared to freeze, her hands tightening on the black shoulder purse she held, and Mary was reminded of the deer that had stopped in front of her and Roger on a trip to Okefenokee Swamp, its eyes huge. Roger had hit the brakes hard enough for their shoulder belts to snap tight across them, and they'd screeched to a stop a couple of feet away from the animal, who'd turned and leapt into the brush, graceful in flight.

This memory had flashed through her brain (and left a pang – oh, she missed her husband!) in an instant. Then the nurse straightened her shoulders and walked to the table. "Hello. May I sit?"

Mary and Celia nodded. The woman dropped down with a sigh. For a moment, the three of them examined the black square table in front of them, no one willing to break the silence.

Finally, Mary spoke up. "Would you like something to drink?"

The nurse shook her head. "Maybe when the crowd lightens up." Another small silence. "My name is Nadine. I'm sorry, but I don't know which of you is which?"

"I'm Mary Beamer," Mary said, looking into Nadine's eyes. She tried to read the woman and gauge her intentions.

"Celia Morris," her friend said. "Francine Winters was my mother."

"Oh," Nadine said, putting a hand on top of Celia's. "I'm so sorry, dear. That was a terrible thing."

Celia nodded. Mary felt a surge of compassion as she saw her friend's jaw tighten.

"Ma'am," she said, her hand tightening on her coffee cup, "you asked us to meet you here. Can I ask why?"

The nurse sighed. She began to twist a silver ring with tiny chips of diamonds and sapphires on her finger. "I need to be up front with you, young woman. I'm not anti-abortion. I believe we provide a service to women in need."

Mary felt frustrated. What did she do? Did this woman have something important to say? If she was honest with her would she close off this final source of information?

"I think abortion is murder," she finally said, softly. "If you were willing, we could talk about it. But that's not why you're here, is it?"

Celia glanced at her and back to the nurse. "I agree with you, but as Mary said, that's not what you're here to talk about, is it?"

"No," Nadine said, staring at her hands. "To be honest, I'm not sure I'm doing the right thing here. I'm so confused . . ." she glanced over at Mary. "You went to the clinic in Atlanta about ten years ago? Is that right?"

"I was taken to the clinic,' Mary corrected. "I – I was having contractions, Celia's mom insisted on taking me there."

"Ah," Nadine sighed, her shoulders slumping. "I always wondered how much she knew. That might explain –" she stopped talking suddenly, her eyes wide.

Celia straightened up. "Explain what?"

Nadine glanced at both women nervously. "If you don't mind, I think I will get something to drink. Just a minute . . ." she stood, accidently jarring the table. Mary grabbed her cup before the contents could go sloshing on the surface while Celia did the same. The nurse ignored them and went to stand behind a pair of teenage boys who were craning their heads to the glass display case of pastries while rattling off an order.

Celia shook her head. "That woman is acting crazy."

"No," Mary said softly, her eyes on the way the plump woman kept shifting her weight and fiddling with her purse strap. "She's nervous. Frightened."

"Of us?" Celia shook her head. "I don't think we're that intimidating." She drank her latte, grimacing. "I need something stronger than this. Why couldn't she ask to meet us at a bar?"

Mary winced at the question. She felt so out of her element here, so far from the safe Christian cocoon she'd lived in for so long. Here she was, in the world, chasing guesses and rumors – and her own tattered conscience, perhaps.

She snorted. Some Christian *soldier* she turned out to be!

"What's up?" Celia asked. Nadine was at the counter now, gazing at the menu high on the wall.

"I'm just thinking what a lousy influence I'm turning out to be," Mary muttered.

"Because I want to go to a bar?" Celia's eyebrow shot up. "Cut yourself some slack, girlfriend."

"Because of all of it," Mary said, bracing her head with a hand. "What kind of witness am I? I've done terrible things and lied about them for ten years!"

"So you're human," Celia shrugged. "Welcome to the club."

"I'm supposed to be better than this," Mary frowned.

Before Celia could respond, Nadine rejoined them with a cup of coffee in her hand. She took a deep breath as she sat down. "I'm very sorry about that. You have to understand this wasn't an easy decision for me."

"Why did you decide to talk to us?" Mary asked. She prayed silently. *God, I know I've messed up. But please, if this woman can help me make some of it right, please let her help me.*

Nadine took a gulp of coffee then wiped her mouth with a napkin. "Because I'm thinking some lines have been crossed. And perhaps you're a part of that." She seemed to struggle with herself for a moment, then the nurse straightened her shoulders and looked straight at Mary. "I think that maybe Ms. Abrams and Dr. Green – that maybe they stole your baby."

- SIXTY-NINE -

Mary stared at Nadine, feeling as if all the breath had left her body. The grinding and hiss of the espresso machine seemed to come from far away. Everything seemed far away, except for this plump woman with the black purse who'd just told her the thing she'd feared ever since she'd first read the note.

"Mary? Mary!"

She blinked, realizing Celia was talking to her – well, almost shouting at her. Mary shook her head, grabbing the table in front of her, suddenly feeling dizzy.

"Excuse me? Is there a problem here?"

Mary glanced up to see a young man in a green Starbuck's apron looking at her with a mixture of concern and alarm on his face. She swallowed, not sure what to say.

Celia had a hand on her arm. "She's just a little hypoglycemic, hasn't eaten for a while. Tell you what, I'll give you some cash and you can bring her something to eat, all right?"

The young man's dark eyes darted from one face to the other. "She ain't gonna throw up, is she? I mean, it'll gross out the customers."

Mary swallowed the bile that bubbled in the back of her throat. "I – I'm all right, really."

Celia made an impatient sound and pulled out a ten dollar bill. "Look, be nice and get her a piece of your chocolate pound cake – get us all a piece and keep the change."

"Sure," he said, his eyes lighting up at the mention of change. The ten went into his jeans pocket and he headed back to the counter.

"Dear, put your head between your knees for a moment," Nadine said, guiding Mary's head down. "You're white as a sheet – no wonder the boy was concerned."

Mary heard Celia snort as she allowed the nurse to bend her forward. "Well, no wonder she's white – you have any other surprises up your sleeve there, Nadine?"

"Celia, please don't," Mary asked, her voice faint. She stared at the large brown tile at her feet and concentrated on breathing normally.

Part of her wanted to run home, run to her bedroom, lock the door, and burrow under the covers. Pull the soft comforter over her head and pretend no one could find her there. Hide for as long as she could.

That might work when she was ten. Or even sixteen. But she was an adult now, and as horrible as this was, she needed to face it like one. With a final deep breath, Mary straightened up.

The Starbucks employee came over balancing three paper plates, each with a thick slice of chocolate pound cake. He distributed the food along with plastic forks and napkins, then scurried back to the counter.

The three women looked at each other. No one spoke, or picked up a fork. It was as if the three of them were waiting for something.

Mary sighed. She grabbed the fork and stabbed at the soft cake. She slipped it into her mouth and closed her eyes, letting the rich chocolate flavor fill her taste buds. Joanne had once joked that God had created chocolate to help them deal with tough times. The memory made her smile, even as the thought of her best friend hurt.

She opened her eyes and saw Celia and Nadine staring at her, both looking to her for where she wanted to take the conversation. She licked some chocolate off her lips and turned to Nadine. "You weren't with the Atlanta clinic, were you?"

"No," Nadine shook her head. "I've lived in Alabama for most of my life." She studied Mary, her gaze thoughtful. "But I heard Dr. Green and Ms. Abrams arguing about you...and I know you both make her nervous."

"I make her nervous?" Celia's eyes widened. "I mean, I have been a pain to her but what's she worried about with me?"

Nadine took a sip of coffee. "Well, that's one of the reasons I decided to approach the two of you," she said, shifting a little in her seat. "I think . . . well, I can't prove it . . . I just happened to hear . . ."

Celia rolled her eyes. "Just spit it out, woman!"

"I think maybe they had something to do with your mother's death," Nadine blurted.

For the second time, a profound silence fell on the table. Only this time it was Celia's face that was draining of color. "What . . . you . . . how?"

Mary shook her head. "Foster suspected, didn't he? That's why he mentioned an autopsy."

Celia glanced over at Mary, and her eyes became hard. "If that's the case . . . if they . . . I swear, I'll –"

"Hush!" Nadine said, putting a hand on Celia's arm.

"Celia," Mary said softly, "you're shouting."

The blond woman glanced around the shop, saw a couple of people shooting a questioning gaze in their direction, and took a deep breath. "Right. Fine. Why would they want to hurt my mother?"

"She knew about the babies, I suspect," Nadine said.

Mary shook her head. "I don't understand. You say they stole my baby. Why? And what other babies are you talking about?"

Nadine drained her coffee quickly, as if she got strength from it. "Well, the babies we recover from late-term abortions..."

Mary and Celia looked at each other, then at Nadine.

Nadine gulped. "You see, Dr. Green . . . he thought their mothers didn't want them, so why not take them and give them to good homes? People who couldn't adopt the regular way."

She spoke more quickly, before either woman could say anything. "It's quite difficult, the rules they have. This was a win-win situation – people who wanted children got them, people who didn't . . . well, that was taken care of as well."

Celia was shaking her head, tears in her eyes. "No! No way my mother would know about that. You've got to be wrong . . ."

"Celia," Mary said, full of pity for her friend.

"She's wrong, Mary," Celia turned to her friend, her voice pleading. "She has to be . . ."

Mary bit her lip. She thought back to the recent conversations she'd had with Francine. Her shoulders sagged. "Celia, she might be right."

Celia stared at her, her lip quivering. Then she sighed and grabbed a napkin. "Yeah, she might be," she muttered, wiping her eyes.

Mary shook her head, trying to think past all the overwhelming emotions. Foster was probably on his way to Montgomery . . . but maybe they couldn't wait . . .

"How do we prove this?" she asked, looking from one woman to the other.

Nadine swallowed. "I could show you the nursery."

"There's a nursery?" Celia asked, her jaw dropping. "You guys have that many babies?"

"We take care of them!" Nadine protested. "They're often premature and need medical attention!"

Mary studied Nadine, who was paler than when she'd first entered the coffee shop. "You'll get in trouble for showing us this, won't you?"

The nurse wouldn't meet her eyes. "I guess. And I wish it wasn't coming to this. I just . . . I just wish they hadn't gone so far."

"What about . . . my son?" Mary asked, swallowing the lump in her throat. "Is there any way we can find out about him, any records . . . ?"

Nadine shook her head. "I don't know. We keep records of the medical side of our business, of course. If there are other records of the adoptions… I've never seen them."

"I'll bet that witch Abrams has them," Celia spat. "She probably has them encrypted on that fancy computer of hers."

"Even those that were destroyed?" Mary asked, her heart beating a little faster.

"Oh yes," Celia said. "She's the type to have them. I bet she sees it as job insurance."

"But if they're encrypted . . ." Mary wondered.

Celia smiled unpleasantly. "Mary, you're talking about my job description. Let me have a few minutes with that computer and a jump drive and we'll get to the bottom of things."

Nadine was shaking her head. "You want to break into Ms. Abrams' office? I – I want to help you but I don't know . . ."

Mary clenched her hands together. "Nadine . . . ten years ago I made a terrible mistake. Then, when I was confused and afraid, someone took advantage of me and told me my child was dead." She swallowed, her grip tightening on the white plastic fork she held.

"All these years I thought that the baby's death was God's way of punishing me. That I was such a wicked person I could never make up for what I did."

A snapping sound made the three women jump. Mary looked down and saw that she'd broken the fork in her hand.

Looking back up to Nadine, she continued, her voice shaking just a little bit, "Now I find out my child isn't dead. I owe it to him to be sure he's all right. The only way to do that is to find out where he is. And the only way to do *that* is to see those records."

The seconds passed as Mary held Nadine's eyes with her own. Mary heard Celia shifting in her seat, the chair making a soft scraping sound.

Then Nadine dropped her eyes. "All right," she said, her voice trembling. "I'll help."

- SEVENTY -

JACK STIFLED A YAWN as he pulled into the hotel parking lot the two women had told him they were staying at. It was a nice hotel – again. This Celia Morris had money to spend; there was no question about that.

He'd tried calling them several times. Once, he'd dropped the phone and grabbed the steering wheel as his car threatened to roll off the side of the road. After that, Jack waited until he had stopped the car at some gas station or fast-food drive-thru before dialing the phone again. He knew he was very tired and that was affecting his driving.

He finally caught Mary Beamer. She was in a hurry but he managed to pry the name of her hotel and the address of the clinic. He asked what was going on and she told him she didn't have time to discuss it, they were meeting someone for coffee. Since then his calls went to voicemail.

Well . . . Jack looked down at his notepad, his handwriting nearly undecipherable. Were they here? Would they be at the clinic? The latter didn't make sense – it was after six, no one would be there, would they?

He got out of the car, hissing as his back and legs complained. Stretching, he examined himself. The white shirt he'd put on that morning now sported a brown coffee stain just above his navel. The material clung to him and he knew he stank.

Well, the hotel would have a men's room near the lobby. He'd go and freshen up best he could before he took his next step. Jack checked to make sure he had his digital recorder and his notebook and headed towards the large brown building.

The lobby's floors were so polished he could see a faint reflection. The reservation desk was of sturdy dark wood, two young men manning it looking a lot better than Jack felt at the moment.

He glanced around, hoping he wouldn't have to ask one of those well-dressed employees for directions to the restroom. A man in his mid-forties and wearing a blue and white security uniform gave him a calculating stare, arms folded as he stood near a comfortable looking aqua couch.

Jack grimaced and finally caught sight of a sign pointing him to his destination. He hurried to it, grateful to find the expensive looking men's room empty. Maybe it was a good sign that things would finally break his way.

Cold water gushed into the marble basin. Jack cupped his hands under the stream and splashed his face again and again, willing the chill to sharpen his mind.

Taking a deep breath, Jack kept his head bowed over the sink, watching water drip from his nose. He was so tired. Not just physically – mentally and emotionally, this story had used him up and almost spit him out. And still he came back for more.

What would Lisa think? Would she understand this was the only way he could deal with losing her? And that he needed this story, needed it to assure himself that he was still the reporter he once was?

"The reporter I *am*," he muttered to the sink. "I'm still a great reporter."

The reflection that stared back at him when he finally looked up in the mirror wasn't reassuring. His eyes were bloodshot, his chin darkened with beard stubble, and he looked so much older then he was.

With a grunt Jack pushed himself away from the sink. He'd come this far – there was no way he was going to quit now. Running damp hands through his hair in an attempt to look a little more put together, Jack grabbed a handful of paper towels and tackled the coffee stain.

Ten minutes later he returned to the lobby, the stain somewhat fainter but his shirt clearly damp. Jack surveyed the large open area again, letting his gaze skip past the security guard who glanced at him yet again, a frown on his weathered face. Jack smiled and nodded at the man while he contemplated his next move.

He'd come to the hotel first because he thought that was the best place to find the two women. Mary Beamer had hung up the phone before he could ask where they were having coffee. He guessed she didn't want him around for that.

Jack slapped his notebook against the palm of his hand as he slowly made his way to the front desk. He hoped that Mary would come through for him –

he'd come close to pushing Wheeler over the edge, and Jack knew that if he did that he'd be on the street, story or no.

He stood patiently at the counter and waited for the tanned blond man in front of him to look up from his computer and acknowledge his existence. After a chilly moment, the desk clerk looked up.

"Can I help you?" the man asked. His narrowed blue eyes and the slight curl of his lip communicated that he believed Jack didn't belong there.

"I'm just looking for a couple of friends of mine," Jack said with an attempt at a smile. "A Ms. Beamer and a Ms. Morris have reservations here, and I'd like to go say hi."

The man's eyebrow went up. "Did they give you their room number, sir?"

Jack swallowed a sarcastic reply. "No. I was hoping you could help me out with that."

The desk clerk's eyes gave Jack's rumpled clothes a once-over. "I'm sorry, sir, but we don't give that information out to people. You'll have to contact them."

The reporter ran his hands through his hair. This snotty kid was getting to him. "Look, can you at least tell me if they're up there?"

"I wouldn't know," the blond replied, his voice cooling. "Now, if you don't mind, I have some work to do. Have a pleasant evening."

"But –" Jack started to argue. He felt a hand clamp his shoulder and shut up.

"Clark," a deep voice asked behind him, "Is this gentleman giving you trouble?"

The blond clerk shook his head, a faint smirk tugging at his lips. "Not at all, Stan, but I think he needs help finding the door."

Jack swore and pulled away, turning to glare at the security guard behind him. "That's okay, I can find my own way out."

The guard's face was impassive. "Then I suggest you do so, sir."

Many possible responses tumbled through Jack's mind. Most of them would more than likely land him in a jail cell. So he settled for clenching his jaw and his fists as he turned on his heel (the move making the shiny floor under him squeak in protest) and strode out of the place.

Once outside in the fading daylight, Jack let his shoulders slump as he trudged across the parking lot to his car. He was tired, uncomfortable, and discouraged. The high he'd felt earlier when he'd learned about the Montgomery connection was no longer fueling him.

He got into his car and sat there a few moments, head back, eyes closed. What should he do now? He was so close, and his gut told him there was something about to break on this story. Yet here he was, half asleep in his old car without a clue.

The notepad was still in his hands. Jack opened his eyes and looked down at it, at the two addresses scribbled on the page.

The clinic. It was where the story was. Where the answers for him were. And even if there was nothing he could do except stare at the exterior tonight, Jack felt compelled to do just that.

It beat sitting here feeling sorry for himself. Jack grabbed the Montgomery map that lay across the dash and began to try to figure out directions. He felt some energy come back to him as he did.

Yeah, the answers were coming. His star would rise again. By this time tomorrow, everything would be better.

They had to be, because Jack couldn't afford for them to get any worse.

- SEVENTY-ONE -

*P*LEASE MAKE SURE YOUR SEATS *are in their upright positions and your seat belts are securely fastened. We will be landing in Montgomery shortly."*

Roger sighed and closed his eyes. His body was crammed into a middle seat in the row, and he'd spent most of the flight trying not to bump the two people on either side of him with his elbows. The woman at the window had spent the flight buried in a best-seller, barely speaking except to accept a drink from the flight attendant. The large man to his right had pulled out a notebook and a financial magazine and kept muttering to himself while he read.

As for Roger, he'd tried to concentrate on the news magazine he'd picked up at one of the airport shops. He'd failed miserably. Every time he tried, his thoughts went back to Mary, how strangely she'd been acting, and how crazy he felt doing this.

Paul had driven him to the airport and helped him get a flight that was priced low enough that Roger had gulped instead of screamed. Before they got to the line for security Paul gripped his hand. "We're praying for you, Roger."

He nodded. "Yeah. Thanks...thanks for everything, Paul. Thank Joanne, too."

His friend grinned. "Hey, no problem. Let us know you got there safely, okay?"

That had been nearly four hours ago. Now it was approaching eight o'clock, and he would soon be able to talk with his wife and maybe get a clue about what was going on. With her. With *them.*

Roger had debated calling her and telling her he was on his way. He'd even punched in her number while he waited to board his connecting flight in Atlanta. But at the last minute he decided that would be counterproductive. What if she told him not to come?

The plane began to descend. Roger felt a slight swoop in his stomach as they slipped through clouds. He began to pray, as he had been on and off ever since he let Paul convince him that going after Mary was the right thing to do.

God, I'm not sure what's going on here. I wish I did. I love Mary and I am praying to You asking for strength and wisdom to deal with what's going on right now. Please, God, help me be a good husband and help Mary and I get through whatever this crisis is so that we can continue to serve you. In Jesus' name, amen.

There was a thud as the plane's wheels made contact with the runway and a scream of sound as the engines reversed. Once the noise let up some a calm voice welcomed everyone to Montgomery and told them the time was 8:21 PM.

Roger pulled his cell phone out of his pocket, nearly jabbing the guy muttering about financials with his elbow. He muttered an apology as he turned on the phone. His seatmate was too busy turning his phone on to do more than grunt something back.

There were no messages, Roger noticed. He called Paul as promised, to let his friend know he was on the ground and safe. Then he decided it was time to call Mary and announce is arrival.

His hands trembled as he punched in her number. How would he find her? What would she say when she found out he was there? Would she be happy? Upset? Angry?

The call went to her voicemail. Roger frowned but decided to leave a message. "Hi, hon. Look, everything's okay, but I need you to call me on my cell as soon as you get this, okay? Love you."

He stood as best as he could – he was tall enough that he couldn't stand straight without knocking his head on the panel above – and waited his turn to get off the plane. Once he was able to move into the aisle, he nabbed the green carry-on that held his stuff from an overhead compartment and followed the line of weary travelers off the plane.

Once off the plane, Roger found himself fighting a surge of loneliness. No one expected him here – for all he knew Mary didn't want him here.

She hadn't called back yet. This bugged him for some reason. They both kept their cell phones on and charged – it wasn't like her to ignore something like this.

Roger snorted at himself. Yeah, and exactly what had been normal about her lately?

A donut shop sent out tantalizing aromas of coffee and cinnamon. Roger's stomach growled in response. He let himself follow his nose to the counter, where he got himself a strong cup of coffee and a frosted cinnamon bun.

An empty table with a couple of crumpled up napkins and a ring of spilled coffee was near the doorway. He sank into a plastic chair, glad for a moment to gather his thoughts.

Roger took his time with his snack. *Come on, Mary, check your phone! Please, sweetheart, call me back!*

Nothing. His phone, which he'd laid on the table, remained silent.

After he popped the last of the cinnamon bun into his mouth, Roger wiped his hands and pulled out his wallet. One of the things he'd done after packing that afternoon was to check their caller ID. He'd found the number that he assumed belonged to the reporter who'd called that morning.

Now he stared at it, scribbled hastily on a sheet of green notepaper that was by the phone in the kitchen. Mary wasn't answering her phone. Maybe this guy would?

What if Mary answered this guy's phone?

Roger shook his head to clear that thought out. He bowed his head and prayed once more. Then he punched in the reporter's number.

Fifteen minutes later he burst out a door to where he'd been told he could get a cab. He jumped into the first free one he came to and stammered out his destination. As the driver pulled away from the curb, Roger buried his face in his hands, trying to pray through his tears.

- SEVENTY-TWO -

MARY TRIED TO HIDE HER UNEASE as Celia parked her car once again in the clinic's parking lot. Unlike earlier, there was no one around. It made the whole thing seem eerie.

Celia glanced over at her friend. "It's gonna be okay, you know."

"We're breaking the law," Mary said. She couldn't help fidgeting.

Her friend shook her head as she reached into the back seat and snagged the small Radio Shack bag she'd tossed there earlier. "Nadine has a key and authority to enter the place. No laws broken."

Mary glanced at the bag her friend held. "And what *you* plan on doing?"

Celia shrugged. "I'm doing it, not you. Stop worrying. It's time to get answers."

Mary watched Celia get out of the car. Answers. Was that why her stomach was in knots and she couldn't stop her palms from sweating? Because she was about to get answers? Or because she was about to participate in something she wasn't entirely comfortable with?

"Hey!" Celia ducked her head back into the car. "You coming or what?"

Mary swallowed and climbed out of the car. Nadine was waiting by the door, shifting from foot to foot. That gave Mary a measure of relief – at least she wasn't the only one somewhat uncomfortable with what they were doing.

"Both your phones are on silent, right?" Nadine asked.

Celia and Mary nodded. Nadine had wanted them to leave their phones in the rental car, but Celia wanted access to her phone's camera and Mary wanted hers in case they needed to call someone quickly. They compromised on putting the phones on silent mode and Celia and Mary promising not to take any calls.

The nurse nodded. "All right. First I'll take you to Ms. Abrams' office, Ms. Morris. Then I'll show Ms. Beamer the nursery."

"Right," Celia said. She glanced around. "You sure the coast is clear?"

Nadine nodded. "I checked around back. Only one here is the nurse on duty." She shuffled her keying a moment, the fading sunlight making the bronze and silver keys wink and twinkle, then said, "I'm taking a big chance doing this. If you're caught, I don't know how much help I can be."

"Gotcha," Celia said, rolling her eyes. "You've only warned us about that ten times already."

Mary bit her lip. It was almost too late to back out. Part of her wanted to run back to the car, get behind the wheel, and drive straight back to Jacksonville. Anything was better than this.

Before she could act on that impulse, Nadine turned and unlocked the clinic door. Cool air wafted out to the women. Nadine stepped in and held the door open to Celia and Mary.

Celia glanced at her friend. "After you," she said, sweeping her hand towards the door. "Let's find out about this son of yours."

At the mention of her son, Mary's impulse to flee died. She took a deep breath, silently asked God for mercy, and once again stepped into the clinic.

The waiting room was dark, only a dim light above the reception desk providing any illumination. Nadine stepped quickly to the door leading to the clinic proper, Mary and Celia behind her.

"I'd like to keep most of the lights off," Nadine whispered. "Just so we don't raise any questions."

Celia frowned. "You're sure taking this being careful thing to the max," she whispered back.

Mary rubbed her arms, wishing they could turn on more lights. The dim hallway made her heart pound, her imagination taking her to the horror movies she and her friends had enjoyed when she was a teen. Bad place for her mind to go right now.

They were soon at the door to Sharon Abrams' office. Nadine tried a key and frowned. "She must have changed the lock."

"What?" Mary felt her breathing speed up.

"Not to worry, ladies," Celia said calmly. She took a credit card out of her purse and began to fiddle with the door. A few long moments later the door swung open with a soft creaking sound. "See? No problem."

Mary shook her head. They were really doing this. She was really breaking the law.

Well, a voice in her head sniped, *you've been breaking God's laws all this time. Why stop at man's laws?*

Celia pulled a silver thumb drive from the bag. "Here, take my phone. It has the better camera. You remember how to work it, right?"

Mary nodded, her throat suddenly too dry to speak. Celia gave her a brief sharp look and then gave Mary a tight hug.

"It's gonna be okay," she whispered into Mary's ear. "Just a little longer, girlfriend."

Mary hugged Celia back, feeling afraid. Would it really be okay? She stepped back and took Celia's iPhone, wiping her eyes.

Celia touched Nadine's shoulder. "You take care of her, okay? Both of you meet me back here after."

When the nurse nodded, Celia turned and slipped into Abrams office. Nadine heaved a huge sigh. "Well, let's go, Ms. Beamer. I gotta say your friend has guts."

"Yeah," Mary managed to force out. She followed Nadine as they snuck through the dim hallways, the only noises the hum of the air conditioner and the soft impact of their shoes on the carpet.

When they got to a door that was marked "Private" Nadine took a moment to listen at the door before unlocking it. After cautiously sticking her head inside she waved Mary through.

There was a door on the left that was slightly ajar. Nadine pointed to it. "That's the bathroom. Stand there and listen good. Don't turn on the lights or make any noise. When we leave, go down the hallway to the second door on the right. I'll try to give you five minutes."

Mary nodded, her heart beating so hard she was surprised she couldn't hear it. She stepped into the dark restroom, closing the door so that only a sliver of light was visible. As Nadine's footsteps faded, Mary tried to bring her breathing and pulse down to a more normal level.

She wanted to pray for God to be with her during this, but could she? Would God really want to bless what she was doing now, helping to do?

"God," she prayed, her voice inaudible, "I'm sorry. If there was another way to find out about this son I didn't know about, I swear I'd do it. This is my last chance to deal with it. Please forgive me, and help me if You can."

Approaching footsteps caused her to clamp her mouth shut. She barely breathed as she saw Nadine walking with another woman, this one somewhat younger and dressed in a white uniform.

"…you sure this is gonna be okay?" the younger woman asked, a whine underlying her words. "They told me I hadda be in there unless I had to go to the john."

"Now Maggie," Nadine's voice was kind. "Don't tell me you couldn't use a smoke and a cup of coffee."

"Well…yeah," Maggie agreed, following Nadine out the door. "I mean, I get they don't want smoke around the babies but why…"

The voices faded. Mary swallowed. It was time. She forced herself to step out of the relative safety of the bathroom and go quickly to the second door on the right.

With a final, terrified glance down the hallway, Mary turned the knob and entered the nursery.

- SEVENTY-THREE -

MARY FROZE AS SHE STOOD IN THE NURSERY. She'd heard Nadine explain what was going on – and the thought had been in the back of her mind, hadn't it, ever since she'd first gotten the note from Martha Thompson? It shouldn't have surprised her.

But it did.

The room had six hospital-style cribs, three to a wall. A table to the right of the door sent heat to Mary's arm – a warming table? A rocking chair in the center of the room, oak with blue and white cushions, still rocked slightly.

A burbling sound made Mary's head whip to the left. She couldn't keep herself from walking towards it, past the chair, to the middle crib of three on this wall.

A baby – no more than a few days old – lay on its back. She – Mary assumed the baby was female by the pink blanket that swaddled it – had a cap of blond hair, fine as fuzz. Soft sounds came from her milky lips.

There was a card at the foot of the crib. It read, "Baby Jane Doe 25," and was dated the day before yesterday.

Mary felt her legs shake. Twenty-five? Did that mean that twenty four other babies had . . .?

She realized her face was wet, that she was weeping for this tiny life, for the mother who probably didn't know she existed, and not only them, but for herself and her son who existed somewhere.

A glance at her watch warned her that she was running out of time. Swallowing her tears, Mary began taking pictures of the nursery and the small Jane Doe. She found another baby – a dark-haired dark skinned child labeled John Doe 12 – sleeping in another crib. He apparently was receiving treatment of some kind; there were leads attached to his chest that went out to a heart monitor.

Mary kept snapping pictures. She found the babies' medical files on a small metal desk in a corner of the room. She considered taking them, but knew that would raise questions too soon. She opened the baby girl's file and began to take pictures of the pages.

She'd taken shots of four or five pages when her phone vibrated. It was a text message from Nadine: *we're coming back. Hide if you haven't!*

Heart pounding, Mary ran out of the room. She ducked into the dark bathroom, her breath coming in short gasps. She leaned against the cool wall and let herself slide to a sitting position.

She heard the door to the main part of the clinic open and Nadine's voice. "...don't know how hard it's been for Dr. Green these past few days. Poor man, he doesn't need the stress."

"I hear that!" Maggie sounded a bit more cheerful than she had earlier. "But how long do you think before he'll be looking for another girlfriend?"

"I have no idea," Nadine said. "Well, I'll let you go back to work. I enjoyed visiting with you Maggie."

"Hey, thanks for the ciggie break!" Maggie said. "And the dirt, too. I promise – lips are sealed."

Mary rested her forehead on her knees and waited. The door to the bathroom opened and she jumped, startled. Nadine was looking at her, a worried frown on her face.

"Let's go!" Nadine whispered. "We need to get to Ms. Abrams' office!"

Mary got to her feet, unable to stop shaking. Nadine blew out an impatient breath and grabbed Mary by the arm, pushing her back into the main part of the clinic. Once the door clicked shut behind them, Nadine took a shaky breath. "Okay. Tell me you got pictures."

Mary nodded. "It . . . there are babies in there."

"Yes, there are," Nadine said, giving Mary a strange look as she led the way back to Sharon Abrams' office. "Two of them at the moment."

"How many...?" Mary tried to ask, but found she couldn't complete the sentence.

Nadine shrugged. "I don't know, to be honest. I don't keep count."

Mary bit her lip. She was badly frightened and wanted nothing more than to get out of this clinic and back home. This wasn't her. Mary Hollister Beamer didn't sneak into abortion clinics after hours to find dirt on the owners.

What was she doing here?

She came out of her thoughts as Nadine opened the door to the office Celia had disappeared into a while ago. The room's lights were on, and Celia was in the office chair, leaning slightly forward as she stared at the computer screen, her fingers dancing over the keyboard.

"Are you ready to go yet?" Nadine asked as she hurried over to Celia's side. Mary joined her and glanced at the computer screen, which made no sense to her with its strings of numbers and letters.

"Patience, ladies," Celia said, frowning slightly as the screen shifted to a login screen. "She's smart enough to have security on these files. Fortunately for us, I'm not stupid."

Mary slipped Celia's phone into her friend's purse. "Are these the files we're looking for?"

Celia shrugged a shoulder. "Well, they're encrypted, so I'm willing to bet they're not Sharon Abrams' cookie recipes." She typed something into the login box and suddenly the screen showed a column of files. "Bingo, ladies!"

Nadine rubbed her arms. "Fine. Copy them and let's get out of here."

"Just a minute," Celia murmured. "Let's make sure the most important file is here."

Mary felt ice shoot down her spine. She thought she knew what Celia would consider the "most important file." She shivered, trying to tamp down her fear.

"Aha," Celia murmured. "Here we go: Mary Hollister." She turned and gave her friend a sympathetic look. "Mary? Want to see it?"

Mary looked at the file icon with her name under it. The cursor was poised on top of it, blinking. Waiting.

"Are you out of your mind?" Nadine hissed. "We have to leave!"

Celia ignored the nurse, her eyes on Mary. "Up to you, hon. This is part of what it's all about."

Mary tried to swallow, wishing she didn't have to decide this right now. She realized she didn't. "Let's get the files copied first. Then . . . maybe I'll take a look."

"Gotcha," Celia said, turning back to the computer and plugging in the thumb drive they'd brought.

There was silence for a few minutes while the three women watched the bar showing the progress of the copy command. Near the end, Mary's head jerked up. "Did you hear that?"

Nadine's eyes widened. "What? What did you hear?"

"I thought I heard a car door," Mary said. She glanced behind them at the window. "We shouldn't have turned on the lights!"

"Too late to worry about that," Celia said, her eyes glued to the computer screen. "Okay, it's done. Mary, grab the memory stick while I close this out."

Mary nodded and pulled the precious memory stick out of the USB port. She was frightened – she could swear she heard something.

Celia was getting to her feet when the doorknob rattled.

Acting on impulse, Mary stuck the memory stick into her shirt, tucking it into her bra. She pulled her hand out just as the door opened, revealing an angry-looking Sharon Abrams.

An angry-looking Sharon Abrams who was pointing a pistol at the three of them.

- SEVENTY-FOUR -

"WELL, WELL, WELL," Sharon Abrams said, her eyes going from one white face to the other, "now what are you all up to?"

Mary felt as if she'd been turned into a statue. She was surprised she was still able to breathe – shouldn't her lungs be as paralyzed as her limbs and her mouth?

She felt Celia trembling next to her. Celia's hands were clenched into fists, and while she looked nearly as afraid as Mary, there was a good measure of anger in her expression as well.

Nadine leaned on the desk, looking as if she might faint. "Ms. Abrams... please, I can explain..."

"Oh really?" Sharon arched an eyebrow, the gun moving to point at the nurse. "That will be interesting. Please, Nadine, explain why you helped two pro-life fanatics break into the clinic and try to destroy it. I'm sure it will be fascinating."

"If that's what you think we're doing, call the police," Celia spat. "We'll be happy to talk to them."

Sharon glared at Celia as she shut the door behind her. "So, let me guess – you're the one who was hacking into my computer. I guess you missed the security application that alerted me to your antics."

Celia shrugged. Mary felt her heart sink. The police...they'd arrest them, because on the surface she and Celia were the criminals. By the time things got sorted out, what would happen to the records they found? Or the babies?

"Ms. Abrams," Nadine stuttered, "please listen. I heard you and Dr. Green arguing, and – and I was worried that maybe, maybe you'd –"

Shut up, Mary thought, watching Abrams' face get darker as Nadine stammered. *You're making it worse. Shut up!*

"Ah, I worried about that," Sharon mused. "Nadine, you should have kept your concerns inside the clinic. You should have talked to me, not these two."

"I – I panicked," Nadine stammered. Her legs shook so hard that Mary didn't know how the woman remained on her feet. "I mean, it sounded like you murdered Ms. Winters."

Sharon cocked her head. "Do you think I'm capable of murder, Nadine?"

Mary felt a chill crawl down her spine. She saw Celia's eyes darting around the room, looking for something to give them an advantage over the office manager. Mary wished she could think of something that would help – she wished she was one of those women she saw on television who knew martial arts and didn't feel like throwing up when faced with a gun.

Tears were sliding down Nadine's face. "Ms. Abrams…please, just let me leave. I'll keep my mouth shut, I promise I will…"

"I know you will," Sharon said, her voice suddenly gentle.

Celia stiffened. Mary held a hand out, fearing what was about to happen. In contrast, Nadine seemed to relax a little, taking a tentative step towards the office manager –

The sound of the gun firing was louder than Mary had thought it would be. She screamed, watching in horror as a bloom of red appeared on Nadine's white blouse. The nurse looked surprised, then her face went slack as she fell to the floor.

Celia moved towards the nurse. Sharon Abrams promptly pointed the gun at Mary. "Stay where you are, or your friend gets the next bullet."

Mary was shaking, partly with fear, but also with a deeply buried anger. "Why did you do that? Why hurt anybody?"

"Shut up!" Sharon snapped. "I'm protecting what's important to me! And no goody-goody hypocrite is going to stop me!"

"And my mother?" Celia's voice was hard. "She tried to stop you?"

Sharon smirked. "Your dear mother…she sold out your friend's baby, did you know that? And she was always eager to help us find others…for an appropriate finder's fee."

Celia went pale. Mary swallowed the bile that filled her throat. She'd been afraid of this, hoped it wasn't true… "You did kill her, didn't you?"

"She got greedy," Sharon shrugged. "Wanted to blackmail Dr. Green. Couldn't permit that."

"We'll end you," Celia said, her voice low. "When the press finds out what you've done -"

"What the press will find out," Sharon said, "is that two crazy anti-abortionists broke into the clinic, killed one of our dear nurses, and tried to burn the place down. Unfortunately for them, they died in the very flames they created."

Gun still trained on the two of them, Sharon stepped back to the doorway and picked up a bright red gas can. She began to splash gasoline on the carpet in front of her, a smile on her face.

"Celia…" Mary moaned. Her friend took a couple of steps forward again.

"Goodbye, ladies," Sharon said. She threw the gun into the room and slammed the door shut.

Celia dove for the gun as Mary staggered over to Nadine. She dropped to her knees and fumbled for a pulse. She saw the nurse's chest rise. "Celia! She's still alive!"

Her friend swore. "Gun's empty. We need to get out of here before –"

There was a quiet fwump! sound outside the door. That was followed by a crackling sound, and the smell of burning.

Mary shared a horrified look with Celia.

Sharon had started the fire.

- SEVENTY-FIVE -

S HARON STEPPED BACK from the pool of gasoline she'd poured on the carpet in front of her office. She pulled out the box of matches she'd brought and scraped on the rough side of the box. She tossed it into the pool, taking a hasty step back as it ignited.

She hadn't expected the heat that reached for her even as she scrambled back, grabbing the gas can as she did. The flames eagerly fed on the gasoline and carpet, caressing the white walls as they traveled.

When they'd chosen to torch the clinic in Atlanta, Sharon had paid someone else to do it. But there hadn't been time for that tonight. When she'd gotten the alert that someone was hacking into her computer, she had to move quickly.

Once again, Thomas would owe her. She was taking steps to protect him and the clinic. After this she was going to make it clear to him that he was not to question her. She was in charge, not him!

She fell back, splashing more gasoline on the walls and carpet. The overhead sprinklers glinted in the light of the flames – she'd made a point of disabling the fire protection system before going to her office. The place had to burn.

Sharon looked over her shoulder. She was angling towards the nursery – she wanted to get the babies out. Their bodies would leave questions she didn't want to answer, and besides, they were a commodity. She didn't want to lose the possible income they would bring.

She got to the door that led the way into the nursery area. She opened the door and coughed deeply. The air was becoming hazy with smoke – the fire was spreading faster than she'd anticipated.

"Ms. Abrams!" Maggie, her eyes wild, was in the hallway. "What's happening?"

"Fire," Sharon said, coughing again. "We need to get the babies, get them out."

The nurse stared past the office manager, seeing the glow down the hall. "Forget the babies. I'm getting out of here!"

Sharon grabbed Maggie by the arm. "Get yourself together! We need to get the babies! Now!"

Maggie stared at her, panicked, then down at the gas can Sharon still held. "You're crazy! Let go of me!"

Sharon swore as she struggled with the woman, Gasoline splashed on the two of them, and she dropped the can so she could use both hands to subdue the nurse.

Maggie swore and punched Sharon in the face, sending the office manager staggering. The nurse followed the blow with a shove, and Sharon tripped over the gas can, her head hitting the wall as she went down. She heard Maggie screaming, but it seemed to come from far way as black stars exploded in her vision and the stench of gasoline and smoke filled her nostrils.

It took Sharon a few precious seconds to clear her head. She was so dizzy. She put her hands on the wall beside her, using it to support her weight as she got to her feet.

The hall seemed darker – had the lights gone out? Or was the smoke that thick that soon? She opened her eyes but shut them quickly as things spun around at sickening speed. She had to get out! Forget the babies, she had to save herself.

Hands on the wall, she began to feel her way. She thought she heard someone calling her, but she ignored them. Why was it getting hotter?

Searing pain! Her eyes flew open and she saw flames dancing on her pants leg, felt it cooking the flesh underneath, smelled the sweet-awful stench of herself burning.

Sharon screamed. She batted at the flames with her hands, stumbling back and falling once again. She screamed as the pain spread, consumed her. She screamed until the pain seized her lungs and dragged her down to everlasting darkness.

- SEVENTY-SIX -

H ERE," CELIA PRESSED A TOWEL onto the bullet wound in Nadine's chest. "I'm gonna wet some more towels and try to break that window."

"What about the security bars?" Mary gasped. Smoke had been slipping under the door, giving the room a slightly hazy look. A glow under the door and the smell of burning wood told her that they were running out of time.

"We'll deal with that when we get some air in here," Celia said. She shot Mary a worried look. "You know, if you think God answers prayer, this might be a good time to send Him an SOS."

Mary pressed the reddening towel to Nadine's chest, bowing her head over the dying woman. She prayed softly, coughing now and then. "God, we need Your help. Please, help us get out of here so we can stop this evil. Help me save this woman's life, and Celia's."

Her voice roughened, and not just from the smoke. "I know I don't deserve anything from You, after all I've done, but please, if You can show me mercy, let me see Roger and Kelly again."

Celia dropped a couple of wet washcloths on Mary's lap. "For the smoke. Put one on Nadine's face and cover your nose and mouth with the other."

Mary nodded. She kept her eyes on Nadine's white face as she covered the woman's nose and mouth with the cloth, and held the other one over her face while keeping pressure on the wound with her other hand.

There was a crash of glass and Celia swearing, then cool air flowed in behind Mary. She saw Celia swing the office chair she'd used to smash a hole in the glass. The hole got bigger and by the third swing most of the glass was gone.

Celia dropped the chair, breathing heavily. She'd wrapped a towel around her head but her efforts had caused it to slip. "Mary, how're you doing?"

"Okay," Mary said. She saw blood streaking her friend's arm. "Celia! You're hurt!"

"It's okay," Celia said. She groped along the window frame, and then gave a triumphant shout. "I thought they'd have a quick release latch! Let's get out of here!"

Mary almost sobbed with relief as she watched Celia push aside the bars. She stood, swaying a little as a wave of dizziness struck her. She then grabbed Nadine under her arms and began to drag her towards the window.

Celia came over and grabbed Nadine's legs. A whoosh caused both women to look towards the other end of the office, where they saw the door hidden under a sheet of flame.

"Let's go!" Celia screamed. Mary nodded, feeling adrenaline rush through her at the sight of the flames. Together she and Celia got Nadine to the window. Mary awkwardly climbed onto the small counter under the window and together she and Celia pushed and pulled the nurse out into the Alabama night.

They staggered a few steps and then Celia gasped, "We gotta put her down. We need help." They lowered Nadine onto the grass and dropped down beside her, breathing heavily.

"Why . . . why aren't the sprinklers working?" Mary asked, watching the flames grow and the smoke rise, obscuring the stars above.

"I bet Ms. Crazy Lady took care of that," Celia said darkly. "We need to call the fire department. Where's my phone?"

Mary felt her heart sink. "In your purse."

"Oh," Celia said, her eyes going to the window where the glow from the fire cast a weird light on the grass. "I guess we'll have to get yours."

A scream made them both look up. The nurse Mary had seen with Nadine earlier ran to them, eyes wide with horror. "Who are you? What happened to Nadine?"

Mary got to her feet. "Where are the babies?"

The nurse looked at Mary with a horrified look on her face. "What? How do you know about –"

Dread went through Mary. She grabbed the woman and shook her. "The babies! Are they still in there?"

"I – I didn't have a chance to get them out . . ." the woman stammered, looking frightened.

There was a screech of tires as a car careened into the parking lot. Mary focused on the nurse in front of her. "How do I get in there? How did you get out?"

"B-back door . . . are you crazy?"

She heard Jack Foster swearing and asking what was going on. She ignored him. "You need to show me. We need to get them out!"

"Are you crazy, lady?" the nurse snapped. "I ain't going back in there!"

"Fine, just show me how I can!" Mary shouted.

Mary heard Celia calling her to stop, heard Foster rattling information to 911. She shoved the nurse in the direction she'd come from, and after a few steps the nurse shook her arm off and began to run around the building, Mary hot on her heels.

She would not stand and wait while babies burned. She couldn't.

- SEVENTY-SEVEN -

THE NURSE STOPPED by a back door, still open slightly. "There," she swallowed. "But the fire's close by – it's too dangerous . . ."

Mary shook her head. "Go back and wait for the firefighters. Send them back here."

"You aren't seriously going in there!" the nurse argued. "They're just babies!"

"Just babies?" Mary asked, shocked. She shook her head in disgust. "Just go."

Turning to the door, Mary took a deep breath. Uttering a prayer for safety and putting the nearly dry towel on her face, she threw the door wide open and ran in.

Noise assaulted her. The not-so-far-away sound of flames. Babies wailing. An alarm.

Mary rushed to the nursery and looked in. Both babies were still there, the air here filling with smoke. She saw the alarm was from the heart monitor. John Doe was in distress.

Mary found herself coughing. She had to get them out of here. But she needed to make sure she didn't pass out first. Hoping the open door would bring in a little fresh air, she sprinted back into the hallway and headed to the bathroom she'd hidden in – had it only been minutes ago? It felt like years.

Mary turned the water in the sink on full blast and dropped the towel into the basin. She searched the oak cabinet beneath and added two washcloths on top, letting them get sopping wet.

She gathered it all up, not bothering to turn off the water. As she stepped out of the bathroom, the sopping fabric clutched to her chest, she heard a sound in the hallway to the main part of the clinic.

Mary stepped to the doorway cautiously. She saw Sharon Abrams pushing herself to her feet. Her back was to Mary and she appeared shaky. To Mary's horror, the office manager took a couple of steps away from the doorway, towards the fire that was getting closer.

"Ms. Abrams!" she screamed. She wanted to run towards the office manager but fear of the woman and the approaching flames kept her feet rooted to the floor. "Ms. Abrams! Please, stop!"

The woman appeared not to hear her. Just as Mary resolved to run after her, a finger of flame ran along the carpet and up her leg. There must have been gasoline on her slacks, because they quickly started burning.

Sharon Abrams screamed, beating on the flames with her hands. Mary started to run towards her, her vocal cords paralyzed by what she saw. She thought she could throw the wet towel and washcloths on the woman, smother the flames. But then Sharon spun and fell back onto a flaming piece of carpet.

Mary shrieked, her voice drowned out by the horrific screams that came from the office manager. Sharon writhed as the flames rushed over her, and Mary felt tears on her own cheeks, knowing there was nothing she could do, wishing there was.

For a moment, she stood there, paralyzed by the death she'd witnessed. A fit of coughing had her bending double and shocked her back to reality. *The babies!*

Mary stumbled back into the nursery. The flames seemed to be coming faster, as if sensing prey. She glanced at the two cribs, the screaming heart monitor, her chest aching, breathing becoming more and more of a chore.

Her eyes fell on several metal tanks that stood in a corner. *What were those? Probably oxygen . . . oh, no!*

Mary ran to Jane Doe's crib, scooping up the baby in her arms. She placed her in John Doe's crib, putting them both close together. Both babies were crying and coughing, their faces dry, their tear ducts not functioning yet.

Mary had a flash of memory: the first time she saw Kelly's tears. How tiny they'd been, small glitters on the infant's soft face . . .

Mary pulled the leads off John Doe – she couldn't move both the crib and the monitor. "It's okay, sweeties, it's okay," she rasped to the babies. "We're going to go now."

She pushed the crib out of the nursery. Heat baked her from the left – the flames were getting closer. It was so hard to push the crib...she couldn't breathe...

Mary focused on the open door in front of her, green grass and fresh air. Just a few more steps . . . *God, please, take my life, but not these little ones...*

Suddenly there were people around her. People helping her rush the crib out into the night air. She had a confused impression of firemen in yellow coats and red helmets and a disheveled-looking Jack Foster around her. Then the world spun out of control and she fell down, down, down, into a smothering blackness.

- SEVENTY-EIGHT -

BEEP . . . BEEP . . .
The sound filtered into Mary's awareness. She was laying down on something soft and the quiet was comforting. Something was irritating her nose, and she raised a hand to pull it away.

"No, Mare," a voice, and a warm hand closing on hers. "That has to stay put, hon."

Her eyes flew open – it *couldn't* be –

Roger's face hovered over hers. His eyes were bloodshot and there were tear tracks on his face. But he was smiling.

"Mary. Thank God," he said, his voice breaking slightly. "Thank God you're gonna be okay."

She looked around, realizing she was in a hospital room. A bed next to hers was empty, white sheets and blanket smoothed neatly over it. The lighting was dim. A large television screen on the wall was dark.

Mary put a hand to her aching head. She tried to order her thoughts. "The – the babies? Celia?"

"The babies are fine," Roger said, caressing her hand as he sat on the edge of her bed. "They're in the neonatal care unit. Doc says you got them out just in time."

"Celia?" Mary asked again.

A small grin tugged her husband's face. "She took ten stitches on her arm and was released. She's in the waiting room and wanted me to tell you she's going to kick your rear end for pulling this stunt."

"She said 'rear end?'" Mary asked, feeling a grin of her own.

"Well, I cleaned it up a little," Roger admitted. He gently smoothed her hair. "Now, aren't you curious about yourself?"

"The nurse . . . Nadine?" Mary asked.

Roger sighed. "She's in critical condition. Not sure if she'll pull through. Now, we need to talk about you."

Mary felt a thread of fear. Not about her condition – she was sure she'd be fine. But Roger being here . . . "We are still in Montgomery? I haven't been out that long, have it?"

Her husband swallowed and blinked hard. "Yes, we're still in Montgomery. Mare – you stopped breathing at the clinic.

She felt her breath catch. "Oh, honey…"

Roger shook his head. "I'd just gotten to Montgomery . . . you weren't answering your phone, so I called Foster. He told me . . . he told me what happened to you and what hospital you were at. I jumped into the first cab I saw and prayed the whole time." She saw a tear slip down his face. "Mary, I was so *scared…*"

"I'm sorry," she whispered, feeling tears of her own. "Roger, I'm so sorry for everything. I know . . . I haven't been a very good wife, or a good Christian . . ."

He put his fingers on her lips. "Wait. I have to tell you something before you say anything else."

The fear inside her grew. *God, give me strength. I know I deserve whatever he says to me.*

She nodded at her husband, her hand squeezing his. Realizing he might not want the contact, she tried to pull away. Before she could, his grip tightened on her fingers.

"Mary," Roger said, looking deeply into her eyes. "I don't know what's been going on the past couple of weeks. I don't know what it is you've buried for so long."

He took a deep breath, and Mary found herself holding her breath.

"I've been angry with you," he continued. "But after praying . . . and this," his hand circled to include the IV pole and monitors by the bedside, "I remembered that when I married you I promised for better or for worse."

He brought his hands to her cheeks, his thumbs wiping the tears that were coursing down her face. "I can't promise I won't be angry, Mare, but I'll promise you this: no matter what you've done, I still choose to love you. And I'll do everything I can to help you deal with it."

Suddenly she could breathe. She looked into Roger's eyes, and knew he wasn't lying. He meant every word.

Was it possible? Had she been wrong, thinking she was unforgivable? Had she underestimated this man who'd dropped everything and come to her, even not knowing what was going on?

He bent down and kissed her lips gently. The floodgates opened, and Mary buried her face in his chest as he pulled her into a tight, reassuring hug.

After the storm of tears passed, Roger gently lowered Mary back on the bed. She wiped her eyes and accepted the cup of water he held for her. The cool liquid soothed her throat and help clear her head.

She took Roger's hands in her own but kept her eyes on his face. Mary knew this was one step of many she'd have to take, but it was an important one.

"When I was sixteen," she began, "I fell in love with a boy named Harold . . ."

- SEVENTY-NINE -

JACK WATCHED AS WHEELER READ the copy he'd written. He tried not to fidget. He leaned back in the hard chair in front of Wheeler's desk and started to count the acoustical ceiling tiles.

A rustle of papers told him the editor was finished. "Looks good. In fact, it might be the best writing you've ever done."

"Thank you," Jack said, lowering his gaze to look at his boss. Wheeler was riffling the pages along his thumb, his expression thoughtful.

"So, Green looking to make a deal?"

Jack shrugged. "Neither he nor his attorney will talk to me. If I read the federal prosecutor correctly, they aren't interested in a deal. In fact, when they saw the copies of the records Ms. Beamer had on that memory stick they found on her, they made up their minds Dr. Green will be in prison for life if at all possible."

"And the feds don't care that Ms. Beamer stole the evidence?" Wheeler asked with a raised eyebrow.

Jack snorted. "Maybe they would've if she hadn't carted out two living babies from the clinic – babies that had been reported dead." He gestured to the story in Wheeler's hands. "Besides, as I wrote, they got a warrant for Ms. Abrams' condo, given there was eyewitness testimony from Ms. Beamer, Ms. Morris, and those two nurses she was trying to kill people. She almost did kill that one gal."

Wheeler nodded and drank some coffee. "Hm. As I said, good job. This will probably put your name back in the spotlight, Jack. Try not to let your head swell too much, okay?"

Jack managed a chuckle. "Yeah, okay, sir." He got to his feet. "If that's all –"

"One thing," Wheeler said, a finger raised in the air. "I'm guessing you took a peek at these records before the cops got them."

"Um, maybe," Jack said, suddenly feeling the need to shift his weight from foot to foot.

Wheeler glared at him. "Maybe, eh? Your story has some details that make me wonder."

"Well…" Jack sighed. "Yeah. I got hold of the stick when they found it on Beamer's body. Everybody was so panicked trying to resuscitate her they didn't notice me copying the files to my laptop." His hands in his pockets, he decided to go for bluster. "You gonna slap my wrist, boss?"

Wheeler leaned back in his desk chair and steepled his fingers. He stared over his hands at Jack, his face unreadable. The reporter found himself starting to sweat at the attention. What more needed to be said?

Finally, Wheeler spoke, his voice uncharacteristically soft. "Did you find records for a Lisa Foster?"

Jack jumped as if Wheeler had stuck a hot poker in his gut. He debated storming out of the office but knew it would only put off the inevitable.

He stared at his shoes and the dirty carpet in between them. "No. She never was his patient."

"But you thought she was." It wasn't a question.

Jack gulped in air, feeling his heart began to race. "When I went over her stuff, I found his card. It made sense – I mean, you know what happened, don't you?"

Wheeler nodded. "Yeah. I know the story was a ruptured appendix, but I'm not the editor around here for nothing."

Jack clenched his jaw. "Yeah. I guess so." He looked up at Wheeler, his eyes blazing. "If she'd talked to me – said something, anything! She didn't have to do that!"

With a frown, Wheeler gestured to the chair Jack had vacated. "Sit back down for a sec."

"Sir, with all due respect –"

"I said sit down!"

With a sigh, Jack dropped back into the chair. He put a shaking hand to his eyes.

Wheeler came from around the desk and sat next to him. "Now listen up. I'm not a touchy-feely guy and I'm only giving this speech once. You repeat it outside this office and I'll swear up and down you're a liar. Got it?"

Jack nodded.

"Okay." Wheeler held up a finger. "One, it's a good thing you didn't find her records, because that would've put this very well written story of yours in jeopardy. It would have been an obvious conflict of interest."

"I was objective!" Jack argued.

"Did I say you could talk?" Wheeler snapped back. "Jack, you let this story practically take over your life. You put everything on the line for it. Don't tell me there wasn't some sort of vendetta going on here!"

Jack clenched his fists. "So, because my wife died from an abortion, I can't write this story?"

"I didn't say that. Two," Wheeler held up a second finger. "You need to find a way to put Lisa's death to rest. Thanks to you, a lot of parents are gonna have closure on their kids – I think you rate a little closure too."

"Really?" Jack's eyebrows shot up. "And how do you suggest I do that?"

Wheeler shrugged. "Search me. I'm your editor, not your pastor. You'll have to figure it out on your own"

"I can't argue that," Jack muttered.

That got him a gentle cuff on the head. "Third: Jack, you're good at what you do. But you use people for you own aims. That only goes so far in this business. Someday, someone's gonna stick a knife in your back because of what you did. And I won't always be there to pull it out."

Jack sighed. "Okay, fine. Anything else?"

Wheeler rolled his eyes. "No, I guess not. Get outta here, take a day off – a real vacation day this time. But keep your phone handy. When this story breaks on Monday I'm gonna need you."

"Got it," Jack said, getting to his feet. "Oh, there may be a follow up story to this pretty soon."

"I sure hope so," Wheeler said returning to his desk and picking up his coffee mug. "About Beamer and her gal pal?"

"About Beamer," Jack said. He gave his boss a sardonic grin. "You mentioned closure – this story may just teach me something about it."

- EIGHTY -

MARY KEPT ONE HAND IN ROGER'S as she sat on the dark blue velour couch. Her heart was pounding and she kept reminding herself to breathe slowly.

Roger rubbed her back. "It's gonna be okay, Mare."

She swallowed. "I was such an idiot." She looked outside the bay window in this suburban Atlanta home. Bonnie Cullen had said that her husband and son would be in by 3:30.

Foster, who sat in a fat recliner, shook his head. "They won't come faster if you keep checking the window every two seconds."

Roger glared at the reporter who suddenly found a need to fiddle with his recorder. Bonnie Cullen, a woman a couple of years older than Mary with short blond hair and freckles, came into the room holding a denim-covered photo album.

Bonnie was nervous, Mary saw. She felt the same way.

As she sat on the couch next to Mary and Roger, she cleared her throat. "We weren't Christians when we adopted him," she said. "We only were baptized four years ago."

Mary nodded. Bonnie opened the album to the first page. There was a copy of a birth certificate with the name "Nathaniel Samuel Cullen."

"Nathaniel," Mary tried out the name.

Bonnie nodded. "We didn't realize it at the time, but it means, 'gift of God.'"

Roger nodded. He had been the one to set up this meeting. Bonnie's husband, Andrew and he had talked a long time and the couple had called back on Monday, when the story broke, and agreed to speak to Mary and Roger.

Mary squeezed Roger's hand more tightly as she saw the first picture of her son – apparently taken when he was adopted. He had a mop of hair that was the shade of her own, and his facial features showed a strong resemblance to Harold's.

She felt Roger's arm go around her as tears dropped onto the album. "I'm sorry," she whispered. "I seem to be crying a lot lately."

Bonnie's voice was choked. "I know. Me too." Her hands were clenched tightly in her lap, and when she spoke again, the fear in her voice was overpowering. "Roger – Roger told us you weren't going to try to take him away. That you weren't going to have the adoption declared invalid."

Mary stared in the woman's green, tear-filled eyes. She and Roger had prayed about that all weekend. When Mary went down in front of the congregation on Sunday and confessed her deception, they'd asked their fellow Christians to pray for wisdom to decide what was best.

"They checked you out –" Jack began but Mary held up a hand to stop him.

She took her hand out of Roger's and took one of Bonnie's into her own. She felt herself steady as she spoke. "We did make inquiries. We know you are good people."

"T-thank you," Bonnie stammered. "We try to be. We're not perfect, not by a long shot –"

"None of us are," Mary said. "You both are lovers of God? And – and Nathaniel?"

A small smile showed through Bonnie's tears. "He loves to sing. He's trying to learn how to lead songs at services. His Bible school teacher makes the kids do memory work and he's very good at it."

"Is he happy?" Mary asked softly. "Is he healthy?"

Bonnie met Mary's gaze with her own. "He had a few health issues when he was younger – I guess from being premature – but yes, he's healthy." Bonnie looked down at the photo album in her lap and sighed. "When Andrew and I discovered we couldn't have any kids and found out how hard it was to adopt a baby…I guess we just decided to take matters into our own hands." She swallowed. "We don't know what to tell Nate. But Mary, we love him as much as if I'd given birth to him."

"I believe that," Mary said. She looked at Roger. He smiled and squeezed her hand. Turning back to Bonnie, she said, "I think the best thing for him is to stay with the mom and dad he's always known."

She saw Bonnie's slender shoulders sag with relief. "I – I can't thank you enough. I thought you must hate us." She swiped her eyes while Mary did the same. "Do you – I mean, they'll be home any minute, do you want us to tell him?"

Mary took a shuddering breath. This choice was one Roger told her was hers, and hers alone. He'd promised to stand by her no matter what she decided.

She took a moment and thought about how Roger had hardly let her out of his sight the past few days, touching her more often, as if to assure the both of them she was there. He'd gone down front with her that Sunday, arm around her shoulder as she wept in the pew.

Mary had been afraid of her friends' reactions. She was shocked and brought to even more tears as person after person came up to her, embraced her, told her God had forgiven her and they would too.

She'd so underestimated how much she was loved – by God, by her fellow Christians, by her husband. How could she have doubted?

Joanne had not been in the auditorium – she and another woman had taken the young children, including Kelly, out of services when Mary went down front. Paul had suggested while letting the adults in on the breaking story, it might be too confusing for the little ones. Mary and Roger had agreed, simply telling Kelly that Mommy had sinned and asked people to pray for her.

Kelly listened with wide eyes. Then she climbed up on Mary's lap and hugged her hard. "Don't cry, Mommy, God will forgive you."

Mary pulled back and looked at her daughter through her tears. "You sure, Princess?"

Kelly nodded. "Sure. You and daddy forgive me when I'm bad, and God's our Heavenly daddy, right?"

Mary knew her daughter wouldn't understand why Mommy suddenly hugged her so tightly she gasped or why Mommy cried harder then before. Why hadn't Mary had the wisdom of a child?

Roger's quiet voice brought Mary back to the present. She saw a green Ford Taurus pulling into the driveway, and Bonnie Cullen's slightly panicked look.

"Just say…" she coughed and tried again, reaching into her purse. She pulled out a DVD and a thick unsealed envelope. "Just say we're new friends of yours. And . . . when you think he's ready for it, give him these."

Mary pressed the items into Bonnie's hands. She glanced down at them, then at Mary. "You're sure?"

"Yes," Mary said. "It's what's best for him." She gestured to the DVD and letter. "You can look at them and make up your own mind."

There was the sound of a door opening and running feet. A ten-year-old boy dashed into the room. "Hey Mom! Can I have –"

He stopped and stared at the strangers in front of him. Mary took a long look at him, drinking him in. His hair had lightened some and was wavy. His eyes were dark brown and inquisitive. He was all arms and legs at the moment, dressed in jeans and a red t-shirt.

A tall man with thick light brown hair came into the room. He said nothing, but his eyes flicked from face to face, waiting to find out what had been discussed.

Bonnie gave herself a little shake. "Come here, sweetie," she said to Nate. When the boy was at her side, she wrapped her arms around him. "Honey, these are some new friends of mine and your dad's: Mr. and Mrs. Beamer. Can you say hello?"

"Hello," he said shyly, sticking out his hand for them both to shake. Mary tried to focus on touching his skin, hoping she could commit it – and him – to memory.

Andrew turned to Jack, who sat quietly in the recliner. "And you are?"

Foster got to his feet. "Oh, I'm with Mary and Roger. Name's Foster." He shook hands with the man and then with Nate. As he straightened up, he caught Mary's eye, raising an eyebrow in question.

She shook her head slightly. He frowned, but she and Roger had warned him it might be this way. Jack sighed.

Andrew Cullen gave the reporter a worried look. "Hey, Nate, go see if there's any cookies left and start your homework, okay? I need to talk to your mom and her friends for a moment."

"Is this a grownup thing?" Nate asked, rolling his eyes. Mary had to smile, as did Roger.

"Yes, Andrew said with a grin that didn't totally hide his tension, "It's a grownup thing. Now scoot!"

Nate nodded, called out a "nice to meet you" to the room and headed to where Mary suspected the kitchen was. She drew a shaky breath. "Thank you for letting me meet him."

Andrew looked from one person to another. "So, what are you planning to do?"

Bonnie stood up and put a hand on her husband's arm. "They're going to leave it alone for now." She held up the DVD and letter. "These are for later – when we feel he's ready."

Andrew seemed to relax a little at that news. He looked at Jack. "You're the reporter who broke this, aren't you?"

Jack nodded. "I was hoping to interview you about this for a follow-up article —"

"No," Andrew said. "No, we don't want our names in the paper. I'm sorry."

"Perhaps I could change your names —"

"I said no!" Andrew snapped. He sighed. "Look, you wanna do your job. But I have my family to consider."

"We should go," Mary said, standing herself. Jack looked as if he wanted to argue about it, but Roger shook his head at the reporter.

"Wait," Bonnie said. She went to the photo album and opened it to the back, where a pocket held pictures. She pulled two out and handed them to Mary. "Here's a baby picture — and last year's school portrait. Please, take them."

Mary swallowed. "Thank you." She bowed her head, and asked softly. "If you wouldn't mind . . . if I could know how he's doing..."

"Of course," Bonnie said, pulling Mary into a hug. "We're friends now."

The women shed a few more tears while the husband exchanged contact information. Then Mary, Roger, and Jack stepped out into the Georgia afternoon and let the Cullens return to their family.

Jack was shaking his head. "You're just going to leave it at that? No contact? You're okay with that?"

They'd reached their cars, parked on the shady street. Mary turned to Jack. "Yes, I am. Because it's what's best. And please, don't try to find a way to report this meeting. That would be wrong."

The reporter's shoulders sagged. "I — I don't understand."

Roger raised an eyebrow. "What don't you understand?"

Jack gestured to Mary. "She was freaking out about this ever since I met her. I mean, she was a head case." Roger's face darkened; Jack spoke more quickly. "But now — now, she's handling it just fine! Like she's put it behind her!"

He turned to Mary, and she saw a hunger in his eyes. "How do I do that, Mary? How do I put an awful past behind me?"

She studied the man in front of her. She realized that Jack Foster, whatever else he was, was a man in pain. A man who needed redemption just as badly as she did.

Like him, she hadn't realized until recently that it was something available to anyone. If God could love and forgive her, why not him?

She looked over at Roger and tilted her head to Jack with a smile. Then putting a hand on his shoulder, she said, "I think I can answer that. Why don't we all go get some coffee?"

ABOUT THE AUTHOR:

LAURA WARE's column "Laura's Look" runs weekly in the News Sun (Highlands County). Along with her numerous epublished works she has sold several short stories to various publications; one appeared in a Pocket Books anthology. Laura lives in Central Florida. Check out her website at www.laurahware.com You can email her at laura@laurahware.com

FREE EBOOK COPY!

For a free ebook copy of REDEMPTION, go to https://www.smashwords.com/books/view/403760 and enter coupon code ZT59D at checkout. Then select your preferred ebook fromat and download.

www.ingramcontent.com/pod-product-compliance
Lightning Source LLC
Chambersburg PA
CBHW030923260626
47169CB00002B/366